In a future less than fifty years away, the world is still as we know it. Time continues to tick by. The truth is that it is ticking away.

A powerful few know what lies ahead.

They are preparing for it.

They are trying to protect us.

They are setting us on a path from which we can never return.

A path that will lead to destruction.

A path that will take us below ground.

The history of the silo is about to be written.

Our future is about to begin.

SHIFT

In a future less than fifty years away, the world is still as we know it. Time continues to tick by. The truth is that it is ticking away.

A powerful few know what lies ahead.

They are preparing for it.

They are trying to protect us.

They are setting us on a path from which we can never return.

A path that will lead to destruction.

A path that will take us below ground.

The history of the silo is about to be written.

Our future is about to begin.

SHIFT

HUGH

HOWEY

CENTURY

Published by Century 2013

2 4 6 8 10 9 7 5 3 1

First published in Great Britain in 2013 by
Century
Random House, 20 Vauxhall Bridge Road,
London SW1V 2SA

www.randomhouse.co.uk

Addresses for companies within The Random House Group Limited can be found at:
www.randomhouse.co.uk

The Random House Group Limited Reg. No. 954009

A CIP catalogue record for this book
is available from the British Library

HB ISBN 9781780891217
TPB ISBN 9781780891224

The Random House Group Limited supports the Forest Stewardship Council® (FSC®),
the leading international forest-certification organisation. Our books carrying the FSC
label are printed on FSC®-certified paper. FSC is the only forest-certification scheme
supported by the leading environmental organisations, including Greenpeace. Our paper
procurement policy can be found at www.randomhouse.co.uk/environment

Typeset in Adobe Caslon by Palimpsest Book Production Limited,
Falkirk, Stirlingshire
Printed and bound in Great Britain by Clays Ltd, St Ives PLC

For all those who find themselves well and truly alone.

*I*n 2007, the Center for Automation in Nanobiotech (CAN) outlined the hardware and software platforms that would one day allow robots smaller than human cells to make medical diagnoses, conduct repairs and even self-propagate.

That same year, CBS re-aired a programme about the effects of propranolol on sufferers of extreme trauma. A simple pill, it had been discovered, could wipe out the memory of any traumatic event.

At almost the same moment in humanity's broad history, mankind had discovered the means for bringing about its utter downfall. And the ability to forget it ever happened.

FIRST SHIFT - LEGACY

Prologue

2110

Beneath the hills of Fulton County, Georgia

Troy returned to the living and found himself inside a tomb. He awoke to a world of confinement, a thick sheet of frosted glass pressed near to his face.

Dark shapes stirred on the other side of the icy murk. He tried to lift his arms, to beat on the glass, but his muscles were too weak. He attempted to scream – but could only cough. The taste in his mouth was foul. His ears rang with the clank of heavy locks opening, the hiss of air, the squeak of hinges long dormant.

The lights overhead were bright, the hands on him warm. They helped him sit while he continued to cough, his breath clouding the chill air. Someone had water. Pills to take. The water was cool, the pills bitter. Troy fought down a few gulps. He was unable to hold the glass without help. His hands trembled as memories flooded back, scenes from long nightmares. The feeling of deep time and yesterdays mingled. He shivered.

A paper gown. The sting of tape removed. A tug on his arm, a tube pulled from his groin. Two men dressed in white helped him out of the coffin. Steam rose all around him, air condensing and dispersing.

Sitting up and blinking against the glare, exercising lids long shut, Troy looked down the rows of coffins full of the living that stretched towards the distant and curved walls. The ceiling felt low; the suffocating press of dirt stacked high above. And the years. So many had passed. Anyone he cared about would be gone.

Everything was gone.

The pills stung his throat. He tried to swallow. Memories faded like dreams upon waking, and he felt his grip loosen on everything he'd known.

He collapsed backwards – but the men in the white overalls saw this coming. They caught him and lowered him to the ground, a paper gown rustling on shivering skin.

Images returned; recollections rained down like bombs and then were gone.

The pills would only do so much. It would take time to destroy the past.

Troy began to sob into his palms, a sympathetic hand resting on his head. The two men in white allowed him this moment. They didn't rush the process. Here was a courtesy passed from one waking soul to the next, something all the men sleeping in their coffins would one day rise to discover.

And eventually . . . forget.

2049

Washington, DC

The tall glass trophy cabinets had once served as bookshelves. There were hints. Hardware on the shelves dated back centuries, while the hinges and the tiny locks on the glass doors went back mere decades. The framing around the glass was cherry, but the cases had been built of oak. Someone had attempted to remedy this with a few coats of stain, but the grain didn't match. The colour wasn't perfect. To trained eyes, details such as these were glaring.

Congressman Donald Keene gathered these clues without meaning to. He simply saw that long ago there had been a great purge, a making of space. At some point in the past, the Senator's waiting room had been stripped of its obligatory law books until only a handful remained. These tomes sat silently in the dim corners of the glass cabinets. They were shut in, their spines laced with cracks, old leather flaking off like sunburned skin.

A handful of Keene's fellow freshmen filled the waiting room, pacing and stirring, their terms of service newly begun. Like Donald, they were young and still hopelessly optimistic. They were bringing change to Capitol Hill. They hoped to deliver where their similarly naive predecessors had not.

While they waited their turns to meet with the great Senator Thurman from their home state of Georgia, they chatted nervously among themselves. They were a gaggle of priests, Donald imagined, all lined up to meet the Pope, to kiss his ring. He let out a heavy breath and focused on the contents of the case, lost himself in the treasures behind the glass while a fellow representative from Georgia prattled on about his district's Centers for Disease Control and Prevention.

'—and they have this detailed guide on their website, this response and readiness manual in case of, okay, get this – a zombie invasion. Can you believe that? Fucking zombies. Like even the CDC thinks something could go wrong and suddenly we'd all be *eating* each other—'

Donald stifled a smile, fearful its reflection would be caught in the glass. He turned and looked over a collection of photographs on the walls, one each of the Senator with the last four presidents. It was the same pose and handshake in each shot, the same background of windless flags and fancy oversized seals. The Senator hardly seemed to change as the presidents came and went. His hair started white and stayed white; he seemed perfectly unfazed by the passing of decades.

Seeing the photographs side by side devalued each of them somehow. They looked staged. Phoney. It was as if this collection of the world's most powerful men had each begged for the opportunity to stand and pose with a cardboard cut-out, a roadside attraction.

Donald laughed, and the congressman from Atlanta joined him.

'I know, right? Zombies. It's hilarious. But think about it, okay? Why would the CDC even *have* this field manual unless—'

Donald wanted to correct his fellow congressman, to tell him what he'd really been laughing about. *Look at the smiles*, he wanted to say. They were on the faces of the *presidents*. The Senator looked as if he'd rather be anyplace else. It looked as if each in this succession of commanders-in-chief knew who the more powerful man was, who would be there long after they had come and gone.

'—it's advice like, everyone should have a baseball bat with their flashlights and candles, right? Just in case. You know, for bashing brains.'

Donald pulled out his phone and checked the time. He

glanced at the door leading off the waiting room and wondered how much longer he'd have to wait. Putting the phone away, he turned back to the cabinet and studied a shelf where a military uniform had been carefully arranged like a delicate work of origami. The left breast of the jacket featured a wall of medals; the sleeves were folded over and pinned to highlight the gold braids sewn along the cuffs. In front of the uniform, a collection of decorative coins rested in a custom wooden rack, tokens of appreciation from men and women serving overseas.

The two arrangements spoke volumes: the uniform from the past and the coins from those currently deployed, bookends on a pair of wars. One that the Senator had fought in as a youth. The other, a war he had battled to prevent as an older and wiser man.

'—yeah, it sounds crazy, I know, but do you know what rabies does to a dog? I mean, what it *really* does, the biological—'

Donald leaned in closer to study the decorative coins. The number and slogan on each one represented a deployed group. Or was it a battalion? He couldn't remember. His sister Charlotte would know. She was over there somewhere, out in the field.

'Hey, aren't you even a little nervous about this?'

Donald realised the question had been aimed at him. He turned and faced the talkative congressman. He must've been in his mid-thirties, around Donald's age. In him, Donald could see his own thinning hair, his own beginnings of a gut, that uncomfortable slide to middle age.

'Am I nervous about zombies?' Donald laughed. 'No. Can't say that I am.'

The congressman stepped up beside Donald, his eyes drifting towards the imposing uniform that stood propped up as if a warrior's chest remained inside. 'No,' the man said. 'About meeting *him*.'

The door to the reception area opened, bleeps from the phones on the other side leaking out.

'Congressman Keene?'

An elderly receptionist stood in the doorway, her white blouse and black skirt highlighting a thin and athletic frame.

'Senator Thurman will see you now,' she said.

Donald patted the congressman from Atlanta on the shoulder as he stepped past.

'Hey, good luck,' the gentleman stammered after him.

Donald smiled. He fought the temptation to turn and tell the man that he knew the Senator well enough, that he had been bounced on his knee back when he was a child. Only – Donald was too busy hiding his own nerves to bother.

He stepped through the deeply panelled door of rich hardwoods and entered the Senator's inner sanctum. This wasn't like passing through a foyer to pick up a man's daughter for a date. This was different. This was the pressure of meeting as colleagues when Donald still felt like that same young child.

'Through here,' the receptionist said. She guided Donald between pairs of wide and busy desks, a dozen phones chirping in short bursts. Young men and women in suits and crisp blouses double-fisted receivers. Their bored expressions suggested that this was a normal workload for a weekday morning.

Donald reached out a hand as he passed one of the desks, brushing the wood with his fingertips. Mahogany. The aides here had desks nicer than his own. And the decor: the plush carpet, the broad and ancient crown cornicing, the antique tile ceiling, the dangling light fixtures that may have been actual crystal.

At the end of the buzzing and bleeping room, a panelled door opened and disgorged Congressman Mick Webb, just finished with his meeting. Mick didn't notice Donald, was too absorbed by the open folder he held in front of him.

Donald stopped and waited for his colleague and old college friend to approach. 'So,' he asked, 'how did it go?'

Mick looked up and snapped the folder shut. He tucked it under his arm and nodded. 'Yeah, yeah. It went great.' He smiled. 'Sorry if we ran long. The old man couldn't get enough of me.'

Donald laughed. He believed that. Mick had swept into office with ease. He had the charisma and confidence that went along with being tall and handsome. Donald used to joke that if his friend wasn't so shit with names, he'd be president someday. 'No problem,' Donald said. He jabbed a thumb over his shoulder. 'I was making new friends.'

Mick grinned. 'I bet.'

'Yeah, well, I'll see you back at the ranch.'

'Sure thing.' Mick slapped him on the arm with the folder and headed for the exit. Donald caught the glare from the Senator's receptionist and hurried over. She waved him through to the dimly lit office and pulled the door shut behind him.

'Congressman Keene.'

Senator Paul Thurman stood from behind his desk and stretched out a hand. He flashed a familiar smile, one Donald had come to recognise as much from photos and TV as from his childhood. Despite Thurman's age – he had to be pushing seventy if he wasn't already there – the Senator was trim and fit. His Oxford shirt hugged a military frame; a thick neck bulged out of his knotted tie; his white hair remained as crisp and orderly as an enlisted man's.

Donald crossed the dark room and shook the Senator's hand.

'Good to see you, sir.'

'Please, sit.' Thurman released Donald's hand and gestured to one of the chairs across from his desk. Donald lowered himself into the bright red leather, the gold grommets along the arm like sturdy rivets in a steel beam.

'How's Helen?'

'Helen?' Donald straightened his tie. 'She's great. She's back in Savannah. She really enjoyed seeing you at the reception.'

'She's a beautiful woman, your wife.'

'Thank you, sir.' Donald fought to relax, which didn't

help. The office had the pall of dusk, even with the overhead lights on. The clouds outside had turned nasty – low and dark. If it rained, he would have to take the underpass back to his office. He hated being down there. They could carpet it and hang those little chandeliers at intervals, but he could still tell he was below ground. The tunnels in Washington made him feel like a rat scurrying through a sewer. It always seemed as if the roof was about to cave in.

'How's the job treating you so far?'

'The job's good. Busy, but good.'

He started to ask the Senator how Anna was doing, but the door behind him opened before he could. The receptionist entered and delivered two bottles of water. Donald thanked her, twisted the cap on his and saw that it had been pre-opened.

'I hope you're not too busy to work on something for me.' Senator Thurman raised an eyebrow. Donald took a sip of water and wondered if that was a skill one could master, that eyebrow lift. It made him want to jump to attention and salute.

'I'm sure I can make the time,' he said. 'After all the stumping you did for me? I doubt I would've made it past the primaries.' He fiddled with the water bottle in his lap.

'You and Mick Webb go back, right? Both Bulldogs.'

It took Donald a moment to realise the Senator was referring to their college mascot. He hadn't spent a lot of time at Georgia following sports. 'Yessir. Go Dawgs.'

He hoped that was right.

The Senator smiled. He leaned forward so that his face caught the soft light raining down on his desk. Donald watched as shadows grew in wrinkles otherwise easy to miss. Thurman's lean face and square chin made him look younger head-on than he did in profile. Here was a man who got places by approaching others directly rather than in ambush.

'You studied architecture at Georgia.'

Donald nodded. It was easy to forget that he knew Thurman better than the Senator knew him. One of them grabbed far more newspaper headlines than the other.

'That's right. For my undergrad. I went into planning for my master's. I figured I could do more good governing people than I could drawing boxes to put them in.'

He winced to hear himself deliver the line. It was a pat phrase from grad school, something he should have left behind with crushing beer cans on his forehead and ogling asses in skirts. He wondered for the dozenth time why he and the other congressional newcomers had been summoned. When he first got the invite, he thought it was a social visit. Then Mick had bragged about his own appointment, and Donald figured it was some kind of formality or tradition. But now he wondered if this was a power play, a chance to butter up the representatives from Georgia for those times when Thurman would need a particular vote in the lower and *lesser* house.

'Tell me, Donny, how good are you at keeping secrets?'

Donald's blood ran cold. He forced himself to laugh off the sudden flush of nerves.

'I got elected, didn't I?'

Senator Thurman smiled. 'And so you probably learned the best lesson there is about secrets.' He picked up and raised his water bottle in salute. '*Denial*.'

Donald nodded and took a sip of his own water. He wasn't sure where this was going, but he already felt uneasy. He sensed some of the back-room dealings coming on that he'd promised his constituents he'd root out if elected.

The Senator leaned back in his chair.

'Denial is the secret sauce in this town,' he said. 'It's the flavour that holds all the other ingredients together. Here's what I tell the newly elected: the truth is going to get out – it always does – but it's going to blend in with all the *lies*.' The Senator twirled a hand in the air. 'You have to deny each lie and every truth with the same vinegar. Let those websites and blowhards who bitch about cover-ups confuse the public *for* you.'

'Uh, yessir.' Donald didn't know what else to say so he drank another mouthful of water instead.

The Senator lifted an eyebrow again. He remained frozen

for a pause, and then asked, out of nowhere: 'Do you believe in aliens, Donny?'

Donald nearly lost the water out of his nose. He covered his mouth with his hand, coughed, had to wipe his chin. The Senator didn't budge.

'Aliens?' Donald shook his head and wiped his wet palm on his thigh. 'No, sir. I mean, not the abducting kind. Why?'

He wondered if this was some kind of debriefing. Why had the Senator asked him if he could keep a secret? Was this a security initiation? The Senator remained silent.

'They're not real,' Donald finally said. He watched for any twitch or hint. 'Are they?'

The old man cracked a smile. 'That's the thing,' he said. 'If they are or they aren't, the chatter out there would be the same. Would you be surprised if I told you they're very much real?'

'Hell, yeah, I'd be surprised.'

'Good.' The Senator slid a folder across the desk.

Donald eyed it and held up a hand. 'Wait. Are they real or aren't they? What're you trying to tell me?'

Senator Thurman laughed. 'Of course they're not real.' He took his hand off the folder and propped his elbows on the desk. 'Have you seen how much NASA wants from us so they can fly to Mars and back? We're not getting to another star. Ever. And nobody's coming here. Hell, why would they?'

Donald didn't know *what* to think, which was a far cry from how he'd felt less than a minute ago. He saw what the Senator meant, how truth and lies seemed black and white, but mixed together they made everything grey and confusing. He glanced down at the folder. It looked similar to the one Mick had been carrying. It reminded him of the government's fondness for all things outdated.

'This is denial, right?' He studied the Senator. 'That's what you're doing right now. You're trying to throw me off.'

'No. This is me telling you to stop watching so many science fiction flicks. In fact, why do you think those eggheads are always dreaming of colonising some other planet? You have any idea what would be involved? It's ludicrous. Not cost-effective.'

Donald shrugged. He didn't think it was ludicrous. He twisted the cap back onto his water. 'It's in our nature to dream of open space,' he said. 'To find room to spread out in. Isn't that how we ended up here?'

'Here? In America?' The Senator laughed. 'We didn't come here and find open space. We got a bunch of people sick, killed them and *made* space.' Thurman pointed at the folder. 'Which brings me to this. I've got something I'd like you to work on.'

Donald placed his bottle on the leather inlay of the formidable desk and took the folder.

'Is this something coming through committee?'

He tried to temper his hopes. It was alluring to think of co-authoring a bill in his first year in office. He opened the folder and tilted it towards the window. Outside, storms were gathering.

'No, nothing like that. This is about CAD-FAC.'

Donald nodded. *Of course.* The preamble about secrets and conspiracies suddenly made perfect sense, as did the gathering of Georgia congressmen outside. This was about the Containment and Disposal Facility, nicknamed CAD-FAC, at the heart of the Senator's new energy bill, the complex that would one day house most of the world's spent nuclear fuel. Or, according to the websites Thurman had alluded to, it was going to be the next Area 51, or the site where a new-and-improved superbomb was being built, or a secure holding facility for libertarians who had purchased one too many guns. Take your pick. There was enough noise out there to hide *any* truth.

'Yeah,' Donald said, deflated. 'I've been getting some entertaining calls from my district.' He didn't dare mention the one about the lizard people. 'I want you to know, sir, that privately I'm behind the facility one hundred per cent.' He looked up at the Senator. 'I'm glad I didn't have to vote on it publicly, of course, but it was about time someone offered up their backyard, right?'

'Precisely. For the common good.' Senator Thurman took a long pull from his water, leaned back in his chair and cleared his throat. 'You're a sharp young man, Donny. Not everyone sees what a boon to our state this'll be. A real lifesaver.' He smiled. 'I'm sorry, you *are* still going by Donny, right? Or is it Donald now?'

'Either's fine,' Donald lied. He no longer enjoyed being called Donny, but changing names in the middle of one's life was practically impossible. He returned to the folder and flipped the cover letter over. There was a drawing underneath that struck him as being out of place. It was . . . too familiar. Familiar, and yet it didn't belong there – it was from another life.

'Have you seen the economic reports?' Thurman asked. 'Do you know how many jobs this bill created overnight?' He snapped his fingers. 'Forty thousand, just like that. And that's only from Georgia. A lot will be from your district, a lot of shipping, a lot of stevedores. Of course, now that it's passed, our less nimble colleagues are grumbling that *they* should've had a chance to bid—'

'I drew this,' Donald interrupted, pulling out the sheet of paper. He showed it to Thurman as if the Senator would be surprised to see that it had snuck into the folder. Donald wondered if this was the Senator's daughter's doing, some kind of a joke or a hello and a wink from Anna.

Thurman nodded. 'Yes, well, it needs more detail, wouldn't you say?'

Donald studied the architectural illustration and wondered what sort of test this was. He remembered the drawing. It was a last-minute project for his biotecture class in his senior year. There was nothing unusual or amazing about it, just a large cylindrical building a hundred or so storeys tall ringed with glass and concrete, balconies burgeoning with gardens, one side cut away to reveal interspersed levels for housing, working and shopping. The structure was spare where he remembered other classmates being bold, utilitarian where he could've taken risks. Green tufts jutted up from the flat roof – a horrible cliché, a nod to carbon neutrality.

In sum, it was drab and boring. Donald couldn't imagine a design so bare rising from the deserts of Dubai alongside the great new breed of self-sustaining skyscrapers. He certainly couldn't see what the Senator wanted with it.

'More detail,' he murmured, repeating the Senator's words. He flipped through the rest of the folder, looking for hints, for context.

'Wait.' Donald studied a list of requirements written up as if by a prospective client. 'This looks like a design proposal.' Words he had forgotten he'd ever learned caught his eye: *interior traffic flow, block plan, HVAC, hydroponics*—

'You'll have to lose the sunlight.' Senator Thurman's chair squeaked as he leaned over his desk.

'I'm sorry?' Donald held the folder up. 'What exactly are you wanting me to do?'

'I would suggest those lights like my wife uses.' He cupped his hand into a tiny circle and pointed at the centre. 'She gets these tiny seeds to sprout in the winter, uses bulbs that cost me a goddamned fortune.'

'You mean grow lights.'

Thurman snapped his fingers again. 'And don't worry about the cost. Whatever you need. I'm also going to get you some help with the mechanical stuff. An engineer. An entire team.'

Donald flipped through more of the folder. 'What is this *for*? And why me?'

'This is what we call a *just-in-case* building. Probably'll never get used, but they won't let us store the fuel rods out there unless we put this bugger nearby. It's like this window in my basement I had to lower before our house could pass inspection. It was for . . . what do you call it . . . ?'

'Egress,' Donald said, the word flowing back unaided.

'Yes. Egress.' He pointed to the folder. 'This building is like that window, something we've gotta build so the rest will pass inspection. This will be where – in the unlikely event of an attack or a leak – facility employees can go. A shelter. And it needs to be *perfect* or this project will be shut down faster than a tick's wink. Just because our bill passed and got signed doesn't mean we're home free, Donny. There was that project out west that got okayed decades ago, scored funding. Eventually, it fell through.'

Donald knew the one he was talking about. A containment facility buried under a mountain. The buzz on the Hill was that the Georgia project had the same chances of success. The folder suddenly tripled in weight as he considered this. He was being asked to be a part of this future failure. He would be staking his newly won office on it.

'I've got Mick Webb working on something related. Logistics and planning. You two will need to collaborate on a few things. And Anna is taking leave from her post at MIT to lend a hand.'

'*Anna?*' Donald fumbled for his water, his hand shaking.

'Of course. She'll be your lead engineer on this project. There are details in there on what she'll need, space-wise.'

Donald took a gulp of water and forced himself to swallow.

'There's a lot of other people I could call in, sure, but this project can't fail, you understand? It needs to be like *family*. That's why I want to use people I know, people I can trust.' Senator Thurman interlocked his fingers. 'If this is the only thing you were elected to do, I want you to do it right. It's why I stumped for you in the first place.'

'Of course.' Donald bobbed his head to hide his confusion. He had worried during the election that the Senator's endorsement stemmed from old family ties. This was somehow worse. Donald hadn't been using the Senator at all; it was the *other way around*. Studying the drawing in his lap, the newly elected congressman felt one job he was inadequately trained for melt away – only to be replaced by a *different* job that seemed equally daunting.

'Wait,' he said. 'I still don't get it.' He studied the old drawing. 'Why the grow lights?'

'Because this building I want you to design for me – it's going to go underground.'

Troy held his breath and tried to remain calm while the doctor pumped the rubber bulb. The inflatable band swelled around his bicep until it pinched his skin. He wasn't sure if slowing his breathing and steadying his pulse affected his blood pressure, but he had a strong urge to impress the man in the white overalls. He wanted his numbers to come back *normal*.

His arm throbbed a few beats while the needle bounced and the air hissed out.

'Eighty over fifty.' The band made a ripping sound as it was torn loose. Troy rubbed the spot where his skin had been pinched.

'Is that okay?'

The doctor made a note on his clipboard. 'It's low, but not outside the norm.' Behind him, his assistant labelled a cup of dark grey urine before placing it inside a small fridge. Troy caught sight of a half-eaten sandwich among the samples, not even wrapped.

He looked down at his bare knees sticking out of the blue paper gown. His legs were pale and seemed smaller than he remembered. Bony.

'I still can't make a fist,' he told the doctor, working his hand open and shut.

'That's perfectly normal. Your strength will return. Look into the light, please.'

Troy followed the bright beam and tried not to blink.

'How long have you been doing this?' he asked the doctor.

'You're my third coming out. I've put two under.' He lowered the light and smiled at Troy. 'I've only been out myself for a few weeks. I can tell you that the strength will return.'

Troy nodded. The doctor's assistant handed him another pill and a cup of water. Troy hesitated. He stared down at the little blue capsule nestled in his palm.

'A double dose this morning,' the doctor said, 'and then you'll be given one with breakfast and dinner. Please do not skip a treatment.'

Troy looked up. 'What happens if I don't take it?'

The doctor shook his head and frowned, but didn't say anything.

Troy popped the pill in his mouth and chased it with the water. A bitterness slid down his throat.

'One of my assistants will bring you some clothes and a fluid meal to kick-start your gut. If you have any dizziness or chills, you're to call me at once. Otherwise, we'll see you back here in six months.' The doctor made a note, then chuckled. 'Well, someone else will see you. My shift will be over.'

'Okay.' Troy shivered.

The doctor looked up from his clipboard. 'You're not cold, are you? I keep it a little extra warm in here.'

Troy hesitated before answering. 'No, doctor. I'm not cold. Not any more.'

Troy entered the lift at the end of the hall, his legs still weak, and studied an array of numbered buttons. The orders they'd given him included directions to his office, but he vaguely remembered how to get there. Much of his orientation had survived the decades of sleep. He remembered studying that same book over and over, thousands of men assigned to various shifts, tours of the facility before being put under like the women. The orientation felt like yesterday; it was older memories that seemed to be slipping away.

The doors to the lift closed automatically. His apartment was on thirty-seven; he remembered that. His office was on thirty-four. He reached for a button, intending to head straight to his desk, and instead found his hand sliding up to the very top. He still had a few minutes before he needed to be anywhere, and he felt some strange urge, some tug, to get as high as possible, to rise through the soil pressing in from all sides.

The lift hummed into life and accelerated up the shaft. There was a whooshing sound as another car or maybe the counterweight zoomed by. The round buttons flashed as the floors passed. There was an enormous spread of them, seventy in all. The centres of many were dull from years of rubbing. This didn't seem right. It seemed like just yesterday the buttons were shiny and new. Just yesterday, *everything* was.

The lift slowed. Troy palmed the wall for balance, his legs still uncertain.

The door dinged and slid open. Troy blinked at the bright lights in the hallway. He left the lift and followed a short walk towards a room that leaked chatter. His new boots were stiff on his feet, the generic grey overalls itchy. He tried to imagine waking up like this nine more times, feeling this weak and disoriented. Ten shifts of six months each. Ten shifts he hadn't volunteered for. He wondered if it would get progressively easier or if it would only get worse.

The bustle in the cafeteria quietened as he entered. A few heads turned his way. He saw at once that his grey overalls weren't so generic. There was a scattering of colours seated at the tables: a large cluster of reds, quite a few yellows, a man in orange; no other greys.

That first meal of sticky paste he'd been given rumbled once more in his stomach. He wasn't allowed to eat anything else for six hours, which made the aroma from the canned foods overwhelming. He remembered the fare, had lived on it during orientation. Weeks and weeks of the same gruel. Now it would be months. It would be hundreds of years.

'Sir.'

A young man nodded to Troy as he walked past, towards the lifts. Troy thought he recognised him but couldn't be sure.

The gentleman certainly seemed to have recognised *him*. Or was it the grey overalls that stood out?

'First shift?'

An older gentleman approached, thin, with white and wispy hair that circled his head. He held a tray in his hands, smiled at Troy. Pulling open a recycling bin, he slid the entire tray inside and dropped it with a clatter.

'Come up for the view?' the man asked.

Troy nodded. It was all men throughout the cafeteria. All men. They had explained why this was safer. He tried to remember as the man with the splotches of age on his skin crossed his arms and stood beside him. There were no introductions. Troy wondered if names meant less amid these short six-month shifts. He gazed out over the bustling tables towards the massive screen that covered the far wall.

Whirls of dust and low clouds hung over a field of scattered and mangled debris. A few metal poles bristled from the ground and sagged lifelessly, the tents and flags long vanished. Troy thought of something but couldn't name it. His stomach tightened like a fist around the paste and the bitter pill.

'This'll be my second shift,' the man said.

Troy barely heard. His watering eyes drifted across the scorched hills, the grey slopes rising up towards the dark and menacing clouds. The debris scattered everywhere was rotting away. Next shift, or the one after, and it would all be gone.

'You can see further from the lounge.' The man turned and gestured along the wall. Troy knew well enough what room he was referring to. This part of the building was familiar to him in ways this man could hardly guess at.

'No, but thanks,' Troy stammered. He waved the man off. 'I think I've seen enough.'

Curious faces returned to their trays, and the chatter resumed. It was sprinkled with the clinking of spoons and forks on metal bowls and plates. Troy turned and left without saying another word. He put that hideous view behind him – turned his back on the unspoken eeriness of it. He hurried, shivering, towards the lift, knees weak from more than the long rest. He needed to be alone, didn't want anyone around him this time, didn't want sympathetic hands comforting him while he cried.

3

2049

Washington, DC

Donald kept the thick folder tucked inside his jacket and hurried through the rain. He had chosen to get soaked crossing the square rather than face his claustrophobia in the tunnels.

Traffic hissed by on the wet asphalt. He waited for a gap, ignored the crossing signals and scooted across.

In front of him, the marble steps of Rayburn, the office building for the House of Representatives, gleamed treacherously. He climbed them warily and thanked the doorman on his way in.

Inside, a security officer stood by impassively while Donald's badge was scanned, red unblinking eyes beeping at bar codes. He checked the folder Thurman had given him, made sure it was still dry, and wondered why such relics were still considered safer than an email or a digital copy.

His office was one floor up. He headed for the stairs, preferring them to Rayburn's ancient and slow lift. His shoes squeaked on the tile as he left the plush runner by the door.

The hallway upstairs was its usual mess. Two high-schoolers from the intern programme hurried past, most likely fetching coffee. A TV crew stood outside Amanda Kelly's office, camera lights bathing her and a young reporter in a daytime glow. Concerned voters and eager lobbyists were identifiable by the guest passes hanging around their necks. They were easy to distinguish from one another, these two groups. The voters wore frowns and invariably seemed lost. The lobbyists were the ones with the Cheshire Cat grins who navigated the halls more confidently than even the newly elected.

Donald opened the folder and pretended to read as he made his way through the chaos, hoping to avoid conversation. He squeezed behind the cameraman and ducked into his office next door.

Margaret, his secretary, stood up from her desk. 'Sir, you have a *visitor*.'

Donald glanced around the waiting room. It was empty. He saw that the door to his office was partway open.

'I'm sorry, I let her in.' Margaret mimed carrying a box, her hands at her waist and her back arched. 'She had a delivery. Said it was from the Senator.'

Donald waved her concerns aside. Margaret was older than him, in her mid-forties, and had come highly recommended, but she did have a conspiratorial streak. Perhaps it came with the years of experience.

'It's fine,' Donald assured her. He found it interesting that there were a hundred senators, two from his state, but only one was referred to as *the Senator*. 'I'll see what it's about. In the meantime, I need you to free up a daily block in my schedule. An hour or two in the morning would be ideal.' He flashed her the folder. 'I've got something that's going to eat up quite a bit of time.'

Margaret nodded and sat down in front of her computer. Donald turned towards his office.

'Oh, sir . . .'

He looked back. She pointed to her head. 'Your *hair*,' she hissed.

He ran his fingers through his hair and drops of water leapt off him like startled fleas. Margaret frowned and lifted her shoulders in a helpless shrug. Donald gave up and pushed his office door open, expecting to find someone sitting across from his desk.

Instead, he saw someone wiggling *underneath* it.

'Hello?'

The door had bumped into something on the floor.

Donald peeked around and saw a large box with a picture of a computer monitor on it. He glanced at the desk, saw the display was already set up.

'Oh, hey!'

The greeting was muffled by the hollow beneath his desk. Slender hips in a herringbone skirt wiggled back towards him. Donald knew who it was before her head emerged. He felt a flush of guilt, of anger at her being there unannounced.

'You know, you should have your cleaning lady dust under here once in a while.' Anna Thurman stood up and smiled. She slapped her palms together, brushing them off before extending one his way. Donald took her hand nervously. 'Hey, stranger.'

'Yeah. Hey.' Rain dribbled down his cheek and neck, hiding any sudden flush of perspiration. 'What's going on?' He walked around his desk to create some space between them. A new monitor stood innocently, a film of protective plastic blurring the screen.

'Dad thought you might need an extra one.' Anna tucked a loose clump of auburn hair behind her ear. She still possessed the same alluring and elfin quality when her ears poked out like that. 'I volunteered,' she explained, shrugging.

'Oh.' He placed the folder on his desk and thought about the drawing of the building he had briefly suspected was from her. And now, here she was. Checking his reflection in the new monitor, he saw the mess he had made of his hair. He reached up and tried to smooth it.

'Another thing,' Anna said. 'Your computer would be better off *on* your desk. I know it's unsightly, but the dust is gonna choke that thing to death. Dust is *murder* on these guys.'

'Yeah. Okay.'

He sat down and realised he could no longer see the chair across from his desk. He slid the new monitor to one side while Anna walked around and stood beside him, her arms crossed, completely relaxed. As if they'd seen each other yesterday.

'So,' he said. 'You're in town.'

'Since last week. I was gonna stop by and see you and Helen on Saturday, but I've been so busy getting settled into my apartment. Unboxing things, you know?'

'Yeah.' He accidentally bumped the mouse, and the old monitor winked on. His computer was running. The terror of being in the same room with an ex subsided just enough for the timing of the day's events to dawn on him.

'Wait.' He turned to Anna. 'You were over here *installing* this while your father was asking me if I was interested in his project? What if I'd declined?'

She raised an eyebrow. Donald realised it wasn't something one learned – it was a talent that ran in the family.

'He practically gift-wrapped the election for you,' she said flatly.

Donald reached for the folder and riffled the pages like a deck of cards. 'The illusion of free will would've been nice, that's all.'

Anna laughed. She was about to tousle his hair, he could sense it. Dropping his hand from the folder and patting his jacket pocket, he felt for his phone. It was as though Helen were there with him. He had an urge to call her.

'Was Dad at least gentle with you?'

He looked up to see that she hadn't moved. Her arms were still crossed, his hair untousled – nothing to panic about.

'What? Oh, yeah. He was fine. Like old times. In fact, it's like he hasn't aged a day.'

'He doesn't really age, you know.' She crossed the room and picked up large moulded pieces of foam, then slid them noisily into the empty box. Donald found his eyes drifting towards her skirt and forced himself to look away.

'He takes his nano treatments almost religiously. Started because of his knees. The military covered it for a while. Now he swears by them.'

'I didn't know that,' Donald lied. He'd heard rumours, of course. It was 'Botox for the whole body', people said. Better than testosterone supplements. It cost a fortune, and you wouldn't live forever, but you sure as hell could delay the pain of ageing.

Anna narrowed her eyes. 'You don't think there's anything *wrong* with that, do you?'

'What? No. It's fine, I guess. I just wouldn't. Wait – why? Don't tell me you've been . . .'

Anna rested her hands on her hips and cocked her head to the side. There was something oddly seductive about the defensive posture, something that whisked away the years since he'd last seen her.

'Do you think I would *need* to?' she asked him.

'No, no. It's not that . . .' He waved his hands. 'It's just that *I* don't think I ever would.'

A smirk thinned her lips. Maturity had hardened Anna's good looks, had refined her lean frame, but the fierceness from her youth remained. 'You say that now,' she said, 'but wait until your joints start to ache and your back goes out from something as simple as turning your head too fast. Then you'll see.'

'Okay. Well.' He clapped his hands together. 'This has been quite the day for catching up on old times.'

'Yes, it has. Now, what day works best for you?' Anna interlocked the flaps on the large box and slid it towards the door with her foot. She walked around the back of the desk and stood beside him, a hand on his chair, the other reaching for his mouse.

'What *day* . . . ?'

He watched while she changed some settings on his computer and the new monitor flashed to life. Donald could feel the pulse in his crotch, could smell her familiar perfume. The breeze she had caused by walking across the room seemed to stir all around him. This felt near enough to a caress, to a physical touch, that he wondered if he was cheating on Helen right at that very moment while Anna did little more than adjust sliders on his control panel.

'You know how to use this, right?' She slid the mouse from one screen to the other, dragging an old game of solitaire with it.

'Uh, yeah.' Donald squirmed in his seat. 'Um . . . what do you mean about a day that works best for me?'

She let go of the mouse. It felt as though she had taken her hand off his thigh.

'Dad wants me to handle the mechanical spaces on the plans.' She gestured towards the folder as if she knew precisely what was inside. 'I'm taking a sabbatical from the Institute until this Atlanta project is up and running. I thought we'd want to meet once a week to go over things.'

'Oh. Well. I'll have to get back to you on that. My schedule here is crazy. It's different every day.'

He imagined what Helen would say to him and Anna getting together once a week.

'We could, you know, set up a shared space in AutoCAD,' he suggested. 'I can link you into my document—'

'We could do that.'

'And email back and forth. Or video-chat. You know?'

Anna frowned. Donald realised he was being too obvious. 'Yeah, let's set up something like that,' she said.

There was a flash of disappointment on her face as she turned for the box, and Donald felt the urge to apologise, but doing so would spell out the problem in neon lights: *I don't trust myself around you. We're not going to be friends. What the fuck are you doing here?*

'You really need to do something about the dust.' She glanced back at his desk. 'Seriously, your computer is going to choke on it.'

'Okay. I will.' He stood and hurried around his desk to walk her out. Anna stooped for the box.

'I can get that.'

'Don't be silly.' She stood with the large box pinned between one arm and her hip. She smiled and tucked her hair behind her ear again. She could've been leaving his dorm room in college. There was that same awkward moment of a morning goodbye in last night's clothes.

'Okay, so you have my email?' he asked.

'You're in the blue pages now,' she reminded him.

'Yeah.'

'You look great, by the way.' And before he could step back or defend himself, she was fixing his hair, a smile on her lips.

Donald froze. When he thawed some time later, Anna was gone, leaving him standing there alone, soaked in guilt.

4

2110

• Silo 1 •

Troy was going to be late. The first day of his first shift, already a blubbering mess, and he was going to be late. In his rush to get away from the cafeteria, to be alone, he had taken the non-express by accident. Now, as he tried to compose himself, the lift seemed intent on stopping at every floor on the way down to load and unload passengers.

He stood in the corner as the lift stopped again and a man wrestled a cart full of heavy boxes inside. A gentleman with a load of green onions crowded behind him and stood close to Troy for a few stops. Nobody spoke. When the man with the onions got off, the smell remained. Troy shivered, one violent quake that travelled up his back and into his arms, but he thought nothing of it. He got off on thirty-four and tried to remember why he had been upset earlier.

The central lift shaft emptied onto a narrow hallway, which funnelled him towards a security station. The floor plan was vaguely familiar and yet somehow alien. It was unnerving to note the signs of wear in the carpet and the patch of dull steel in the middle of the turnstile where thighs had rubbed against it over the years. These were years that hadn't existed for Troy. This wear and tear had shown up as if by magic, like damage sustained from a night of drunkenness.

The lone guard on duty looked up from something he was reading and nodded in greeting. Troy placed his palm on a screen that had grown hazy from use. There was no chit-chat, no small talk, no expectation of forming a lasting relationship. The light above the console flashed green, the pedestal gave a loud click, and a little more sheen was rubbed off the revolving bar as Troy pushed through.

At the end of the hallway, Troy paused and pulled his orders out of his breast pocket. There was a note on the back from the doctor. He flipped it over and turned the little map around to face the right direction; he was pretty sure he knew the way, but everything was dropping in and out of focus.

The red dash marks on the map reminded him of fire safety plans he'd seen on walls somewhere else. Following the route took him past a string of small offices. Clacking keyboards, people talking, phones ringing – the sounds of the workplace made him feel suddenly tired. It also ignited a burn of insecurity, of having taken on a job he surely couldn't perform.

'Troy?'

He stopped and looked back at the man standing in a doorway he'd passed. A glance at his map showed him he'd almost missed his office.

'That's me.'

'Merriman.' The gentleman didn't offer his hand. 'You're late. Step inside.'

Merriman turned and disappeared into the office. Troy followed, his legs sore from the walk. He recognised the man, or thought he did. Couldn't remember if it was from the orientation or some other time.

'Sorry I'm late,' Troy started to explain. 'I got on the wrong elevator—'

Merriman raised a hand. 'That's fine. Do you need a drink?'

'They fed me.'

'Of course.' Merriman grabbed a clear Thermos off his desk, the contents a bright blue and took a sip. Troy remembered the foul taste. The older man smacked his lips and let out a breath as he lowered the Thermos.

'That stuff's awful,' he said.

'Yeah.' Troy looked around the office, his post for the next six months. The place, he figured, had aged quite a bit.

Merriman, too. If he was a little greyer from the past six months, it was hard to tell, but he had kept the place in order. Troy resolved to extend the same courtesy to the next guy.

'You remember your briefing?' Merriman shuffled some folders on his desk.

'Like it was yesterday.'

Merriman glanced up, a smirk on his face. 'Right. Well, there hasn't been anything exciting for the last few months. We had some mechanical issues when I started my shift but worked through those. There's a guy named Jones you'll want to use. He's been out a few weeks and is a lot sharper than the last guy. Been a lifesaver for me. He works down on sixty-eight with the power plant, but he's good just about anywhere, can fix pretty much anything.'

Troy nodded. 'Jones. Got it.'

'Okay. Well, I left you some notes in these folders. There have been a few workers we had to deep-freeze, some who aren't fit for another shift.' He looked up, a serious expression on his face. 'Don't take that lightly, okay? Plenty of guys here would love to nap straight through instead of work. Don't resort to the deep freeze unless you're sure they can't handle it.'

'I won't.'

'Good.' Merriman nodded. 'I hope you have an uneventful shift. I've got to run before this stuff kicks in.' He took another fierce swig and Troy's cheeks sucked in with empathy. He walked past Troy, slapped him on the shoulder and started to reach for the light switch. He stopped himself at the last minute and looked back, nodded, then was gone.

And just like that, Troy was in charge.

'Hey, wait!' He glanced around the office, hurried out and caught up with Merriman, who was already turning down the main hall towards the security gate. Troy jogged to catch up.

'You leave the light on?' Merriman asked.

Troy glanced over his shoulder. 'Yeah, but—'

'Good habits,' Merriman said. He shook his Thermos. 'Form them.'

A heavyset man hurried out of one of the offices and laboured to catch up with them. 'Merriman! You done with your shift?'

The two men shared a warm handshake. Merriman smiled and nodded. 'I am. Troy here will be taking my place.'

The man shrugged, didn't introduce himself. 'I'm off in two weeks,' he said, as if that explained his indifference.

'Look, I'm running late,' Merriman said, his eyes darting towards Troy with a trace of blame. He pushed the Thermos into his friend's palm. 'Here. You can have what's left.' He turned to go and Troy followed along.

'No thanks!' the man called out, waving the Thermos and laughing.

Merriman glanced at Troy. 'I'm sorry, did you have a question?' He passed through the turnstile and Troy went through behind him. The guard never looked up from his tablet.

'A few, yeah. You mind if I ride down with you? I was a little . . . behind at orientation. Sudden promotion. Would love to clarify a few things.'

'Hey, I can't stop you. You're in charge.' Merriman jabbed the call button on the express.

'So, basically, I'm just here in case something goes wrong?'

The lift opened. Merriman turned and squinted at Troy almost as if to gauge if he was being serious.

'Your job is to *make sure* nothing goes wrong.' They both stepped into the lift and the car raced downward.

'Right. Of course. That's what I meant.'

'You've read the Order, right?'

Troy nodded. *But not for this job*, he wanted to say. He had studied to run just a single silo, not the one that oversaw them all.

'Just follow the script. You'll get questions from the other silos now and then. I found it wise to say as little as possible. Just be quiet and listen. Keep in mind that these are mostly second- and third-generation survivors, so their vocabulary is already a little different. There's a cheat-sheet and a list of forbidden words in your folder.'

Troy felt a bout of dizziness and nearly sagged to the ground as weight was added, the lift slowing to a stop. He was still incredibly weak.

The door opened; he followed Merriman down a short hallway, the same one he had emerged from hours earlier. The doctor and his assistant waited in the room beyond, preparing an IV. The doctor looked curiously at Troy, as if he hadn't planned on seeing him again so soon, if ever.

'You finish your last meal?' the doctor asked, waving Merriman towards a stool.

'Every vile drop of it.' Merriman unclasped the tops of his overalls and let them flop down around his waist. He sat and held out his arm, palm up. Troy saw how pale Merriman's skin was, the loose tangle of purple lines weaving past his elbow. He tried not to watch the needle go in.

'I'm repeating my notes here,' Merriman told him, 'but you'll want to meet with Victor in the psych office. He's right across the hall from you. There's some strange things going on in a few of the silos, more fracturing than we thought. Try and get a handle on that for the next guy.'

Troy nodded.

'We need to get you to your chamber,' the doctor said. His young assistant stood by with a paper gown. The entire procedure looked very familiar. The doctor turned to Troy as if he were a stain that needed scrubbing away.

Troy backed out of the door and glanced down the hall in the direction of the deep freeze. The women and children were kept there, along with the men who couldn't make it through their shifts. 'Do you mind if I . . . ?' He felt a very real tug pulling him in that direction. Merriman and the doctor both frowned.

'It's not a good idea—' the doctor began.

'I wouldn't,' Merriman said. 'I made a few visits the first weeks. It's a mistake. Let it go.'

Troy stared down the hallway. He wasn't exactly sure what he would find there, anyway.

'Get through the next six months,' Merriman said. 'It goes by fast. It all goes by fast.'

Troy nodded. The doctor shooed him away with his eyes while Merriman began tugging off his boots. Troy turned, gave the heavy door down the hall one last glance, then headed in the other direction for the lift.

He hoped Merriman was right. Jabbing the button to call the express, he tried to imagine his entire shift flashing by. And the one after that. And the next one. Until this insanity had run its course, little thought to what came after.

5

2049

Washington, DC

Time flew by for Donald Keene. Another day came to an end, a week, and still he needed more time. It seemed the sun had just gone down when he looked up and it was past eleven.

Helen. There was a rush of panic as he fumbled for his phone. He had promised his wife he would always call before ten. A guilty heat wedged around his collar. He imagined her sitting around, staring at her phone, waiting and waiting.

It didn't even ring on his end before she picked up.

'There you are,' she said, her voice soft and drowsy, her tone hinting more at relief than anger.

'Sweetheart. God, I'm really sorry. I totally lost track of time.'

'That's okay, baby.' She yawned, and Donald had to fight the infectious urge to do the same. 'You write any good laws today?'

He laughed and rubbed his face. 'They don't really let me do that. Not yet. I'm mostly staying busy with this little project for the Senator—'

He stopped himself. Donald had dithered all week on the best way to tell her, what parts to keep secret. He glanced at the extra monitor on his desk. Anna's perfume was somehow frozen in the air, still lingering a week later.

Helen's voice perked up: 'Oh?'

He could picture her clearly: Helen in her nightgown, his side of the bed still immaculately made, a glass of water within her reach. He missed her terribly. The guilt he felt, despite his innocence, made him miss her all the more.

'What does he have you doing? It's legal, I hope.'

'What? Of course it's legal. It's . . . some architectural stuff, actually.' Donald leaned forward to grab the finger of gold Scotch left in his tumbler. 'To be honest, I'd forgotten how much I love the work. I would've been a decent architect if I'd stuck with it.' He took a burning sip and eyed his monitors, which had gone dark to save the screens. He was dying to get back to it. Everything fell away, disappeared, when he lost himself in the drawing.

'Sweetheart, I don't think designing a new bathroom for the Senator's office is why the taxpayers sent you to Washington.'

Donald smiled and finished the drink. He could practically hear his wife grinning on the other end of the line. He set the glass back on his desk and propped up his feet. 'It's nothing like that,' he insisted. 'It's plans for that facility they're putting in outside of Atlanta. Just a minor portion of it, really. But if I don't get it just right, the whole thing could fall apart.'

He eyed the open folder on his desk. His wife laughed sleepily.

'Why in the world would they have you doing something like that?' she asked. 'If it's so important, wouldn't they pay someone who knows what they're doing?'

Donald laughed dismissively, however much he agreed. He couldn't help but feel victim to Washington's habit for assigning jobs to people who weren't qualified for them. 'I'm actually quite good at this,' he told his wife. 'I'm starting to think I'm a better architect than a congressman.'

'I'm sure you're wonderful at it.' His wife yawned again. 'But you could've stayed *home* and been an architect. You could work late *here*.'

'Yeah, I know.' Donald remembered their discussions on whether or not he should run for office, if it would be worth them being apart. Now he was spending his time away doing the very thing they'd agreed he should give up. 'I think this is just something they put us through our first year,' he said. 'Think of it like your internship. It'll get better. And besides, I think it's a *good* sign he wants me in on this. He sees the Atlanta thing as a family project, something to keep in-house. He actually took notice of some of my work at—'

'*Family* project.'

'Well, not *literally* family, more like—' This wasn't how he wanted to tell her. It was a bad start. It was what he got for putting it off, for waiting until he was exhausted and tipsy.

'Is this why you're working late? Why you're calling me after ten?'

'Baby, I lost track of the time. I was on my computer.' He looked to his tumbler, saw that it held the barest of sips, just the golden residue that had slid down the glass after his last pull. 'This is good news for us. I'll be coming home more often because of this. I'm sure they'll need me to check out the job site, work with the foremen—'

'That *would* be good news. Your dog misses you.'

Donald smiled. 'I hope you *both* do.'

'You know I do.'

'Good.' He swilled the last drop in the glass and gulped it down. 'And listen, I know how you're gonna feel about this, and I swear it's out of my control, but the Senator's daughter is working on this project with me. Mick Webb, too. You remember him?'

Cold silence.

Then, 'I remember the Senator's daughter.'

Donald cleared his throat. 'Yeah, well, Mick is doing some of the organisational work, securing land, dealing with contractors. It's practically his district, after all. And you know neither of us would be where we are today without the Senator stumping for us—'

'What I remember is that you two used to date. And that she used to flirt with you even when I was around.'

Donald laughed. 'Are you serious? Anna Thurman? C'mon, honey, that was a lifetime ago—'

'I thought you were going to come home more often, anyway. On the weekends.' He heard his wife let out a breath. 'Look, it's late. Why don't we both get some sleep? We can talk about this tomorrow.'

'Okay. Yeah, sure. And sweetheart?'

She waited.

'Nothing's gonna come between us, okay? This is a huge opportunity for me. And it's something I'm really good at. I'd forgotten how good at it I am.'

A pause.

'There's a lot you're good at,' his wife said. 'You're a good husband, and I know you'll be a good congressman. I just don't trust the people you're surrounding yourself with.'

'But you know I wouldn't be here if it wasn't for him.'

'I know.'

'Look, I'll be careful. I promise.'

'Okay. I'll talk to you tomorrow. Sleep tight. I love you.'

She hung up, and Donald looked down at his phone, saw that he had a dozen emails waiting for him. He decided to ignore them until morning. Rubbing his eyes, he willed himself awake, to think clearly. He shook the mouse to stir his monitors. They could afford to nap, to go dark awhile, but he couldn't.

A wireframe apartment sat in the middle of his new screen. Donald zoomed out and watched the apartment sink away and a hallway appear, then dozens of identical wedge-shaped living quarters squeeze in from the edges. The building specs called for a bunker that could house ten thousand people for at least a year – utter overkill. Donald approached the task as he would any design project. He imagined himself in their place, a toxic spill, a leak or some horrible fallout, a terrorist attack, something that might send all of the facility workers underground where they would have to stay for weeks or months until the area was cleared.

The view pulled back further until other floors appeared above and below, empty floors he would eventually fill with storerooms, hallways, more apartments. Entire other floors and mechanical spaces had been left empty for Anna—

'Donny?'

His door opened – the knock came after. Donald's arm jerked so hard his mouse went skidding off the pad and across his desk. He sat up straight, peered over his monitors and saw Mick Webb grinning at him from the doorway. Mick had his jacket tucked under one arm, tie hanging loose, a peppery stubble on his dark skin. He laughed at Donald's harried expression and sauntered across the room. Donald fumbled for the mouse and quickly minimised the AutoCAD window.

'Shit, man, you haven't taken up day-trading, have you?'

'Day-trading?' Donald leaned back in his chair.

'Yeah. What's with the new set-up?' Mick walked around behind the desk and rested a hand on the back of Donald's chair. An abandoned game of Freecell sat embarrassingly on the smaller of the two screens.

'Oh, the extra monitor.' Donald minimised the card game and turned in his seat. 'I like having a handful of programs up at the same time.'

'I can see that.' Mick gestured at the empty monitors, the wallpaper of cherry blossoms framing the Jefferson Memorial.

Donald laughed and rubbed his face. He could feel his own stubble, had forgotten to eat dinner. The project had only begun a week ago and he was already a wreck.

'I'm heading out for a drink,' Mick told him. 'You wanna come?'

'Sorry. I've got a little more to do here.'

Mick clasped his shoulder and squeezed until it hurt. 'I hate to break it to you, man, but you're gonna have to start over. You bury an ace like that, there's no coming back. C'mon, let's get a drink.'

'Seriously, I can't.' Donald twisted out from his friend's grasp and turned to face him. 'I'm working on those plans for Atlanta. I'm not supposed to let anyone see them. It's top secret.'

For emphasis, he reached out and closed the folder on

his desk. The Senator had told him there would be a division of labour and that the walls of that divide needed to be a mile high.

'Ohhh. *Top secret.*' Mick waggled both hands in the air. 'I'm working on the same project, asshole.' He waved at the monitor. 'And you're doing the plans? What gives? My GPA was higher than yours.' He leaned over the desk and stared at the taskbar. 'AutoCAD? Cool. C'mon, let's see it.'

'Yeah, right.'

'Come the fuck on. Don't be a child about this.'

Donald laughed. 'Look, even the people on my team aren't going to see the entire plan. And neither will I.'

'That's ridiculous.'

'No, it's how government shit like this gets done. You don't see me prying into your part in all this.'

Mick waved a hand dismissively. 'Whatever. Grab your coat. Let's go.'

'Fine, sure.' Donald patted his cheeks with his palms, trying to wake up. 'I'll work better in the morning.'

'Working on a Saturday. Thurman must love you.'

'Let's hope so. Just give me a couple of minutes to shut this down.'

Mick laughed. 'Go ahead. I'm not looking.' He walked over to the door while Donald finished up.

When Donald stood to go, his desk phone rang. His secretary wasn't there, so it was someone with his direct line. Donald reached for it and held up a finger to Mick.

'Helen—'

Someone cleared their throat on the other end. A deep and rough voice apologised: 'Sorry, no.'

'Oh.' Donald glanced up at Mick, who was tapping his watch. 'Hello, sir.'

'You boys going out?' Senator Thurman asked.

Donald turned to the window. 'Excuse me?'

'You and Mick. It's a Friday night. Are you hitting the town?'

'Uh, just the one drink, sir.'

What Donald wanted to know was how the hell the Senator knew Mick was there.

'Good. Tell Mick I need to see him first thing Monday morning. My office. You too. We need to discuss your first trip down to the job site.'

'Oh. Okay.'

Donald waited, wondering if that was all.

'You boys will be working closely on this moving forward.'

'Good. Of course.'

'As we discussed last week, there won't be any need to share details about what you're working on with other project members. The same goes for Mick.'

'Yes, sir. Absolutely. I remember our talk.'

'Excellent. You boys have a good time. Oh, and if Mick starts blabbing, you have my permission to kill him on the spot.'

There was a breath of silence, and then the hearty laugh of a man whose lungs sounded much younger than his years.

'Ah.' Donald watched Mick, who had taken out the plug from a decanter to take a sniff. 'Okay, sir. I'll be sure to do that.'

'Great. See you Monday.'

The Senator hung up abruptly. As Donald returned the phone to its cradle and grabbed his coat, his new monitor remained quietly perched on his desk, watching him blankly.

6

2110

• Silo 1 •

Troy's beaten-up plastic meal tray slid down the line behind the spattered sheet of glass. Once his badge was scanned, a measured portion of canned string beans fell out of a tube and formed a steaming pile on his plate. A perfectly round cut of turkey plopped from the next tube, the ridges still visible from the tin. Mashed potatoes spat out at the end of the line like a spit wad from a child's straw. Gravy followed with an unappetising squirt.

Behind the serving line stood a heavyset man in white overalls, hands clasped behind his back. He didn't seem interested in the food. He concentrated on the workers as they lined up for their meals.

When Troy's tray reached the end of the line, a younger man in pale green overalls and probably not out of his twenties arranged silverware and napkins by the plate. A glass of water was added from a tightly packed tray nearby. The final step was like a ritualised handshake, one Troy remembered from the months of orientation: a small plastic shot glass was handed over, a pill rattling in the bottom, a blurry blue shape barely visible through the translucent cup.

Troy shuffled into place.

'Hello, sir.'

A young grin. Perfect teeth. Everyone called him sir, even those much older. It was discomfiting no matter who it came from.

The pill rattled in the plastic. Troy took the cup and tossed the pill down. He swallowed it dry, grabbed his tray and tried not to hold up the line. Searching for a seat, he caught the heavyset man watching him. Everyone in the facility seemed to think Troy was in charge, but he wasn't fooled. He was just another person doing a job, following a script. He found an empty spot facing the screen. Unlike that first day, it no longer bothered him to see the scorched world outside. The view had grown oddly comforting. It created a dull ache in his chest, which was near to feeling *something*.

A mouthful of potatoes and gravy washed away the taste of the pill. Water was never up to the task, could never take away the bitterness. Eating methodically, he watched the sun set on the first week of his first shift. Twenty-five more weeks to go. It was a countable number phrased like that. It seemed shorter than half a year.

An older gentleman in blue overalls with thinning hair sat down diagonally across from him, polite enough not to block the view. Troy recognised the man, had spoken with him once by the recycling bin. When he looked up, Troy nodded in greeting.

The cafeteria hummed pleasantly as they both ate. A few hushed conversations rose and faded. Plastic, glass and metal beat out a rhythmless tune.

Troy glanced at the view and felt there was something he was supposed to know, something he kept forgetting. He awoke each morning with familiar shapes at the edges of his vision, could feel memories nearby, but by the time breakfast came, they were already fading. By dinner, they were lost. It left Troy with a sadness, a cold sensation, and a feeling like a hollow stomach – different from hunger – like rainy days as a child when he didn't know how to fill his time.

The gentleman across from him slid over a little and cleared his throat. 'Things going okay?' he asked.

He reminded Troy of someone. Blotchy skin hung slightly loose around his weathered face. He had a drooping neck, an unsightly pinch of flesh hanging from his Adam's apple.

'Things?' Troy repeated. He returned the smile.

'Anything, I suppose. Just checking in. I go by Hal.' The

gentleman lifted his glass. Troy did the same. It was as good as a handshake.

'Troy,' he said. He supposed to some people it still mattered what they called themselves.

Hal took a long pull from his glass. His neck bobbed, the gulp loud. Self-conscious, Troy took a small sip and worked on the last of his beans and turkey.

'I've noticed some people sit facing it and some sit with their backs to it.' Hal jerked his thumb over his shoulder.

Troy looked up at the screen. He chewed his food, didn't say anything.

'I reckon those who sit and watch, they're trying to remember something,' Hal said.

Troy swallowed and forced himself to shrug.

'And those of us who don't want to watch,' Hal continued. 'I figure we're trying our best to forget.'

Troy knew they shouldn't be having this conversation, but now it had begun, and he wanted to see where it would lead.

'It's the bad stuff,' Hal said, staring off towards the lifts. 'Have you noticed that? It's just the bad stuff that slips away. All the unimportant things, we remember well.'

Troy didn't say anything. He jabbed his beans, even though he didn't plan on eating them.

'It makes you wonder, don't it? Why we all feel so rotten inside?'

Hal finished up his food, nodded a wordless goodbye and got up to leave. Troy was left alone. He found himself staring at the screen, a dull ache inside that he couldn't name. It was the time of evening just before the hills disappeared, before they darkened and faded into the cloud-filled sky.

7

2049

Washington, DC

Donald was glad he had decided to walk to his meeting with the Senator. The rain from the week before had finally let up, and the traffic in Dupont Circle was at a crawl. Heading up Connecticut and leaning into a stiffening breeze, Donald wondered why the meeting had been moved to Kramerbooks of all places. There were a dozen superior coffee houses much closer to the office.

He crossed a side street and hurried up the short flight of stone steps to the bookshop. The front door to Kramer's was one of those ancient wooden affairs older establishments hung like a boast, a testament to their endurance. Hinges squeaked and actual bells jangled overhead as he pushed open the door, and a young woman straightening books on a centre table of bestsellers glanced up and smiled hello.

The cafe, Donald saw, was packed with men and women in business suits sipping from white porcelain cups. There was no sign of the Senator. Donald started to check his phone, see if he was too early, when a Secret Service agent caught his eye.

The agent stood broad-shouldered at the end of an aisle of books in the small corner of Kramer's that acted as the cafe's bookshop. Donald laughed at how conspicuously hidden the man was: the earpiece, the bulge by his ribs, the sunglasses indoors. Donald headed the agent's way, the wooden boards underfoot groaning with age.

The agent's gaze shifted his way, but it was hard to tell if he was looking at Donald or towards the front door.

'I'm here to see Senator Thurman,' Donald said, his voice cracking a little. 'I have an appointment.'

The agent turned his head to the side. Donald followed the gesture and peered down an aisle of books to see Thurman browsing through the stacks at the far end.

'Ah. Thanks.' He stepped between the towering shelves of old books, the light dimming and the smell of coffee replaced with the tang of mildew mixed with leather.

'What do you think of this one?'

Senator Thurman held out a book as Donald approached. No greeting, just the question.

Donald checked the title embossed in gold on the thick leather cover. 'Never heard of it,' he admitted.

Senator Thurman laughed. 'Of course not. It's over a hundred years old – and it's French. I mean, what do you think of the *binding*?' He handed Donald the book.

Donald was surprised by how heavy the volume was. He cracked it open and flipped through a few pages. It felt like a law book, had that same dense heft, but he could see by the white space between lines of dialogue that it was a novel. As he turned a few pages, he admired how thin the individual sheets were. Where the pages met at the spine, they had been stitched together with tiny ropes of blue and gold thread. He had friends who still swore by physical books – not for decoration, but to actually read. Studying the one in his hand, Donald could understand their nostalgic affection.

'The binding looks great,' he said, brushing it with the pads of his fingers. 'It's a beautiful book.' He handed the novel back to the Senator. 'Is this how you shop for a good read? You mostly go by the cover?'

Thurman tucked the book under his arm and pulled another from the shelf. 'It's just a sample for another project I'm working on.' He turned and narrowed his eyes at Donald. It was an uncomfortable gaze. He felt like prey.

'How's your sister doing?' he asked.

The question caught Donald off guard. A lump formed in his throat at the mention of her.

'Charlotte? She's . . . she's fine, I guess. She redeployed. I'm sure you heard.'

'I did.' Thurman slotted the book in his hand back into a gap and weighed the one Donald had appraised. 'I was proud of her for re-upping. She does her country proud.'

Donald thought about what it cost a family to do a country proud.

'Yeah,' he said. 'I mean, I know my parents were really looking forward to having her home, but she was having trouble adjusting to the pace back here. It . . . I don't think she'll be able to really *relax* until the war's over. You know?'

'I do. And she may not find peace even then.'

That wasn't what Donald wanted to hear. He watched the Senator trace his finger down an ornate spine adorned with ridges, bumps and recessed lettering. The old man's eyes seemed to focus beyond the rows of books.

'I can drop her a line if you want. Sometimes a soldier just needs to hear that it's okay to see someone.'

'If you mean a shrink, she won't do it.' Donald recalled the changes in his sister around the time of her sessions. 'We already tried.'

Thurman's lips pursed into a thin, wrinkled line, his worry revealing hidden signs of age. 'I'll talk to her. I'm familiar enough with the hubris of youth, believe me. I used to have the same attitude when I was younger. I thought I didn't need any help, that I could do everything on my own.' He turned to face Donald. 'The profession's come a long way. They have pills now that can help her with the battle fatigue.'

Donald shook his head. 'No. She was on those for a while. They made her too forgetful. And they caused a . . .' He hesitated, didn't want to talk about it. '. . . a *tic*.'

He wanted to say tremors, but that sounded too severe. And while he appreciated the Senator's concern – this feeling as if the man was family – he was uncomfortable discussing his sister's problems. He remembered the last time she was home, the disagreement they'd had while going through his and Helen's photographs from Mexico. He had asked

Charlotte if she remembered Cozumel from when they were kids, and she had insisted she'd never been. The disagreement had turned into an argument, and he had lied and said his tears were ones of frustration. Parts of his sister's life had been erased, and the only way the doctors could explain it was to say that it must've been something she *wanted* to forget. And what could be wrong with that?

Thurman rested a hand on Donald's arm. 'Trust me on this,' he said quietly. 'I'll talk to her. I know what she's going through.'

Donald bobbed his head. 'Yeah. Okay. I appreciate it.' He almost added that it wouldn't do any good, could possibly cause harm, but the gesture was a nice one. And it would come from someone his sister looked up to, rather than from family.

'And hey, Donny, she's piloting drones.' Thurman studied him, seemed to be picking up on his worry. 'It's not like she's in any physical danger.'

Donald rubbed the spine of a shelved book. 'Not physical, no.'

They fell silent, and Donald let out a heavy breath. He could hear the chatter from the cafe, the clink of a spoon stirring in some sugar, the clang of bells against the old wooden door, the squeal and hiss of milk being steamed.

He had seen videos of what Charlotte did, camera feeds from the drones and then from the missiles as they were guided in to their targets. The video quality was amazing. You could see people turning to look up to the heavens in surprise, could see the last moments of their lives, could cycle through the video frame by frame and decide – after the fact – if this had been your man or not. He knew what his sister did, what she dealt with.

'I spoke with Mick earlier,' Thurman said, seeming to sense that he'd brought up a sore topic. 'You two are going to head down to Atlanta and see how the excavation is going.'

Donald snapped to. 'Of course. Yeah, it'll be good to get the lay of the land. I got a nice head start on my plans last week, gradually filling in the dimensions you set out. You do realise how deep this thing goes, right?'

'That's why they're already digging the foundations. The outer walls should be getting a pour over the next few weeks.' Senator Thurman patted Donald's shoulder and nodded towards the end of the aisle, signalling that they were finished looking through books.

'Wait. They're already *digging*?' Donald walked alongside Thurman. 'I've only got an outline ready. I hope they're saving mine for last.'

'The entire complex is being worked on at the same time. All they're pouring are the outer walls and foundations, the dimensions of which are fixed. We'll fill each structure from the bottom up, the floors craned down completely furnished before we pour the slabs between. But look, this is why I need you boys to go check things out. It sounds like a damned nightmare down there with the staging. I've got a hundred crews from a dozen countries working on top of one another while materials pile up everywhere. I can't be in ten places at once, so I need you to get a read on things and report back.'

When they reached the Secret Service agent at the end of the aisle, the Senator handed him the old book with the French embossing. The man in the dark shades nodded and headed towards the counter.

'While you're down there,' Thurman said, 'I want you to meet up with Charlie Rhodes. He's handling delivery of most of the building materials. See if he needs anything.'

'*Charles* Rhodes? As in the governor of Oklahoma?'

'That's right. We served together. And hey, I'm working on transitioning you and Mick into some of the higher levels of this project. Our leadership team is still short a few dozen members. So keep up the good work. You've impressed some important people with what you've put together so far, and Anna seems confident you'll be able to stay ahead of schedule. She says the two of you make a great team.'

Donald nodded. He felt a blush of pride – and also the

inevitability of extra responsibilities, more bites out of his ever-dwindling time. Helen wouldn't like hearing that his involvement with the project might grow. In fact, Mick and Anna might be the only people he could share the news with, the only ones he could talk to. Every detail about the build seemed to require convoluted layers of clearance. He couldn't tell if it was the fear of nuclear waste, the threat of a terrorist attack or the likelihood that the project would fall through.

The agent returned and took up a position beside the Senator, shopping bag in hand. He looked over at Donald and seemed to study him through those impenetrable sunglasses. Not for the first time, Donald felt watched.

Senator Thurman shook Donald's hand and said to keep him posted. Another agent materialised from nowhere and formed up on Thurman's flank. They marched the Senator through the jangling door, and Donald only relaxed once they were out of view.

8

2110

• Silo 1 •

The Book of the Order lay open on his desk, the pages curling up from a spine stitched to last. Troy studied the upcoming procedure once again, his first official act as head of Operation Fifty, and it brought to mind a ribbon-cutting ceremony, a grand display where the man with the shears took credit for the hard work of others.

The Order, he had decided, was more recipe book than operations manual. The shrinks who had written it had accounted for everything, every quirk of human nature. And like the field of psychology, or any field that involved human nature, the parts that made no sense usually served some deeper purpose.

It made Troy wonder what *his* purpose was. How necessary his position. He had studied for a much different job, was meant to be head of a single silo, not all of them. He had been promoted at the last minute, and that made him feel arbitrary, as if anyone could be slotted into his place.

Of course, even if his office was mostly titular, perhaps it served some symbolic purpose. Maybe he wasn't there to lead so much as to provide an illusion to the others that *they were being led.*

Troy skipped back two paragraphs in the Order. His eyes had passed over every word, but none of them had registered. Everything about his new life made him prone to distraction, made him think too much. It had all been perfectly arranged – all the levels and tasks and job descriptions – but for what? For maximum *apathy?*

Glancing up, he could see Victor sitting at his desk in the Office for Psychological Services across the hall. It would be easy enough to walk over there and ask. They, more than any one architect, had designed this place. He could ask them how they had done it, how they had managed to make everyone feel so empty inside.

Sheltering the women and the children played some part; Troy was sure of that. The women and children of silo one had been gifted with a long sleep while the men stayed and took shifts. It removed the passion from the plans, forestalled the chance that the men might fight among themselves.

And then there was the routine, the mind-numbing routine. It was the castration of thought, the daily grind of an office worker who drooled at the clock, punched out, watched TV until sleep overtook him, slapped an alarm three times, did it again. It was made worse by the absence of weekends. There were no free days. It was six months on and *decades* off.

It made him envious of the rest of the facility, all the other silos, where hallways must echo with the laughter of children, the voices of women, the passion and happiness missing from this bunker at the heart of it all. Here, all he saw was stupor, dozens of communal rooms with movies playing in loops on flat-panel TVs, dozens of unblinking eyes in comfortable chairs. No one was truly awake. No one was truly alive. They must have wanted it that way.

Checking the clock on his computer, Troy saw that it was time to go. Another day behind him. Another day closer to the end of his shift. He closed his copy of the Order, locked it away in his desk and headed for the communications room down the hall.

A pair of heads looked up from the radio stations as he walked in, all frowns and lowered brows in their orange coveralls. Troy took a deep breath, pulled himself together. This was an office. It was a job. And he was the man in charge. He just had to keep his shit together. He was there to cut a ribbon.

Saul, one of the lead radio techs, took off his headset and

rose to greet him. Troy vaguely knew Saul; they lived on the
same executive wing and saw each other in the gym from
time to time. While they shook hands, Saul's wide and handsome face tickled some deeper memory, an itch Troy had
learned to ignore. Maybe this was someone he had met at
his orientation, from before his long sleep.

Saul introduced him to the other tech in comm room
orange, who waved and kept his headset on. The name faded
immediately. It didn't matter. An extra headset was pulled
from a rack. Troy accepted it and lowered it around his neck,
keeping the muffs off his ears so he could still hear. Saul
found the silvery jack at the end of the headset and ran his
fingers across an array of fifty numbered receptacles. The
layout and the room reminded Troy of ancient photographs
of phone operators back before they were replaced with
computers and automated voices.

The mental image of a bygone day mixed and fizzed with
his nerves and the shivers brought on by the pills, and Troy
felt a sudden bout of giggles bubble beneath the surface. The
laughter nearly burst out of him, but he managed to hold it
together. It wouldn't be a good sign for the head of overall
operations to lurch into hysterics when he was about to gauge
the fitness of a future silo head.

'—and you'll just run through the set questions,' Saul was
telling him. He held out a plastic card to Troy, who was pretty
sure he didn't need it but took it anyway. He'd been memor-
ising the routine for most of the day. Besides, he was sure it
didn't matter what he said. The task of gauging a candidate's
fitness was better left to the machines and the computers, all
the sensors embedded in a distant headset.

'Okay. There's the call.' Saul pointed to a single flashing
light on a panel studded with flashing lights. 'I'm patching
you through.'

Troy adjusted the muffs around his ears as the tech made
the connection. He heard a few beeps before the line clicked
over. Someone was breathing heavily on the other end. Troy
reminded himself that this young man would be far more

nervous than he was. After all, he had to *answer* the questions – Troy simply had to ask them.

He glanced down at the card in his hand, his mind suddenly blank, thankful that he'd been given the thing.

'Name?' he asked the young man.

'Marcus Dent, sir.'

There was a quiet confidence in his young voice, the sound of a chest thrust out with pride. Troy remembered feeling that once, a long time ago. And then he thought of the world Marcus Dent had been born into, a legacy *he* would only ever know from books.

'Tell me about your training,' Troy said, reading the lines. He tried to keep his voice even, deep, full of command, although the computers were designed to do that for him. Saul made a hoop with his finger and thumb, letting him know he was getting good data from the boy's headset. Troy wondered if his was similarly equipped. Could anyone in that room – or any other room – tell how nervous he was?

'Well, sir, I shadowed under Deputy Willis before transferring to IT Security. That was a year ago. I've been studying the Order for six weeks. I feel ready, sir.'

Shadowing. Troy had forgotten it was called that. He had meant to bring the latest vocabulary card with him.

'What is your primary duty to the . . . silo?' He had nearly said *facility.*

'To maintain the Order, sir.'

'And what do you protect above all?' He kept his voice flat. The best readings would come from not imparting too much emotion into the man being measured.

'Life and Legacy,' Marcus recited.

Troy had a difficult time seeing the next question. It was obscured by an unexpected blur of tears. His hand trembled. He lowered the shaking card to his side before anyone noticed.

'And what does it take to protect the things we hold dear?' he asked. His voice sounded like someone else's. He ground his teeth together to keep them from chattering. Something was wrong with him. Powerfully wrong.

'Sacrifice,' Marcus said, steady as a rock.

Troy blinked rapidly to clear his vision, and Saul held up his hand to let him know he could continue, that the measures were coming through. Now they needed baselines so the biometrics could tease out the boy's sincerity towards the first questions.

'Tell me, Marcus, do you have a girlfriend?'

He didn't know why that was the first thing that came to mind. Maybe it was the envy that other silos didn't freeze their women, didn't freeze anyone at all. Nobody in the comm room seemed to react or care. The formal portion of the test was over.

'Oh, yessir,' Marcus said, and Troy heard the boy's breathing change, could imagine his body relaxing. 'We've applied to be married, sir. Just waiting to hear back.'

'Well, I don't think you'll have to wait too much longer. What's her name?'

'Melanie, sir. She works here in IT.'

'That's great.' Troy wiped at his eyes. The shivers passed. Saul waved his finger in a circle over his head, letting him know he could wrap it up. They had enough.

'Marcus Dent,' he said, 'welcome to Operation Fifty of the World Order.'

'Thank you, sir.' The young man's voice lifted an octave.

There was a pause, then the sound of a deep breath being taken and held.

'Sir? Is it okay if I ask a question?'

Troy looked to the others. There were shrugs and not much else. He considered the role this young man had just assumed, knew well the sensation of being promoted to new responsibilities, that mix of fear, eagerness and confusion.

'Sure, son. One question.' He figured he was in charge. He could make a few rules of his own.

Marcus cleared his throat, and Troy pictured this shadow and his silo head sitting in a distant room together, the master studying his student.

'I lost my great-grandmother a few years ago,' Marcus

said. 'She used to let slip little things about the world before. Not in a forbidden way, but just as a product of her dementia. The doctors said she was resistant to her medication.'

Troy didn't like the sound of this, that third-generation survivors were gleaning anything about the past. Marcus may be newly cleared for such things, but others weren't.

'What's your question?' Troy asked.

'The Legacy, sir. I've done some reading in it as well – not neglecting my studies of the Order and the Pact, of course – and there's something I have to know.'

Another deep breath.

'Is everything in the Legacy true?'

Troy thought about this. He considered the great collection of books that contained the world's history – a carefully edited history. In his mind, he could see the leather spines and the gilded pages, the rows and rows of books they had been shown during their orientation.

He nodded and found himself once again needing to wipe his eyes.

'Yes,' he told Marcus, his voice dry and flat. 'It's true.'

Someone in the room sniffled. Troy knew the ceremony had gone on long enough.

'Everything in there is absolutely true.'

He didn't add that not *every* true thing was written in the Legacy. Much had been left out. And there were other things he suspected that *none* of them knew, that had been edited out of books and brains alike.

The Legacy was the allowed truth, he wanted to say, the truth that was carried from each generation to the next. But the lies, he thought to himself, were what they carried there in silo one, in that drug-hazed asylum charged somehow with humanity's survival.

9

2049

Fulton County, Georgia

The front-end loader let out a throaty blat as it struggled up the hill, a charcoal geyser streaming from its exhaust pipe. When it reached the top, a load of dirt avalanched out of its toothy bucket, and Donald saw that the loader wasn't climbing the hill so much as creating it.

Hills of fresh dirt were taking shape like this all over the site. Between them – through temporary gaps left open like an ordered maze – burdened dump trucks carried away soil and rock from the cavernous pits being hollowed from the earth. These gaps, Donald knew from the topographical plans, would one day be pushed closed, leaving little more than a shallow crease where each hill met its neighbour.

Standing on one of these growing mounds, Donald watched the ballet of heavy machinery while Mick Webb spoke with a contractor about the delays. In their white shirts and flapping ties, the two congressmen seemed out of place. The men in hard hats with the leather faces, calloused hands and busted knuckles belonged there. He and Mick, blazers tucked under their arms, sweat stains spreading in the humid Georgia heat, were somehow – nominally, at least – supposed to be in charge of that ungodly commotion.

Another loader released a mound of soil as Donald shifted his gaze towards downtown Atlanta. Past the massive clearing of rising hills and over the treetops still stripped bare from fading winter rose the glass-and-steel spires of the old Southern city. An entire corner of sparsely populated Fulton County had been cleared. Remnants of a golf course were still visible at one end where the machines had yet to disturb the land.

Down by the main parking lot, a staging zone the size of several football fields held thousands of shipping containers packed with building supplies, more than Donald thought necessary. But he was learning by the hour that this was the way of government projects, where public expectations were as high as the spending limits. Everything was done in excess or not at all. The plans he had been ordered to draw up practically begged for proportions of insanity, and his building wasn't even a necessary component of the facility. It was only there for the worst-case scenario.

Between Donald and the field of shipping containers stood a sprawling city of trailers; a few functioned as offices, but most of them served as housing. This was where the thousands of men and women working on the construction could ditch their hard hats, clock off and take their well-earned rest.

Flags flew over many of the trailers, the workforce as multinational as an Olympic village. Spent nuclear fuel rods from the world over would one day be buried beneath the pristine soil of Fulton County. It meant that the world had a stake in the project's success. The logistical nightmare this ensured didn't seem to concern the back-room dealers. He and Mick were finding that many of the early construction delays could be traced to language barriers, as neighbouring work crews couldn't communicate with one another and had evidently given up trying. Everyone simply worked on their set of plans, heads down, ignoring the rest.

Beside this temporary city of tin cans sat the vast parking lot he and Mick had trudged up from. He could see their rental car down there, the only quiet and electric thing in sight. Small and silver, it seemed to cower among the belching dump trucks and loaders on all sides. The overmatched car looked precisely how Donald felt, both on that little hill at the construction site and back at the Hill in Washington.

'Two months behind.'

Mick smacked him on the arm with his clipboard. 'Hey, did you hear me? Two months behind already, and they just broke ground six months ago. How is that even possible?'

Donald shrugged as they left the frowning foremen and trudged down the hill to the parking lot. 'Maybe it's because they have elected officials pretending to do jobs that belong to the private sector,' he offered.

Mick laughed and squeezed his shoulder. 'Jesus, Donny, you sound like a goddamned Republican!'

'Yeah? Well, I feel like we're in over our heads here.' He waved his arm at the depression in the hills they were skirting, a deep bowl scooped out of the earth. Several mixer trucks were pouring concrete into the wide hole at its centre. More trucks waited in line behind them, their butts spinning impatiently.

'You do realise,' Donald said, 'that one of these holes is going to hold the building they let *me* draw up? Doesn't that scare you? All this money? All these people. It sure as hell scares me.'

Mick's fingers dug painfully into Donald's neck. 'Take it easy. Don't go getting all philosophical on me.'

'I'm being serious,' Donald said. 'Billions of taxpayer dollars are gonna nestle in the dirt out there in the shape that *I* drew up. It seemed so . . . *abstract* before.'

'Christ, this isn't about you or your plans.' He popped Donald with the clipboard and used it to point towards the container field. Through a fog of dust, a large man in a cowboy hat waved them over. 'Besides,' Mick said, as they angled away from the parking lot, 'what're the chances anyone even uses your little bunker? This is about energy independence. It's about the death of coal. You know, it feels like the rest of us are building a nice big house over here, and you're over in a corner stressing about where you're gonna hang the fire extinguisher—'

'*Little bunker?*' Donald held his blazer up over his mouth as a cloud of dust blew across them. 'Do you know how many floors *deep* this thing is gonna be? If you set it on the ground, it'd be the tallest building in the world.'

Mick laughed. 'Not for long it wouldn't. Not if you designed it.'

The man in the cowboy hat drew closer. He smiled widely as he kicked through the packed dirt to meet them, and Donald finally recognised him from TV: Charles Rhodes, the governor of Oklahoma.

'You Senator Thawman's boys?'

Governor Rhodes had the authentic drawl to go with the authentic hat, the authentic boots and the authentic buckle. He rested his hands on his wide hips, a clipboard in one of them.

Mick nodded. 'Yessir. I'm Congressman Webb. This is Congressman Keene.'

The two men shook hands. Donald was next. 'Governor,' he said.

'Got your delivery.' He pointed the clipboard at the staging area. 'Just shy of a hundred containers. Should have somethin' rollin' in about every week. Need one of you to sign right here.'

Mick reached out and took the clipboard. Donald saw an opportunity to ask something about Senator Thurman, something he figured an old war buddy would know.

'Why do some people call him Thawman?' he asked.

Mick flipped through the delivery report, a breeze pinning back the pages for him.

'I've heard others call him that when he wasn't around,' Donald explained, 'but I've been too scared to ask.'

Mick looked up from the report with a grin. 'It's because he was an ice-cold killer in the war, right?'

Donald cringed. Governor Rhodes laughed.

'Unrelated,' he said. 'True, but unrelated.'

The governor glanced back and forth between them. Mick passed the clipboard to Donald, tapped a page that dealt with the emergency housing facility. Donald looked over the materials list.

'You boys familiar with his anti-cryo bill?' Governor Rhodes asked. He handed Donald a pen, seemed to expect him to just sign the thing and not look over it too closely.

Mick shook his head and shielded his eyes against the Georgia sun. 'Anti-cryo?' he asked.

'Yeah. Aw, hell, this probably dates back before you squirts were even born. Senator Thawman penned the bill that put down that cryo fad. Made it illegal to take advantage of rich folk and turn them into ice cubes. It went to the big court, where they voted five–four, and suddenly tens of thousands of popsicles with more money than sense were thawed out and buried proper. These were people who'd frozen themselves in the hopes that doctors from the future would discover some medical procedure for extracting their rich heads from their own rich asses!'

The governor laughed at his own joke and Mick joined him. A line on the delivery report caught Donald's eye. He turned the clipboard around and showed the governor. 'Uh, this shows two thousand spools of fibre optic. I'm pretty sure my plans call for forty spools.'

'Lemme see.' Governor Rhodes took the clipboard and procured another pen from his pocket. He clicked the top of it three times, then scratched out the quantity. He wrote in a new number to the side.

'Wait, will the price reflect that?'

'Price is the same,' he said. 'Just sign the bottom.'

'But—'

'Son, this is why hammers cost the Pentagon their weight in gold. It's government accounting. Just a signature, please.'

'But that's *fifty times* more fibre than we'll need,' Donald complained, even as he found himself scribbling his name. He passed the clipboard to Mick, who signed for the rest of the goods.

'Oh, that's all right.' Rhodes took the clipboard and pinched the brim of his hat. 'I'm sure they'll find a use for it somewhere.'

'Hey, you know,' Mick said, 'I remember that cryo bill. From law school. There were lawsuits, weren't there? Didn't a group of families bring murder charges against the Feds?'

The governor smiled. 'Yeah, but it didn't get far. Hard to

prove you killed people who'd already been pronounced dead. And then there were Thawman's bad business investments. Those turned out to be a lifesaver.'

Rhodes tucked his thumb in his belt and stuck out his chest.

'Turned out he'd sunk a fortune into one of these cryo companies before digging deeper and reconsidering the . . . *ethical* considerations. Old Thawman may have lost most of his money, but it ended up savin' his ass in Washington. Made him look like some kinda saint, suffering a loss like that. Only defence better woulda been if he'd unplugged his dear momma with all them others.'

Mick and the governor laughed. Donald didn't see what was so funny.

'All right, now, you boys take care. The good state of Oklahoma'll have another load for ya in a few weeks.'

'Sounds good,' Mick said, grasping and pumping that huge Midwestern paw.

Donald shook the governor's hand as well, and he and Mick trudged off towards their rental. Overhead, against the bright blue Southern sky, vapour trails like stretched ropes of white yarn revealed the flight lines of the numerous jets departing the busy hub of Atlanta International. And as the throaty noise of the construction site faded, the chants from the anti-nuke protestors could be heard outside the tall mesh of security fences beyond. They passed through the security gate and into the parking lot, the guard waving them along.

'Hey, you mind if I drop you off at the airport a little early?' Donald asked. 'It'd be nice to get a jump on traffic and get down to Savannah with some daylight.'

'That's right,' Mick said with a grin. 'You've got a hot date tonight.'

Donald laughed.

'Sure, man. Abandon me and go have a good time with your wife.'

'Thanks.'

Mick fished out the keys to the rental. 'But you know, I

was really hoping you'd invite me to come along. I could join you two for dinner, crash at your place, hit some bars like old times.'

'Not a chance,' Donald said.

Mick slapped the back of Donald's neck and squeezed. 'Yeah, well, happy anniversary anyway.'

Donald winced as his friend pinched his neck. 'Thanks,' he said. 'I'll be sure to give Helen your regards.'

10

2110

• Silo 1 •

Troy played a hand of solitaire while silo twelve collapsed. There was something about the game that he found blissfully numbing. The repetition held off the waves of depression even better than the pills. The lack of skill required moved beyond distraction and into the realm of complete mindlessness. The truth was, the player won or lost the very moment the computer shuffled the deck. The rest was simply a process of finding out.

For a computer game, it was absurdly low-tech. Instead of cards, there was just a grid of letters and numbers with an asterisk, ampersand, per cent or plus sign to designate the suit. It bothered Troy not to know which symbol stood for hearts or clubs or diamonds. Even though it was arbitrary, even though it didn't really matter, it frustrated him not to know.

He had stumbled upon the game by accident while digging through some folders. It took a bit of experimenting to learn how to flip the draw deck with the space bar and place the cards with the arrow keys, but he had plenty of time to work things like this out. Besides meeting with department heads, going over Merriman's notes and refreshing himself on the Order, all he had was time. Time to collapse in his office bathroom and cry until snot ran down his chin, time to sit under a scalding shower and shiver, time to hide pills in his cheek and squirrel them away for when the hurt was the worst, time to wonder why the drugs weren't working like they used to, even when he doubled the dosage on his own.

Perhaps the game's numbing powers were the reason it existed at all, why someone had spent the effort to create it, and why subsequent heads had kept it secreted away. He had seen it on Merriman's face during that lift ride at the end of his shift. The chemicals only cut through the worst of the pain, that indefinable ache. But lesser wounds resurfaced. The bouts of sudden sadness had to be coming from somewhere.

The last few cards fell into place while his mind wandered. The computer had shuffled for a win, and Troy got all the credit for verifying it. The screen flashed GOOD JOB! in large block letters. It was strangely satisfying to be told this by a home-made game – told that he had done a good job. There was a sense of completion, of having *done* something with his day.

He left the message flashing and glanced around his office for something else to do. There were amendments to be made in the Order, announcements to write up for the heads of the other silos, and he needed to make sure the vocabulary in these memos adhered to the ever-changing standards.

He got it wrong himself, often calling them bunkers instead of silos. It was difficult for those who had lived in the time of the Legacy. An old vocabulary, a way of seeing the world, persisted despite the medication. He felt envious of the men and women in the other silos, those who were born and who would die in their own little worlds, who would fall in and out of love, who would keep their hurts in memory, feel them, learn from them, be changed by them. He was jealous of these people even more than he envied the women of his silo who remained in their long-sleep lifeboats—

There was a knock on his open door. Troy looked up and saw Randall, who worked across the hall in the psych office, standing in the doorway. Troy waved him inside with one hand and minimised the game with the other. He fidgeted with the copy of the Order on his desk, trying to look busy.

'I've got that beliefs report you wanted.' Randall waved a folder.

'Oh, good. Good.' Troy took the folder. Always with the folders. He was reminded of the two groups that had built that place: the politicians and the doctors. Both were stuck in a prior era, a time of paperwork. Or was it possible that neither group trusted any data they couldn't shred or burn?

'The head of silo six has a new replacement picked out and processed. He wants to schedule a talk with you, make the induction formal.'

'Oh. Okay.' Troy flipped through the folder and saw typed transcripts from the comm room about each of the silos. He looked forward to another induction ceremony. Any task he had already done once before filled him with less dread.

'Also, the population report on silo thirty-two is a little troubling.' Randall came around Troy's desk and licked his thumb before sorting through the reports, and Troy glanced at his monitor to make sure he'd minimised the game. 'They're getting close to the maximum and fast. Doc Haines thinks it might be a bad batch of birth control implants. The head of thirty-two, a Biggers . . . Here we go.' Randall pulled out the report. 'He denies this, says no one with an active implant has gotten pregnant. He thinks the lottery is being gamed or that there's something wrong with our computers.'

'Hmm.' Troy took the report and looked it over. Silo thirty-two had crept above nine thousand inhabitants, and the median age had fallen into the low twenties. 'Let's set up a call for first thing in the morning. I don't buy the lottery being gamed. They shouldn't even be running the lottery, right? Until they have more space?'

'That's what I said.'

'And all the population accounts for every silo are run from the same computer.' Troy tried not to make this sound like a question, but it was. He couldn't remember.

'Yup,' Randall confirmed.

'Which means we're being lied to. I mean, this doesn't happen overnight, right? Biggers had to see this coming, which means he knew about it earlier, so either he's complicit, or he's lost control over there.'

'Exactly.'

'Okay. What do we know about Biggers's second?'

'His shadow?' Randall hesitated. 'I'd have to pull that file, but I know he's been in place for a while. He was there before we started our shifts.'

'Good. I'll speak with him tomorrow. Alone.'

'You think we should replace Biggers?'

Troy nodded grimly. The Order was clear on problems that defied explanation: *Start at the top. Assume the explanation is a lie.* Because of the rules, he and Randall were talking about a man being put out of commission as if he were broken machinery.

'Okay, one more thing—'

The thunder of boots down the hallway interrupted the thought. Randall and Troy looked up as Saul bolted into the room, his eyes wide with fear.

'Sirs—'

'Saul. What's going on?'

The communications officer looked like he'd seen a thousand ghosts.

'We need you in the comm room, sir. Right now.'

Troy pushed away from his desk. Randall was right behind him.

'What is it?' Troy asked.

Saul hurried down the hallway. 'It's silo twelve, sir.'

The three of them ran past a man on a ladder who was replacing a long light bulb that had gone dim, the large rectangular plastic cover above him hanging open like a doorway to the heavens. Troy found himself breathing hard as he struggled to keep up.

'What *about* silo twelve?' he huffed.

Saul flashed a look over his shoulder, his face screwed up with worry. 'I think we're losing it, sir.'

'What, like contact? You can't reach them?'

'No. Losing *it*, sir. The *silo*. The whole damn thing.'

11

2049

Savannah, Georgia

Donald wasn't one for napkins, but he obeyed decorum by shaking the folded cloth loose and draping it in his lap. Each of the napkins at the other settings around the table had been bent into a decorative pyramid that stood upright amid the silverware. He didn't remember the Corner Diner having cloth napkins when he was in high school. Didn't they used to have those paper napkin dispensers that were all dented up from years of abuse? And those little salt and pepper shakers with the silver caps, even those had gotten fancier. A dish of what he assumed was sea salt sat near the flower arrangement, and if you wanted pepper, you had to wait for someone to come around and crack it on your food for you.

He started to mention this to his wife, and saw that she was gazing past him at the booth behind. Donald turned in his seat, the original vinyl squeaking beneath him. He glanced back at the older couple sitting in the booth where he and Helen had sat on their first date.

'I swear I asked them to reserve it for us,' Donald said.

His wife's gaze drifted back to him.

'I think they might've gotten confused when I described which one it was.' He stirred the air with his finger. 'Or maybe I got turned around when I was on the phone.'

She waved her hand. 'Sweetie, forget about it. We could be eating grilled cheese at home and I'd be thrilled. I was just staring off into space.'

Helen unfolded her own napkin with delicate care, almost as if she were studying the folds, seeing how to piece it back together, how to return a disassembled thing to its original state. The waiter came over in a bustle and filled their glasses with water, careless drips spotting the white tablecloth. He apologised for the wait, and then left them to wait some more.

'This place sure has changed,' he said.

'Yeah. It's more grown-up.'

They both reached for their waters at the same time. Donald smiled and held his glass up. 'Fifteen years to the day that your father made the mistake of extending your curfew.'

Helen smiled and tapped her glass against his. 'To fifteen more,' she said.

They took sips.

'If this place keeps up, we won't be able to afford to eat here in fifteen years,' Donald said.

Helen laughed. She had barely changed since that first date. Or maybe it was because the changes were so subtle. It wasn't like coming to a restaurant every five years and seeing the leaps all at once. It was how siblings aged rather than distant cousins.

'You fly back in the morning?' Helen asked.

'Yeah, but to Boston. I have a meeting with the Senator.'

'Why Boston?'

He waved his hand. 'He's having one of those nano treatments of his. I think he stays locked up in there for a week or so at a time. He still somehow gets his work done—'

'Yeah, by having his minions go out of *their* way—'

'We're not his minions,' Donald said, laughing.

'—to come kiss his ring and leave gifts of myrrh.'

'C'mon, it's not like that.'

'I just worry that you're pushing yourself too hard. How much of your free time are you spending on this project of his?'

A lot, he wanted to say. He wanted to tell his wife how gruelling the hours were, but he knew how she would react. 'It's not as time-consuming as you'd think.'

'Really? Because it seems like it's the only thing I hear you talking about. I don't even know what else it is you do.'

Their waiter came past with a tray full of drinks and said it would be just a moment longer. Helen studied the menu.

'I'll be done with my portion of the plans in another few months,' he told her. 'And then I won't bore you with it any more.'

'Honey, you don't bore me. I just don't want him taking advantage of you. This isn't what you signed up for. You decided *not* to become an architect, remember? Otherwise, you could've stayed home.'

'Baby, I want you to know . . .' He dropped his voice. 'This project we're working on is—'

'It's really important, I know. You've told me, and I believe you. And then in your moments of self-doubt, you admit that your part in the entire scheme of things is superfluous anyway and will never be used.'

Donald had forgotten they'd had that conversation.

'I'll just be glad when it's done,' she said. 'They can truck the fuel rods through our *neighbourhood* for all I care. Just bury the whole thing and smooth the dirt over and stop talking about it.'

This was something else. Donald thought about the phone calls and emails he'd been getting from the district, all the headlines and fear-mongering over the route the spent rods would take from the port as the trucks skirted Atlanta. Every time Helen heard a peep about the project, all she could likely think of was him wasting his time on it rather than doing his real job. Or the fact that he could've stayed in Savannah and done the same work.

Helen cleared her throat. 'So . . .' She hesitated. 'Was Anna at the job site today?'

She peered over the lip of her glass, and Donald realised, in that moment, what his wife was *really* thinking when the CAD-FAC project and the fuel rods came up. It was the insecurity of him working with *her*, of being so far from home.

'No.' He shook his head. 'No, we don't really see each other. We send plans back and forth. Mick and I went, just the two of us. He's coordinating a lot of the materials and crews—'

The waiter arrived, pulled his black folio from his apron and clicked his pen. 'Can I start you off with drinks?'

Donald ordered two glasses of the house Merlot. Helen declined the offer of an appetiser.

'Every time I bring her up,' she said, once their waiter had angled off towards the bar, 'you mention Mick. Stop changing the subject.'

'Please, Helen, can we not talk about her?' Donald folded his hands together on the table. 'I've seen her once since we started working on this. I set it up so that we didn't have to meet, because I knew you wouldn't like it. I have no feelings for her, honey. Absolutely none. Please. This is our night.'

'Is working with her giving you second thoughts?'

'Second thoughts about what? About taking on this job? Or about being an architect?'

'About . . . *anything*.' She glanced at the other booth, the booth he should've reserved.

'No. God, no. Honey, why would you even say something like that?'

The waiter came back with their wine. He flipped open his black notebook and eyed the two of them. 'Have we decided?'

Helen opened her menu and looked from the waiter to Donald. 'I'm going to get my usual,' she said. She pointed to what had once been a simple grilled cheese sandwich with fries that now involved fried green heirloom tomatoes, Gruyère cheese, a honey-maple glaze and matchstick frites with tartar.

'And for you, sir?'

Donald looked over the menu. The conversation had him flustered, but he felt the pressure to choose and to choose swiftly.

'I think I'm going to try something different,' he said, picking his words poorly.

12

2110

· Silo 1 ·

S ilo twelve was collapsing, and by the time Troy and the
others arrived, the communication room was awash in
overlapping radio chatter and the stench of sweat. Four
men crowded around a comm station normally manned by a
single operator. The men looked precisely how Troy felt:
panicked, out of their depth, ready to curl up and hide somewhere. It had a calming effect on him. Their panic was his
strength. He could fake this. He could hold it together.

Two of the men wore sleepshirts rather than their orange
overalls, suggesting that the late shift had been woken up
and called in. Troy wondered how long silo twelve had been
in trouble before they finally came and got *him*.

'What's the latest?' Saul asked an older gentleman, who
held a headphone to one ear.

The gentleman turned, his bald head shining in the
overhead light, sweat in the wrinkles of his brow, his white
eyebrows high with concern. 'I can't get anyone to answer
the server,' he said.

'Give us *just* the feeds from twelve,' Troy said, pointing
to one of the other three workers. A man he had met just a
week or so ago pulled off his headset and flipped a switch.
The speakers in the room buzzed with overlapping shouts
and orders. The others stopped what they were doing and
listened.

One of the other men, in his thirties, cycled through
dozens of video feeds. It was chaos everywhere. There was a
shot of a spiral staircase crammed with people pushing and

shoving. A head disappeared, someone falling down, presumably being trampled as the rest moved on. Eyes were wide with fear, jaws clenched or shouting.

'Let's see the server room,' Troy said.

The man at the controls typed something on his keypad. The crush of people disappeared and was replaced with a calm view of perfectly still cabinets. The server casings and the grating on the floor throbbed from the blinking overhead lights of an unanswered call.

'What happened?' Troy asked. He felt unusually calm.

'Still trying to determine that, sir.'

A folder was pressed into his hands. A handful of people gathered in the hallway, peering in. News was spreading, a crowd gathering. Troy felt a trickle of sweat run down the back of his neck, but still that eerie calmness, that resignation to this statistical inevitability.

A desperate voice from one of the radios cut through the rest, the panic palpable:

'—they're coming through. Dammit, they're bashing down the door. They're gonna get through—'

Everyone in the comm room held their breath, all the jitters and activity ceasing as they listened and waited. Troy was pretty sure he knew which door the panicked man was talking about. A lone door stood between the cafeteria and the airlock. It should have been made stronger. A lot of things should have been made stronger.

'—I'm on my own up here, guys. They're gonna get through. Holy shit, they're gonna get through—'

'Is that a deputy?' Troy asked. He flipped through the folder. There were status updates from silo twelve's IT head. No alarms. Two years since the last cleaning. The fear index had been pegged at an eight the last time it'd been measured. A little high, but not too low.

'Yeah, I think that's a deputy,' Saul said.

The man at the video feed looked back at Troy. 'Sir, we're gonna have a mass exodus.'

'Their radios are locked down, right?'

Saul nodded. 'We shut down the repeaters. They can talk among themselves, but that's it.'

Troy fought the urge to turn and meet the curious faces peering in from the hallway. 'Good,' he said. The priority in this situation was to contain the outbreak: don't let it spread to neighbouring cells. This was a cancer. Excise it. Don't mourn the loss.

The radio crackled:

'—*they're almost in, they're almost in, they're almost in*—'

Troy tried to imagine the stampede, the crush of people, how the panic had spread. The Order was clear on not intervening, but his conscience was muddled. He held out a hand to the radioman.

'Let me speak to him,' Troy said.

Heads swivelled his way. A crowd that thrived on protocol sat stunned. After a pause, the receiver was pressed into his palm. Troy didn't hesitate. He squeezed the mic.

'Deputy?'

'*Hello? Sheriff?*'

The video operator cycled through the feeds, then waved his hand and pointed to one of the monitors. The floor number '72' sat in the corner of the screen, and a man in silver overalls lay slumped over a desk. There was a gun in his hand, a pool of blood around a keyboard.

'That's the sheriff?' Troy asked.

The operator wiped his forehead and nodded.

'*Sheriff? What do I do?*'

Troy clicked the mic. 'The sheriff is dead,' he told the deputy, surprised by the steadiness of his own voice. He held the transmit button and pondered this stranger's fate. It dawned on him that most of these silo dwellers thought they were alone. They had no idea about each other, about their true purpose. And now Troy had made contact, a disembodied voice from the clouds.

One of the video feeds clicked over to the deputy, who was gripping a handset, the cord spiralling to a radio mounted on the wall. The floor number in the corner read '1'.

'You need to lock yourself in the holding cell,' Troy radioed, seeing that the least obvious solution was the best. It was a temporary solution, at least. 'Make sure you have every set of keys.'

He watched the man on the video screen. The entire room, and those in the hallway, watched the man on the video screen.

The door to the upper security office was just visible in the warped bubble of the camera's view. The edges of the door seemed to bulge outward because of the lens. And then the centre of the door bulged *inward* because of the mob. They were beating the door down. The deputy didn't respond. He dropped the microphone and hurried around the desk. His hands shook so violently as he reached for the keys that the grainy camera was able to capture it.

The door cracked along the centre. Someone in the comm room drew in an audible breath. Troy wanted to launch into the statistics. He had studied and trained to be on the *other* end of this, to lead a small group of people in the event of a catastrophe, not to lead them *all*.

Maybe that's why he was so calm. He was watching a horror that he should have been in the middle of, that he should have lived and died through.

The deputy finally secured the keys. He ran across the room and out of sight. Troy imagined him fumbling with the lock on the cell as the door burst in, an angry mob forcing their way through the splintered gap in the wood. It was a solid door, strong, but not strong enough. It was impossible to tell if the deputy had made it to safety. Not that it mattered. It was temporary. It was all temporary. If they opened the doors, if they made it out, the deputy would suffer a fate far worse than being trampled.

'The inner airlock door is open, sir. They're trying to get out.'

Troy nodded. The trouble had probably started in IT, had spread from there. Maybe the head – but more likely his shadow. Someone with override codes. Here was the curse:

a person had to be in charge, had to guard the secrets. Some wouldn't be able to. It was statistically predictable. He reminded himself that it was inevitable, the cards already shuffled, the game just waiting to play out.

'Sir, we've got a breach. The outer door, sir.'

'Fire the canisters now,' Troy said.

Saul radioed the control room down the hall and relayed the message. The view of the airlock filled with a white fog.

'Secure the server room,' Troy added. 'Lock it down.'

He had this portion of the Order memorised.

'Make sure we have a recent backup just in case. And put them on our power.'

'Yessir.'

Those in the room who had something to do seemed less anxious than the others, who were left shifting about nervously while they watched and listened.

'Where's my outside view?' Troy asked.

The mist-filled scene of people pushing on one another's backs through a white cloud was replaced by an expansive shot of the outside, of a claustrophobic crowd scampering across a dry land, of people collapsing to their knees, clawing at their faces and their throats, a billowing fog rising up from the teeming ramp.

No one in the comm room moved or said a word. There was a soft cry from the hallway. Troy shouldn't have allowed them to stay and watch.

'Okay,' he said. 'Shut it down.'

The view of the outside went black. There was no point in watching the crowd fight their way back in, no reason to witness the frightened men and women dying on the hills.

'I want to know why it happened.' Troy turned and studied those in the room. 'I want to know, and I want to know what we do to prevent this next time.' He handed the folder and the microphone back to the men at their stations. 'Don't tell the other silo heads just yet. Not until we have answers for the questions they'll have.'

Saul raised his hand. 'What about the people still inside twelve?'

'The only difference between the people in silo twelve and the people in silo thirteen is that there won't be future generations growing up in silo twelve. That's it. Everyone in all the silos will eventually die. We all die, Saul. Even us. Today was just their day.' He nodded to the dark monitor and tried not to picture what was really going on over there. 'We knew this would happen, and it won't be the last. Let's concentrate on the others. Learn from it.'

There were nods around the room.

'Individual reports by the end of this shift,' Troy said, feeling for the first time that he was actually in charge of something. 'And if anyone from twelve's IT staff can be raised, debrief them as much as you can. I want to know who, why and how.'

Several of the exhausted people in the room stiffened before trying to look busy. The gathering in the hallway shrank back as they realised the show was over and the boss was heading their way.

The boss.

Troy felt the fullness of his position for the first time, the heavy weight of responsibility. There were murmurs and sidelong glances as he headed back to his office. There were nods of sympathy and approval, men thankful that they occupied lower posts. Troy strode past them all.

More will try to escape, Troy thought. For all their careful engineering, there was no way to make a thing infallible. The best they could do was plan ahead, stockpile spares, not mourn the dark and lifeless cylinder as it was discarded and others were turned to with hope.

Back in his office, he closed the door and leaned back against it for a moment. His shoulders stuck to his overalls with the light sweat worked up from the swift walk. He took a few deep breaths before crossing to his desk and resting his hand on his copy of the Order. The fear persisted that they'd gotten it all wrong. How could a room full of doctors plan for everything? Would it really get easier as the generations went along, as people forgot and the whispers from the original survivors faded?

Troy wasn't so sure. He looked over at his wall of schematics, that large blueprint showing all the silos spread out amid the hills, fifty circles spaced out like stars on an old flag he had once served.

A powerful tremor coursed through Troy's body: his shoulders, elbows and hands twitched. He gripped the edge of his desk until it passed. Opening the top drawer, he picked up a red marker and crossed to the large schematic, the shivers still wracking his chest.

Before he could consider the permanence of what he was about to do, before he could consider that this mark of his would be on display for every future shift, before he could consider that this may become a trend, an action taken by his replacements, he drew a bold 'X' through silo twelve.

The marker squealed as it was dragged violently across the paper. It seemed to cry out. Troy blinked away the blurry vision of the red X and sagged to his knees. He bent forward until his forehead rested against the tall spread of papers, old plans rustling and crinkling as his chest shook with heavy sobs.

With his hands in his lap, shoulders bent with the weight of another job he'd been pressured into, Troy cried. He bawled as silently as he could so those across the hall wouldn't hear.

13

2049

RYT Hospital, Dwayne Medical Center

Donald had toured the Pentagon once, had been to the White House twice, went in and out of the Capitol building a dozen times a week, but nothing he'd seen in DC prepared him for the security around RYT's Dwayne Medical Center. The lengthy checks hardly made the hour-long meeting with the Senator seem worthwhile.

By the time he passed through the full body scanners leading into the nanobiotech wing, he'd been stripped, given a pair of green medical scrubs to wear, had a blood sample taken, and had allowed every sort of scanner and bright light to probe his eyes and record – so they said – the infrared capillary pattern of his face.

Heavy doors and sturdy men blocked every corridor as they made their way deeper and deeper into the NBT wing. When Donald spotted the Secret Service agents – who had been allowed to keep their dark suits and shades – he knew he was getting close. A nurse scanned him through a final set of stainless steel doors. The nanobiotic chamber awaited him inside.

Donald eyed the massive machine warily. He'd only ever seen them on TV dramas, and this one loomed even larger in person. It looked like a small submarine that had been marooned on the upper floors of the RYT. Hoses and wires led away from the curved and flawless white exterior in bundles. Studded along the length were several small glass windows that brought to mind the portholes of a ship.

'And you're sure it's safe for me to go in?' He turned to the nurse. 'Because I can always wait and visit him later.'

The nurse smiled. She couldn't be out of her twenties, had her brown hair wrapped in a knot on the back of her head, was pretty in an uncomplicated way. 'It's perfectly safe,' she assured him. 'His nanos won't interact with your body. We often treat multiple patients in a single chamber.'

She led him to the end of the machine and spun open the locking wheel at the end. A hatch opened with a sticky, ripping sound from the rubber seals and let out a slight gasp of air from the difference in pressure.

'If it's so safe, then why are the walls so *thick*?'

A soft laugh. 'You'll be fine.' She waved him towards the hatch. 'There'll be a slight delay and a little buzz after I seal this door, and then the inner hatch will unlock. Just spin the wheel and push to open.'

'I'm a little claustrophobic,' Donald admitted.

God, listen to himself. He was an adult. Why couldn't he just say he didn't want to go in and have that be enough? Why was he allowing himself to be pressured into this?

'Just step inside please, Mr Keene.'

The nurse placed her hand on the small of Donald's back. Somehow, the pressure of a young and pretty woman watching was stronger than his abject terror of the oversized capsule packed with its invisible machines. He wilted and found himself ducking through the small hatch, his throat constricting with fear.

The door behind him thumped shut, leaving him in a curved space hardly big enough for two. The locks clanked into the jamb. There were tiny silver benches set into the arching walls on either side of him. He tried to stand up, but his head brushed the ceiling.

An angry hum filled the chamber. The hair on the back of his neck stood on end, and the air felt charged with electricity. He looked for an intercom, some way to communicate with the Senator through the inner door so he didn't have to go in any further. It felt as though he couldn't breathe; he needed to get *out*. There was no wheel on the outer door. Everything had been taken out of his control—

The inner locks clanked. Donald lunged for the door and tried the handle. Holding his breath, he opened the hatch and escaped the small airlock for the larger chamber in the centre of the capsule.

'Donald!' Senator Thurman looked up from a thick book. He was sprawled out on one of the benches running the length of the long cylinder. A notepad and pen sat on a small table; a plastic tray held the remnants of dinner.

'Hello, sir,' he said, barely parting his lips.

'Don't just stand there, get in. You're letting the buggers out.'

Against his every impulse, Donald stepped through and pushed the door shut, and Senator Thurman laughed. 'You might as well breathe, son. They could crawl right through your skin if they wanted to.'

Donald let out his held breath and shivered. It may have been his imagination, but he thought he felt little pinpricks all over his skin, bites like Savannah's no-see-ums on summer days.

'You can't feel 'em,' Senator Thurman said. 'It's all in your head. They know the difference between you and me.'

Donald glanced down and realised he was scratching his arm.

'Have a seat.' Thurman gestured to the bench opposite his. He had the same colour scrubs on and a few days' growth on his chin. Donald noticed the far end of the capsule opened onto a small bathroom, a showerhead with a flexible hose clipped to the wall. Thurman swung his bare feet off the bench and grabbed a half-empty bottle of water, took a sip. Donald obeyed and sat down, a nervous sweat tickling his scalp. A stack of folded blankets and a few pillows sat at the end of the bench. He saw how the frames folded open into cots but couldn't imagine being able to sleep in this tight coffin.

'You wanted to see me, sir?' He tried to keep his voice from cracking. The air tasted metallic, a hint of the machines on his tongue.

'Drink?' The Senator opened a small fridge below the bench and pulled out a bottle of water.

'Thanks.' Donald accepted the water but didn't open it, just enjoyed the cool against his palm. 'Mick said he filled you in.' He wanted to add that this meeting felt unnecessary.

Thurman nodded. 'He did. Met with him yesterday. He's a solid boy.' The Senator smiled and shook his head. 'The irony is, this class we just swore in? Probably the best bunch the Hill has seen in a very long time.'

'The irony?'

Thurman waved his hand, shooing the question away. 'You know what I love about this treatment?'

Practically living for ever? Donald nearly blurted.

'It gives you time to think. A few days in here, nothing with batteries allowed, just a few books to read and something to write on – it really clears your head.'

Donald kept his opinions to himself. He didn't want to admit how uncomfortable the procedure made him, how terrifying it was to be in that room right then. Knowing that tiny machines were coursing through the Senator's body, picking through his individual cells and making repairs, repelled him. Supposedly, your urine turned the colour of charcoal once all the machines shut down. He trembled at the thought.

'Isn't that nice?' Thurman asked. He took a deep breath and let it out. 'The quiet?'

Donald didn't answer. He realised he was holding his breath again.

Thurman looked down at the book in his lap, then lifted his gaze to study Donald.

'Did you know your grandfather taught me how to play golf?'

Donald laughed. 'Yeah. I've seen the pictures of you two together.' He flashed back to his grandmother flipping through old albums. She had this outmoded obsession with printing the pictures from her computer and stuffing them in books. Said they became more real once they were displayed like that.

'You and your sister have always felt like family to me,' the Senator said.

The sudden openness was uncomfortable. A small vent in the corner of the pod circulated some air, but it still felt warm in there. 'I appreciate that, sir.'

'I want you in on this project,' Thurman said. 'All the way in.'

Donald swallowed. 'Sir. I'm fully committed, I promise.'

Thurman raised his hand and shook his head. 'No, not like—' He dropped his hand to his lap, glanced at the door. 'You know, I used to think you couldn't hide anything any more. Not in this age. It's all out there, you know?' He waggled his fingers in the air. 'Hell, you ran for office and squeezed through that mess. You know what it's like.'

Donald nodded. 'Yeah, I had a few things I had to own up to.'

The Senator cupped his hands into the shape of a bowl. 'It's like trying to hold water and not letting a single drop through.'

Donald nodded.

'A president can't even get a blow job any more without the world finding out.'

Donald's confused squint had Thurman waving at the air. 'Before your time. But here's the thing, here's what I've found, both overseas and in Washington. It's the *unimportant* drips that leak through. The peccadilloes. Embarrassments, not life-and-death stuff. You want to invade a foreign country? Look at D-Day. Hell, look at Pearl Harbor. Or 9/11. Not a problem.'

'I'm sorry, sir, I don't see what—'

Thurman's hand flew out, his fingers thudding shut as he pinched the air. Donald thought for a moment that he meant for him to keep quiet, but then the Senator leaned forward and held the pinched pads of his fingers for Donald to see, as if he had snatched a mosquito.

'Look,' he said.

Donald leaned closer, but he still couldn't make anything out. He shook his head. 'I don't see, sir . . .'

'That's right. And you wouldn't see it coming, either. That's what they've been working on, those snakes.'

Senator Thurman released the invisible pinch and studied the pad of his thumb for a moment. He blew a puff of air across it. 'Anything these puppies can stitch, they can *unstitch*.'

He peered across the pod at Donald. 'You know why we went into Iran the first time? It wasn't about nukes, I'll tell you that. I crawled through every hole that's ever been dug in those dunes over there, and those rats had a bigger prize they were chasing than nukes. You see, they've figured out how to attack us without being *seen*, without having to blow themselves up, and with *zero* repercussions.'

Donald was sure he didn't have the clearance to hear any of this.

'Well, the Iranians didn't figure it out for themselves so much as steal what Israel was working on.' He smiled at Donald. 'So, of course, we had to start playing catch-up.'

'I don't understa—'

'These critters in here are programmed for my DNA, Donny. Think about that. Have you ever had your ancestry tested?' He looked Donald up and down as if he were surveying a mottled mutt. 'What are you, anyway? Scottish?'

'Maybe Irish, sir. I honestly couldn't tell you.' He didn't want to admit that it was unimportant to him; it seemed like a topic close to Thurman's heart.

'Well, these buggers can tell. If they ever get them perfected, that is. They could tell you what clan you came from. And that's what the Iranians are working on: a weapon you can't see, that you can't stop, and if it decides you're Jewish, even a *quarter* Jew . . .' Thurman drew his thumb across his own neck.

'I thought we were wrong about that. We never found any NBs in Iran.'

'That's because they self-destructed. *Remotely.* Poof.' The old man's eyes widened.

Donald laughed. 'You sound like one of those conspiracy theorists—'

Senator Thurman leaned back and rested his head against the wall. 'Donny, the conspiracy theorists sound like *us.*'

Donald waited for the Senator to laugh. Or smile. Neither came.

'What does this have to do with me?' he asked. 'Or our project?'

Thurman closed his eyes, his head still tilted back. 'You know why Florida has such pretty sunrises?'

Donald wanted to scream. He wanted to beat on the door until they hauled him out of there in a straightjacket. Instead, he took a sip of water.

Thurman cracked an eye. Studied him again.

'It's because the sand from Africa blows clear across the Atlantic.'

Donald nodded. He saw what the Senator was getting at. He'd heard the same fear-mongering on the twenty-four-hour news programmes, how toxins and tiny machines can circle the globe, just like seeds and pollens have done for millennia.

'It's coming, Donny. I know it is. I've got eyes and ears everywhere, even in here. I asked you to meet me here because I want you to have a seat at the *after* party.'

'Sir?'

'You and Helen both.'

Donald scratched his arm and glanced at the door.

'It's just a contingency plan for now, you understand? There are plans in place for anything. Mountains for the president to crawl inside of, but we need something else.'

Donald remembered the congressman from Atlanta prattling on about zombies and the CDC. This sounded like more of that nonsense.

'I'm happy to serve on any committee you think is important—'

'Good.' The Senator took the book from his lap and handed it to Donald. 'Read this,' Thurman said.

Donald checked the cover. It was familiar, but instead of French script, it read: *The Order*. He opened the heavy tome to a random page and started skimming.

'That's your bible from now on, son. When I was in the war, I met boys no higher than your knee who had the entire Qur'an memorised, every stinkin' verse. You need to do better.'

'Memorise?'

'As near as you can. And don't worry, you've got a couple of years.'

Donald raised his eyebrows in surprise, then shut the book and studied the spine. 'Good. I'll need it.' He wanted to know if there would be a raise involved or a ton of committee meetings. This sounded ludicrous, but he wasn't about to refuse the old man, not with his re-election coming up every two years.

'All right. Welcome.' Thurman leaned forward and held out his hand. Donald tried to get his palm deep into the Senator's. It made the older man's grip hurt a lot less. 'You're free to go.'

'Thank you, sir.'

He stood and exhaled in relief. Cradling the book, he moved to the airlock door.

'Oh, and Donny?'

He turned back. 'Yessir?'

'The National Convention is in a couple of years. I want you to go ahead and pencil it into your schedule. And make sure Helen is there.'

Donald felt goosebumps run down his arms. Did that mean a real possibility of promotion? Maybe a speech on the big stage?

'Absolutely, sir.' He knew he was smiling.

'Oh, and I'm afraid I haven't been completely honest with you about the critters in here.'

'Sir?' Donald swallowed. His smile melted. He had one hand on the hatch's wheel. His mind resumed playing tricks on him, the taste on his tongue metallic, the pricks everywhere on his skin.

'Some of the buggers in here are very much for you.'

Senator Thurman stared at Donald for a beat, and then he started laughing.

Donald turned, sweat glassy on his brow as he worked the wheel in the door with a free hand. It wasn't until he secured the airlock, the seals deadening the Senator's laughter, that he could breathe again.

The air around him buzzed, a jolt of static to kill any strays. Donald blew out his breath, harder than usual, and unsteadily walked away.

14

2110

• Silo 1 •

The shrinks kept Troy's door locked and delivered his meals while he went through the silo twelve reports alone. He spread the pages across his keyboard – safely away from the edge of his desk. This way, when stray tears fell, they didn't smudge the paper.

For some reason, Troy couldn't stop crying. The shrinks with the strict meal plans had taken him off his meds for the last two days, long enough to compile his findings with Troy sober, free from the forgetfulness the pills brought about. He had a deadline. After he put his final notes together, they would get him something to cut through the pain.

Images of the dying interfered with his thoughts, the picture of the outside, of people suffocating and falling to their knees. Troy remembered giving the order. What he regretted most was making someone else push the button.

Coming off his meds had brought back other random haunts. He began to remember his father, events from before his orientation. And it worried him that the billions who had been wiped out could be felt as an ache in his gut while the few thousand of silo twelve who had scrambled to their deaths made him want to curl up and die.

The reports on his keyboard told a story of a shadow who had lost his nerve, an IT head who couldn't see the darkness rising at her feet, and an honest enough Security chief who had chosen poorly. All it took was for a lot of seemingly decent people to put the wrong person in power, and then pay for their innocent choice.

The keycodes for each video feed sat in the margins. It reminded him of an old book he had once known; the references had a similar style.

Jason 2:17 brought up a slice of the feed from the IT head's shadow. Troy followed the action on his monitor. A young man, probably in his late teens or early twenties, sat on a server-room floor. His back was to the camera, the corners of a plastic tray visible in his lap. He was bent over a meal, the bony knots of his spine casting dots of shadow down the back of his overalls.

Troy watched. He glanced at the report to check the timecode. He didn't want to miss it.

In the video, Jason's right elbow worked back and forth. He looked to be eating. The moment was coming. Troy willed himself not to blink, could feel tears coat his eyes from the effort.

A noise startled Jason. The young IT shadow glanced to the side, his profile visible for a moment, an angular and gaunt face from weeks of privation. He grabbed the tray from his lap; it was the first time Troy could spot the rolled-up sleeve. And there, as he fought with the cuff to roll it back down, were the dark parallel lines across his forearm, and nothing on his tray that called for a knife.

The rest of the clip was of Jason speaking to the IT head, her demeanour motherly and tender, a touch on his shoulder, a squeeze of his elbow. Troy could imagine her voice. He had spoken to her once or twice to take down a report. In a few more weeks, they would've scheduled a time to speak with Jason and induct him formally.

The clip ended with Jason descending back into the space beneath the server-room floor, a shadow swallowing a shadow. The head of IT – the *true* head of silo twelve – stood alone for a moment, hand on her chin. She looked so *alive*. Troy had a childlike impulse to reach out and brush his fingers across the monitor, to acknowledge this ghost, to apologise for letting her down.

Instead, he saw something the reports had missed. He

watched her body twitch towards the hatch, stop, freeze for a moment, then turn away.

Troy clicked the slider at the bottom of the video to see it again. There she was rubbing her shadow's shoulder, talking to him, Jason nodding. She squeezed his elbow, was concerned about him. He was assuring her everything was fine.

Once he was gone, once she was alone, the doubts and fears overtook her. Troy couldn't know it for sure, but he could *sense* it. She knew a darkness was brewing beneath her feet, and here was her chance to destroy it. It was a mask of concern, a twitch in that direction, reconsidering, turning away.

Troy paused the video and made some notes, jotted down the times. The shrinks would have to verify his findings. Shuffling the papers, he wondered if there was anything he needed to see again. A decent woman had been murdered because she could not bring herself to do the same, to kill in order to protect. And a Security chief had let loose a monster who had mastered the art of concealing his pain, a young man who had learned how to manipulate others, who wanted *out*.

He typed up his conclusions. It was a dangerous age for shadowing, he noted in his report. Here was a boy between his teens and twenties, an age deep in doubts and shallow in control. Troy asked in his report if anyone at that age could ever be ready. He made mention of the first head of IT he had inducted, the question the boy had asked after hearing tales from his demented great-grandmother. Was it right to expose anyone to these truths? Could men at such a fragile age be expected to endure such blows without shattering?

What he didn't add, what he asked himself, was if anyone at *any* age could ever be ready.

There was precedence, he typed, for limiting certain positions of authority by age. And while this would lead to shorter terms – which meant subjecting more unfortunate souls to the abuse of being locked up and shown their Legacy – wasn't it better to go through a damnable process more often rather than take risks such as these?

He knew this report would matter little. There was no planning for insanity. With enough revolutions and elections, enough transfers of power, eventually a madman would take the reins. It was inevitable. These were the odds they had planned for. This was why they had built so many.

He rose from his desk and walked to the door, slapped it soundly with the flat of his palm. In the corner of his office, a printer hummed and shot four pages out of its mouth. Troy took them; they were still warm as he slid them into the folder, these reports on the newly dead and still dying. He could feel the life and warmth draining from those printed pages. Soon, they would be as cool as the air around them. He grabbed a pen from his desk and signed the bottom.

A key rattled in his lock before the door opened.

'Done already?' Victor asked. The grey-haired psychiatrist stood across from his desk, keys jangling as they returned to his pocket. He held a small plastic cup in his hand.

Troy handed him the folder. 'The signs were there,' he told the doctor, 'but they weren't acted upon.'

Victor took the folder with one hand and held out the plastic cup with the other.

Troy typed a few commands on his computer and wiped his copy of the videos. The cameras were of no use for predicting and preventing these kinds of problems. There were too many to watch all at once. You couldn't get enough people to sit and monitor an entire populace. They were there to sort through the wreckage, the aftermath.

'Looks good,' Victor said, flipping through the folder. The plastic cup sat on Troy's desk, two pills inside. They had increased the dosage to what he had taken at the start of his shift, a little extra to cut through the pain.

'Would you like me to fetch you some water?'

Troy shook his head. He hesitated. Looking up from the cup, he asked Victor a question: 'How long do you think it'll take? Silo twelve, I mean. Before all of those people are gone.'

Victor shrugged. 'Not long, I imagine. Days.'

Troy nodded. Victor watched him carefully. Troy tilted

his head back and rattled the pills past his trembling lips. There was the bitter taste on his tongue. He made a show of swallowing.

'I'm sorry that it was your shift,' Victor said. 'I know this wasn't the job you signed up for.'

Troy nodded. 'I'm actually glad it was mine,' he said after a moment. 'I'd hate for it to have been anyone else's.'

Victor rubbed the folder with one hand. 'You'll be given a commendation in my report.'

'Thank you,' Troy said. He didn't know what the fuck for.

With a wave of the folder, Victor finally turned to leave and go back to his desk across the hall where he could sit and glance up occasionally at Troy.

And in that brief moment it took for Victor to walk over, with his back turned, Troy spat the pills into the palm of his hand.

Shaking his mouse with one hand, waking up his monitor so he could boot a game of solitaire, Troy smiled across the hallway at Victor, who smiled back. And in his other hand, still sticky from the outer coating dissolved by his saliva, the two pills nestled in his palm. Troy was tired of forgetting. He had decided to remember.

15

2049

Savannah, Georgia

Donald sped down highway 17, a flashing red light on his dash warning him as he exceeded the local speed limit. He didn't care about being pulled over, didn't care about being wired a ticket or his insurance rates creeping up. It all seemed trivial. The fact that there were circuits riding along in his car keeping track of everything he did paled in comparison to the suspicion that machines in his *blood* were doing the same.

The tyres squealed as he spiralled down his exit ramp too fast. He merged onto Berwick Boulevard, the overhead lights strobing through the windshield as he flew beneath them. Glancing down at his lap, he watched the gold inlay text on the book throb with the rhythm of the passing lights.

Order. Order. Order.

He had read enough to worry, to wonder what he'd gotten himself mixed up in. Helen had been right to warn him, had been wrong about the scale of the danger.

Turning into his neighbourhood, Donald remembered a conversation from long before – he remembered her begging him not to run for office, saying that it would change him, that he couldn't fix anything up there, but that he could sure as hell come home broken.

How right had she been?

He pulled up to the house and had to leave the car by the kerb. Her Jeep was in the middle of the driveway. One more habit formed in his absence, a reminder that he didn't live there any more, didn't have a real home.

Leaving his bags in the boot, he took just the book and his keys. The book was heavy enough.

The motion light came on as he neared the porch. He saw a form by the window, heard frantic scratching on the other side. Helen opened the door, and Karma rushed out, tail whacking the side of the jamb, tongue lolling, so much bigger in just the few weeks that he'd been away.

Donald crouched down and rubbed her head, let the dog lick his cheek.

'Good girl,' he said. He tried to sound happy. The cool emptiness in his chest intensified from being home. The things that should have felt comforting only made him feel worse.

'Hey, honey.' He smiled up at his wife.

'You're early.'

Helen wrapped her arms around his neck as he stood. Karma sat down and whined at them, tail swishing on the concrete. Helen's kiss tasted like coffee.

'I took an earlier flight.'

He glanced over his shoulder at the dark streets of his neighbourhood. As if anyone needed to follow him.

'Where're your bags?'

'I'll get 'em in the morning. C'mon, Karma. Let's go inside.' He steered his dog through the door.

'Is everything okay?' Helen asked.

Donald went to the kitchen. He set the book down on the island and fished in the cabinet for a glass. Helen watched him with concern as he pulled a bottle of brandy out of the cabinet.

'Baby? What's going on?'

'Maybe nothing,' he said. 'Lunatics—' He poured three fingers of brandy, looked to Helen and raised the bottle to see if she wanted any. She shook her head. 'Then again,' he continued, 'maybe there's something to it.' He took more than a sip. His other hand hadn't left the neck of the bottle.

'Baby, you're acting strange. Come sit down. Take off your coat.'

He nodded and let her help him remove his jacket. He slid his tie off, saw the worry on her face, knew it to be a reflection of his own.

'What would you do if you thought it all might end?' he asked his wife. 'What would you do?'

'If what? You mean us? Oh, you mean life. Honey, did someone pass away? Tell me what's going on.'

'No, not someone. Everyone. Everything.'

He tucked the bottle under his arm, grabbed his drink and the book and went to the living room. Helen and Karma followed. Karma was already on the sofa waiting for him to sit down before he got there, oblivious to anything he was saying, just thrilled for the pack to be reunited.

'It sounds like you've had a very long day,' Helen said, trying to find excuses for him.

Donald sat on the sofa and put the bottle and book on the coffee table. He pulled his drink away from Karma's curious nose.

'I have something I have to tell you,' he said.

Helen stood in the middle of the room, her arms crossed. 'That'd be a nice change.' She smiled to let him know she was joking. Donald nodded.

'I know, I know,' he said. His eyes fell to the book. 'This isn't about that project. And honestly, do you think I enjoy keeping my life from you?'

Helen crossed to the recliner next to the sofa and sat down. 'What is this about?' she asked.

'I've been told it's okay to tell you about a . . . promotion. Well, more of an assignment than a promotion. Not an assignment, really, more like being on the National Guard. Just in case—'

Helen reached over and squeezed his knee. 'Take it easy,' she whispered. Her eyebrows were lowered, confusion and worry lurking in the shadows there.

Donald took a deep breath. He was still revved up from running the conversation over in his head, from driving too fast. In the weeks since his meeting with Thurman he had been reading too much into the book – and too much into that conversation. He couldn't tell if he was piecing something together, or just falling apart.

'How much have you followed what's going on in Iran?' he asked, scratching his arm. 'And Korea?'

She shrugged. 'I see blurbs online.'

'Mmm.' He took a burning gulp of the brandy, smacked his lips and tried to relax and enjoy the numbing chill as it travelled through his body. 'They're working on ways to take everything out,' he said.

'Who? *We* are?' Helen's voice rose. 'We're thinking of taking *them* out?'

'No, no—'

'Are you sure I'm allowed to hear this—'

'No, sweetheart, they're designing weapons to take *us* out. Weapons that can't be stopped, that can't be defended against.'

Helen leaned forward, her hands clasped, elbows on her knees. 'Is this stuff you're learning in Washington? Classified stuff?'

He waved his hand. 'Beyond classified. Look, you know why we went into Iran—'

'I know why they *said* we went in—'

'It wasn't bullshit,' he said, cutting her off. 'Well, maybe it was. Maybe they hadn't figured it out yet, hadn't mastered how—'

'Honey, slow down.'

'Yeah.' He took another deep breath. He had an image in mind of a large mountain out west, a concrete road disappearing straight into the rock, thick vault doors standing open as files of politicians crowded inside with their families.

'I met with the Senator a few weeks ago.' He stared down into the ginger-coloured liquor in his glass.

'In Boston,' Helen said.

He nodded. 'Right. Well, he wants us to be on this alert team—'

'You and Mick.'

He turned to his wife. 'No – us.'

'*Us?*' Helen placed a hand on her chest. 'What do you mean, us? You and me?'

'Now listen—'

'You're volunteering *me* for one of his—'

'Sweetheart, I had no idea what this was all about.' He set his glass on the coffee table and grabbed the book. 'He gave me this to read.'

Helen frowned. 'What is that?'

'It's like an instruction manual for the – well, for the *after*. I think.'

Helen got up from the recliner and stepped between him and the coffee table. She nudged Karma out of the way, the dog grunting at being disturbed. Sitting down beside him, she put a hand on his back, her eyes shiny with worry.

'Donny, were you drinking on the plane?'

'No.' He pulled away. 'Just please listen to me. It doesn't matter *who* has them, it only matters *when*. Don't you see? This is the ultimate threat. A world-ender. I've been reading about the possibilities on this website—'

'A website,' she said, voice flat with scepticism.

'Yeah. Listen. Remember those treatments the Senator takes? These nanos are like synthetic life. Imagine if someone turned them into a virus that didn't care about its host, that didn't need *us* in order to spread. They could be out there already.' He tapped his chest, glanced around the room suspiciously, took a deep breath. 'They could be in every one of us right now, little timer circuits waiting for the right moment—'

'Sweetheart—'

'Very bad people are working on this, trying to make this happen.' He reached for his glass. 'We can't sit back and let them strike first. So we're gonna do it.' There were ripples in the liquor. His hand was shaking. 'God, baby, I'm pretty sure we're gonna do it before *they* can.'

'You're scaring me, honey.'

'Good.' Another burning sip. He held the glass with both hands to keep it steady. 'We should be scared.'

'Do you want me to call Dr Martin?'

'Who?' He tried to make room between them, bumped up against the armrest. 'My sister's doctor? The *shrink*?'

She nodded gravely.

'Listen to what I'm telling you,' he said, holding up a finger. 'These tiny machines are *real*.' His mind was racing. He was going to babble and convince her of nothing but his paranoia. 'Look,' he said. 'We use them in medicine, right?'

Helen nodded. She was giving him a chance, a slim one. But he could tell she really wanted to go call someone. Her mother, a doctor, *his* mother.

'It's like when we discovered radiation, okay? The first thing we thought was that this would be a cure, a medical discovery. X-rays, but then people were taking drops of radium like an elixir—'

'They poisoned themselves,' Helen said. 'Thinking they were doing something good.' She seemed to relax a little. 'Is this what you're worried about? That the nanos are going to mutate and turn on us? Are you still freaked out from being inside that machine?'

'No, nothing like that. I'm talking about how we looked for medicinal uses first, then ended up building the bomb. This is the *same thing*.' He paused, hoping she would get it. 'I'm starting to think we're building them too. Tiny machines, just like the ones in the nanobaths that stitch up people's skin and joints. Only *these* would tear people apart.'

Helen didn't react. Didn't say a word. Donald realised he sounded crazy, that every bit of this was already online and in podcasts that radiated out from lonely basements on lonely airwaves. The Senator had been right. Mix truth and lies and you couldn't tell them apart. The book on his coffee table and a zombie survival guide would be treated the same way.

'I'm telling you they're real,' he said, unable to stop himself. 'They'll be able to reproduce. They'll be invisible. There won't be any warning when they're set loose, just dust in the breeze, okay? Reproducing and reproducing, this invisible war will wage itself all around us while we're turned to mush.'

Helen remained silent. He realised she was waiting for him to finish, and then she would call her mom and ask what to do. She would call Dr Martin and get his advice.

Donald started to complain, could feel the anger welling up, and knew that anything he said would confirm her fears rather than convince her of his own.

'Is there anything else?' she whispered. She was looking for permission to leave and make her phone calls, to talk to someone rational.

Donald felt numb. Helpless and alone.

'The National Convention is going to be held in Atlanta.' He wiped underneath his eyes, tried to make it look like weariness, like the strain of travel. 'The DNC hasn't announced it yet, but I heard from Mick before I got on the flight.' He turned to Helen. 'The Senator wants us both there, is already planning something big.'

'Of course, baby.' She rested her hand on his thigh and looked at him as if he were her patient.

'And I'm going to ask that I spend more time down here, maybe do some of my work from home on weekends, keep a closer eye on the project.'

'That'd be great.' She rested her other hand on his arm.

'I want us to be good to each other,' he said. 'For whatever time we have left—'

'Shh, baby, it's okay.' She wrapped her arm around his back and shushed him again, trying to soothe him. 'I love you,' she said.

He wiped at his eyes again.

'We'll get through this,' she told him.

Donald bobbed his head. 'I know,' he said. 'I know we will.'

The dog grunted and nuzzled her head into Helen's lap, could sense something was wrong. Donald scratched the pup's neck. He looked up at his wife, tears in his eyes. 'I know we'll get through this,' he said, trying to calm himself. 'But what about everyone *else*?'

16

2110

• Silo 1 •

Troy needed to see a doctor. Ulcers had formed in both sides of his mouth, down between his gums and the insides of his cheeks. He could feel them like little wads of tender cotton embedded in his flesh. In the morning, he kept the pill tucked down on the left side. At supper, on the right. On either side, it would burn and dry out his mouth with the bitter bite of the medicine, but he would endure it.

He rarely employed napkins during meals, a bad habit he had formed long ago. They went into his lap to be polite and then onto his plate when he was finished. Now he had a different routine. One quick small bite of something, wipe his mouth, spit out the burning blue capsule, take a huge gulp of water, swish it around.

The hard part was not checking to see if anyone was watching while he spat it out. He sat with his back to the wall screen, imagining eyes drilling through the side of his head, but he kept his gaze in front of him and chewed his food.

He remembered to use his napkin occasionally, to wipe with both hands, always with both hands, pinching across his mouth, staying consistent. He smiled at the man across from him and made sure the pill didn't fall out. The man's gaze drifted over Troy's shoulder as he stared at the view of the outside world on the screen.

Troy didn't turn to look. There was still the same draw to the top of the silo, the same compulsion to be as high as possible, to escape the suffocating depths, but he no longer felt any desire to see outside. Something had changed.

He spotted Hal at the next table over – recognised his bald and splotchy scalp. The old man was sitting with his back to Troy. Troy waited for him to turn and catch his eye, but Hal never looked around.

He finished his corn and worked on his beets. It had been long enough since spitting out his pill to risk a glance towards the serving line. Tubes spat food; plates rattled on trays; one of the doctors from Victor's office stood beyond the glass serving line, arms crossed, a wan smile on his face. He was scanning the men in line and looking out over the tables. Why? What was there to keep an eye on? Troy wanted to know. He had dozens of burning questions like this. Answers sometimes presented themselves, but they skittered away if he trained his thoughts on them.

The beets were awful.

He ate the last of them while the gentleman across the table stood with his tray. It wasn't long before someone took his place. Troy looked up and down the row of adjoining tables. The vast majority of the workers sat on the *other* side so they could see out. Only a handful sat like Hal and himself. It was strange that he'd never noticed this before.

In the past weeks, it seemed patterns were becoming easier to spot, even as other faculties slipped and stumbled. He cut into a rubbery hunk of canned ham, his knife screeching against his plate, and wondered when he'd get some real sleep. He couldn't ask the doctors for anything to help, couldn't show them his gums. They might find out he was off his meds. The insomnia was awful. He might doze off for a minute or two, but deep sleep eluded him. And instead of remembering anything concrete, all he had were these dull aches, these bouts of terrible sadness, and the inescapable feeling that something was deeply wrong.

He caught one of the doctors watching him. Troy looked down the table and saw men shoulder to shoulder on the other side, eyeing the view. It wasn't long ago that he'd wanted to sit and stare, mesmerised by the grey hills on the screen.

And now he felt sick when he caught even a glimpse; the view brought him close to tears.

He stood with his tray, then worried he was being obvious. The napkin fell from his lap and landed on the floor, and something skittered away from his foot.

Troy's heart skipped a beat. He bent and snatched the napkin, hurried down the line, looking for the pill. He bumped into a chair that had been pulled back from the table, felt all the room's eyes on him.

The pill. He found it and scooped it up with his napkin, the tray teetering dangerously in his palm. He stood and composed himself. A trickle of sweat itched his scalp and ran down the back of his neck. Everyone knew.

Troy turned and walked towards the water fountain, not daring to glance up at the cameras or over at the doctors. He was losing it. Growing paranoid. And there was just over a month left on this shift. A month that would test every inch of will he had left.

Trying to walk naturally with so many eyes on him was impossible. He rested the edge of his tray on the water fountain, stepped on the lever with his foot and topped up his glass. This was why he had gotten up: he was thirsty. He felt like announcing the fact out loud.

Returning to the tables, Troy squeezed between two other workers and sat down facing the screen. He balled up his napkin, felt the pill hidden within its folds, and tucked it between his thighs. He sat there, sipping his water, facing the screen like everyone else, like he was supposed to. But he didn't dare look.

17

2051

Washington, DC

The fat raindrops on the canopy outside De'Angelo's restaurant sounded like rhythmless fingers tapping on a drum. The traffic on L Street hissed through puddles gathering against the kerb, and the asphalt that flashed between the cars gleamed shiny and black from the street-lights. Donald shook two pills out of a plastic vial and into his palm. Two years on the meds. Two years completely free of anxiety, gloriously numb.

He glanced at the label and thought of Charlotte, of the necessity of fulfilling the prescription under his sister's name, then popped them in his mouth. Donald swallowed. He was sick of the rain, preferred the cleanliness of the snow. Winter had been too warm again.

Keeping out of the foot traffic flowing through the front doors, he cradled his phone against his ear and listened patiently while his wife urged Karma to pee.

'Maybe she doesn't need to go,' he suggested. He dropped the vial into his coat pocket and cupped his hand over the phone as the lady beside him wrestled with her umbrella, water flicking everywhere.

Helen continued to cajole Karma with words the poor dog didn't understand. This was typical of Helen and Donald's conversations of late. There was nothing real to say to one another.

'But she hasn't been since *lunch*,' Helen insisted.

'She didn't go somewhere in the house, did she?'

'She's four years old.'

Donald had forgotten. Lately, time felt locked in a bubble. He wondered if his medication was causing that or if it was the workload. Whenever anything seemed . . . off any more, he always assumed it must be the medication. Before, it could have been the vagaries of life; it could have been anything. Somehow, it felt worse to have something concrete and new to pin it on.

There was shouting across the street, two homeless men yelling at each other in the rain, squabbling over a bag of tin cans. More umbrellas were shaken and more fancy dresses flowed into the restaurant. Here was a city charged with governing all the others, and it couldn't even take care of itself. These things used to worry him more. He patted the capsule in his jacket pocket, a comforting twitch he'd developed.

'She won't go,' his wife said exhaustedly.

'Baby, I'm sorry I'm up here and you have all that to take care of. But look, I really need to get inside. We're trying to wrap up final revisions on these plans tonight.'

'How is everything going with that? Are you almost done?'

A file of taxis drove by, hunting for fares, fat tyres rolling across sheets of water like hissing snakes. Donald watched as one of them slowed to a stop, brakes squealing from the wet. He didn't recognise the man stepping out, coat held over his head. It wasn't Mick.

'Huh? Oh, it's going great. Yeah, we're basically done, maybe a few tweaks here and there. The outer shells are poured, and the lower floors are in—'

'I meant, are you almost done working with *her*?'

He turned away from the traffic to hear better. 'Who, Anna? Yeah. Look, I've told you. We've only consulted here and there. Most of it's done electronically.'

'And Mick is there?'

'Yup.'

Another cab slowed as it passed by. Donald turned, but the car didn't stop.

'Okay. Well, don't work too late. Call me tomorrow.'

'I will. I love you.'

'Love you— Oh! Good girl! That's a good girl, Karma—'

'I'll talk to you tomorr—'

But the line was already dead. Donald glanced at his phone before putting it away, shivered once from the cool evening and from the moisture in the air. He pressed through the crowd outside the door and made his way to the table.

'Everything okay?' Anna asked. She sat alone at a table with three settings. A wide-necked sweater had been pulled down to expose one shoulder. She pinched her second glass of wine by its delicate stem, a pink half-moon of lipstick on its rim. Her auburn hair was tied up in a bun, the freckles across her nose almost invisible behind a thin veil of make-up. She looked, impossibly, more alluring than she had in college.

'Yeah, everything's fine.' Donald twisted his wedding ring with his thumb – a habit. 'Have you heard from Mick?' He reached into his pocket and pulled out his phone, checked his texts. He thought of firing off another, but there were already four unanswered messages sitting there.

'Nope. Wasn't he flying in from Texas this morning? Maybe his flight was delayed.'

Donald saw that his glass, which he'd left near empty when he made the call outside, had been topped up. He knew Helen would disapprove of him sitting there alone with Anna, even though nothing was going to happen. Nothing ever would.

'We could always do this another time,' he suggested. 'I'd hate for Mick to be left out.'

She set down her glass and studied the menu. 'Might as well eat while we're here. Be a little late to find something else. Besides, Mick's logistics are independent of our design. We can send him our materials report later.'

Anna leaned to the side and reached for something in her bag, her sweater falling dangerously open. Donald looked away quickly, a flush of heat on the back of his neck. She pulled out her tablet and placed it on top of his Manilla folder, the screen flashing to life.

'I think the bottom third of the design is solid.' She spun the tablet for him to see. 'I'd like to sign off on it so they can start layering the next few floors in.'

'Well, a lot of these are yours,' he said, thinking of all the mechanical spaces at the bottom. 'I trust your judgement.'

He picked the tablet up, relieved that their conversation hadn't veered away from work. He felt like a fool for thinking Anna had anything else in mind. They had been exchanging emails and updating each other's plans for over two years and there had never been a hint of impropriety. He warned himself not to let the setting, the music, the white tablecloths, fool him.

'There *is* one last-minute change you're not going to like,' she said. 'The central shaft needs to be modified a little. But I think we can still work with the same general plan. It won't affect the floors at all.'

He scrolled through the familiar files until he spotted the difference. The emergency stairwell had been moved from the side of the central shaft to the very middle. The shaft itself seemed smaller, or maybe it was because all the other gear they'd filled it with was gone. Now there was empty space, the discs turned to doughnuts. He looked up from the tablet and saw their waiter approaching.

'What, no lift?' He wanted to make sure he was seeing this right. He asked the waiter for a water and said he'd need more time with the menu.

The waiter bowed and left. Anna placed her napkin on the table and slid over to the adjacent chair. 'The board said they had their reasons.'

'The medical board?' Donald exhaled. He had grown sick of their meddling and their suggestions, but he had given up fighting with them. He never won. 'Shouldn't they be more worried about people falling over these railings and breaking their necks?'

Anna laughed. 'You know they're not into that kind of medicine. All they can think about is what these workers might go through, emotionally, if they're ever trapped in there for a few weeks. They wanted the plan to be simpler. More . . . *open*.'

'More open.' Donald chuckled and reached for his glass of wine. 'And what do they mean, trapped for a few weeks?'

Anna shrugged. 'You're the elected official. I figure you should know more about this government silliness than I do. I'm just a consultant. I'm just getting paid to lay out the pipes.'

She finished her wine, and the waiter returned with Donald's water and to take their orders. Anna raised her eyebrow, a familiar twitch that begged a question: *Are you ready?* It used to mean much more, Donald thought, as he glanced at the menu.

'How about you pick for me?' he finally said, giving up.

Anna ordered and the waiter jotted down her selections.

'So now they want a single stairwell, huh?' Donald imagined the concrete needed for this, then thought of a spiral design made of metal. Stronger and cheaper. 'We can keep the service lift, right? Why couldn't we slide this over and put it in right here?'

He showed her the tablet.

'No. No lifts. Keep everything simple and open. That's what they said.'

He didn't like this. Even if the facility would never be used, it should be built as if it might. Why else bother? He'd seen a partial list of supplies they were going to stockpile inside. Lugging them by stair seemed impossible, unless they planned to stock the floors before the prebuilt sections were craned inside. That was more Mick's department. It was one of many reasons he wished his friend were there.

'You know, this is why I didn't go into architecture.' He scrolled through their plans and saw all the places where his design had been altered. 'I remember the first class we had where we had to go out and meet with mock clients, and they always wanted either the impossible or the downright stupid – or both. And that's when I knew it wasn't for me.'

'So you went into politics.' Anna laughed.

'Yeah. Good point.' Donald smiled, saw the irony. 'But hey, it worked for your father.'

'My dad went into politics because he didn't know what else to do. He got out of the army, sank too much money into busted venture after busted venture, then figured he'd serve his country some other way.'

She studied him a long moment.

'This is *his* legacy, you know.' She leaned forward and rested her elbows on the table, bent a graceful finger at the tablet. 'This is one of those things they said would never get done, and *he's* doing it.'

Donald put the tablet down and leaned back in his chair. 'He keeps telling me the same thing,' he said. 'That this is our legacy, this project. I told him I feel too young to be working on my crowning achievement.'

Anna smiled. They both took sips of wine. A basket of bread was dropped off, but neither of them reached for it.

'Speaking of legacies and leaving things behind,' Anna asked, 'is there a reason you and Helen decided not to have kids?'

Donald placed his glass back on the table. Anna lifted the bottle, but he waved her off. 'Well, it's not that we don't want them. We just both went directly from grad school to our careers, you know? We kept thinking—'

'That you'll have for ever, right? That you'll always have time. There's no hurry.'

'No. It's not that . . .' He rubbed the tablecloth with the pads of his fingers and felt the slick and expensive fabric slide over the other tablecloth hidden below. When they were finished with their meals and out the door, he figured this top layer would be folded back and carried off with their crumbs, a new layer revealed beneath. Like skin. Or the generations. He took a sip of wine, the tannins numbing his lips.

'I think that's it exactly,' Anna insisted. 'Every generation is waiting longer and longer to pull the trigger. My mom was almost forty when she had me, and that's getting more and more common.'

She tucked a loose strand of hair behind her ear.

'Maybe we all think we might be the first generation that simply doesn't die,' she continued, 'that lives for ever.' She raised her eyebrows. 'Now we all *expect* to hit a hundred and thirty, maybe longer, like it's our right. And so this is my theory—' She leaned closer. Donald was already uncomfortable with where the conversation was going. 'Children *used* to be our legacy, right? They were our chance to cheat death, to pass these little bits of ourselves along. But now we hope it can simply be *us*.'

'You mean like cloning? That's why it's illegal.'

'I don't mean cloning – and besides, just because it's illegal, you and I both know people do it.' She took a sip of her wine and nodded at a family in a distant booth. 'Look. He has daddy's *everything*.'

Donald followed her gaze and watched the kid for a moment, then realised she was just making a point.

'Or how about *my* father?' she asked. 'Those nano baths, all the stem-cell vitamins he takes. He truly thinks he's gonna live for ever. You know he bought a load of stock in one of those cryo firms years back?'

Donald laughed. 'I heard. And I heard it didn't work out so well. Besides, they've been trying stuff like that for years—'

'And they keep getting closer,' she said. 'All they ever needed was a way to stitch up the cells damaged from the freezing, and now that's not so crazy a dream, right?'

'Well, I hope the people who dream such things get whatever it is they're looking for, but you're wrong about us. Helen and I talk about having kids all the time. I know people having their first kid in their fifties. We've got time.'

'Mmm.' She finished what was in her glass and reached for the bottle. 'You think that,' she said. 'Everyone thinks they've got all the time left in the world.' She levelled her cool grey eyes at him. 'But they never stop to ask just how much time that is.'

After dinner, they waited under the awning for Anna's car service. Donald declined to share a ride, saying he needed to get back to the office and would just take a cab. The rain hitting the awning had changed, had grown sombre.

Her ride pulled up, a shiny black Lincoln, just as Donald's phone began vibrating. He fumbled in his jacket pocket while she leaned in for a hug and kissed his cheek. He felt a flush of heat despite the cool air, saw that it was Mick calling and picked up.

'Hey, you just land or what?' Donald asked.

A pause.

'Land?' Mick sounded confused. There was noise in the background. The driver hurried around the Lincoln to get the door for Anna. 'I took a red-eye,' Mick said. 'My flight got in early this morning. I'm just walking out of a movie and saw your texts. What's up?'

Anna turned and waved. Donald waved back.

'You're getting out of a movie? We just wrapped up our meeting at De'Angelo's. You missed it. Anna said she emailed you like three times.'

He glanced up at the car as Anna drew her leg inside. Just a glimpse of her red heels, and then the driver pushed the door shut. The rain on the tinted glass stood out like jewels.

'Huh. I must've missed them. Probably went to junk mail. Not a big deal. We'll catch up. Anyway, I just got out of this trippy movie. If you and I were still in our getting-high days, I would totally force you to blast one with me right now and go to the midnight showing. My mind is totally bent—'

Donald watched the driver hurry around the car to get out of the rain. Anna's window lowered a crack. One last wave, and the car pulled out into light traffic.

'Yeah, well, those days are long gone, my friend,' Donald

said distractedly. Thunder grumbled in the distance. An umbrella opened with a pop as a gentleman prepared to brave the storm. 'Besides,' Donald told Mick, 'some things are better off back in the past. Where they belong.'

18

2110

• Silo 1 •

The exercise room on level twelve smelled of sweat, of having been used recently. A line of iron weights sat in a jumble in one corner, and a forgotten towel had been left draped over the bar of the bench press, over a hundred pounds of iron discs still in place.

Troy eyed the mess as he worked the last bolt free from the side of the exercise bike. When the cover plate came off, washers and nuts rained down from recessed holes and bounced across the tile. Troy scrambled for them and pushed the hardware into a tidy pile. He peered inside the bike's innards and saw a large cog, its jagged teeth conspicuously empty.

The chain that did all the work hung slack around the cog's axle. Troy was surprised to see it there, would have thought the thing ran on belts. This seemed too fragile. Not a good choice for the length of time it would be expected to serve. It was strange, in fact, to think that this machine was already fifty years old – and that it needed to last centuries more.

He wiped his forehead. Sweat was still beading up from the handful of miles he'd gotten in before the machine broke. Fishing around in the toolbox Jones had loaned him, he found the flathead screwdriver and began levering the chain back onto the cog.

Chains on cogs. *Chains on cogs.* He laughed to himself. Wasn't that the way?

'Excuse me, sir?'

Troy turned to find Jones, his chief mechanic for another week, standing in the gym's doorway.

'Almost done,' Troy said. 'You need your tools back?'

'Nossir. Dr Henson is looking for you.' He raised his hand, had one of those clunky radios in it.

Troy grabbed an old rag out of the toolbox and wiped the grease from his fingers. It felt good to be working with his hands, getting dirty. It was a welcome distraction, something to do besides checking the blisters in his mouth with a mirror or hanging out in his office or apartment waiting to cry again for no reason.

He left the bike and took the radio from Jones. Troy felt a wave of envy for the older man. He would love to wake up in the morning, put on those denim overalls with the patches on the knees, grab his trusty toolbox and work down a list of repairs. Anything other than sitting around while he waited for something much bigger to break.

Squeezing the button on the side of the radio, he held it up to his mouth.

'This is Troy,' he said.

The name sounded strange. In recent weeks, he hadn't liked saying his own name, didn't like hearing it. He wondered what Dr Henson and the shrinks would say about that.

The radio crackled. 'Sir? I hate to disturb you—'

'No, that's fine. What is it?' Troy walked back to the exercise bike and grabbed his towel from the handlebars. He wiped his forehead and saw Jones hungrily eyeing the disassembled bike and scattering of tools. When he lifted his brows questioningly, Troy waved his consent.

'We've got a gentleman in our office who's not responding to treatment,' Dr Henson said. 'It looks like another deep freeze. I'll need you to sign the waiver.'

Jones glanced up from the bike and frowned. Troy rubbed the back of his neck with the towel. He remembered Merriman saying to be careful handing these out. There were plenty of good men who would just as soon sleep through all this mess than serve out their shifts.

'You're sure?' he asked.

'We've tried everything. He's been restrained. Security is taking him down the express right now. Can you meet us down here? You'll have to sign off before he can be put away.'

'Sure, sure.' Troy rubbed his face with his towel, could smell the detergent in the clean cloth cut through the odour of sweat in the room and the tinge of grease from the open bike. Jones grabbed one of the pedals with his thick hands and gave it a turn. The chain was back on the cog, the machine operational again.

'I'll be right down,' Troy said before releasing the button and handing the radio back to the mechanic. Some things were a pleasure to fix. Others weren't.

The express had already passed when Troy reached the lifts; he could see the floor display racing down. He pressed the call button for the other one and tried to imagine the sad scene playing out below. Whoever it was had his sympathies.

He shook violently, blamed it on the cool air in the hallway and his damp skin. A ping-pong ball clocked back and forth in the rec room around the corner, sneakers squeaking as players chased the next shot. From the same room, a television was playing a movie, the sound of a woman's voice.

Looking down, Troy was self-conscious about his shorts and T-shirt. The only authority he really felt was lent by his overalls, but there was no time to ride up and change.

The lift beeped and opened, and the conversation inside fell quiet. Troy nodded a greeting, and two men in yellow said hello. The three of them rode in silence for a few levels until the men got off on forty-four, a general living level. Before the doors could close, Troy saw a bright ball skitter across the hallway, two men racing after it. There were shouts and laughter followed by guilty silence when they noticed Troy.

The metal doors squeezed shut on the brief glimpse of lower and more normal lives.

With a shudder, the lift sank deeper into the earth. Troy could feel the dirt and concrete squeezing in from all sides, piling up above. Sweat from nerves mixed with that from his exercise. He was coming out of the other side of the medication, he thought. Every morning, he could feel some semblance of his old self returning, and it lasted longer and longer into the day.

The fifties went by. The lift never stopped on the fifties. Emergency supplies he hoped would never be needed filled the corridors beyond. He remembered parts of the orientation, back when everyone had been awake. He remembered the code names they came up with for everything, the way new labels obscured the past. There was something here nagging him, but he couldn't place it.

Next were the mechanical spaces and the general storerooms, followed by the two levels that housed the reactor. Finally, the most important storage of all: the Legacy, the men and women asleep in their shiny coffins, the survivors from the *before*.

There was a jolt as the lift slowed and the doors chimed open. Troy immediately heard a commotion in the doctor's office, Henson barking commands to his assistant. He hurried down the hallway in his gym attire, sweat cooling on his skin.

When he entered the ready room, he saw an elderly man being restrained on a gurney by two men from Security. It was Hal – Troy recognised him from the cafeteria, remembered speaking with him the first day of his shift and several times since. The doctor and his assistant fumbled through cabinets and drawers, gathering supplies.

'My name is Carlton!' Hal roared, his thin arms flailing while unbuckled restraints dangled from the table and swayed from the commotion. Troy assumed they would've had him under control to get him down the lift, wondered if he had broken free when he had come to. Henson and his assistant found what they needed and gathered by the gurney. Hal's eyes widened at the sight of the needle; the fluid inside was a blue the colour of open sky.

Dr Henson looked up and saw Troy standing there in his exercise clothes, paralysed and watching the scene. Hal screamed once more that his name was Carlton and continued to kick at the air, his heavy boots slamming against the table. The two security men jerked with effort as they held him down.

'A hand?' Henson grunted, teeth clenched as he began to wrestle with one of Hal's arms.

Troy hurried to the gurney and grabbed one of Hal's legs. He stood shoulder to shoulder with the security officers and wrestled with a boot while trying not to get kicked. Hal's legs felt like a bird's inside the baggy overalls, but they kicked like a mule's. One of the officers managed to work a strap across his thighs. Troy leaned his weight on Hal's shin while a second strap was pulled tight.

'What's wrong with him?' he asked. His concerns about himself vanished in the presence of true madness. Or was this where he was heading?

'Meds aren't taking,' Henson said.

Or he's not taking them, Troy thought.

The medical assistant used his teeth to pull the cap off the sky-coloured syringe. Hal's wrist was pinned. The needle disappeared into his trembling arm, the plunger moving the bright blue liquid into his pale and blotchy flesh.

Troy cringed at the sight of the needle being stabbed into Hal's jerking arm – but the power in the old man's legs faded immediately. Everyone seemed to take deep breaths as he wilted into unconsciousness, his head drifting to the side, one last incomprehensible scream fading into a moan, and then a deep and breathy exhalation.

'What the hell?' Troy wiped his forehead with the back of his arm. He was dripping with sweat, partly from the exertion but mostly from the scene before him, from feeling a man go under like that, sensing the life and will drain from his kicking boots as he was forced asleep. His own body shook with a sudden and violent tremor, gone before he knew it was coming. The doctor glanced up and frowned.

'I apologise for that,' Henson said. He glared at the officers, directing his blame.

'We had him no problem,' one of them said, shrugging.

Henson turned to Troy. His jowls sagged with disappointment. 'I hate to ask you to sign off on this . . .'

Troy wiped his face with the front of his shirt and nodded. The losses had been accounted for – individual losses as well as silos, spares stocked accordingly – but they all stung.

'Of course,' he said. This was his job, right? Sign this. Say these words. Follow the script. It was a joke. They were all reading lines from a play none of them could remember. But he was beginning to. He could feel it.

Henson shuffled through a drawer of forms while his assistant unbuckled Hal's overalls. The men from Security asked if they were needed, checked the restraints a final time and were waved away. One of them laughed out loud over something the other said as the sound of their boots faded towards the lift.

Troy, meanwhile, lost himself in Hal's slack face, the slight rise and fall of his old and narrow chest. *Here* was the reward for remembering, he thought. This man had woken up from the routine of the asylum. He hadn't gone crazy; he'd had a sudden bout of *clarity*. He'd cracked open his eyes and seen through the mist.

A clipboard was procured from a peg on the wall, the right form shoved into its metal jaws. Troy was handed a pen. He scratched his name, passed the clipboard back and watched the two doctors work; he wondered if they felt any of what he felt. What if they were all playing the same part? What if each and every one of them was concealing the same doubts, none of them talking because they all felt so completely alone?

'Could you get that one for me?'

The medical assistant was down on his knees, twisting a knob on the base of the table. Troy saw that it was on wheels. The assistant nodded at Troy's feet.

'Of course.' Troy crouched down to free the wheel. He

was a part in this. It was his signature on the form. It was him twisting the knob that would free the table and allow it to roll down the hall.

With Hal under, the restraints were loosened, his overalls peeled off with care. Troy volunteered with the boots, unknotting the laces and setting them aside. There was no need for a paper gown – his modesty was no longer a concern. An IV needle was inserted and taped down; Troy knew it would plug into the cryopod. He knew what it felt like to have ice crawl through his veins.

They pushed the gurney down the hall and to the reinforced steel doors of the deep freeze. Troy studied the doors. They seemed familiar. He seemed to remember speccing something similar for a project once, but that was for a room full of machines. No – computers.

The keypad on the wall chirped as the doctor entered his code. There was the heavy *thunk* of rods withdrawing into the thick jamb.

'The empties are at the end,' Henson said, nodding into the distance.

Rows and rows of gleaming and sealed beds filled the freezing chamber. His eyes fell to the readout screens on the bases of each pod. There were green lights solid with life, no space needed for a pulse or heartbeat, first names only, no way to connect these strangers to their past lives.

Cassie, Catherine, Gabriella, Gretchen.

Made-up names.

Gwynn. Halley. Heather.

Everyone in order. No shifts for them. Nothing for the men to fight over. It would all be done in an instant. Step inside the lifeboat, dream a moment, step out onto dry land.

Another Heather. Duplicates without last names. Troy wondered how that would work. He steered blindly between the rows, the doctor and his assistant chatting about the procedure, when a name caught his peripheral vision and a fierce tremor vibrated through his limbs.

Helen. And another: *Helen.*

Troy lost his grip on the gurney and nearly fell. The wheels squealed to a stop.

'Sir?'

Two Helens. But before him, on a crisp display showing the frozen temps of a deep, deep slumber, another:

Helena.

Troy staggered away from the gurney and Hal's naked body. The echo of the old man's feeble screams came back to him, insisting he was someone named Carlton. Troy ran his hands along the curved top of the cryopod.

She was *here.*

'Sir? We really need to keep moving—'

Troy ignored the doctor. He rubbed the glass shield, the cold inside leaching into his hand.

'Sir—'

A spiderweb of frost covered the glass. He wiped the frozen film of condensation away so he could see inside.

'We need to get this man installed—'

Closed eyes lay inside that cold and dark place. Blades of ice clung to her lashes. It was a familiar face, but this was not his wife.

'Sir!'

Troy stumbled, hands slapping at the cold coffin for balance, bile rising in his throat with remembrance. He heard himself gag, felt his limbs twitch, his knees buckle. He hit the ground between two of the pods and shook violently, spit on his lips, strong memories wrestling with the last residue of the drugs still in his veins.

The two men in white shouted at each other. Footsteps slapped frosted steel and faded towards the distant and heavy door. Inhuman gurgles hit Troy's ears and sounded faintly as though they came from him.

Who was he? What was he doing there? What were any of them doing?

This was not Helen. His name was not Troy.

Footsteps stomped towards him in a hurry. The name was on his tongue as the needle bit his flesh.

Donny.

But that wasn't right, either.

And then the darkness took him, tightening down around anything from his past that his mind deemed too awful to bear.

19

2052

Fulton County, Georgia

Some mash-up of music festival, family reunion and state fair had descended on the southernmost corner of Fulton County. For the past two weeks, Donald had watched while colourful tents sprang up over a brand-new nuclear containment facility. Fifty state flags flew over fifty depressions in the earth. Stages had been erected, an endless parade of supplies flowing over the rolling hills, golf carts and four-wheelers forming convoys of food, Tupperware containers, baskets of vegetables – some even pulled small enclosed trailers loaded with livestock.

Farmers' markets had been staked out in winding corridors of tents and booths, chickens clucking and pigs snorting, children petting rabbits, dogs on leashes. Owners of the latter guided dozens of breeds through the crowds. Tails wagged happily, and wet noses sniffed the air.

On Georgia's main stage, a local rock band performed a sound check. When they fell quiet to adjust levels, Donald could hear the twangs of bluegrass spilling over from the general direction of North Carolina's delegation. In the opposite direction, someone was giving a speech on Florida's stage while the convoys moved supplies over the rise, and families spread blankets and picnicked on the banks of sweeping bowls. The hills, Donald saw, formed stadium seating, as if they'd been designed for the task.

What he couldn't figure out was where they were putting all those supplies. The tents seemed to keep gobbling them up with no end in sight. The four-wheelers with their little boxed trailers had been rumbling up and down the slopes the entire two weeks he'd been there helping prep for the National Convention.

Mick rumbled to a stop beside him, sitting atop one of the ubiquitous all-terrain vehicles. He grinned at Donald and goosed the throttle while still holding the brakes. The Honda lurched, tyres growling against the dirt.

'Wanna go for a ride to South Carolina?' he yelled over the engine. He shifted forward on the seat to make room.

'You got enough gas to make it there?' Donald held his friend's shoulder and stepped on the second set of pegs. He threw his leg over the seat.

'It's just over that hill, you idiot.'

Donald resisted the urge to assure Mick he'd been joking. He held on to the metal rack behind him as Mick shifted through the gears. His friend stuck to the dusty highway between the tents until they reached the grass, then angled towards the South Carolina delegation, the tops of the buildings of downtown Atlanta visible off to one side.

Mick turned his head as the Honda climbed the hill. 'When is Helen getting here?' he yelled.

Donald leaned forward. He loved the feel of the crisp October morning air. It reminded him of Savannah that time of year, the chill of a sunrise on the beach. He had just been thinking of Helen when Mick asked about her.

'Tomorrow,' he shouted. 'She's coming on a bus with the delegates from Savannah.'

They crested the hill, and Mick throttled back and steered along the ridgeline. They passed a loaded-down ATV heading in the opposite direction. The network of ridges formed an interlocked maze of highways high above each containment facility's sunken bowl.

Peering into the distance, Donald watched the ballet of scooting ATVs weave across the landscape. One day, he imagined, the flat roads on top of the hills would rumble with much larger trucks bearing hazardous waste and radiation warnings.

And yet, seeing the flags waving over the Florida delegation to one side and the Georgia stage to the other, and noting the way the slopes would carry record crowds and afford everyone a perfect view of each stage, Donald couldn't help but think that all the happy accidents had some larger purpose. It was as if the facility had been planned from the beginning to serve the 2052 National Convention, as if it had been built with more than its original goal in mind.

A large blue flag with a white tree and crescent moon swayed lazily over the South Carolina stage. Mick parked the four-wheeler in a sea of other ATVs ringing the large hospitality tent.

Following Mick through the parked vehicles, Donald saw that they were heading towards a smaller tent, which was swallowing a ton of traffic.

'What kind of errand are we on?' he asked.

Not that it mattered. In recent days they'd done a little of everything around the facility: running bags of ice to various state headquarters, meeting with congressmen and senators to see if they needed anything, making sure all the volunteers and delegates were settling into their trailers okay – whatever the Senator needed.

'Oh, we're just taking a little tour,' Mick said cryptically. He waved Donald into the small tent where workers were filing through in one direction with their arms loaded and coming out the other side empty-handed.

The inside of the small tent was lit up with floodlights, the ground packed hard from the traffic, the grass matted flat. A concrete ramp led deep into the earth, workers with volunteer badges trudging up one side. Mick jumped into the line heading down.

Donald knew where they were going. He recognised the ramp. He hurried up beside Mick.

'This is one of the rod storage facilities.' He couldn't hide the excitement in his voice, didn't even try. He'd been dying to see the other design, either on paper or in person. All he was privy to was his bunker project; the rest of the facility remained shrouded in mystery. 'Can we just go *in*?'

As if to answer, Mick started down the ramp, blending with the others.

'I begged for a tour the other day,' Donald hissed, 'but Thurman spouted all this national security crap—'

Mick laughed. Halfway down the slope, the roof of the tent seemed to recede into the darkness above, and the concrete walls on either side funnelled the workers towards gaping steel doors.

'You're not going to see inside one of those other facilities,' Mick told him. He put his hand on Donald's back and ushered him through the industrial-looking and familiar entrance chamber. The foot traffic ground to a halt as people took turns entering or leaving through the small hatch ahead. Donald felt turned around.

'Wait.' Donald caught glimpses through the hatch. 'What the hell? This is my design.'

They shuffled forward. Mick made room for the people coming out. He had a hand on Donald's shoulder, guiding him along.

'What're we doing here?' Donald asked. He could've sworn his own bunker design was in the bowl set aside for Tennessee. Then again, they'd been making so many last-minute changes the past weeks, maybe he'd been mixed up.

'Anna told me you wimped out and skipped the tour of this place.'

'That's bullshit.' Donald stopped at the oval hatch. He recognised every rivet. 'Why would she say that? I was right here. I cut the damn ribbon.'

Mick pushed at his back. 'Go. You're holding up the line.'

'I don't want to go.' He waved the people out. The workers behind Mick shifted in place, heavy Tupperware containers in their hands. 'I saw the top floor last time,' he said. 'That was enough.'

His friend clasped his neck with one hand and gripped his wrist with the other. As his head was bent forward, Donald had to move along to avoid falling on his face. He tried to reach for the jamb of the interior door, but Mick had his wrist.

'I want you to see what you *built*,' his friend said.

Donald stumbled through to the security office. He and Mick stepped aside to let the congestion they'd caused ease past.

'I've been looking at this damn thing every day for three years,' Donald said. He patted his pocket for his pills, wondered if it was too soon to take another. What he didn't tell Mick was that he'd forced himself to envision his design being *above* ground the entire time he'd worked on it, more a skyscraper than a buried straw. No way could he share that with his best friend, tell him how terrified he felt right then with no more than ten metres of dirt and concrete over his head. He seriously doubted Anna had used the phrase 'wimped out', but that's exactly what he had done after cutting the ribbon. While the Senator led dignitaries through the complex, Donald had hurried up to find a patch of grass with nothing but bright blue sky above.

'This is really fucking important,' Mick said. He snapped his fingers in front of Donald. Two lines of workers filed past. Beyond them, a man sat in a small cubicle, a brush in one hand and a can of paint in the other. He was applying a coat of flat grey to a set of steel bars. A technician behind him worked to wire some kind of massive screen into the wall. Not everything looked as if it was being finished precisely the way Donald had drawn it.

'Donny, listen to me. I'm serious. Today is the last day we can have this talk, okay? I need you to see what you built.' Mick's permanent and mischievous grin was gone, his eyebrows tilted. He looked, if anything, sad. 'Will you please come inside?'

Taking a full breath and fighting the urge to rush out to the hills and fresh air, away from the stifling crowds, Donald found himself agreeing. It was the look on Mick's face, the feeling that he needed to tell Donald about a loved one who had just passed away, something deathly serious.

Mick patted his shoulder in gratitude as Donald nodded. 'This way.'

Mick led him towards the central shaft. They passed through the cafeteria, which was being used. It made sense. Workers sat at tables and ate off plastic trays, taking a break. The smell of food drifted from the kitchens beyond. Donald laughed. He never thought they'd be used at all. Again, it felt as though the convention had given this place a purpose. It made him happy. He thought of the entire complex devoid of life one day, all the workers milling about outside storing away nuclear rods, while this massive building that would have touched the clouds had it been above ground, would sit perfectly empty.

Down a short hallway, the tile gave way to metal grating, and a broad cylinder dived straight through the heart of the facility. Anna had been right. It really was worth seeing.

They reached the railing of the central shaft, and Donald paused to peer over. The vast height made him forget for a moment that he was underground. On the other side of the landing, a conveyor lift rattled on its gears while a never-ending series of flat loading trays spun empty over the top. It reminded Donald of the buckets on a waterwheel. The trays flopped over before descending back down through the building.

The men and women from outside deposited each of their containers onto one of the empty trays before turning and heading back out. Donald looked for Mick and saw him disappearing down the staircase.

He hurried after, his fear of being buried alive chasing him.

'Hey!'

His shoes slapped the freshly painted stairs, the diamond plating keeping him from skidding off in his haste. He caught up with Mick as they made a full circuit of the thick inner post. Tupperware containers full of emergency supplies – supplies Donald figured would rot, unused – drifted eerily downward beyond the rail.

'I don't want to go any deeper than this,' he insisted.

'Two levels down,' Mick called back up. 'C'mon, man, I want you to see.'

Donald numbly obeyed. It would've been worse to make his way out alone.

At the first landing they came to, a worker stood by the conveyor with some type of gun. As the next container passed by, he shot its side with a flash of red, the scanner buzzing. The worker leaned on the railing, waiting for the next one while the container continued its ratcheting plummet.

'Did I miss something?' Donald asked. 'Are we still fighting deadlines? What's with all the supplies?'

Mick shook his head. 'Deadlines, lifelines,' he said.

At least, that's what Donald thought his friend said. Mick seemed lost in thought.

They spiralled down another level to the next landing, ten more metres of reinforced concrete between, thirty-three feet of wasted depth. Donald knew the floor. And not just from the plans he'd drawn. He and Mick had toured a floor like this in the factory where it had been built.

'I've been here before,' he told Mick.

Mick nodded. He waved Donald down the hallway until it made a turn. Mick picked one of the doors, seemingly at random, and opened it for Donald. Most of the floors had been prefabbed and furnished before being craned into place. If that wasn't the exact floor the two of them had toured, it had been one of the many just like it.

Once Donald was inside, Mick flicked on the apartment's overhead lights and closed the door. Donald was surprised to see that the bed was made. Stacks of linen were piled up in a chair. Mick grabbed the linens and moved them to the floor. He sat down and nodded to the foot of the bed.

Donald ignored him and poked his head into the small bathroom. 'This is actually pretty cool to see,' he told his friend. He reached out and turned the knob on the sink, expecting nothing. When clear water gurgled out, he found himself laughing.

'I knew you'd dig it once you saw it,' Mick said quietly.

Donald caught sight of himself in the mirror, the joy still on his face. He tended to forget how the corners of his eyes wrinkled up when he smiled. He touched his hair, sprinkles of grey even though he had another five years before he was over that proverbial hill. His job was ageing him prematurely. He had feared it might.

'Amazing that we built this, huh?' Mick asked. Donald turned and joined his friend in the tight quarters. He wondered if it was the work they'd been elected to perform that had aged them both or if it had been this one project, this all-consuming build.

'I appreciate you forcing me down here.' He almost added that he would love to see the rest, but he figured that would be pushing it. Besides, the crews back in the Georgia tents were probably looking for them already.

'Look,' Mick said, 'there's something I want to tell you.'

Donald looked at his friend, who seemed to be searching for the words. He glanced at the door. Mick was silent. Donald finally relented and sat at the foot of the bed.

'What's up?' he asked.

But he thought he knew. The Senator had included Mick in his other project, the one that had driven Donald to seek help from the doctor. Donald thought of the thick book he had largely memorised. Mick had done the same. And he'd brought him there not just to let him see what they'd accomplished, but to find a spot of perfect privacy, a place where secrets could be divulged. He patted his pocket where he kept his pills, the ones that kept his thoughts from running off to dangerous places.

'Hey,' Donald said, 'I don't want you saying anything you're not supposed to—'

Mick looked up, eyes wide with surprise.

'You don't need to say *anything*, Mick. Assume I know what *you* know.'

Mick shook his head sadly. 'You don't,' he said.

'Well, assume it anyway. I don't want to know anything.'

'I *need* you to know.'

'I'd rather not—'

'It's not a secret, man. It's just . . . I want you to know that I love you like a brother. I always have.'

The two of them sat in silence. Donald glanced at the door. The moment was uncomfortable, but it somehow filled his heart to hear Mick say it.

'Look—' Donald started.

'I know I'm always hard on you,' Mick said. 'And hell, I'm sorry. I really do look up to you. And Helen.' Mick turned to the side and scratched at his cheek. 'I'm happy for the two of you.'

Donald reached across the narrow space and squeezed his friend's arm.

'You're a good friend, Mick. I'm glad we've had this time together, the last few years, running for office, building this—'

Mick nodded. 'Yeah. Me too. But listen, I didn't bring you down here to get all sappy like this.' He reached for his cheek again, and Donald saw that he was wiping at his eyes. 'I had a talk with Thurman last night. He – a few months ago, he offered me a spot on a team, a top team, and I told him last night that I'd rather you take it.'

'What? A committee?' Donald couldn't imagine his friend giving up an appointment, *any* kind of appointment. 'Which one?'

Mick shook his head. 'No, something else.'

'What?' Donald asked.

'Look,' Mick said, 'when you find out about it, and you understand what's going on, I want you to think of me right here.' Mick glanced around the room. There were a few breaths of complete silence punctuated by drips of water from the bathroom sink. 'If I could choose to be anywhere, *anywhere* in the coming years, it would be right down here with the first group.'

'Okay. Yeah, I'm not sure what you mean—'

'You will. Just remember this, all right? That I love you like a brother and that everything happens for a reason. I wouldn't have wanted it any other way. For you or for Helen.'

'Okay.' Donald smiled. He couldn't tell if Mick was fucking with him or if his friend had consumed a few too many Bloody Marys from the hospitality tent that morning.

'All right.' Mick stood abruptly. He certainly moved as though he were sober. 'Let's get the hell out of here. This place gives me the creeps.'

Mick threw open the door and flicked off the lights.

'Wimping out, eh?' Donald called after his friend.

Mick shook his head and the two of them headed back down the hallway. Behind them, they left the small, random apartment in darkness, its little sink dripping. And Donald tried to sort out how he'd gotten turned around, how the Tennessee tent where he'd cut the ribbon had become the one from South Carolina. He almost had it, his subconscious flashing to a delivery of goods, to fifty times more fibre optic than needed, but the connection was lost.

Meanwhile, containers loaded with supplies rumbled down the mammoth shaft. And empty trays rattled up.

20

2110

• Silo 1 •

Troy woke up in a fog, groggy and disoriented, his head pulsing. He lifted his hands and groped in front of his face, expecting to find the chill of icy glass, the press of domed steel, the doom of a deep freeze. His hands found only empty air. The clock beside his bed showed it was a little after three in the morning.

He sat up and saw that he had on a pair of gym shorts. He couldn't remember changing the night before, couldn't remember going to bed. Planting his feet on the floor, he rested his elbows on his knees, sank his head into his palms and sat there a moment. His entire body ached.

After a few minutes slipped by, he dressed himself in the dark, buckling up his overalls. Light would be bad for his headache. It wasn't a theory he needed to test.

The hallway outside was still dimmed for the evening, just bright enough to grope one's way to the shared bathrooms. Troy stole down the hall and headed for the lift.

He hit the 'up' button, hesitated, wasn't sure if that was right. Something tugged at him. He pressed the 'down' button as well.

It was too early to go into his office, not unless he wanted to fiddle on the computer. He wasn't hungry, but he could go up and watch the sun rise. The late shift would be up there drinking coffee. Or he could hit the rec room and go for a jog. That would mean going back to his room to change.

The lift arrived with a beep while he was still deciding.

Both lights went off, the up and the down. He could take this lift anywhere.

Troy stepped inside. He didn't know where he wanted to go.

The lift closed. It waited on him patiently. Eventually, he figured, it would whisk off to heed some other call, pick up a person with purpose, someone with a destination. He could stand there and do nothing and let that other soul decide.

Running his finger across the buttons, he tried to remember what was on each level. There was a lot he'd memorised, but not everything he knew felt accessible. He had a sudden urge to head for one of the lounges and watch TV, just let the hours slide past until he finally needed to be somewhere. This was how the shift was supposed to go. Waiting and then doing. Sleeping and then waiting. Make it to dinner and then make it to bed. The end was always in sight. There was nothing to rebel against, just a routine.

The lift shook into motion. Troy jerked his hand away from the buttons and took a step back. It didn't show where he was going but it felt as if it had started downwards.

Only a few floors passed before the lift lurched to a halt. The doors opened on a lower apartment level. A familiar face from the cafeteria, a man in reactor red, smiled as he stepped inside.

'Morning,' he said.

Troy nodded.

The man turned and jabbed one of the lower buttons, one of the reactor levels. He studied the otherwise blank array, turned and gave Troy a quizzical look.

'You feeling okay, sir?'

'Hmm? Oh, yeah.'

Troy leaned forward and pressed sixty-eight. The man's concern for his well-being must've had him thinking of the doctor, even though Henson wouldn't be on shift for several hours. But there was something else nagging him, something he felt he needed to see, a dream slipping away.

'Must not have taken the first time,' he explained, glancing at the button.

'Mmm.'

The silence lasted one or two floors.

'How much longer you got?' the reactor mechanic asked.

'Me? Just another couple of weeks. How about you?'

'I just got on a week ago. But this is my second shift.'

'Oh?'

The lights counted downward in floors but upward in number. Troy didn't like this; he felt as if the lowest level should be level one. They should count *up*.

'Is the second shift easier?' he asked. The question came out unbidden. It was as though the part of him dying to know was more awake than the part of him praying for silence.

The mechanic considered this.

'I wouldn't say it's easier. How about . . . less uncomfortable?' He laughed quietly. Troy felt their arrival in his knees, gravity tugging on him. The doors beeped open.

'Have a good one,' the mechanic said. They hadn't shared their names. 'In case I don't see you again.'

Troy raised his palm. 'Next time,' he said. The man stepped out, and the doors winked shut on the halls to the power plant. With a hum, the lift continued its descent.

The doors dinged on the medical level. Troy stepped out and heard voices down the corridor. He crept quietly across the tile, and the voices became louder. One was female. It wasn't a conversation; it must have been an old movie. Troy peeked into the main office and saw a man lounging on a gurney, his back turned, a TV set up in the corner. Troy slunk past so as not to disturb him.

The hallway split in two directions. He imagined the layout, could picture the pie-shaped storerooms, the rows of deep-freeze coffins, the tubes and pipes that led from the walls to the bases, from the bases into the people inside.

He stopped at one of the heavy doors and tried his code. The light changed from red to green. He dropped his hand, didn't need to enter this room, didn't feel the urge, just wanted to see if it would work. The urge was elsewhere.

He meandered down the hall past a few more doors. Wasn't he just here? Had he ever left? His arm throbbed. He rolled back his sleeve and saw a spot of blood, a circle of redness around a pinprick scab.

If something bad had happened, he couldn't remember. That part of him had been choked off.

He tried his code on this other pad, this other door, and waited for the light to turn green. This time, he pushed the button that opened the door. He didn't know what it was, but there was something inside that he needed to see.

21

2052

Fulton County, Georgia

L ight rains on the morning of the convention left the
man-made hills soggy, the new grass slick, but did
little to erode the general festivities. Parking lots had
been emptied of construction vehicles and mud-caked pickups.
Now they held hundreds of idling buses and a handful of
sleek black limos, the latter splattered with mud.

The lot where temporary trailers had served as offices and
living quarters for construction crews had been handed over
to the staffers, volunteers, delegates and dignitaries who had
laboured for weeks to bring that day to fruition. The area was
dotted with welcoming tents that served as the headquarters
for the event coordinators. Throngs of new arrivals filed from
the buses and made their way through the CAD-FAC's security
station. Massive fences bristled with coils of razor wire that
seemed outsized and ridiculous for the convention but made
sense for the storing of nuclear material. These barriers and
gates held at bay an odd union of protestors: those on the
Right who disagreed with the facility's current purpose and
those on the Left who feared its future one.

There had never been a National Convention with such
energy, such crowds. Downtown Atlanta loomed beyond the
treetops, but the city seemed far removed from the sudden
bustle in lower Fulton County.

Donald shivered beneath his umbrella at the top of a
knoll and gazed out over the sea of people gathering across
the hills, heading towards whichever stage flew their state's
flag, umbrellas bobbing and jostling like water bugs.

Somewhere, a marching band blared a practice tune and stomped another hill into mud. There was a sense in the air that the world was about to change – a woman was about to win nomination for president, only the second such nomination in Donald's lifetime. And if the pollsters could be believed, this one had more than a chance. Unless the war in Iran took a sudden turn, a milestone would be reached, a final glass ceiling shattered. And it would happen right there in those grand divots in the earth.

More buses churned through the lot and let off their passengers, and Donald pulled out his phone and checked the time. He still had an error icon, the network choked to death from the overwhelming demand. He was surprised, with so much other careful planning, that the committee hadn't accounted for this and erected a temporary tower or two.

'Congressman Keene?'

Donald started and turned to find Anna walking along the ridgeline towards him. He glanced down at the Georgia stage but didn't see her ride. He was surprised she would just walk up. And yet, it was like her to do things the difficult way.

'I couldn't tell if that was you,' she said, smiling. 'Everyone has the same umbrella.'

'Yeah, it's me.' He took a deep breath, found his chest still felt constricted with nerves whenever he saw her, as though any conversation could get him into trouble.

Anna stepped close as if she expected him to share his umbrella. He moved it to his other hand to give her more space, the drizzle peppering his exposed arm. He scanned the bus lot and searched impossibly for any sign of Helen. She should have been there by now.

'This is gonna be a mess,' Anna said.

'It's supposed to clear up.'

Someone on the North Carolina stage checked her microphone with a squawk of feedback. 'We'll see,' Anna said. She wrapped her coat tighter against the early morning breeze. 'Isn't Helen coming?'

'Yeah. Senator Thurman insisted. She's not gonna be happy when she sees how many people are here. She hates crowds. She won't be happy about the mud, either.'

Anna laughed. 'I wouldn't worry about the conditions of the grounds after this.'

Donald thought about all the loads of radioactive waste that would be trucked in. 'Yeah.' He saw her point.

He peered down the hill again at the Georgia stage. It would be the site of the first national gathering of delegates later that day, all the most important people under one tent. Behind the stage and among the smoking food tents, the only sign of the underground containment facility was a small concrete tower rising up from the ground, a bristle of antennae sprouting from the top. Donald thought of how much work it would take to haul away all the flags and soaked buntings before the first of the spent fuel rods could finally be brought in.

'It's weird to think of a few thousand people from the state of Tennessee stomping around on top of something *we* designed,' Anna said. Her arm brushed against Donald's. He stood perfectly still, wondering if it had been an accident. 'I wish you'd seen more of the place.'

Donald shivered, more from fighting to remain still than from the cold and moist morning air. He hadn't told anyone about Mick's tour the day before. It felt too sacred. He would probably tell Helen about it and no one else. 'It's crazy how much time went into something nobody will ever use,' he said.

Anna murmured her agreement. Her arm was still touching his. There was still no sign of Helen. Donald felt irrationally that he would somehow spot her among the crowds. He usually could. He remembered the high balcony of a place they'd stayed in during their honeymoon in Hawaii. Even from up there, he could spot her taking her early morning walks along the foam line, looking for seashells. There might be a few hundred strollers out on the beach, and yet his eyes would be drawn immediately to her.

'I guess the only way they were going to build any of this

was if we gave them the right kind of insurance,' Donald said, repeating what the Senator had told him. But it still didn't feel right.

'People want to feel safe,' Anna said. 'They want to know, if the worst happens, they'll have someone – *something* – to fall back on.'

Again, Anna rested against his arm. Definitely not an accident. Donald felt himself withdraw and knew she would sense it too.

'I was really hoping to tour one of the *other* bunkers,' he said, changing the subject. 'It'd be interesting to see what the other teams came up with. Apparently, though, I don't have the clearance.'

Anna laughed. 'I tried the same thing. I'm dying to see our competition. But I can understand them being sensitive. There's a lot of eyes on this joint.' She leaned into him once more, ignoring the space he'd made.

'Don't you feel that?' she asked. 'Like there's some huge bull's-eye over this place? I mean, even with the fences and walls down there, you can bet the whole world is gonna be keeping an eye on what happens here.'

Donald nodded. He knew she wasn't talking about the convention but about what the place would be used for afterwards.

'Hey, it looks like I've got to get back down there.'

He turned to follow her gaze, saw Senator Thurman climbing the hill on foot, a massive black golf umbrella shedding the rain around him. The man seemed impervious to the mud and grime in a way no one else was, the same way he seemed oblivious to the passing of time.

Anna reached over and squeezed Donald's arm. 'Congrats again. It was fun working together on this.'

'Same,' he said. 'We make a good team.'

She smiled. He wondered for a moment if she would lean over and kiss his cheek. It would feel natural in that moment. But it came and went. Anna left his protective cover and headed off towards the Senator.

Thurman lifted his umbrella, kissed his daughter's cheek and watched her descend the hill. He hiked up to join Donald.

They stood beside each other for a pause, the rain dripping off their umbrellas with a muted patter.

'Sir,' Donald finally said. He felt newly comfortable in the man's presence. The last two weeks had been like summer camp, where being around the same people almost every hour of the day brought a level of familiarity and intimacy that knowing them casually for years could never match. There was something about forced confinement that brought people together. Beyond the obvious, physical ways.

'Damn rain,' was Thurman's reply.

'You can't control everything,' Donald said.

The Senator grunted as if he disagreed. 'Helen not here yet?'

'No, sir.' Donald fished in his pocket and felt for his phone. 'I'll message her again in a bit. Not sure if my texts are getting through or not – the networks are absolutely crushed. I'm pretty sure this many people descending on this corner of the county is unprecedented.'

'Well, this will be an unprecedented day,' Thurman said. 'Nothing like it ever before.'

'It was mostly your doing, sir. I mean, not just building this place, but choosing not to run. This country could've been yours for the taking this year.'

The Senator laughed. 'That's true most years, Donny. But I've learned to set my sights higher than that.'

Donald shivered again. He couldn't remember the last time the Senator had called him that. Maybe that first meeting in his office, more than two years ago? The old man seemed unusually tense.

'When Helen gets here, I want you to come down to the state tent and see me, okay?'

Donald pulled out his phone and checked the time. 'You know I'm supposed to be at the Tennessee tent in an hour, right?'

'There's been a change of plans. I want you to stay close

to home. Mick is going to cover for you over there, which means I need you with me.'

'Are you sure? I was supposed to meet with—'

'I know. This is a good thing, trust me. I want you and Helen near the Georgia stage with me. And look—'

The Senator turned to face him. Donald peeled his eyes away from the last of the unloading buses. The rain had picked up a little.

'You've contributed more to this day than you know,' Thurman said.

'Sir?'

'The world is going to change today, Donny.'

Donald wondered if the Senator had been skipping his nanobath treatments. His eyes seemed dilated and focused on something in the distance. He appeared older somehow.

'I'm not sure I understand—'

'You will. Oh, and a surprise visitor is coming. She should be here any moment.' He smiled. 'The national anthem starts at noon. There'll be a flyover from the 141st after that. I want you nearby when that happens.'

Donald nodded. He had learned when to stop asking questions and just do what the Senator expected of him.

'Yes, sir,' he said, shivering against the cold.

Senator Thurman left. Turning his back to the stage, Donald scanned the last of the buses and wondered where in the world Helen was.

22

2110

· Silo 1 ·

Troy walked down the line of cryopods as if he knew where he was going. It was just like the way his hand had drifted to the button that had brought him to that floor. There were made-up names on each of the panels. He knew this somehow. He remembered coming up with his name. It had something to do with his wife, some way to honour her, or some kind of secret and forbidden link so that he might one day remember.

That all lay in the past, deep in the mist, a dream forgotten. Before his shift there had been an orientation. There were familiar books to read and reread. That's when he had chosen his name.

A bitter explosion on his tongue brought him to a halt. It was the taste of a pill dissolving. Troy stuck out his tongue and scraped it with his fingers, but there was nothing there. He could feel the ulcers on his gums against his teeth but couldn't recall how they'd formed.

He walked on. Something wasn't right. These memories weren't supposed to return. He pictured himself on a gurney, screaming, someone strapping him down, stabbing him with needles. That wasn't him. He was holding that man's boots.

Troy stopped at one of the pods and checked the name. *Helen.* His gut lurched and groped for its medicine. He didn't want to remember. That was a secret ingredient: the *not wanting to remember.* Those were the parts that slipped away, the parts the drugs wrapped their tentacles around and pulled beneath the surface. But now, there was some small part of

him that was dying to know. It was a nagging doubt, a feeling
of having left some important piece of himself behind. It was
willing to drown the rest of him for the answers.

The frost on the glass wiped away with a squeak. He
didn't recognise the person inside and moved on to the next
pod, a scene from before orientation coming back to him.

Troy recalled halls packed with people crying, grown men
sobbing, pills that dried their eyes. Fearsome clouds rose on
a video screen. Women were put away for safety. Like a lifeboat, women and children first.

Troy remembered. It wasn't an accident. He remembered
a talk in another pod, a bigger pod with another man there, a
talk about the coming end of the world, about making *room*,
about ending it all before it ended on its own.

A controlled explosion. Bombs were sometimes used to
put out fires.

He wiped another frost-covered sheet of glass. The
sleeping form in the next chamber had eyelashes that glittered
with ice. She was a stranger. He moved on, but it was coming
back to him. His arm throbbed. The shakes were gone.

Troy remembered a calamity, but it was all for show.
The real threat was in the air, invisible. The bombs were
to get people to move, to make them afraid, to get them
crying and forgetting. People had spilled like marbles down
a bowl. Not a bowl – a *funnel*. Someone explained why they
were spared. He remembered a white fog, walking through
a white fog. The death was already in them. Troy remembered a taste on his tongue, metallic.

The ice on the next pane was already disturbed, had been
wiped away by someone recently. Beads of condensation stood
like tiny lenses warping the light. He rubbed the glass and
knew what had happened. He saw the woman inside with
the auburn hair that she sometimes kept in a bun. This was
not his wife. This was someone who wanted that, wanted
him like that.

'Hello?'

Troy turned towards the voice. The night-shift doctor

was heading his way, weaving between the pods, coming for him. Troy clasped his hand over the soreness on his arm. He didn't want to be taken again. They couldn't make him forget.

'Sir, you shouldn't be in here.'

Troy didn't answer. The doctor stopped at the foot of the pod. Inside, a woman who wasn't his wife lay in slumber. Wasn't his wife, but had wanted to be.

'Why don't you come with me?' the doctor asked.

'I'd like to stay,' Troy said. He felt a bizarre calmness. All the pain had been ripped away. This was more forceful than forgetting. He remembered everything. His soul had been cut free.

'I can't have you in here, sir. Come with me. You'll freeze in here.'

Troy glanced down. He had forgotten to put on shoes. He curled his toes away from the floor . . . then allowed them to settle.

'Sir? Please.' The young doctor gestured down the aisle. Troy let go of his arm and saw that things were handled as needed. No kicking meant no straps. No shivering meant no needles.

He heard the squeak of hurrying boots out in the hallway. A large man from Security appeared by the open vault door, visibly winded. Troy caught a glimpse of the doctor waving the man down. They were trying not to scare him. They didn't know that he couldn't be scared any more.

'You'll put me away for good,' Troy said. It was something between a statement and a question. It was a realisation. He wondered if he was like Hal – like *Carlton* – if the pills would never take again. He glanced towards the far end of the room, knew the empties were kept there. This was where he would be buried.

'Nice and easy,' the doctor said.

He led Troy to the exit; he would embalm him with that bright blue sky. The pods slid by as the two of them walked in silence.

The man from Security took deep breaths as he filled

the doorway, his great chest heaving against his overalls. There was a squeak from more boots as he was joined by another. Troy saw that his shift was over. Two weeks to go. He'd nearly made it.

The doctor waved the large men out of the way, seemed to hope they wouldn't be needed. They took up positions to either side, seemed to think otherwise. Troy was led down the hallway, hope guiding him and fear flanking him.

'You *know*, don't you?' Troy asked the doctor, turning to study him. 'You remember everything.'

The doctor didn't turn to face him. He simply nodded.

This felt like a betrayal. It wasn't fair.

'Why are you allowed to remember?' Troy asked. He wanted to know why those dispensing the medicine didn't have to take some of their own.

The doctor waved him into his office. His assistant was there, wearing a sleepshirt and hanging an IV bag bulging with blue liquid.

'Some of us remember,' the doctor said, 'because we know this isn't a bad thing we've done.' He frowned as he helped Troy onto the gurney. He seemed truly sad about Troy's condition. 'We're doing good work here,' he said. 'We're saving the world, not ending it. And the medicine only touches our regrets.' He glanced up. 'Some of us don't have any.'

The doorway was stuffed with security. It overflowed. The assistant unbuckled Troy's overalls. Troy watched numbly.

'It would take a different kind of drug to touch what *we* know,' the doctor said. He pulled a clipboard from the wall. A sheet of paper was fed into its jaws. There was a pause, and then a pen was pressed into Troy's palm.

Troy laughed as he signed off on himself.

'Then why me?' he asked. 'Why am I here?' He had always wanted to ask this of someone who might know. These were the prayers of youth, but now with a chance of some reply.

The doctor smiled and took the clipboard. He was probably in his late twenties, had come on shift just a few weeks ago. Troy was a few years shy of forty. And yet this man had all the wisdom, all the answers.

'It's good to have people like you in charge,' the doctor said, and he seemed to genuinely mean it. The clipboard was returned to its peg. One of the security men yawned and covered his mouth. Troy watched as his overalls were unsnapped and flopped to his waist. A fingernail makes a distinctive click when it taps against a needle.

'I'd like to think about this,' Troy said. He felt a sudden panic wash over him. He knew this needed to happen, but wanted just a few more minutes alone with his thoughts, to savour this brief bout of comprehension. He wanted to sleep, certainly, but not quite yet.

The men in the doorway stirred as they sensed Troy's doubts, could see the fear in his eyes.

'I wish there was some other way,' the doctor said sadly. He rested a hand on Troy's shoulder, guided him back against the table. The men from Security stepped closer.

There was a prick on his arm, a deep bite without warning. He looked down and saw the silver barb slide into his vein, the bright blue liquid pumped inside.

'I don't want—' he said.

There were hands on his shins, his knees, weight on his shoulders. The heaviness against his chest was from something else.

A burning rush flowed through his body, chased immediately by numbness. They weren't putting him to sleep. *They were killing him.* Troy knew this as suddenly and swiftly as he knew that his wife was dead, that some other person had tried to take her place. He would go into a coffin *for good* this time. And all the dirt piled over his head would finally serve some purpose.

Darkness squeezed in around his vision. He closed his eyes, tried to yell for it to stop, but nothing came out. He wanted to kick and fight it, but more than mere hands had a hold of him now. He was sinking.

His last thoughts were of his beautiful wife, but the

thoughts made little sense – they were the dream world invading.

She's in Tennessee, he thought. He didn't know why or how he knew this. But she was there – and waiting. She was already dead and had a spot hollowed out by her side just for him.

Troy had just one more question, one name he hoped to grope for and seize before he went under, some part of himself to take with him to those depths. It was on the tip of his tongue like a bitter pill, so close that he could taste it—

But then he forgot.

23

2052

Fulton County, Georgia

The rain finally let up just as warring announcements and battling tunes filled the air above the teeming hills. While the main stage was prepped for the evening's gala, it sounded to Donald as though the real action was taking place at all the other states. Opening bands ripped into their sets as the buzz of ATVs subsided to a trickle.

It felt vaguely claustrophobic to be down in the bottom of the bowl by the Georgia stage. Donald sensed an unquenchable urge for height, to be up on the ridge where he could see what was going on. It left him imagining the sight of thousands of guests arrayed across each of the hills, picturing the political fervour in the air everywhere, the gelling of like-minded families celebrating the promise of something new.

As much as Donald wanted to celebrate new beginnings with them, he was mostly looking forward to the *end*. He couldn't wait for the convention to wrap up. The weeks had worn on him. He was looking forward to a real bed, to some privacy, his computer, reliable phone service, dinners out and, most of all: time alone with his wife.

Fishing his phone out of his pocket, he checked his messages for the umpteenth time. They were minutes away from the anthem, and then the flyover from the 141st. He had also heard someone mention fireworks to start the convention off with a bang.

His phone showed that the last half-dozen messages still hadn't gone through. The network was clogged, an error message popping up that he'd never seen before. At least some of the earlier ones looked as if they'd been sent. He scanned the wet banks for her, hoping to see her making her way down, a smile he could spot from any distance.

Someone stepped up beside him. Donald looked away from the hills to see that Anna had joined him by the stage.

'Here we go,' she said quietly, scanning the crowd.

She looked and sounded nervous. Maybe it was for her father, who had done so much to arrange the main stage and make sure everyone was in the right place. Glancing back, he saw that people were taking their seats, chairs wiped down from the morning drizzle, not nearly as many people as it seemed before. They must be either working in the tents or off to the other stages. This was the quiet brewing before the—

'*There* she is.'

Anna waved her arms. Donald felt his heart swell up into his neck as he turned and followed Anna's gaze. His relief was mixed with the panic of Helen seeing him there with her, the two of them waiting side by side.

Shuffling down the hill was certainly someone familiar. A young woman in a pressed blue uniform, a hat tucked under one arm, a dark head of hair wrapped up in a crisp bun.

'Charlotte?' Donald shielded his eyes from the glare of the noonday sun filtering through wispy clouds. He gaped in disbelief. All other events and concerns melted away as his sister spotted them and waved back.

'She sure as hell cut this close,' Anna muttered.

Donald hurried over to his four-wheeler and turned the key. He hit the ignition, gave the handle some gas, and raced across the wet grass to meet her.

Charlotte beamed as he hit the brakes at the base of the hill. He killed the engine.

'Hey, Donny.'

His sister leaned in to him before he could dismount. She threw her arms around his neck and squeezed.

He returned her embrace, worried about denting the

creases of her neat uniform. 'What the hell are you doing here?' he asked.

She let go and took a step back, smoothed the front of her shirt. The air-force dress hat disappeared back under her arm, every motion like an ingrained and precise habit.

'Are you surprised?' she asked. 'I thought the Senator would've let it slip by now.'

'Hell, no. Well, he said something about a visitor but not who. I thought you were in Iran. Did he swing this?'

She nodded, and Donald felt his cheeks cramping from smiling so hard. Every time he saw her, there came a relief from discovering that she was still the same person. The sharp chin and splash of freckles across her nose, the shine in her eyes that had not yet dulled from the horrible things she'd seen. She had just turned thirty, had been half a world away with no family on her birthday, but she was frozen in his mind as the young teen who had enlisted.

'I think I'm supposed to be on the stage for this thing tonight,' she said.

'Of course.' Donald smiled. 'I'm sure they'll want you on camera. You know, to show support for the troops.'

Charlotte frowned. 'Oh, God, I'm one of *those* people, aren't I?'

He laughed. 'I'm sure they'll have someone from the army, navy and marines there with you.'

'Oh, God. And I'm the *girl*.'

They laughed together, and one of the bands beyond the hills finished their set. Donald scooted forward and told his sister to hop on, his chest suddenly less constricted. There had been a shift in the weather, these breaking clouds, the quietening stages, and now the arrival of family.

He cranked the engine and raced through the least muddy path on the way back to the stage, his sister holding on tight behind him. They pulled up beside Anna, his sister hopping off and into her arms. While they chatted, Donald killed the ignition and checked his phone for messages. Finally, one had gotten through.

Helen: *In Tennessee. where r u?*

There was a jarring moment as his brain tried to make sense of the message. It was from Helen. What the hell was she doing in *Tennessee?*

Another stage fell silent. It took only a heartbeat or two for Donald to realise that she wasn't hundreds of miles away. She was just over the hill. None of his messages about meeting at the Georgia stage had gone through.

'Hey, I'll be right back.'

He cranked the ATV. Anna grabbed his wrist.

'Where are you going?' she asked.

He smiled. 'Tennessee. Helen just texted me.'

Anna glanced up at the clouds. His sister was inspecting her hat. On the stage, a young girl was being ushered up to the mic. She was flanked by a colour guard, and the seats facing the stage were filling up, necks stretched with anticipation.

Before he could react or put the ATV in gear, Anna reached across, twisted the key and pulled it out of the ignition.

'Not now,' she said.

Donald felt a flash of rage. He reached for her hands, for the key, but it disappeared behind her back.

'Wait,' she hissed.

Charlotte had turned towards the stage. Senator Thurman stood with a microphone in hand, the young girl, maybe sixteen, beside him. The hills had grown deathly quiet. Donald realised what a racket the ATV had been making. The girl was about to sing.

'*Ladies and gentlemen, fellow Democrats—*'

There was a pause. Donald got off the four-wheeler, took a last glance at his phone, then tucked it away.

'*—and our handful of Independents.*'

Laughter from the crowd. Donald set off at a jog across the flat at the bottom of the bowl. His shoes squished in the wet grass and the thin layer of mud. Senator Thurman's voice continued to roar through the microphone:

'*Today is the dawn of a new era, a new time.*'

Donald was out of shape, his shoes growing heavy with mud.

'*As we gather in this place of future independence—*'

By the time the ground sloped upward, he was already winded.

'*—I'm reminded of the words from one of our enemies. A Republican.*'

Distant laughter, but Donald paid no heed. He was concentrating on the climb.

'*It was Ronald Reagan who once said that freedom must be fought for, that peace must be earned. As we listen to this anthem, written a long time ago as bombs dropped and a new country was forged, let's consider the price paid for our freedom and ask ourselves if any cost could be too great to ensure that these liberties never slip away.*'

A third of the way up – and Donald had to stop and catch his breath. His calves were going to give out before his lungs did. He regretted puttering around on the ATV the past weeks while some of the others slogged it on foot. He promised himself he'd get in better shape.

He started back up the hill, and a voice like ringing crystal filled the bowl. It spilled in synchrony over the looming rise. He turned towards the stage below where the national anthem was being sung by the sweetest of young voices—

And he saw Anna hurrying up the hill after him, a scowl of worry on her face.

Donald knew he was in trouble. He wondered if he was dishonouring the anthem by scurrying up the hill. Everyone had assigned places for the anthem and he was ignoring his. He turned his back on Anna and set off with renewed resolve.

'*—o'er the ramparts we watched—*'

He laughed, out of breath, wondering if these mounds of earth could be considered ramparts. It was easy to see the bowls for what they'd become in the last weeks, individual states full of people, goods and livestock, fifty state fairs bustling at once, all for this shining day, all to be gone once the facility was up and running.

'—*and the rockets' red glare, the bombs bursting in air*—'

He reached the top of the hill and sucked in deep lung-fuls of crisp, clean air. On the stage below, flags swayed idly in a soft breeze. A large screen showed a video of the girl singing about *proof* and *still being there*.

A hand seized his wrist.

'Come back,' Anna hissed.

He was panting. Anna was also out of breath, her knees covered in mud and grass stains. She must've slipped on the way up.

'Helen doesn't know where I am,' he said.

'—*bannerrr yet waaaaave*—'

Applause stirred before the end, a compliment. The jets streaking in from the distance caught his eye even before he heard their rumble. A diamond pattern with wing tips nearly touching.

'Get the fuck back down here,' Anna yelled. She yanked on his arm.

Donald twisted his wrist away. He was mesmerised by the sight of the jets approaching.

'—*o'er the laaand of the freeeeeee*—'

That sweet and youthful voice lifted up from fifty holes in the earth and crashed into the thunderous roar of the powerful jets, those soaring and graceful angels of death.

'Let go,' Donald demanded, as Anna grabbed him and scrambled to pull him back down the hill.

'—*and the hooome of the . . . braaaaave . . .*'

The air shook from the grumble of the perfectly timed fly-by. Afterburners screamed as the jets peeled apart and curved upward into the white clouds.

Anna was practically wrestling him, arms wrapped around his shoulders. Donald snapped out of a trance induced by the passing jets, the beautiful rendition of the anthem amplified across half a county, the struggle to spot his wife in the bowl below.

'Goddammit, Donny, we've got to get *down*—'

The first flash came before she could get her hands over

his eyes. A bright spot in the corner of his vision in the direction of downtown Atlanta. It was a daytime strike of lightning. Donald turned towards it, expecting thunder. The flash of light had become a blinding glow. Anna's arms were around his waist, jerking him backward. His sister was there, panting, covering her eyes, screaming, '*What the fuck?*'

Another flash of light, starbursts in one's vision. Sirens spilled out of all the speakers. It was the recorded sound of air-raid klaxons.

Donald felt half blinded. Even when the mushroom clouds rose up from the earth – impossibly large to be so distant – it still took a heartbeat to realise what was happening.

They pulled him down the hill. Applause had turned to screams audible over the rise and fall of the blaring siren. Donald could hardly see. He stumbled backward and nearly fell as the three of them slipped and slid down the bowl, the wet grass funnelling them towards the stage. The puffy tops of the swelling clouds rose up higher and higher, staying in sight even as the rest of the hills and the trees disappeared from view.

'Wait!' he yelled.

There was something he was forgetting. He couldn't remember what. He had an image of his ATV sitting up on the ridge. He was leaving it behind. How did he get up there? What was happening?

'Go. Go. Go,' Anna was saying.

His sister was cussing. She was frightened and confused, just like him. He had never known his sister to be either one.

'The main tent!'

Donald spun around, his heels slipping in the grass, hands wet with rain and studded with mud and grass. When had he fallen?

The three of them tumbled down the last of the slope as the sound of distant thunder finally reached them. The clouds overhead seemed to race away from the blasts, pushed aside by an unnatural wind. The undersides of the clouds strobed and flashed as if more strikes of lightning were hitting, more bombs detonating. Down by the stage, people weren't running to escape the bowl – they were instead running into the tents, guided by volunteers with waving arms, the markets and food stalls clearing out, the rows of wooden chairs now a heaped and upturned tangle, a dog still tied to a post, barking.

Some people still seemed to be aware, to have their faculties intact. Anna was one of them. Donald saw the Senator by a smaller tent coordinating the flow of traffic. Where was everyone going? Donald felt empty as he was ushered along with the others. It took long moments for his brain to process what he'd seen. Nuclear blasts. The live view of what had for ever been resigned to grainy wartime video. Real bombs going off in the real air. Nearby. He had seen them. Why wasn't he completely blind? Was that even what happened?

The raw fear of death overtook him. Donald knew, in some recess of his mind, that they were all dead. The end of all things was coming. There was no outrunning it. No hiding. Paragraphs from a book he'd read came to mind, thousands of memorised paragraphs. He patted his pants for his pills, but they weren't there. Looking over his shoulder, he fought to remember what he'd left behind—

Anna and his sister pulled him past the Senator, who wore a hard scowl of determination. He frowned at his daughter. The tent flap brushed Donald's face, the darkness within interspersed with a few hanging lights. The spots in his vision from the blasts made themselves known in the blackness. There was a crush of people, but not as many as there should have been. Where were the crowds? It didn't make sense until he found himself shuffling downward.

A concrete ramp, bodies on all sides, shoulders jostling, people wheezing, yelling for one another, hands outstretched as the flowing crush drove loved ones away, husband and wife separated, some people crying, some perfectly poised—

Husband and wife.

Helen!

Donald yelled her name over the crowd. He turned and tried to swim against the flowing torrent of the frightened mob. Anna and his sister pulled on him. People fighting to get below pushed from above. Donald was forced downward, into the depths. He wanted to go under with his wife. He wanted to drown with her.

'*Helen!*'

Oh, God, he remembered.

He remembered what he had left behind.

Panic subsided and fear took its place. He could see. His vision had cleared. But he could not fight the push of the inevitable.

Donald remembered a conversation with the Senator about how it would all end. There was an electricity in the air, the taste of dead metal on his tongue, a white mist rising around him. He remembered most of a book. He knew what this was, what was happening.

His world was gone.

A new one swallowed him.

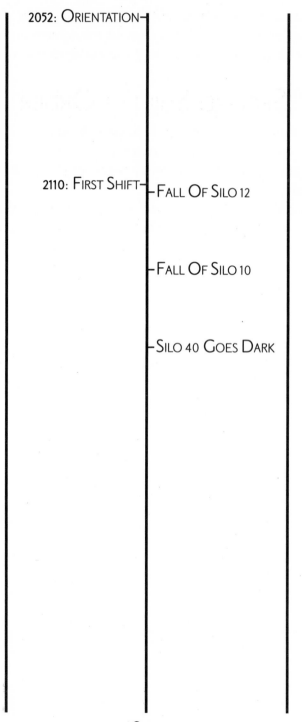

2052: ORIENTATION

2110: FIRST SHIFT
FALL OF SILO 12

FALL OF SILO 10

SILO 40 GOES DARK

SILO
1

SECOND SHIFT – ORDER

24

2212

• Silo 1 •

Troy started awake from a series of terrible dreams. The world was on fire, and the people who had been sent to extinguish it were all asleep. Asleep and frozen stiff, smoking matches still in their hands, wisps and grey curls of evil deeds.

He had been buried, was enveloped in darkness, could feel the tight walls of his small coffin hemming him in.

Dark shapes moved beyond the frosted glass, the men with their shovels trying to free him.

Troy's eyelids seemed to rip and crack as he fought to open them fully. There was crust in the corners of his eyes, melting frost coursing down his cheeks. He tried to lift his arms to wipe it away, but they responded feebly. An IV tugged at his wrist as he managed to raise one hand. He was aware of his catheter. Every inch of his body tingled as he emerged from the numbness and into the cold.

The lid popped with a hiss of air. There was a crack of light to his side that grew as the shadows folded away.

A doctor and his assistant reached in to tend to him. Troy tried to speak but could only cough. They helped him up, brought him the bitter drink. Swallowing took effort. His hands were so weak, arms trembling, that they had to help him with the cup. The taste on his tongue was metallic. It tasted like death.

'Easy,' they said when he tried to drink too fast. Tubes and IVs were carefully removed by expert hands, pressure applied, gauze taped to frigid skin. There was a paper gown.

'What year?' he asked, his voice a dry rasp.

'It's early,' the doctor said, a different doctor. Troy blinked against the harsh lights, didn't recognise either man tending to him. The sea of coffins around him remained a hazy blur.

'Take your time,' the assistant said, tilting the cup.

Troy managed a few sips. He felt worse than last time. It had been longer. The cold was deep within his bones. He remembered that his name wasn't Troy. He was supposed to be dead. Part of him regretted being disturbed. Another part hoped he had slept through the worst of it.

'Sir, we're sorry to wake you, but we need your help.'

'Your report—'

Two men were talking at once.

'Another silo is having problems, sir. Silo eighteen—'

Pills were produced. Troy waved them away. He no longer wished to take them.

The doctor hesitated; the two capsules rested in his palm. He turned to consult with someone else, a third man. Troy tried to blink the world into focus. Something was said. Fingers curled around the pills, filling him with relief.

They helped him up, had a wheelchair waiting. A man stood behind it, his hair as stark white as his overalls, his square jaw and iron frame familiar. Troy recognised him. This was the man who woke the freezing.

Another sip of water as he leaned against the pod, knees trembling from being weak and cold.

'What *about* silo eighteen?' Troy whispered the question as the cup was lowered.

The doctor frowned and said nothing. The man behind the wheelchair studied him intently.

'I know you,' Troy said.

The man in white nodded. The wheelchair was waiting for Troy. Troy felt his stomach twist as dormant parts of him stirred.

'You're the Thaw Man,' he said, even though this didn't sound quite right.

The paper gown was warm. It rustled as his arms were

guided through the sleeves. The men working on him were nervous. They chattered back and forth, one of them saying a silo was falling, the other that they needed his help. Troy cared only about the man in white. They helped him towards the wheelchair.

'Is it over?' he asked. He watched the colourless man, his vision clearing, his voice growing stronger. He dearly hoped that he had slept through it all.

The Thaw Man shook his head sadly as Troy was lowered into the chair.

'I'm afraid, son,' a familiar voice said, 'that it's only begun.'

25

The year of the Great Uprising

• Silo 18 •

Deathdays were birthdays. That's what they said to ease their pain, those who were left behind. An old man dies and a lottery is won. Children weep while hopeful parents cry tears of joy. Deathdays were birthdays, and no one knew this better than Mission Jones.

Tomorrow was his seventeenth. Tomorrow, he would grow a year older. It would also mark seventeen years to the day since his mother had died.

The cycle of life was everywhere – it wrapped around all things like the great spiral staircase – but nowhere was it more evident, nowhere could it be seen so clearly that a life given was one taken away, than in him. And so Mission approached his birthday without joy, with a heavy load on his young back, thinking on death and celebrating nothing.

Three steps below him and matching his pace, Mission could hear his friend Cam wheezing from his half of the load. When Dispatch assigned them a tandem, the two boys had flipped a coin – heads for heads, and Cam had lost. That left Mission out in front with a clear view of the stairs. It also gave him rights to set the pace, and his dark thoughts made for an angry one.

Traffic was light on the stairwell that morning. The children were not yet up and heading to school, those of them who still went any more. A few bleary-eyed shopkeeps staggered to work. There were service workers with grease stains on their bellies and patches sewn into their knees coming off late shifts. One man descended bearing more than a non-porter should, but Mission was in no mood to set down his burden and weigh another's. It was enough to glare at the gentleman, to let him know that he'd been seen.

'Three more to go,' he huffed to Cam as they passed the thirty-fifth. His porter's strap was digging into his shoulders, the load a heavy one. Heavier still was its destination. Mission hadn't been back to the farms in near on four months, hadn't seen his father in just as long. His brother, of course, he saw at the Nest now and then, but it'd still been a few weeks. To arrive so near to his birthday would be awkward, but there was no avoiding it. He trusted his father to do as he always had and ignore the occasion altogether, to ignore the fact that he was getting any older.

Past the thirty-fifth they entered another gap between the levels full of graffiti. The noxious odour of home-mixed paint hung in the air. Recent work dribbled in places, parts of it done the night before. Bold letters wrapped across the curving wall of concrete far beyond the stairway railing that read:

This is our 'Lo.

The slang for silo felt dated, even though the paint was not yet dry. Nobody said that any more. Not for years. Further up and much older:

Clean this, Mother—

The rest was obscured in a wash of censoring paint. As if anyone could read it and not fill in the blank. It was the first half that was the killing offence, anyway.

Down with the Up Top!

Mission laughed at this one. He pointed it out to Cam. Probably painted by some kid born above the mids and full of self-loathing, some kid who couldn't abide their own good fortune. Mission knew the kind. They were his kind. He studied all this graffiti painted over last year's graffiti and that from all the many years before. It was here between the levels, where the steel girders stretched out from the stairwell to the cement beyond, that such slogans went back generations.

The End is Coming . . .

Mission marched past this one, unable to argue. The end *was* coming. He could feel it in his bones. He could hear it in the wheezing rattle of the silo with its loose bolts and its rusty joints, could see it in the way people walked of late with their shoulders up around their ears, their belongings clutched to their chests. The end was coming for them all.

His father would laugh and disagree, of course. Mission could hear his father's voice from all the levels away, telling him how people had thought the same thing long before he and his brother were born, that it was the hubris of each generation to think this anew, to think that their time was special, that all things would come to an end with them. His father said it was *hope* that made people feel this, not dread. People talked of the end coming with barely concealed smiles. Their prayer was that when they went, they wouldn't go alone. Their hope was that no one would have the good fortune to come after and live a happy life without them.

Thoughts such as these made Mission's neck itch. He held the hauling strap with one hand and adjusted the 'chief around his neck with the other. It was a nervous habit, hiding his neck when he thought about the end of things.

'You doing okay up there?' Cam asked.

'I'm fine,' Mission called back, realising he'd slowed. He gripped his strap with both hands and concentrated on his pace, on the job. There was a metronome in his head from his shadowing days, a tick-tock, tick-tock for tandem hauls. Two porters with good timing could fall into a rhythm and wind their way up a dozen flights, never feeling a heavy load.

Mission and Cam weren't there yet. Now and then one of them would have to shuffle his feet or adjust his pace to match the other. Otherwise, their load might sway dangerously.

Their load. It was easier to think of it that way. Better not to think of it as a body – a dead man.

Mission thought of his grandfather, whom he'd never known. He had died in the uprising of '78, had left behind a son to take over the farm and a daughter to become a chipper. Mission's aunt had quit that job a few years back; she no longer banged out spots of rust and primed and painted raw steel. Nobody did. Nobody bothered. But his father was still farming that same plot of soil, that same plot generations of Jones boys had farmed, forever insisting that things would never change.

'That word means something else, you know,' his father had told him once, when Mission had spoken of revolution. 'It also means to go around and around. To revolve. One revolution, and you get right back to where you started.'

This was the sort of thing Mission's father liked to say when the priests came to bury a man beneath his corn. His dad would pack the dirt with a shovel, say that's how things go, and plant a seed in the neat depression his thumb made.

Mission had told his friends this other meaning of revolution. He had pretended to come up with it himself. It was just the sort of pseudo-intellectual nonsense they regaled each other with late at night on dark landings while they inhaled potato glue out of plastic bags.

His best friend Rodny had been the only one unimpressed. 'Nothing changes until we *make* it change,' he had said with a serious look in his eye.

Mission wondered what his best friend was doing now. He hadn't seen Rodny in months. Whatever he was shadowing for in IT kept him from getting out much.

He thought back to better days, growing up in the Nest with friends tight as a fist. He remembered thinking they would all stay together and grow old in the up top.

They would live along the same hallways, watch their eventual kids play the way they had.

But they had all gone their separate ways. It was hard to remember who had done it first, who had shaken off the expectations of their parents to follow in their footsteps, but eventually most of them had. Each of them had left home to choose a new fate. Sons of plumbers took up farming. Daughters of the cafeteria learned to sew. Sons of farmers became porters.

Mission remembered being angry when he left home. He remembered a fight with his father, throwing down his shovel, promising he'd never dig a trench again. He'd learned in the Nest that he could be anything he wanted, that he was in charge of his own fate. And so when he grew miserable, he assumed it was the farms that made him feel that way; he assumed it was his family.

He and Cam had flipped a dime back in Dispatch, heads for heads, and Mission had wound up with a dead man's shoulders pressed against his own. When he lifted his gaze to survey the steps ahead, the back of his skull touched a corpse's crown through a plastic bag – birthdays and deathdays pressed tight, two halves of a single coin. Mission carried them both, this load meant for two. He took the stairs a pair at a time, a brutal pace, up towards the farm of his youth.

26

• Silo 18 •

The coroner's office was on thirty-two, just below the dirt farm, tucked away at the end of those dark and damp halls that wound their way beneath the roots. The ceiling was low in that half-level. Pipes hung visible from above and rattled angrily as pumps kicked on and moved nutrients to distant and thirsty roots. Water dripped from dozens of small leaks into buckets and pots. A recently emptied pot banged metallic with each strike. Another overflowed. The floors were slick, the walls damp like sweaty skin.

Inside the coroner's office, the boys lifted the body onto a slab of dented metal, and the coroner signed Mission's work log. She tipped them for the speedy delivery, and when Cam saw the extra chits, his grumpiness over the pace dissolved. Back in the hallway, he bid Mission good day and splashed towards the exit.

Mission watched him go, feeling much more than a year older than his friend. Cam hadn't been told of the evening's plans, the midnight rendezvous of porters. It made him envy the lad for what he didn't know.

Not wanting to arrive at the farms deadheading and have his father lecture him on laziness, Mission stopped by the maintenance room down the hall to see if anything needed carrying up. Winters was on duty, a dark man with a white beard and a knack with pumps. He regarded Mission suspiciously and claimed he hadn't the budget for portering. Mission explained he was going up anyway and that he was glad to take whatever he had.

'In that case . . .' Winters said. He hoisted a huge water pump onto his workbench.

'Just the thing,' Mission told him, smiling.

Winters narrowed his eyes as if Mission had worked a bolt loose.

The pump wouldn't fit inside his porter's pack, but the haul straps on the outside of the pack looped nicely across the jutting pipes and sharp fittings. Winters helped him get his arms through the straps and the pump secured to his back. He thanked the old man, which drew another worried frown, and set off and up the half-level. Back at the stairwell, the odour of mildew from the wet halls faded, replaced by the smell of loam and freshly tilled soil, scents of home that pulled Mission back in time.

The landing on thirty-one was crowded as a jam of people attempted to squeeze inside the farms for the day's food. Standing apart from them was a mother in farmer green cradling a wailing child. She had the stains on her knees of a picker and the agitated look of one sent out of the grow plots to soothe her noisy brood. As Mission crowded past, he heard the mother sing the words of a familiar nursery rhyme. She rocked the child frightfully close to the railing, the infant's eyes wide with what looked to Mission like unadulterated fear.

He worked his way through the crowd, and the cries from the infant receded amid the general din. It occurred to Mission how few kids he saw any more. It wasn't like when he was young. There had been an explosion of newborns after the violence the last generation had wrought, but these days it was just the trickle of natural deaths and the handful of lottery winners. It meant fewer babies crying and fewer parents rejoicing.

He eventually made it through the doors and into the main hall. Using his 'chief, Mission wiped the sweat from his lips. He'd forgotten to top up his canteen a level below, and his mouth was dry. The reasons for pushing so swift a pace felt silly now. It was as if his looming birthday were some deadline to beat, and so the sooner he visited his father and departed, the better. But now, in the wash of sights and sounds from his childhood, his dark and angry thoughts melted away. It was home, and Mission hated how good it felt to be there.

There were a few hellos and waves as he worked his way towards the gates. Some porters he knew were loading sacks of fruits and vegetables to haul up to the cafeteria. He saw his aunt working one of the vending stalls outside the security gate. After giving up chipping, she now performed the questionably legal act of vending, something she'd never shadowed for and had no right to do. Mission did his best not to catch her eye; he didn't want to get sucked into a lecture or have his hair mussed and his 'chief straightened.

Beyond the stalls, a handful of younger kids clustered in the far corner where it was dark, probably dealing seeds, not looking nearly as inconspicuous as they likely thought. The entire scene in the entrance hall was one of a second bazaar, of farmers selling direct, of people crowding in from distant levels to get food they feared would never make it to their shops and stores. It was fear begetting fear, crowds becoming throngs, and it was easy to see how mobs came next.

Working the main security gate was Frankie, a tall, lanky kid Mission had grown up with. Mission wiped his forehead with the front of his undershirt, which was already cool and damp with sweat. 'Hey, Frankie,' he called out.

'Mission.' A nod and a smile. No hard feelings from another kid who'd jumped shadows long ago. Frankie's father worked in security, down in IT. Frankie had wanted to become a farmer, which Mission never understood. Their teacher, Mrs Crowe, had been delighted and had encouraged Frankie to follow his dreams. And now Mission found it ironic that Frankie had ended up working security for the farms. It was as if he couldn't escape what he'd been born to do.

Mission smiled and nodded at Frankie's shoulder-length hair. 'Did someone splash you with grow quick?'

Frankie tucked his hair behind his ear self-consciously. 'I

know, right? My mother threatens to come up here and knife it in my sleep.'

'Tell her I'll hold you down while she does it,' Mission said, laughing. 'Buzz me through?'

There was a wide gate to the side for wheelbarrows and trolleys. Mission didn't feel like squeezing through the turnstiles with the massive pump strapped to his back. Frankie hit a button, and the gate buzzed. Mission pushed his way through.

'Whatcha haulin'?' Frankie asked.

'Water pump from Winters. How've you been?'

Frankie scanned the crowds beyond the gate. 'Hold on a sec,' he said, looking for someone. Two farmers swiped their work badges and marched through the turnstiles, jabbering away. Frankie waved over someone in green and asked if they could cover for him.

'C'mon,' Frankie told Mission. 'Walk me.'

The two old friends headed down the main hall towards the bright aura of distant grow lights. The smells were intoxicating and familiar. Mission wondered what those same smells meant to Frankie, who had grown up near the fetid stink of the water plant. Perhaps this reeked to him the way the plant did to Mission. Perhaps the water plant brought back fond memories for Frankie, instead.

'Things are going nuts around here,' Frankie whispered once they were away from the gates.

Mission nodded. 'Yeah, I saw a few more stalls had sprouted up. More of them every day, huh?'

Frankie held Mission's arm and slowed their pace so they'd have more time to talk. There was the smell of fresh bread from one of the offices. It was too far from the bakery on seven for warm bread, but such was the new way of things. The flour was probably ground somewhere deep in the farms.

'You've seen what they're doing up in the cafeteria, right?' Frankie asked.

'I took a load up that way a few weeks ago,' Mission said. He tucked his thumbs under his shoulder straps and wiggled the heavy pump higher onto his hips. 'I saw they were building something by the wall screens. Didn't see what.'

'They're starting to grow sprouts up there,' Frankie said. 'Corn too, supposedly.'

'I guess that'll mean fewer runs for us between here and there,' Mission said, thinking like a porter. He tapped the wall with the toe of his boot. 'Roker'll be pissed when he hears.'

Frankie bit his lip and narrowed his eyes. 'Yeah, but wasn't Roker the one who started growin' his own beans down in Dispatch?'

Mission wiggled his shoulders. His arms were going numb. He wasn't used to standing still with a load – he was used to moving. 'That's different,' he argued. 'That's food for climbing.'

Frankie shook his head. 'Yeah, but ain't that hypercritical of him?'

'You mean hypocritical?'

'Whatever, man. All I'm saying is everyone has an excuse. "We're doing it because they're doing it and someone else started it. So what if we're doing it a little more than they are?" That's the attitude, man. But then we get in a twist when the next group does it a little more. It's like a ratchet, the way these things work.'

Mission glanced down the hall towards the glow of distant lights. 'I dunno,' he said. 'The mayor seems to be letting things slide lately.'

Frankie laughed. 'You really think the mayor's in charge? The mayor's scared, man. Scared and old.' Frankie glanced back down the hall to make sure nobody was coming. The nervousness and paranoia had been with him since his youth. It'd been amusing when he was younger; now it was sad and a little worrisome. 'You remember when we talked about being in charge one day? How things would be different?'

'It doesn't work like that,' Mission said. 'By the time we're in charge, we'll be old like them and won't care any more. And then *our* kids can hate *us* for pulling the same crap.'

Frankie laughed, and the tension in his wiry frame seemed to subside. 'I bet you're right.'

'Yeah, well, I need to go before my arms fall off.' Mission shrugged the pump higher up his back.

Frankie slapped his shoulder. 'Yeah. Good seeing you, man.'

'Same.' Mission nodded and turned to go.

'Oh, hey, Mish . . .'

He stopped and looked back.

'You gonna see the Crow anytime soon?'

'I'll pass that way tomorrow,' he said, assuming he'd live through the night.

Frankie smiled. 'Tell her I said hey, wouldya?'

'I will,' Mission promised.

One more name to add to the list. If only he could charge his friends for all the messages he ran for them, he'd have way more than the three hundred and eighty-four chits already saved up. Half a chit for every hello he passed to the Crow, and he'd have his own apartment by now. He wouldn't need to stay in the way stations. But messages from friends weighed far less than dark thoughts, so Mission didn't mind them taking up space. They crowded out the other. And Lord knew, Mission hauled his fair share of the heavier kind.

27

• Silo 18 •

It would've made more sense and been kinder on Mission's back to drop off the pump before visiting his father, but the whole point of hauling it up was so that his old man would see him with the load. And so he headed into the planting halls and towards the same growing station his grandfather had worked and supposedly his great-grandfather too. Past the beans and the blueberry vines, beyond the squash and the potatoes. In a spot of corn that appeared ready for harvest, he found his old man on his hands and knees looking how Mission would always remember him: with a small spade working the soil, his hands picking at weeds like a habit, the way a girl might curl her fingers in her hair over and over without even knowing she was doing it.

'Father.'

His old man turned his head to the side, sweat glistening on his brow under the heat of the grow lights. There was a flash of a smile before it melted. Mission's half-brother Riley appeared behind a back row of corn, a little twelve-year-old mimic of his dad, hands covered in dirt. He was quicker to call out a greeting, shouting 'Mission!' as he hurried to his feet.

'The corn looks good,' Mission said. He rested a hand on the railing, the weight of the pump settling against his back, and reached out to bend a leaf with his thumb. Moist. The ears were a few weeks from harvest, and the smell took him right back. He saw a midge running up the stalk and killed the parasite with a deft pinch.

'Wadya bring me?' his little brother squealed.

Mission laughed and tussled his brother's dark hair, a gift from the boy's mother. 'Sorry, bro. They loaded me down this time.' He turned slightly so that Riley – and his father – could see. His brother stepped onto the lowest rail and leaned over for a better look.

'Why dontcha set that down for a while?' his father asked. He slapped his hands together to keep the precious dirt on the proper side of the fence, then reached out and shook Mission's hand. 'You're looking good.'

'You too, Dad.' Mission would've thrust his chest out and stood taller if it hadn't meant toppling back on his rear from the weight of the pump. 'So what's this I hear about the cafeteria starting in their own sprouts?'

His father grumbled and shook his head. 'Corn, too, from what I hear. More goddamn up-sourcing.' He jabbed a finger at Mission's chest. 'This affects you lads, you know.'

His father meant the porters, and there was a tone of having told him so. There was always that tone.

Riley tugged on Mission's overalls and asked to hold his knife. Mission slid the blade from its sheath and handed it over while he studied his father, a silence brewing between them. His dad looked older. His skin was the colour of oiled wood, an unhealthy darkness from working too long under the grow lights. It was called a 'tan', and you could spot a farmer two landings away because of it.

An intense heat radiated from the bulbs overhead, and the anger Mission carried when he was away from home melted into a hollow sadness. The space his mother had left empty could be felt. It was a reminder to Mission of what his being born had cost. More was the pity he felt for his old man with his damaged skin and dark spots on his nose from years of abuse. These were the signs of all those in green who worked the soil, toiling among the silo's dead.

Mission flashed back to his first solid memory as a boy: wielding a small spade that in those days had seemed to him a giant shovel. He had been playing between the rows of corn, turning over scoops of soil, mimicking his father, when without warning his old man had grabbed his wrist.

'Don't dig there,' his father had said with an edge to his voice. This was back before Mission had witnessed his first funeral, before he had seen for himself what was laid beneath the seeds. After that day, he learned to spot the mounds where the soil was darker from having been disturbed.

'They've got you doing the heavy lifting, I see,' his father said, breaking the quiet. He assumed the load Mission had carried had been assigned by Dispatch. Mission didn't correct him.

'They let us carry what we can handle,' he said. 'The older porters get mail delivery. We each haul what we can.'

'I remember when I first stepped out of the shadows,' his dad said. He squinted and wiped his brow, nodded down the line. 'Got stuck with potatoes while my caster went back to plucking blueberries. Two for the basket and one for him.'

Not this again. Mission watched as Riley tested the tip of the knife with the pad of his finger. He reached to take back the blade, but his brother twisted away from him.

'The older porters get mail duty because they *can* get mail duty,' his father explained.

'You don't know what you're talking about,' Mission said, the sadness gone, the anger back. 'The old ports have bad knees is why we get the heavy loads. Besides, my bonus pay is judged by the pound and the time I make, so I don't mind.'

'Oh, yes.' His father waved at Mission's feet. 'They pay you in bonuses and you pay them with your knees.'

Mission could feel his cheeks tighten, could sense the burn of the whelp around his neck.

'All I'm saying, son, is that the older you get and the more seniority you have, you'll earn your own choice of rows to hoe. That's all. I want you to watch out for yourself.'

'I'm watching out for myself, Dad.'

Riley climbed up, sat on the top rail and flashed his teeth at his reflection in the knife. The kid already had a freckled band of spots across his nose, the start of a farmer's tan.

Damaged flesh from damaged flesh, father like son. And Mission could easily picture Riley years hence, on the other side of that rail, all grown up with a kid of his own. It made him thankful that he'd wormed his way out of the farms and into a job he didn't take home every night beneath his fingernails.

'Are you joining us for lunch?' his father asked, sensing perhaps that he was pushing Mission away.

'If you don't mind,' Mission said. He felt a twinge of guilt that his father expected to feed him, but he appreciated not having to ask. And it would hurt his stepmom's feelings if he didn't pay her a visit. 'I'll have to run afterward, though. I've got a . . . delivery tonight.'

His father frowned. 'You'll have time to see Allie though, right? She's forever asking about you. The boys here are lined up to marry that girl if you keep her waiting.'

Mission wiped his face to hide his expression. Allie was a great friend – his first and briefest romance – but to marry her would be to marry the farms, to return home, to live among the buried dead. 'Probably not this time,' he said. He felt bad for admitting it.

'Okay. Well, go drop that off. Don't squander your bonus sitting here jawing with us.' The disappointment in the old man's voice was hotter than the lights and not so easy to shade. 'We'll see you in the feeding hall in half an hour?' He reached out, took his son's hand one more time and gave it a squeeze. 'It's good to see you, son.'

'Same.' Mission shook his father's hand, then clapped his palms together over the grow pit to knock loose any dirt. Riley reluctantly gave the knife back and Mission slipped it into its sheath. He fastened the clasp around the handle, thinking on how he might need to use it that night. He pondered for a moment if he should warn his father, thought of telling him and Riley both to stay inside until morning, not to dare go out.

But he held his tongue, patted his brother on the shoulder and made his way to the pump room down the hall. As he walked through rows of planters and pickers, he thought about farmers selling their own vegetables in makeshift stalls and grinding their own flour. He thought about the cafeteria growing its own sprouts and corn. And he thought of the recently discovered plans to move something heavy from one landing to another without involving the porters.

Everyone was trying to look after themselves in case the violence returned. Mission could feel it brewing, the suspicion and the distrust, the walls being built. Everyone was trying to get a little less reliant on the others, preparing for the inevitable, hunkering down.

He loosened the straps on his pack as he approached the pump room, and a dangerous thought occurred to him, a revelation: if everyone was trying to get to where they didn't *need* one another, how exactly was that supposed to help them all get along?

28

• Silo 18 •

The lights of the great spiral staircase were dimmed at night so man and silo might sleep. It was in those wee hours when children were long hushed with sing-song lullabies and only those with trouble in mind crept about. Mission held very still in that darkness and waited. Somewhere above him, there came the sound of rope wound tight and sliding across metal, the squeaking of fibres as they gripped steel and strained under some great weight.

A gang of porters huddled with him on the stairway. Mission pressed his cheek against the inner post, the steel cooling his skin. He controlled his breathing and listened for the rope. He well knew the sounds they made, could feel the burn on his neck, that raised weal healed over by the years, a mark glanced at by others but rarely mentioned aloud. And again in that thick grey of the dim-time there came a recognisable squeak as the load from above was steadily lowered.

He waited for the signal. He thought on rope, on his own life – and other forbidden things. There was a book in Dispatch down on seventy-four that kept accounts. In the main way station for all the porters, a massive ledger fashioned out of a fortune in paper was kept under lock and key. It contained a careful tally of certain types of deliveries, handwritten so the information couldn't slip off into wires.

Mission had heard the senior porters kept track of certain kinds of pipe in this ledger, but he didn't know why. Brass too, and various types of fluids and powders coming out of Chemical. Order these – or too much rope – and you were put on the watching list. Porters were the lords of rumour. They knew where everything went. And their whisperings gathered like condensation in Dispatch Main where they were written down.

Mission listened to the rope creak and sing in the darkness. He knew what it felt like to have a length of it cinched tightly around his neck. It seemed strange to him that if you ordered enough to hang yourself, nobody cared. Enough to span a few levels, and eyebrows were raised.

He adjusted his 'chief and thought on this in the dim-time. A man may take his own life, he supposed, as long as he didn't take another's job.

'Ready yourself,' came the whisper from above.

Mission tightened the grip on his knife and concentrated on the task at hand. His eyes strained to see in the wan light. He could hear the steady breathing of his fellow porters around him. No doubt they would be squeezing their own knives in anticipation.

The knives came with the job. A porter's knife for slicing open delivered goods, for cutting fruit to eat on the climb, and for keeping peace as its owner strayed across all the silo's heights and depths, taking its dangers two at a time. Now, Mission tensed his in his hand, waiting for the order.

Up the stairwell two full turns, on a dim landing, a group of farmers argued in soft voices as they handled the other end of that rope, performing a porter's job in the dark of night to save a hundred chits or two. Beyond the rail, the rope was invisible in the darkness. He would have to lean out and grope blindly for it. He felt a ring of heat by his collar, and the hilt of his blade was unsure in his sweaty palm.

'Not yet,' Morgan whispered, and Mission felt his old caster's hand on his shoulder, holding him back. Mission cleared his mind. Another soft squeak, the sound of line taking the strain of a heavy generator, and a dense patch of grey drifted through the black. The men above shouted in whispers as they handled the load, as they did in green the work of men in blue.

While the patch of grey inched past, Mission thought of the night's danger and marvelled at the fear in his heart. He possessed a sudden care for a life he had once laboured to end, a life that never should have been. He thought of his mother and wondered what she had been like, beyond the disobedience that had cost her life. That was all he knew of his mom. He knew the implant in her hip had failed, as one in ten thousand might. And instead of reporting the malfunction – and the pregnancy – she had hidden him in loose clothes until it was past the time the Pact allowed a child to be treated as a cyst.

'Ready yourself,' Morgan hissed.

The grey mass of the generator crept down and out of sight. Mission clutched his knife and thought of how he should've been cut out of her and discarded. But past a certain date, and one life was traded for another. Such was the Pact. Born behind bars, Mission had been allowed free while his mother had been sent outside to clean.

'Now,' Morgan commanded, and Mission started. Soft and well-worn boots squeaked on the stairs above, the sounds of men lurching into action. Mission concentrated on his part. He pressed himself against the curved rail and reached out into the space beyond. His palm found rope as stiff as steel. He pressed his blade to the taut line.

There was a pop like sinew snapping, the first of the braids parting with just a touch of his sharp blade.

Mission had but a moment to think of those on the landing below, the farmers' accomplices waiting two levels down. Men were storming up the staircase. Mission longed to join them. With the barest of sawing motions, the rope parted the rest of the way, and Mission thought he heard the heavy generator whistle as it picked up speed. There was a ferocious crash a moment later, men screaming in alarm down below. Above, the fighting had broken out.

With one hand on the rail and another gripping his knife, Mission took the stairs three at a time. He rushed to join the melee above, this midnight lesson on breaking the Pact, on doing another's job. Grunts and groans and slapping thuds spilled from the landing, and Mission threw himself into the scuffle, thinking not of consequences, but only of this one fight.

29

2212

• Silo 1 •

The wheelchair squeaked as its wheels circled around. With each revolution there was a sharp peal of complaint followed by a circuit of deathly silence. Donald lost himself in this rhythmic sound as he was pushed along. His breath puffed out into the air, the room harbouring the same deep chill as his bones.

There were rows and rows of pods stretched out to either side. Names glowed orange on tiny screens, made-up names designed to sever the past from the present. Donald watched them slide by as they pushed him to the exit. His head felt heavy, the weight of remembrance replacing the dreams that coiled away and vanished like wisps of smoke.

The men in the pale blue overalls guided him through the door and into the hallway. He was steered into a familiar room with a familiar table. The wheelchair shimmied as they removed his bare feet from the footrests. He asked how long it'd been, how long he'd been asleep.

'A hundred years,' someone said. Which would make a hundred and sixty since orientation. No wonder the wheelchair felt unsteady – it was older than he was. Its screws had worked loose over the long decades that Donald had been asleep.

They helped him stand. His feet were still numb from his hibernation, the cold fading to painful tingles. A curtain was drawn. They asked him to urinate in a cup, which came as glorious relief. The sample was the colour of charcoal, dead machines flushed from his system. The paper gown wasn't enough to warm him, even though he knew the cold was in his flesh, not in the room. They gave him more of the bitter drink.

'How long before his head is clear?' someone asked.

'A day,' the doctor said. 'Tomorrow at the earliest.'

They had him sit while they took his blood. An old man in white overalls with hair just as stark stood in the doorway, frowning. 'Save your strength,' the man in white said. He nodded to the doctor to continue his work and disappeared before Donald could place him in his faltering memory. He felt dizzy as he watched his blood, blue from the cold, being taken from him.

They rode a familiar lift. The men around him talked, but their voices seemed distant. Donald felt as though he had been drugged, but he remembered that he had stopped taking their pills. He reached for his bottom lip, finger and mouth both tingling, and felt for an ulcer, that little pocket where he kept his pills unswallowed.

But the ulcer wasn't there. It would've healed in his sleep decades ago. The elevator doors parted, and Donald felt more of that dreamtime fade.

They pushed him down another hall, scuff marks on the walls the height of the wheels, black arcs where rubber had once met the paint. His eyes roamed the walls, the ceiling, the tiles, all bearing centuries of wear. It seemed like yesterday that they had been almost new. Now they were heaped with abuse, a sudden crumbling into ruin. Donald remembered designing halls just like these. He remembered thinking they were making something to last for ages. The truth was there all along. The truth was in the design, staring back at him, too insane to be taken seriously.

The wheelchair slowed.

'The next one,' a gruff voice behind him said, a familiar voice. Donald was pushed past one closed door to another. One of the orderlies bustled around the wheelchair, a ring of keys jangling from his hip. A key was selected and slotted into the lock with a series of neat clicks. Hinges cried out as the door was pushed inward. The lights inside were turned on.

It was a room like a cell, musky with the scent of disuse. The light overhead flickered before it came on. There was a narrow double bunk in the corner, a side table, a dresser, a bathroom.

'Why am I here?' Donald asked, his voice cracking.

'This will be your room,' the orderly said, putting away his keys. His young eyes darted up to the man steering the wheelchair as if seeking assurances for his answer. Another young man in pale blue hurried around and removed Donald's feet from the stirrups and placed them on carpet worn flat by the years.

Donald's last memory was of being chased by snarling dogs with leathery wings, chased up a mountain of bones. But that was a dream. What was his last *real* memory? He remembered a needle. He remembered dying. That felt real.

'I mean—' Donald swallowed painfully. 'Why am I . . . *awake*?'

He almost said *alive*. The two orderlies exchanged glances as they helped him from the chair to the lower bunk. The wheelchair squeaked once as it was pushed back into the hallway. The man guiding it paused, his broad shoulders making the doorway appear small.

One of the orderlies held Donald's wrist – two fingers pressing lightly on ice-blue veins, lips moving as he silently counted. The other orderly dropped two pills into a plastic cup and fumbled with the cap on a bottle of water.

'That won't be necessary,' the silhouette in the doorway said.

The orderly with the pills glanced over his shoulder as the older man stepped inside the small room and some of the air was displaced. The room shrank. It became more difficult for Donald to breathe.

'You're the Thaw—' Donald whispered.

The old man with the white hair waved a hand at the

two orderlies. 'Give us a moment,' he said. The one with a grip on Donald's wrist finished his counting and nodded to the other. Unswallowed pills rattled in a paper cup as they were put away. The old man's face had awoken something in Donald, pierced through the muddle of visions and dreams.

'I remember you,' Donald said. 'You're the Thaw Man.'

A smile was flashed, as white as his hair, wrinkles forming around his lips and eyes. The chair in the hallway squeaked as it was pushed away. The door clicked shut. Donald thought he heard the lock engage, but his teeth chattered occasionally and his hearing was still hazy.

'Thurman,' the man said, correcting him.

'I remember,' Donald said. He remembered his office, the one upstairs and some other office far away, someplace where it still rained, where the grass grew and the cherry blossoms came once a year. This man had been a senator, once.

'That you remember is a mystery we need to solve.' The old man tilted his head. 'For now, it's good that you do. We need you to remember.'

Thurman leaned against the metal dresser. He looked as though he hadn't slept in days. His hair was unkempt, not quite how Donald remembered it. There were dark circles beneath his sad eyes. He seemed much . . . older, somehow.

Donald peered down at his own palms, the springs in the bed making the room feel as though it were swaying. He flashed again to the horrible sight of a man remembering his own name and wanting to be free.

'My name is Donald Keene.'

'So you do remember. And you know who I am?' He produced a folded piece of paper and waited for an answer.

Donald nodded.

'Good.' The Thaw Man turned and placed the folded piece of paper on the dresser. He arranged it on its bent legs so it tented upward, towards the ceiling. 'We need you to remember everything,' he said. 'Study this report when the fog clears, see if it jars anything loose. Once your stomach is settled, I'll have a proper meal brought down.'

Donald rubbed his temples.

'You've been gone for some time,' the Thaw Man said. He rapped his knuckles on the door.

Donald wiggled his bare toes against the carpet. The sensation was returning to his feet. The door clicked before swinging open, and the Senator once again blocked the light from the hallway. He became a shadow for a moment.

'Rest, and then we'll get our answers together. There's someone who wants to see you.'

The room was sealed tight before Donald could ask what that meant. And somehow, with the door shut and him gone, there was more air to breathe in that small space. Donald took a few deep breaths. Gathering himself, he grabbed the frame of the bed and struggled to his feet. He stood there a moment, swaying.

'Get our answers,' he repeated aloud. Someone wanted to see him.

He shook his head, which made the world spin. As if he had any answers. All he had were questions. He remembered the orderlies who woke him saying something about a silo falling. He couldn't remember which one. Why would they wake him for that?

He moved unsteadily to the door, tried the knob, confirmed what he already knew. He went to the dresser where the piece of paper stood on its remembered folds.

'Get some rest,' he said, laughing at the suggestion. As if he could sleep. He felt as though he'd been asleep for ever. He picked up the piece of paper and unfolded it.

A report. Donald remembered this. It was a copy of a report. A report about a young man doing horrible things. The room twisted around him as if he stood on some great pivot, the memory of men and women trampled and dying, of giving some awful order, faces peering in at him from a hallway somewhere far in the past.

Donald blinked away a curtain of tears and studied the

trembling report. Hadn't he written this? He had signed it, he remembered. But that wasn't his name at the bottom. It was his handwriting, but it wasn't his name.

Troy.

Donald's legs went numb. He sought the bed – but collapsed to the floor instead as the memories washed over him. Troy and Helen. Helen and Troy. He remembered his wife. He imagined her disappearing over a hill, her arm raised to the sky where bombs were falling, his sister and some dark and nameless shadow pulling him back as people spilled like marbles down a slope, funnelling into some deep hole filled with white mist.

Donald remembered. He remembered all that he had helped do to the world. There was a troubled boy in a silo full of the dead, a shadow among the servers. That boy had brought an end to silo number twelve, and Donald had written a report. But Donald – what had he done? He had killed more than a silo full of people; he had drawn the plans that helped end the world. The report in his hand trembled as he remembered. And the tears that fell and struck the paper were tinged a pale blue.

30

• Silo 1 •

A doctor brought soup and bread a few hours later, and a tall glass of water. Donald ate hungrily while the man checked his arm. The warm soup felt good. It slid to his centre and seemed to radiate its heat outward. Donald tore at the bread with his teeth and chased it with the water. He ate with the desperation of so many years of fasting.

'Thank you,' he said between bites. 'For the food.'

The doctor glanced up from checking his blood pressure. He was an older man, heavyset, with great bushy eyebrows and a fine wisp of hair that clung to his scalp like a cloud to a hilltop.

'I'm Donald,' he said, introducing himself.

There was a wrinkle of confusion on the old man's brow. His grey eyes strayed to his clipboard as if either it or his patient couldn't be trusted. The needle on the gauge jumped with Donald's pulse.

'Who're you?' Donald asked.

'I'm Dr Sneed,' he finally said, though without confidence.

Donald took a long swig on his water, thankful they'd left it at room temperature. He didn't want anything cold inside him ever again. 'Where're you from?'

The doctor removed the cuff from Donald's arm with a loud rip. 'Level ten. But I work out of the shift office on sixty-eight.' He put his equipment back in his bag and made a note on the clipboard.

'No, I mean where are you from? You know . . . before.'

Dr Sneed patted Donald's knee and stood. The clipboard went on a hook on the outside of the door. 'You might have some dizziness the next few days. Let us know if you experience any trembling, okay?'

Donald nodded. He remembered being given the same advice earlier. Or was that his last shift? Maybe the repetition was for those who had trouble remembering. He wasn't going to be one of those people. Not this time.

A shadow fell into the room. Donald looked up to see the Thaw Man in the doorway. He gripped the meal tray to keep it from sliding off his knees.

The Thaw Man nodded to Dr Sneed, but these were not their names. Thurman, Donald told himself. Senator Thurman. He knew this.

'Do you have a moment?' Thurman asked the doctor.

'Of course.' Sneed grabbed his bag and stepped outside. The door clicked shut, leaving Donald alone with his soup.

He took quiet spoonfuls, trying to make anything of the murmurs on the other side of the door. Thurman, he reminded himself again. And not a senator. Senator of what? Those days were gone. Donald had drawn the plans.

The report stood tented on the dresser, returned to its spot. Donald took a bite of bread and remembered the floors he'd laid out. Those floors were now real. They existed. People lived inside them, raising their children, laughing, having fights, singing in the shower, burying their dead.

A few minutes passed before the knob tilted and the door swung inward. The Thaw Man entered the room alone. He pressed the door shut and frowned at Donald. 'How're you feeling?'

The spoon clacked against the rim of the bowl. Donald set the utensil down and gripped the tray with both hands to keep them from shaking, to keep them from forming fists.

'You know,' Donald hissed, teeth clenched together. 'You know what we did.'

Thurman showed his palms. 'We did what had to be done.'

'No. Don't give me that.' Donald shook his head. The water in his glass trembled as if something dangerous approached. 'The world . . .'

'We saved it.'

'That's not true!' Donald's voice cracked. He tried to remember. 'There is no world any more.' He recalled the view from the top, from the cafeteria. He remembered the hills a dull brown, the sky full of menacing clouds. 'We ended it. We killed everyone.'

'They were already dead,' Thurman said. 'We all were. Everyone dies, son. The only thing that matters is—'

'Stop.' Donald waved the words away as if they were buzzing things that could bite him. 'There's no justifying this—' He felt spittle form on his lips, wiped it away with his sleeve. The tray on his lap slid dangerously and Thurman moved quickly – quicker than one would expect of a man his age – to catch it. He placed what was left of the meal on the bedside table, and up close, Donald could see that he had gotten older. The wrinkles were deeper, the skin hanging from the bones. He wondered how much time Thurman had spent awake while Donald had slept.

'I killed a lot of men in the war,' Thurman said, looking down at the tray of half-eaten food.

Donald found himself focused on the old man's neck. He closed his hands together to keep them still. This sudden admission about killing made it seem as if Thurman could read Donald's mind, as though this was some kind of a warning for him to stay his murderous plans.

Thurman turned to the dresser and picked up the folded report. He opened it and Donald caught sight of the pale blue smudges, his ice-tinged tears from earlier.

'Some say killing gets easier the longer you're at it,' he said. And he sounded sad, not threatening. Donald looked down at his own knees and saw that they were bouncing. He forced his heels against the carpet and tried to pin them there.

'For me, it only got worse. There was a man in Iran—'

'The entire goddamn planet,' Donald whispered, stressing each word. This was what he said, but all he could think about was his wife Helen pulled down the wrong hill, everything that had ever existed crumbling to ruin. 'We killed everyone.'

The Senator took in a deep breath and held it a moment. 'I told you,' he said. 'They were already dead.'

'You'll never convince me. You can drug me or kill me, but I promise you, you will never convince me.'

Thurman studied the report. He seemed unsure of something. The paper faintly shook, but maybe it was the vent overhead. Finally, he nodded as if he agreed. 'Drugging you doesn't work. I've read up on your first shift. There's a small percentage of people with some kind of resistance. We'd love to know why.'

Donald could only laugh. He settled against the wall behind the cot and nestled into the darkness the top bunk provided. 'Maybe I've seen too much to forget,' he said.

'No, I don't think so.' Thurman lowered his head so he could still make eye contact. Donald took a sip of water, both hands wrapped around the glass. 'The more you see – the worse the trauma is – the better the medication works. It makes it easier to forget. Except for some people. Which is why we took a sample.'

Donald glanced down at his arm. A small square of gauze had been taped over the spot of blood left by the doctor's needle. He felt a caustic mix of helplessness and fear well up inside him. 'You woke me to take my blood?'

'Not exactly.' Thurman hesitated. 'Your resistance to the meds is something I'm curious about but the reason you're awake is because I was *asked* to wake you. We are losing silos—'

'I thought that was the plan,' Donald spat. 'Losing silos. I thought that was what you wanted.' He remembered crossing silo twelve out with red ink, all those many lives lost. They had accounted for this. Silos were expendable. That's what he'd been told.

Thurman shook his head. 'Whatever's happening out there, we need to understand it. And there's someone here who . . . who thinks you may have stumbled onto the answer. We have a few questions for you, and then we can put you back under.'

Back under. So he wasn't going to be out for long. They had only woken him to take his blood and to peer into his mind, and would then put him back to sleep. Donald rubbed his arms, which felt thin and atrophied. He was dying in that pod. Only more slowly than he would like.

'We need to know what you remember about this report.' Thurman held it out. Donald waved the thing away.

'I already looked it over,' he said. He didn't want to see it again. He could close his eyes and see the desperate people spilling out onto the dusty land, the people that he had ordered dead.

'We have other medications that might ease the—'

'No. No more drugs.' Donald crossed his wrists and spread his arms out, slicing the air with both hands. 'Look, I don't have a resistance to your drugs.' The truth. He was sick of the lies. 'There's no mystery. I just stopped taking the pills.'

It felt good to admit it. What were they going to do, anyway? Put him back to sleep? He took another sip of water while he let the confession sink in. He swallowed.

'I kept them in my gums and spat them out later. It's as simple as that. Probably the case with anyone else remembering. Like Hal, or Carlton, or whatever his name was.'

Thurman regarded him coolly. He tapped the report against his open palm, seeming to digest this. 'We know you stopped taking the pills,' he finally said. 'And when.'

Donald shrugged. 'Mystery solved, then.' He finished his water and put the empty glass back on the tray.

'The drugs you have a resistance to are not in the pills, Donny. The reason people stop taking the pills is because they begin to remember, not the other way around.'

Donald studied Thurman, disbelieving.

'Your urine changes colour when you stop taking them.

You develop sores on your gums where you hide them. These are the signs we look for.'

'What?'

'There are no drugs in the pills, Donny.'

'I don't believe you.'

'We medicate everyone. There are those of us who are immune. But you shouldn't be.'

'Bullshit. I remember. The pills made me woozy. As soon as I stopped taking them, I got better.'

Thurman tilted his head to the side. 'The reason you stopped taking them was because you were . . . I won't say getting better. It was because the fear had begun leaking through. Donny, the medication is in the water.' He waved at the empty glass on the tray. Donald followed the gesture and immediately felt sick.

'Don't worry,' Thurman said. 'We'll get to the bottom of it.'

'I don't want to help you. I don't want to talk about this report. I don't want to see whoever it is you need me to see.'

He wanted Helen. All he wanted was his wife.

'There's a chance that thousands will die if you don't help us. There's a chance that you stumbled onto something with this report of yours, even if I don't believe it.'

Donald glanced at the door to the bathroom, thought about locking himself inside and forcing himself to throw up, to expunge the food and the water. Maybe Thurman was lying to him. Maybe he was telling the truth. A lie would mean the water was just water. The truth would mean that he did have some sort of resistance.

'I barely remember writing the damn thing,' he admitted. And who would want to see him? He assumed it would be another doctor, maybe a silo head, maybe whoever was running this shift.

He rubbed his temples, could feel the pressure building between them. Perhaps he should just do as they wanted and be put back to sleep, back to his dreams. Now and then, he had dreamed of Helen. It was the only place he could be with her.

'Okay,' he said. 'I'll go. But I still don't understand what I could possibly know.' He rubbed his arm where they'd taken the blood. There was an itch there. An itch so deep it felt like a bruise.

Senator Thurman nodded. 'I tend to agree with you. But that's not what she thinks.'

Donald stiffened. 'She?' He searched Thurman's eyes, wondering if he'd heard correctly. 'She who?'

The old man frowned. 'The one who had me wake you.' He waved his hand at the bunk. 'Get some rest. I'll take you to her in the morning.'

31

• Silo 1 •

H e couldn't rest. The hours were cruel, slow and unknowable. There was no clock to mark their passing, no answer to his frustrated slaps on the door. Donald was left to lie in his bunk and stare at the diamond patterns of interlocking wires holding the mattress above him, to listen to the gurgle of water in hidden pipes as it rushed to another room. He couldn't sleep. He had no idea if it was the middle of the night or the middle of the day. The weight of the silo pressed down upon him.

When the boredom grew intolerable, Donald eventually gave in and looked over the report a second time. He studied it more closely. It wasn't the original; the signature was flat, and he remembered using a blue pen.

He skimmed the account of the silo's collapse and his theory that IT heads shadowed too young. His recommendation was to raise the age. He wondered if they had. Maybe so, but the problems were persisting. There was also mention of a young man he had inducted, a young man with a question. This young man's great-grandmother was one of those who remembered, much like Donald. His report suggested allowing one question from each inductee. They were given the Legacy, after all. Why not show them, in that final stage of indoctrination, that there were more truths to be had?

The tiny clicks of a key entering a lock. Thurman opened the door as Donald folded the report away.

'Feeling better?' Thurman asked.

Donald didn't say.

'Can you walk?'

He nodded. A walk. When what he really wanted was to run screaming down the hallway and punch holes in walls. But a walk would do. A walk before his next long sleep.

They rode the lift in silence. Donald noticed Thurman had scanned his badge before pressing the button for level fifty-four. Its number stood bright and new while so many others had been worn away. There was nothing but supplies on that level if Donald remembered correctly, supplies they weren't ever supposed to need. The lift slowed as it approached a level it normally skipped. The doors opened on a cavernous expanse of shelves stocked with instruments of death.

Thurman led him down the middle of it all. There were wooden crates with 'AMMO' stencilled on the side, longer crates beside them with military designations like 'M22' and 'M19'. There were rows of shelves with armour and helmets, with boxes marked 'MEDICAL' and 'RATIONS', many more boxes un-labelled. And beyond the shelves, tarps covered bulbous and winged forms that he knew to be drones. UAVs. His sister had flown them in a war that now seemed pointless and distant, part of ancient history. But here these relics stood, oiled and covered, reeking of grease and fear.

Beyond the drones, Thurman led the way through a murky dimness that made the storehouse seem to go on for ever. At the far end of the wide room, a glow of light leaked from an open-doored office. There were sounds of paper stirring, a chair squeaking as someone turned. Donald reached the doorway and saw, inexplicably, her sitting there.

'Anna?'

She sat behind a wide conference table ringed with identical chairs, looked up from a spread of paperwork and a computer monitor. There was no shock on her part, just a smile of acknowledgement and a weariness that her smile could not conceal.

Her father crossed the room while Donald gaped.

Thurman squeezed her arm and kissed her on the cheek, but Anna's eyes did not leave Donald's. The old man whispered something to his daughter, then announced that he had work of his own to see to. Donald did not budge until the Senator had left the room.

'Anna—'

She was already at the massive table, wrapping her arms around him. She began whispering things, comforting words as Donald sagged into her embrace, suddenly exhausted. He felt her hand caress the back of his head and come to a rest on his neck. His own arms interlocked around her back.

'What're you doing here?' he whispered.

'I'm here for the same reason you are.' She pulled back from the embrace. 'I'm looking for answers.' She stepped away and surveyed the mess on the table. 'To different questions, perhaps.'

A familiar schematic — a grid of fifty silos — covered the table. Each silo was like a small plate, all of them trapped under glass. A dozen chairs were gathered around. Donald realised that this was a war room, where generals stood and pushed plastic models and grumbled over lives lost by the thousands. He glanced up at the maps and schematics plastered on the walls. There was an adjoining bathroom, a towel hanging from a hook on the door. A cot had been set up in the far corner and was neatly made. There was a lamp beside it sitting on one of the wooden crates from the storeroom. Extension cords snaked here and there, signs of a room long converted into an apartment of sorts.

He turned to the nearest wall and flipped through some of the drawings. They were three layers deep in places and covered in notes. It didn't look as if a war was being planned. It looked like a scene from the crime shows that used to lull him to sleep in a former life.

'You've been up longer than me,' he said.

Anna stood beside him. Her hand alighted on his shoulder, and Donald felt himself startle at being touched at all.

'Almost a year now.' Her hand slid down his back before

falling away. 'Can I get you a drink? Water? I also have a stash of Scotch down here. Dad doesn't know half the stuff they hid away in these crates.'

Donald shook his head. He turned and watched as she disappeared into the bathroom and ran the tap. She emerged, sipping from a glass.

'What's going on here?' he asked. 'Why am I up?'

She swallowed and waved her glass at the walls. 'It's—' She laughed and shook her head. 'I was about to say it's nothing, but this is the hell that keeps me out of one box and in another. It doesn't concern you, most of this.'

Donald studied the room again. A year, living like this. He turned his attention to Anna, the way her hair was balled up in a bun, a pen sticking out of it. Her skin was pale except for the dark rings beneath her eyes. He wondered how she was able to do this, live like this.

There was a printout on the far wall that matched the table, a grid of circles, the layout of the facilities. A familiar red X had been drawn across what he knew to be silo twelve in the upper left corner. There was another X nearby, a new one in what looked to be silo ten. More lives lost. And in the lower right-hand corner of the grid, a mess that made no sense. The room seemed to wobble as he took a step closer.

'Donny?'

'What happened here?' he asked, his voice a whisper. Anna turned to see what he was looking at. She glanced at the table, and he realised that her paperwork was scattered around the same corner of the facility. The glass surface crawled with notes written in red and blue wax.

'Donny—' She stepped closer. 'Things aren't well.'

He turned and studied the scrawl of red marks on the wall schematic. There were Xs and question marks. There were notes in red ink with lines and arrows. Ten or a dozen of the silos were heavily marked up.

'How many?' he asked, trying to count, to figure the thousands of lives lost. 'Are they gone?'

She took a deep breath. 'We don't know.' She finished

her water, walked down the long table and reached into one of the chairs pushed up against it. She procured a bottle and poured a few fingers into her plastic cup.

'It started with silo forty,' she said. 'It went dark about a year ago—'

'Went dark?'

Anna took a sip of the Scotch and nodded. She licked her lips. 'The camera feeds went out first. Not at once, but eventually they got them all. We lost contact with the heads over there. Couldn't raise anyone. Erskine was running the shift at the time. He followed the Order and gave the okay to shut the silo down—'

'You mean kill everyone.'

Anna shot him a look. 'You know what had to be done.'

Donald remembered silo twelve. He remembered making that same decision. As if there had been a decision to make. The system ran automatically. Wasn't he just doing what came next, following a set of procedures written down by someone else?

He studied the poster with the red marks. 'And the rest of them? The other silos?'

Anna finished the drink with one long pull and gasped for air afterward. Donald caught her eyeing the bottle. 'They woke up Dad when forty-two went. Two more silos had gone dark by the time he came for me.'

Two more silos. 'Why you?' he asked.

She tucked a strand of loose hair behind her ear. 'Because there was no one else. Because everyone who had a hand in designing this place was either gone or at their wits' end. Because Dad was desperate.'

'He wanted to see you.'

She laughed. 'It wasn't that. Trust me.' She waved her empty cup at the arrangement of circles on the table and the spread of papers. 'They were using the radios at high frequencies. We think it started with forty, that maybe their IT head went rogue. They hijacked their antenna and began communicating with the other silos around them, and we couldn't cut them off. They had taken care of that as well. As soon as Dad suspected this, he argued with the others that wireless networks were my speciality. They eventually relented. No one wanted to use the drones.'

'Argued with what others? Who knows you're here?' Donald couldn't help but think how dangerous this could get, but maybe that was his own weakness screaming at him.

'My dad, Erskine, Dr Sneed, his assistants who brought me out. But those assistants won't work another shift—'

'Deep freeze?'

Anna frowned and splashed her cup, and it struck Donald how much had been lost while he had slept. Entire shifts had gone by. Another silo had gone dark, another red X drawn on the map. An entire corner of silos had run into some kind of trouble. Thurman, meanwhile, had been awake for a year, dealing with it. His daughter as well. Donald waved his arm at the room. 'You've been stuck in here for a year? Working on this?'

She jerked her head at the door and laughed. 'I've been cooped up in worse for a lot longer. But yeah, it sucks. I'm sick of this place.' She took another sip, her cup hiding her expression, and Donald wondered if perhaps he was awake because of her weakness just as she might be awake because of her father's. What was next? Him searching the deep freeze for his sister Charlotte?

'We've lost contact with eleven silos so far.' Anna peered into her cup. 'I think I've got it contained, but we're still trying to figure out how it happened or if anyone's still alive over there. I personally don't think so, but Dad wants to send scouts or drones. Everyone says that's too big a risk. And now it looks like eighteen is going to burn itself to the ground.'

'And I'm supposed to help? What does your father think I know?' He stepped around the planning table and waved for the bottle. Anna splashed her cup and handed the drink to him; she reached for another cup by her monitor while Donald collapsed onto her cot. It was a lot to take in.

'It's not Dad who thinks you know anything. He didn't

want you up at all. No one's supposed to come out of deep freeze.' She screwed the cap back on the bottle. 'It was his boss.'

Donald nearly choked on his first sip of the Scotch. He sputtered and wiped his chin with his sleeve while Anna looked on with concern.

'His *boss*?' he asked, gasping for air.

She narrowed her eyes. 'Dad told you why you're here, right?'

He fumbled in his pocket for the report. 'Something I wrote during my last . . . during my shift. Thurman has a boss? I thought he was in charge.'

Anna laughed humourlessly. 'Nobody's in charge,' she told him. 'The system's in charge. It just runs. We built it to just *go*.' She got up from her desk and walked over to join him on the cot. Donald slid over to give her more room.

'Dad was in charge of digging the holes, that was his job. There were three of them who planned most of this. The other two had ideas for how to hide this place. Dad convinced them they should just build it in plain sight. The nuclear containment facility was his idea, and he was in a position to make it happen.'

'You said three. Who were the others?'

'Victor and Erskine.' Anna adjusted a pillow and leaned back against the wall. 'Not their real names, of course. But what does it matter? A name is a name. You can be anyone down here. Erskine was the one who discovered the original threat, who told Victor and Dad about the nanos. You'll meet him. He's been on a double shift with me, working on the loss of these silos, but it's not his area of expertise. Do you need more?' She nodded at his cup.

'No. I'm already feeling dizzy.' He didn't add that it wasn't from the alcohol. 'I remember a Victor from my shift. He worked across the hall from me.'

'The same.' She looked away for a moment. 'Dad refers to him as the boss, but I've been working with Victor for a while, and he never thought of himself that way. He thought of himself as a steward, joked once about feeling like Noah. He wanted to wake you months ago because of what's happening in silo eighteen, but Dad vetoed the idea. I think Victor was fond of you. He talked about you a lot.'

'Victor talked about *me*?' Donald remembered the man across the hall from him, the shrink. Anna reached up and wiped underneath her eyes.

'Yes. He was a brilliant man, could tell what you were thinking, what anyone was thinking. He planned most of this. Wrote the Order, the original Pact. It was all his design.'

'What do you mean *was*?'

Her lip trembled. She tipped her cup, but there was little left in the bottom.

'Victor's dead,' she said. 'He shot himself at his desk two days ago.'

32

• Silo 1 •

'Victor? Shot himself?' Donald tried to imagine the composed man who had worked across the hall from him doing such a thing. 'Why?'

Anna sniffed and slid closer to Donald. She twisted the empty cup in her hands. 'We don't know. He was obsessed with that first silo we lost. Obsessed. It broke my heart to see how he blamed himself. He used to say that he could see certain things coming, that there were . . . probabilistic certainties.' She said these two words in a mimic of his voice, which brought the old man's face even more vividly to Donald's mind.

'But it killed him not to know the precise when and where.' She dabbed her eyes. 'He would've been better off if it'd happened on someone else's shift. Not his. Not where he'd feel guilty.'

'He blamed me,' Donald said, staring at the floor. 'It was on my shift. I was such a mess. I couldn't think straight.'

'What? No. Donny, no.' She rested a hand on his knee. 'There's no one to blame.'

'But my report—' He still had it in his hand, folded up and dotted here and there with pale blue.

Anna's eyes fell to the piece of paper. 'Is that a copy?' She reached for it, brushed the loose strands of hair off her face. 'Dad had the courage to tell you about this but not about what Vic did.' She shook her head. 'Victor was strong in some ways, so weak in others.' She turned to Donald. 'He was found at his desk, surrounded by notes, everything he had on this silo, and your report was on top.'

She unfolded the page and studied the words. 'Just a copy,' she whispered.

'Maybe it was—' Donald began.

'He wrote notes all over the original.' She slid her finger across the page. 'Right about here, he wrote: "This is why."'

'This is why? As in why he did it?' Donald waved his hand at the room. 'Shouldn't *this* be why? Maybe he realised he'd made a mistake.' He held Anna's arm. 'Think about what we've done. What if we followed a crazy man down here? Maybe Victor had a sudden bout of *sanity*. What if he woke up for a second and saw what we'd done?'

'No.' Anna shook her head. 'We had to do this.'

He slapped the wall behind the cot. 'That's what everyone keeps saying.'

'Listen to me.' She placed a hand on his knee, tried to soothe him. 'You need to keep it together, okay?' She glanced at the door, a fearful look in her eyes. 'I asked him to wake you because I need your help. I can't do this alone. Vic was working on the situation in silo eighteen. If Dad has his way, he'll just terminate the place not to have to deal with it. Victor didn't want that. *I* don't want that.'

Donald thought of silo twelve, which he'd terminated. But it was already falling, wasn't it? It was already too late. They had opened the airlock. He looked at the schematic on the wall and wondered if it was too late for silo eighteen as well.

'What did he see in my report?' he asked.

'I don't know. But he wanted to wake you weeks ago. He thought you had touched on something.'

'Or maybe it was just because I was around at the time.'

Donald looked at the room of clues. Anna had been digging, tearing into a different problem. So many questions and answers. His mind was clear, not like last time. He had questions of his own. He wanted to find his sister, find out what had happened to Helen, dispel this crazy thought that she was still out there somewhere. He wanted to know more about this damnable place he'd helped build.

'You'll help us?' Anna asked. She rested her hand on his back, and her comforting touch brought back the memory of his wife, of the moments she would soothe and care for him. He started as if bitten, some part of him thinking for a moment that he was still married, that she was alive out there, maybe frozen and waiting for him to wake her.

'I need . . .' He jumped up and glanced around the room. His eyes fell to the computer on the desk. 'I need to look some things up.'

Anna rose beside him. 'Of course. I can fill you in with what we know so far. Victor left a series of notes. He wrote all over your report. I can show you. And maybe you can convince Dad that he was on to something, that this silo is worth saving—'

'Yes,' Donald said. He would do it. But only so he could stay awake. And he wondered for a moment if that was Anna's intention as well. To keep him around, near to her.

An hour earlier, all he had wanted was to go back to sleep, to escape the world he had helped create. But now he wanted answers. He would look into silo eighteen, but he would find Helen as well. Find out what had happened to her, where she was. He thought of Mick, and Tennessee flashed in his mind. He turned to the wall schematic with all the silos and tried to remember which state went with which number.

'What can we access from here?' he asked. His skin flushed with heat as he thought of the answers at his disposal.

Anna turned towards the door. There were footsteps out there in the darkness.

'Dad. He's the only one with access to this level any more.'

'Any more?' He turned back to Anna.

'Yeah. Where do you think Victor got the gun?' She lowered her voice. 'I was in here when he came down and cracked open one of the crates. I never heard him. Look, my father blames himself for what happened to Victor, and he still doesn't believe this has anything to do with you or your report. But I knew Vic. He wasn't crazy. If there's anything you can do, please. For me.'

She squeezed his hand. Donald looked down, didn't realise she'd been holding it. The folded report was in her other hand. The footsteps approached. Donald nodded his assent.

'Thank you,' she said. She dropped his hand, grabbed his empty cup from the cot and nested hers with it. She tucked the cups and the bottle into one of the chairs and slid it under the table. Thurman arrived at the door and rapped the jamb with his knuckles.

'Come in,' Anna said, brushing loose hair off her face.

Thurman studied the two of them for a moment. 'Erskine is planning a small ceremony,' he said. 'Just us. Those of us who know.'

Anna nodded. 'Of course.'

Thurman narrowed his eyes and glanced from his daughter to Donald. Anna seemed to take it as a question.

'Donny thinks he can help,' she said. 'We both think it's best for him to work down here with me. At least until we make some progress.'

Donald turned to her in shock. Thurman said nothing.

'We'll need another computer,' she added. 'If you bring one down, I can set it up.'

That, Donald liked the sound of.

'And another cot, of course,' Anna added with a smile.

33

• Silo 18 •

Mission slunk away after the scuffle with the farmers, and the rest of the porters scattered. He stole a few hours of sleep at the upper way station on level ten, his nose numb and lips throbbing from a blow he'd taken. Tossing and turning, too restless to stay put, he rose in the dim-time and realised it was too early yet to go to the Nest; the Crow would still be asleep. And so he headed to the cafeteria for a sunrise and a decent breakfast, the coroner's bonus burning in his pockets the way his knuckles burned from their scrapes.

He nursed his aches with a welcome hot meal, eating with those coming off a midnight shift, and watched the clouds boil and come to life across the hills. The towering husks in the distance – the Crow called them skyscrapers – were the first to catch the rising sun. It was a sign that the world would wake one more day. His birthday, Mission realised. He left his dishes on the table, a chit for whoever cleaned after him, and tried not to think of cleaning at all. Instead, he rushed down the eight flights of stairs before the silo fully woke. He headed towards the Nest, feeling not a day older at all.

Familiar words greeted him at the landing on level thirteen. There, above the door, rather than a level number it read:

THE CROW'S NEST

The words were painted in bright and blocky letters. They followed the outlines from years and generations prior, colour piled on colour and letters crooked from more than one young hand's involvement. The children of the silo came and went and left their marks with bristles, but the Old Crow remained.

Her nest comprised the nursery, day school and classrooms that served the up top. She had been perched there for longer than any alive could remember. Some said she was as old as the silo itself, but Mission knew that was just a legend. Nobody knew how old the silo was.

He entered the Nest to find the hallways empty and quiet, the hour early still. There was a soft screech from one classroom as desks were put back into order. Mission caught a glimpse of two teachers conferring in another classroom, their faces scrunched up with worry, probably wondering what to do with a younger version of himself. The scent of strong tea mixed with the odour of paste and chalk. There were rows of metal lockers in dire need of paint and stippled with dents from tiny fists; they transported Mission back to another age. It felt like just yesterday that he had terrorised that hall. He and all his friends whom he didn't see any more – or at least not as often as he'd like.

The Crow's room was at the far end and adjoined the only apartment on the entire level. The apartment had been built especially for her, converted from a classroom, or so they said. And while she taught only the youngest children any more, the entire school was hers. This was her nest.

Mission remembered coming to her at various stages of his life. Early on, for comfort, feeling so very far from the farms. Later, for wisdom, when he was finally old enough to admit he had none. And more than once he had come for both, like the day he had learned the truth of his birth and his mother's death – that she had been sent to clean because of him. Mission remembered that day well. It was the only time he'd ever seen the Old Crow cry.

He knocked on her classroom door before entering and found her at the blackboard that had been lowered so she could write on it from her chair. Mrs Crowe stopped erasing yesterday's lessons, turned and beamed at him.

'My boy,' she croaked. She waved with the eraser to beckon him closer. A chalky haze filled the air. 'My boy, my boy.'

'Hello, Mrs Crowe.' Mission passed between the handful of desks to get to her. The power line for her electric chair drooped from the centre of the ceiling to a pole that rose up from the chair's back. Mission ducked beneath it as he got closer and bent to give the Crow a hug. His hands wrapped around her, and he breathed in her smell – one of childhood and innocence. The yellow gown she wore, spotted with flowers, was her outfit for Wednesdays, as good as any calendar. It had faded since Mission's time, as all things had.

'I do believe you've grown,' she said, smiling up at him. Her voice was barely a whisper, and he recalled how it kept even the young ones quiet so they could hear what was being said. She brought her hand up and touched her own cheek. 'What happened to your face?'

Mission laughed and shrugged off his porter's pack. 'Just an accident,' he said, lying to her like old times. He placed his pack at the foot of one of the tiny desks, could imagine squeezing into the thing and staying for the day's lesson.

'How've you been?' he asked. He studied her face, the deep wrinkles and dark skin like a farmer's but from age rather than grow lights. Her eyes were rheumy, but there was life still behind them.

'Not so good,' Mrs Crowe said. She twisted the lever on her armrest, and the chair built for her decades ago by some long-gone former student whirred around to face him better. Pulling back her sleeve, she showed Mission a gauze bandage taped to her thin and splotchy arm. 'Those doctors came and took my blood away.' Her hand shook as she indicated the evidence. 'Took half of it, by my reckoning.'

Mission laughed. 'I'm pretty sure they didn't take half your blood, Mrs Crowe. The doctors are just looking out for you.'

She twisted up her face, an explosion of wrinkles. She didn't seem so sure. 'I don't trust them,' she said.

Mission smiled. 'You don't trust anyone. And hey, maybe they're just trying to figure out why you can't die like everyone else does. Maybe they'll come up with a way for everyone to live as long as you someday.'

Mrs Crowe rubbed the bandage on her withering arm. 'Or they're figuring out how to kill me,' she said.

'Oh, don't be so sinister.' Mission reached forward and pulled her sleeve down to keep her from messing with the bandage. 'Why would you think such a thing?'

She frowned and declined to answer. Her eyes fell to his near-empty pack. 'Day off?' she asked.

Mission turned and followed her gaze. 'Hmm? Oh, no. I dropped something off last night. I'll pick up another delivery in a little bit, take it wherever they tell me to.'

'Oh, to be so young and free again.' Mrs Crowe spun her chair around and steered it behind her desk. Mission ducked beneath the pivoting wire out of habit; the pole at the back of the chair was made with younger heads in mind. She picked up a container of the vile vegetable pulp she preferred over water and took a sip. 'Allie stopped by last week.' She set the greenish-black fluid down. 'She was asking about you. Wanted to know if you were still single.'

'Oh?' Mission could feel his temperature shoot up. Mrs Crowe had caught them kissing once, back before he knew what kissing was for. She had left them with a warning and a knowing smile. 'Everyone's so spread out,' Mission said, changing the subject, hoping she might take the hint.

'As it should be.' The Crow opened a drawer on her desk and rummaged around, came out with an envelope. Mission could see a half-dozen names scratched out across the thing. It had been used a handful of times. 'You're heading down from here? Maybe you could drop off something for Rodny?'

She held out the letter. Mission took it, saw his best friend's name written on the outside, all the other names crossed out.

'I can leave it for him, sure. But the last two times I stopped by there, they said he was unavailable.'

Mrs Crowe nodded as if this was to be expected. 'Ask for Jeffery, he's the head of Security down there, one of my boys. You tell him that this is from me and that I said you should hand it to Rodny yourself. In person.' She waved her hands in the air, little trembling blurs. 'I'll write Jeffery a note.'

Mission glanced up at the clock on the wall while she dug into her desk for a pen and ink. Soon the hallways would begin filling with youthful chatter and the opening and slamming of lockers. He waited patiently while she scratched her note and scanned old posters and banners on the walls, the 'motivators', as Mrs Crowe liked to call them.

You can be anything, one of them said. It featured a crude drawing of a boy and a girl standing on a huge mound. The mound was green and the sky blue, just like in the picture books. Another one said: *Dream to your heart's delight*. It had bands of colour in a graceful arcing sweep. The Crow had a name for the shape, but he'd forgotten what it was called. Another familiar one: *Go new places*. It featured a drawing of a crow perched in an impossibly large tree, its wings spread as if it were about to take flight.

'Jeffery is the bald one,' Mrs Crowe said. She waved a hand over her own white and thinning hair to demonstrate.

'I know,' Mission said. It was a strange reminder that so many of the adults and elders throughout the silo had been her students as well. A locker was slammed in the hallway. Mission remembered when he was a kid how the rows and rows of tiny desks had filled the room. There were cubbies full of rolled mats for nap time, reminding him of the daily routine of clearing a space in the middle of the floor, finding his mat, and drifting off to sleep while the Crow sang forgotten songs. He missed those days. He missed the Old Time stories about a world full of impossible things. Leaning against that little desk, Mission suddenly felt as ancient as the Crow, just as impossibly distant from his youth.

'Give Jeffery this, and then see that Rodny gets my note. From you personally, okay?'

He grabbed his pack and slid both pieces of correspondence into his courier pouch. There was no mention of payment, just the twinge of guilt Mission felt for even thinking of it. Digging into the pack reminded him of the items he had brought her, forgotten due to the previous night's brawl.

'Oh, I brought you these from the farm.' He pulled out a few small cucumbers, two peppers and a large tomato, bearing a bruise. He placed them on her desk. 'For your veggie drinks,' he said.

Mrs Crowe clasped her hands together and smiled with delight.

'Is there anything else you need next time I'm passing by?'

'These visits,' she said, her face a wrinkle of smiles. 'All I care about are my little ones. Stop by whenever you can, okay?'

Mission squeezed her arm, which felt like a broomstick tucked into a sleeve. 'I will,' he said. 'And that reminds me: Frankie told me to tell you hello.'

'He should come more often,' she told him, her voice aquiver.

'Not everyone gets around like I do,' he said. 'I'm sure he'd like to see you more often as well.'

'You tell him,' she said. 'Tell him I don't have much time left—'

Mission laughed and waved off the morbid thought. 'You probably told my grandfather the same thing when he was young, and his father before him.'

The Crow smiled as if this were true. 'Predict the inevitable,' she said, 'and you're bound to be right one day.'

Mission smiled. He liked that. 'Still, I wish you wouldn't talk about dying. Nobody likes to hear it.'

'They may not like it, but a reminder is good.' She held out her arms, the sleeves of her flowered dress falling away and revealing the bandage once more. 'Tell me, what do you see when you look at these hands?' She turned them over, back and forth.

'I see time,' Mission blurted out, not sure where the thought came from. He tore his eyes away, suddenly finding her skin to be grotesque. Like shrivelled potatoes found deep in the soil long after harvest time. He hated himself for feeling it.

'Time, sure,' Mrs Crowe said. 'There's time here aplenty. But there's *remnants* too. I remember things being better, once. You think on the bad to remind yourself of the good.'

She studied her hands a moment longer, as if looking for something else. When she lifted her gaze and peered at Mission, her eyes were shining with sadness. Mission could feel his own eyes watering, partly from discomfort, partly due to the sombre pall that had been cast over their conversation. It reminded him that today was his birthday, a thought that tightened his neck and emptied his chest. He was sure the Crow knew what day it was. She just loved him enough not to say.

'I was beautiful, once, you know.' Mrs Crowe withdrew her hands and folded them in her lap. 'Once that's gone, once it leaves us for good, no one will ever see it again.'

Mission felt a powerful urge to soothe her, to tell Mrs Crowe that she was still beautiful in plenty of ways. She could still make music. Could paint. Few others remembered how. She could make children feel loved and safe, another bit of magic long forgotten.

'When I was your age,' the Crow said, smiling, 'I could have any boy I wanted.'

She laughed, dispelling the tension and casting away the shadows, but Mission believed her, even though he couldn't picture it, couldn't imagine away the wrinkles and the spots and the long strands of hair on her knuckles. Still, he believed her. He always did.

'The world is a lot like me.' She lifted her gaze to the ceiling and perhaps beyond. 'The world was beautiful once too.'

Mission sensed an Old Time story brewing like a storm of clouds. More lockers were slammed in the hallway, little voices gathering.

'Tell me,' Mission said, remembering the hours that had

passed like eyeblinks at her feet, the songs she sang while children slept. 'Tell me about the old world.'

The Old Crow's eyes narrowed and settled on a dark corner of the room. Her lips, furrowed with the wrinkles of time, parted and a story began, a story Mission had heard a thousand times before. But it never got old, visiting this land of the Crow's imagination. And as the little ones skipped into the room and slipped into their tiny desks, they too fell silent and gathered around, following along with the widest of eyes and the most open of minds these tales of a world, once beautiful, and now fairly forgotten.

34

• Silo 18 •

The stories Mrs Crowe made up were straight from the children's books. There were blue skies and lands of green, animals like dogs and cats but bigger than people. Juvenile stuff. And yet, these fantastic tales of a better place left Mission angry at the world he lived in. As he left the up top behind and wound his way down, past the farms and the levels of his youth, he thought of this better world and was dismayed at the one he knew. The promise of an *elsewhere* highlighted the flaws of the familiar. He had gone off to be a porter, to fly away and be all that he wished, and now what he wished was to be further away than this world would allow.

These were dangerous thoughts. They reminded him of his mother and where she had been sent seventeen years ago to the day.

Past the farms, Mission noted a hint of something burning further down the silo. The air was hazy, and there was the bitter tinge of smoke on the back of his tongue. A trash pile, maybe. Someone who didn't want to pay the fee to have it ported to recycling. Or someone who didn't think the silo would be around long enough to *need* to recycle.

It could be an accident, of course, but Mission doubted it. Nobody thought that way any more. He could see it on the faces of those on the stairwell. He could see by the way belongings were clutched, children sheltered, that the future of the silo hung in the balance. Last night's fight seemed to prove it.

Mission adjusted his pack and hurried down to the IT levels on thirty-four. When he arrived, there was a crowd gathering on the landing. It was mostly boys his age or a little older, many that he recognised, a lot from the mids. Several stood with computers tucked under their arms, wires dangling, jostling with the throng. Mission picked his way through. Inside, he found a barrier had been set up just beyond the door. Two men from Security manned the temporary gate and allowed only crumpled IT workers through.

'Delivery,' Mission shouted. He worked his way to the front, carefully extracting the note Mrs Crowe had written. 'Delivery for Officer Jeffery.'

One of the security men took the note. Mission was pressed against the barrier by the crush behind him. A woman was waved through. She hurried towards the proper security gate leading into the main hall, smoothing her overalls with obvious relief. There were crowds of young men being given instructions in one corner of the wide hall. They stood to attention in neat rank and file, but their wide eyes gave away their obvious fear.

'What the hell is going on?' Mission asked as the barrier was parted for him.

'What the hell isn't?' one of the security guards answered. 'Power spike last night took out a load of computers. Every one of our techs is pulling a double. There's a fire down in Mechanical or something, and some kinda violence up in the farms. Did you get the wire?'

Mechanical. That was a long way away to nose a fire. And word was out about last night's raid, making him self-conscious of the cut on his nose. 'What wire?' he asked.

The security guard pointed to the groups of boys. 'We're hiring. New techs.'

All Mission saw were young men, and the guy talking to them was with Security, not IT. The security guard handed the note back to Mission and pointed towards the main gate. The woman from earlier was already beeping her way through, a large and familiar bald head swivelling to watch her ass as she headed down the hall.

'Sir?' Mission called out as he approached the gate.

Jeffery turned his head, the deep wrinkles and folds of flesh disappearing from his neck.

'Hmm? Oh—' he snapped his fingers, trying to place the name.

'Mission.'

He wagged his finger. 'That's right. You need to leave something with me, porter?' He held out a palm but seemed disinterested.

Mission handed him the note. 'Actually, I have orders from Mrs Crowe to deliver something in person.' He pulled the sealed envelope with the crossed-out names from his courier pouch. 'Just a letter, sir.'

The old guard glanced at the envelope, then continued reading the note addressed to him. 'Rodny isn't available.' He shook his head. 'I can't give you a timeframe, either. Could be weeks. You wanna leave it with me?'

Again, an outstretched palm, but this time with more interest. Mission pulled the envelope back warily. 'I can't. There's no way I can just hand it to him? This is the Crow, man. If it were the mayor asking me, I'd say no problem.'

Jeffery smiled. 'You were one of her boys too?'

Mission nodded. The head of Security looked past him at a man approaching the gate with his ID out. Mission stepped aside as the gentleman scanned his way through, nodding good morning to Jeffery.

'Tell you what. I'm taking Rodny his lunch in a little bit. When I do, you can come with me, hand him the letter with me standing there, and I won't have to worry about the Crow nipping my hide later. How's that sound?'

Mission smiled. 'Sounds good, man. I appreciate it.'

The officer pointed across the noisy entrance hall. 'Why don't you go grab yourself some water and hang in the conference room. There's some boys in there filling out paperwork.' Jeffery looked Mission up and down. 'In fact, why don't you fill out an application? We could use you.'

'I . . . uh, don't know much about computers,' Mission said.

Jeffery shrugged as if that were irrelevant. 'Suit yourself. One of the lads will be relieving me in a little bit. I'll come get you.'

Mission thanked him again. He crossed the large entrance hall where neat columns and rows of young men listened to barked instructions. Another guard waved him inside the conference room while holding out a sheet of paper and a shard of charcoal. Mission saw that the back of the paper was blank and took it with no plan for filling it out. Half a chit right there in usable paper.

There were a few empty chairs around the wide table. He chose one. A number of boys scribbled with their charcoals on the pages, faces scrunched up in concentration. Mission sat with his back to the only window and placed his sack on the table, kept the letter in his hands. He slid the application inside his pack for future use and studied the Crow's letter for the first time.

The envelope was old but addressed only a handful of times. One edge was worn tissue thin, a small tear revealing a folded piece of paper inside. Peering more closely, Mission saw that it was pulp paper, probably made in the Crow's Nest by one of her kids – water and handfuls of torn paper blended up, pressed down on screens and left overnight to dry.

'Mission,' someone at the table hissed.

He looked up to see Bradley sitting across from him. The fellow porter had his blue 'chief tied around his biceps. Mission had thought he was running a regular route in the down deep.

'You applying?' Bradley hissed.

One of the other boys coughed into his fist as if he were asking for quiet. It looked as though Bradley was already done with his application.

Mission shook his head. There was a knock on the window behind him and he nearly dropped the letter as he whirled around. Jeffery stuck his head in the door. 'Two minutes,' the security guard said to Mission. He jabbed his thumb over his shoulder. 'I'm just waiting on his tray.'

Mission bobbed his head as the door was pulled shut. The other boys looked at him curiously.

'Delivery,' Mission explained to Bradley loud enough for the others to hear. He pulled his pack closer and hid the envelope behind it. The boys went back to their scribbling. Bradley frowned and watched the others.

Mission studied the envelope again. Two minutes. How long would he have with Rodny? He tickled the corner of the sealed flap. The milk paste the Crow had used didn't stick very well to the months-old – maybe years-old – dried glue from before. He worked one corner loose without glancing down at the envelope. Instead, he watched Bradley as he disobeyed the third cardinal rule of porting, telling himself this was different, that this was two old friends talking and he was just in the room with them, overhearing.

Even so, his hands trembled as he pulled the letter out. He glanced down, keeping the note hidden. Purple and red string lay strewn in with the dark grey of cheap paper. The writing was in chalk. It meant the words had to be big. White powder gathered in the folds as it shivered loose from the words like dust falling from old pipes:

> Soon, soon, the momma bird sings.
> *Take flight, take flight!*

Part of an old nursery rhyme. *Beat your wings*, Mission whispered silently, remembering the rest, a story about a young crow learning to be free.

> Beat your wings and fly away to brighter things.
> *Fly, fly with all your might!*

He started to check the back for a real note, something beyond this fragment of a rhyme, when someone banged on the window again. Several of the other boys dropped their charcoals, visibly startled. One boy cursed under his breath. Mission whirled around to see Jeffery on the other side of the glass, a covered meal tray balanced on one palm, his bald head jerking impatiently.

Mission folded the letter up and stuffed it back in the envelope. He raised his hand over his head to let Jeffery know he'd be right there, licked one finger and ran it across the sticky paste, resealing the envelope as best he could. 'Good luck,' he told Bradley, even though he had no clue what the kid thought he was doing. He dragged his pack off the table, was careful to wipe away the chalk dust that had spilled, and hurried out of the conference room.

'Let's go,' Jeffery said, clearly annoyed.

Mission hurried after him. He glanced back once at the window, then over at the noisy crowd jostling against the temporary barriers by the door. An IT tech approached the crowd with a computer, wires coiled neatly on top, and a woman reached out desperately from behind the barrier like a mother yearning for her baby.

'Since when did people start bringing their own computers up?' he asked, his profession having made him curious about how things got from there to here and back again. It felt as though this was yet another loop the porters were being cut out of. Roker would have a fit.

'Yesterday. Wyck decided he wouldn't be sending his techs out to fix them any more. Says it's safer this way. People are being robbed out there and there's not enough security to go around.'

They were waved through the gates and wound in silence through the hallways, every office full of clacking sounds or people arguing. Mission saw electrical parts and paper strewn everywhere. He wondered which office Rodny was in and why nobody else was having their food delivered. Maybe his friend was in trouble. That was it. That would make sense of everything. Maybe he had pulled one of his stunts. Did they have a holding cell on thirty-four? He didn't think so.

He was about to ask Jeffery if Rodny was in the pen when the old security guard stopped at an imposing steel door.

'Here.' He held the tray out to Mission, who stuck the letter between his lips and accepted it. Jeffery glanced back, blocked Mission's view of the door's keypad with his body and tapped in a code. A series of clunks sounded in the jamb of the heavy door. Fucking right, Rodny was in trouble. What kind of pen was this?

The door swung inward. Jeffery grabbed the tray and told Mission to wait there. Mission still had the taste of milk paste on his lips as he watched the Security chief step inside a room that seemed to go back quite a way. The lights inside pulsed as if something was wrong, red warning lights like a fire alarm. Jeffery called out for Rodny while Mission tried to peek around the guard for a better look.

Rodny arrived a moment later, almost as if he were expecting them. His eyes widened when he saw Mission standing there. Mission fought to close his own mouth, which he could feel hanging open at the sight of his friend.

'Hey.' Rodny pulled open the heavy door a little further and glanced down the hallway. 'What're you doing here?'

'Good to see you too,' Mission said. He held out the letter. 'The Crow sent this.'

'Ah, official business.' Rodny smiled. 'You're here as a porter, eh? Not a friend?'

Rodny smiled, but Mission could see that his friend was beat. He looked as if he hadn't slept for days. His cheeks were sunk in, dark rings under his eyes, and there was the shadow of a beard on his chin. Hair that Rodny had once taken pains to keep in style had been chopped short. Mission glanced into the room, wondering what they had him doing in there. Tall black metal cabinets were all he could see. They stretched out of sight, neatly spaced.

'You learning to fix refrigerators?' Mission asked.

Rodny glanced over his shoulder. He laughed. 'Those are computers.' He still had that condescending tone. Mission nearly reminded his friend that today was his birthday, that they were the same age. Rodny was the only one he ever felt like reminding. Jeffery cleared his throat impatiently, seemed annoyed by the chatter.

Rodny turned to the Security chief. 'You mind if we have a few seconds?' he asked.

Jeffery shifted his weight, the stiff leather of his boots squeaking. 'You know I can't,' he said. 'I'll probably get chewed out for allowing even this.'

'You're right.' Rodny shook his head as if he shouldn't have asked. Mission studied the exchange. Even though it had been months since he'd last seen him, he sensed that Rodny was the same as always. He was in trouble for something, probably being forced to do the most reviled task in all of IT for a brash thing he'd said or done. He smiled at the thought.

Rodny tensed suddenly, as though he'd heard something deep inside the room. He held up a finger to the others and asked them to wait there. 'Just a second,' he said, rushing off, bare feet slapping on the steel floors.

Jeffery crossed his arms and looked Mission up and down unhappily. 'You two grow up down the hall from each other?'

'Went to school together,' Mission said. 'So what did Rod do? You know, Mrs Crowe used to make us sweep the entire Nest and clean the blackboards if we cut up in class. We did our fair share of sweeping, the two of us.'

Jeffery appraised him for a moment. And then his expressionless face shattered into tooth and grin. 'You think your friend is in trouble?' he said. He seemed on the verge of laughing. 'Son, you have no idea.'

Before Mission could question him, Rodny returned, smiling and breathless.

'Sorry,' he said to Jeffery. 'I had to get that.' He turned to Mission. 'Thanks for coming by, man. Good to see you.'

That was it?

'Good to see you too,' Mission sputtered, surprised that their visit would be so brief. 'Hey, don't be a stranger.' He went to give his old friend a hug, but Rodny stuck out a hand instead. Mission looked at it for a pause, confused, wondering if they'd grown apart so far, so fast.

'Give my best to everyone,' Rodny said, as if he expected never to see any of them again.

Jeffery cleared his throat, clearly annoyed and ready to go.

'I will,' Mission said, fighting to keep the sadness out of his voice. He accepted his friend's hand. They shook like strangers, the smile on Rodny's face quivering, the folds of the note hidden in his palm digging sharply into Mission's hand.

35

· Silo 18 ·

It was a miracle Mission didn't drop the note as it was passed to him, a miracle that he knew something was amiss, to keep his mouth closed, to not stand there like a fool in front of Jeffery and say, 'Hey, what's this?' Instead, he kept the wad of paper balled in his fist as he was escorted back to the security station. They were nearly there when someone called 'Porter!' from one of the offices.

Jeffery placed a hand on Mission's chest, forcing him to a stop. They turned, and a familiar man strode down the hallway to meet them. It was Mr Wyck, the head of IT, familiar to most porters. The endless shuffle of broken and repaired computers kept the Upper Dispatch on ten as busy as Supply kept the Lower Dispatch on one-twenty. Mission gathered that may have changed since yesterday.

'You on duty, son?' Mr Wyck studied the porter's 'chief knotted around Mission's neck. He was a tall man with a tidy beard and bright eyes. Mission had to crane his neck to meet Wyck's gaze.

'Yessir,' he said, hiding the note from Rodny behind his back. He pressed it into his pocket with his thumb, like a seed going into soil. 'You need something moved, sir?'

'I do.' Mr Wyck studied him for a moment, stroked his beard. 'You're the Jones boy, right? The zero.'

Mission felt a flash of heat around his neck at the use of the term, a reference to the fact that no lottery number had been pulled for him. 'Yessir. It's Mission.' He offered his hand. Mr Wyck accepted it.

'Yes, yes. I went to school with your father. And your mother, of course.'

He paused to give Mission time to respond. Mission ground his teeth together and said nothing. He let go of the man's hand before his sweaty palms had a chance to speak for him.

'Say I wanted to move something without going through Dispatch.' Mr Wyck smiled. His teeth were white as chalk. 'And say I wanted to avoid the sort of nastiness that took place last night a few levels up . . .'

Mission glanced over at Jeffery, who seemed disinterested in the conversation. It was strange to hear this sort of offer from a man of authority, especially in front of a member of Security, but there was one thing Mission had discovered since emerging from his shadowing days: things only got darker.

'I don't follow,' Mission said. He fought the urge to turn and see how far they were from the security gate. A woman emerged from an office down the hall, behind Mr Wyck. Jeffery made a gesture with his hand and she stopped and kept her distance, out of earshot.

'I think you do, and I admire your discretion. Two hundred chits to move a package a half-dozen levels from Supply.'

Mission tried to remain calm. Two hundred chits. A month's pay for half a day's work. He immediately feared this was some sort of test. Maybe Rodny had gotten in trouble for flunking a similar one.

'I don't know—' he said.

'It's an open invitation,' Wyck said. 'The next porter who comes through here will get the same offer. I don't care who does it, but only one will get the chits.' Wyck raised a hand. 'You don't have to answer me. Just show up and ask for Joyce at the Supply counter. Tell her you're doing a job for Wyck. There'll be a delivery report detailing the rest.'

'I'll think about it, sir.'

'Good.' Mr Wyck smiled.

'Anything else?' Mission asked.

'No, no. You're free to go.' He nodded to Jeffery, who snapped back from wherever he'd checked out to.

'Thank you, sir.' Mission turned and followed the chief.

'Oh, and happy birthday, son,' Mr Wyck called out.

Mission glanced back, didn't say thanks, just hurried after Jeffery and through the security gate, past the crowds and out onto the landing, down two turns of stairs, where he finally reached into his pocket for the note from Rodny. Paranoid that he might drop it and watch it bounce off the stairs and through the rail, he carefully unfolded the scrap of paper. It looked like the same rag blend Mrs Crowe's note had been written on, the same threads of purple and red mixed in with the rough grey weave. For a moment, Mission feared the note would be addressed to the Crow rather than to him, maybe more lines of old nursery rhymes. He worked the piece of paper flat. One side was blank; he turned it over to read the other.

It wasn't addressed to anyone. Just two words, which reminded Mission of the way his friend's smile had quivered when they shook hands.

Mission felt suddenly alone. There was a burning smell lingering in the stairwell, a tinge of smoke that mixed with the paint from drying graffiti. He took the small note and tore it into ever smaller pieces. He kept tearing until there was nothing left to shred, and then sprinkled the dull confetti over the rail to drift down and disappear into the void. The evidence was gone, but the message lingered vividly in his mind. The hasty scrawl, the shadowy scratch the edge of a coin or a spoon had made as it was dragged across the paper, two words barely legible from his friend who never needed anybody or asked for anything.

Help me.

And that was all.

36

• Silo 1 •

Finding the right silo was easy enough. Donald could study the old schematic and remember standing on those hills, peering down into the wide bowls that held each facility. The sound of grumbling ATVs came back, the plumes of dust kicked up as they bounced across the ridges where the grass had not yet filled in. He remembered that they had been growing grass over those hills, straw and seed spread everywhere, a task hindsight made both unnecessary and sad.

Standing on that ridge in his memory, he was able to picture the Tennessee delegation. It would be silo two. Once he had this, he dug deeper. It took a bit of fumbling to remember how the computer program worked, how to sift through lives that lived in databases. There was an entire history there of each silo if you knew how to read it, but it only went so far. It went back to made-up names, back to the orientation. It didn't stretch to the Legacy beyond. The old world was hidden behind bombs and a fog of mist and forgetting.

He had the right silo, but locating Helen might prove impossible. He worked frantically while Anna sang in the shower.

She had left the bathroom door open, steam billowing out. Donald ignored what he took to be an invitation. He ignored the throbbing, the yearning, the hormonal rush of being near an ex-lover after centuries of need, and searched instead for his wife.

There were four thousand names in that first generation of silo two. Four thousand exactly. Roughly half were female. There were three Helens. Each had a grainy picture taken for her work ID stored on the servers. None of the Helens matched what he remembered his wife looking like, what he thought she looked like. Tears came unbidden. He wiped them away, furious at himself. From the shower, Anna sang a sad song from long ago while Donald flipped through random photos. After a dozen, the faces of strangers began to meld together and threaten to erode the vision he held of Helen in his memory. He went back to searching by name. Surely he could guess the name she would've chosen. He had picked Troy for himself those many years ago, a clue leading him back to her. He liked to think she would've done the same.

He tried Sandra, her mother's name, but neither of the two hits were right. He tried Danielle, her sister's name. One hit. Not her.

She wouldn't come up with something random, would she? They had talked once of what they might name their kids. It was gods and goddesses, a joke at first, but Helen had fallen in love with the name Athena. He did a search. Zero hits in that first generation.

The pipes squealed as Anna turned off the shower. Her singing subsided back into a hum, a hymn for the funeral they were about to attend. Donald tried a few more names, anxious to discover something, anything. He would search every night if he had to. He wouldn't sleep until he found her.

'Do you need to shower before the service?' Anna called out from the bathroom.

He didn't want to go to the service, he nearly said. He only knew Victor as someone to fear: the grey-haired man across the hall, always watching, dispensing drugs, manipulating him. At least, that's how the paranoia of his first shift made it all seem.

'I'll go like this,' he said. He still wore the beige overalls they'd given him the day before. He flipped through random pictures again, starting at the top of the alphabet. What other name? The fear was that he'd forget what she looked like. Or that she'd look more and more like Anna in his mind. He couldn't let that happen.

'Find anything?'

She snuck up behind him and reached for something on the desk. A towel was wrapped around her breasts and reached the middle of her thighs. Her skin was wet. She grabbed a hairbrush and walked, humming, back to the bathroom. Donald forgot to answer. His body responded to Anna in a way that made him furious and full of guilt.

He was still married, he reminded himself. He would be until he knew what'd happened to Helen. He would be loyal to her for ever.

Loyalty.

On a whim, he searched for the name Karma.

One hit. Donald sat up straight. He hadn't imagined a hit. It was their dog's name, the nearest thing he and Helen ever had to a child of their own. He brought up the picture.

'I guess we're all wearing these horrid outfits to the funeral, right?' Anna passed the desk as she snapped up the front of her white overalls. Donald only noticed in the corner of his tear-filled vision. He covered his mouth and felt his body tremble with suppressed sobs. On the monitor, in a tiny square of black and white pixels in the middle of a work badge, was his wife.

'You'll be ready to go in a few minutes, won't you?'

Anna disappeared back into the bathroom, brushing her hair. Donald wiped his cheeks, salt on his lips while he read.

Karma Brewer. There were several occupations listed, with a badge photo for each. *Teacher, School Master, Judge* – more wrinkles in each picture but always the same half-smile. He opened the full file, thinking suddenly what it would've been like to have been on the very first shift in silo one, to watch her life unfold next door, maybe even reach out and contact her somehow. A judge. It'd been a dream of hers to be a judge one day. Donald wept while Anna hummed, and through a lens of tears, he read about his wife's life without him.

Married, it said, which didn't throw up any flags at first. Married, of course. To him. Until he read about her death. Eighty-two years old. Survived by Rick Brewer and two children, Athena and Mars.

Rick Brewer.

The walls and ceiling bulged inward. Donald felt a chill. There were more pictures. He followed the links to other files. To her husband's files.

'Mick,' Anna whispered behind him.

Donald started and turned to find her reading over his shoulder. Drying tears streaked his face, but he didn't care. His best friend and his wife. Two kids. He turned back to the screen and pulled up the daughter's file. Athena's. There were several pictures from different careers and phases of her life. She had Helen's mouth.

'Donny. Please don't.'

A hand on his shoulder. Donald flinched from it and watched an animation wrought by furious clicks, this child growing into an approximation of his wife, until the girl's own children appeared in her file.

'Donny,' Anna whispered. 'We're going to be late for the funeral.'

Donald wept. Sobs tore through him as if he were made of tissue. 'Late,' he cried. 'A hundred years too late.' He sputtered this last, overcome with misery. There was a granddaughter on the screen that was not his, a great-granddaughter one more click away. They stared out at him, all of them, none with eyes like his own.

37

• Silo 1 •

onald went to Victor's funeral numb. He rode the lift in silence, watched his boots kick ahead of himself as he teetered forward, but what he found on the medical level wasn't a funeral at all – it was body disposal. They were storing the remains back in a pod because they had no dirt in which to bury their dead. The food in silo one came from cans. Their bodies returned to the same.

Donald was introduced to Erskine, who explained unprompted that the body would not rot. The same invisible machines that allowed them to survive the freezing process and turned their waking piss the colour of charcoal would keep the dead as soft and fresh as the living. The thought wasn't a pleasant one. He watched as the man he had known as Victor was prepped for deep freeze.

They wheeled the body down a hall and through a sea of pods. The deep freeze was a cemetery, Donald saw. A grid of bodies laid flat, only a name to feebly encapsulate all that lay within. He wondered how many of the pods contained the dead. Some men must die on their shifts from natural causes. Some must break down and take their own lives as Victor had.

Donald helped the others move the body into the pod. There were only five of them present, only five who could know how Victor had died. The illusion that someone was in charge must be maintained. Donald thought of his last job, sitting at a desk, hands on a rudderless wheel, pretending. He watched Thurman as the old man kissed his palm and pressed his fingers to Victor's cheek. The lid was closed. The cold of the room fogged their breath.

The others took turns eulogising, but Donald paid no heed. His mind was elsewhere, thinking of a woman he had loved long ago, of children he had never had. He did not cry. He had sobbed in the lift, with Anna gently holding him. Helen had died over a century ago. It had been longer than that since he'd lost her over that hill, since missing her messages, since not being able to get through to her. He remembered the national anthem and the bombs filling the air. He remembered his sister, Charlotte being there.

His sister. Family.

Donald knew Charlotte had been saved. He was overcome with a fierce urge to find her and wake her, to bring someone he loved back to life.

Erskine paid his final respects. Only five of them present to mourn this man who had killed billions. Donald felt Anna's presence beside him and realised the lack of a crowd was in fact due to her. The five present were the only ones who knew that a woman had been woken. Her father, Dr Sneed, who had performed the procedure, Anna, Erskine, whom she spoke of as a friend, and himself.

The absurdity of Donald's existence, of the state of the world, swooped down on him in that gathering. He did not belong. He was only there because of a girl he had dated in college, a girl whose father was a senator, whose affections had likely gotten him elected, who had dragged him into a murderous scheme, and had now pulled him from a frozen death. All the great coincidences and marvellous achievements of his life disappeared in a flash. In their place were puppet strings.

'A tragic loss, this.'

Donald emerged from his thoughts to discover that the ceremony was over. Anna and her father stood two rows of pods away discussing something. Dr Sneed was down by the base of the pod, the panel beeping as he made adjustments. That left Donald with Erskine, a thin man with glasses and a British accent. He surveyed Donald from the opposite side of the pod.

'He was on my shift,' Donald said inanely, trying to explain why he was present for the service. There was little else he could think to say of the dead man. He stepped closer and peered through the little window at the calm face within.

'I know,' Erskine said. This wiry man, probably in his early to mid-sixties, adjusted the glasses on his narrow nose and joined Donald in peering through the small window. 'He was quite fond of you, you know.'

'I didn't. I mean . . . he never said as much to me.'

'He was peculiar that way.' Erskine studied the deceased with a smile. 'Brilliant perhaps for knowing the minds of others, just not so keen on communicating with them.'

'Did you know him from before?' Donald asked. He wasn't sure how else to broach the subject. The *before* seemed taboo with some, freely spoken of by others.

Erskine nodded. 'We worked together. Well, in the same hospital. We orbited each other for quite a few years until my discovery.' He reached out and touched the glass, a final farewell to an old friend, it seemed.

'What discovery?' He vaguely remembered Anna mentioning something.

Erskine glanced up. Looking closer, Donald thought he may have been in his seventies. It was hard to tell. He had some of the agelessness of Thurman, like an antique that patinas and will grow no older.

'I'm the one who discovered the great threat,' he said. It sounded more an admission of guilt than a proud claim. His voice was tinged with sadness. At the base of the pod, Dr Sneed finished his adjustments, stood and excused himself. He steered the empty gurney towards the exit.

'The nanos.' Donald remembered; Anna had said as much. He watched Thurman debate something with his daughter, his fist coming down over and over into his palm, and a question came to mind. He wanted to hear it from someone else. He wanted to see if the lies matched, if that meant they might contain some truth.

'You were a medical doctor?' he asked.

Erskine considered the question. It seemed a simple enough one to answer.

'Not precisely,' he said, his accent thick. 'I *built* medical doctors. Very small ones.' He pinched the air and squinted through his glasses at his own fingers. 'We were working on ways to keep soldiers safe, to keep them patched up. And then I found someone else's handiwork in a sample of blood. Little machines trying to do the opposite. Machines made to fight our machines. An invisible battle raging where no one could see. It wasn't long before I was finding the little bastards everywhere.'

Anna and Thurman headed their way. Anna donned a cap, her hair in a bun that bulged noticeably through the top. It was little disguise for what she was, useful perhaps at a distance.

'I'd like to ask you about that sometime,' Donald said hurriedly. 'It might help my . . . help me with this problem in silo eighteen.'

'Of course,' Erskine said.

'I need to get back,' Anna told Donald. She set her lips in a thin grimace from the argument with her father, and Donald finally appreciated how trapped she truly was. He imagined a year spent in that warehouse of war, clues scattered across that planning table, sleeping on that small cot, not able even to ride up to the cafeteria to see the hills and the dark clouds or have a meal at the time of her own choosing, relying on others to bring her everything.

'I'll escort the young man up in a bit,' Donald heard Erskine say, his hand resting on Donald's shoulder. 'I'd like to have a chat with our boy.'

Thurman narrowed his eyes but relented. Anna squeezed Donald's hand a final time, glanced at the pod and headed towards the exit. Her father followed a few paces behind.

'Come with me.' Erskine's breath fogged the air. 'I want to show you someone.'

38

• Silo 1 •

Erskine picked his way through the grid of pods with purpose as though he'd walked the route dozens of times. Donald followed after, rubbing his arms for warmth. He had been too long in that crypt-like place. The cold was leaching back into his bones.

'Thurman keeps saying we were already dead,' he told Erskine, attacking the question head-on. 'Is that true?'

Erskine looked back over his shoulder. He waited for Donald to catch up, seemed to consider this question.

'Well?' Donald asked. 'Were we?'

'I never saw a design with a hundred per cent efficiency,' Erskine said. 'We weren't there yet with our own work, and everything from Iran and Syria was much cruder. Now, North Korea had some elegant designs. I had my money on them. What they had already built could've taken out most of us. That part's true enough.' He resumed his walk through the field of sleeping corpses. 'Even the most severe epidemics burn themselves out,' he said, 'so it's difficult to say. I argued for countermeasures. Victor argued for this.' He spread his arms over the quiet assembly.

'And Victor won.'

'Indeed.'

'Do you think he . . . had second thoughts? Is that why . . . ?'

Erskine stopped at one of the pods and placed both hands on its icy surface. 'I'm sure we all have second thoughts,' he said sadly. 'But I don't think Vic ever doubted the rightness of this mission. I don't know why he did what he did in the end. It wasn't like him.'

Donald peered inside the pod Erskine had led him to. There was a middle-aged woman inside, her eyelids covered in frost.

'My daughter,' Erskine said. 'My only child.'

There was a moment of silence. It allowed the faint hum of a thousand pods to be heard.

'When Thurman made the decision to wake Anna, all I could dream about was doing the same. But why? There was no reason, no need for her expertise. Caroline was an accountant. And besides, it wouldn't be fair to drag her from her dreams.'

Donald wanted to ask if it would ever be fair. What world did Erskine expect his daughter to ever see again? When would she wake to a normal life? A happy life?

'When I found nanos in her blood, I knew this was the right thing to do.' He turned to Donald. 'I know you're looking for answers, son. We all are. This is a cruel world. It's always been a cruel world. I spent my whole life looking for ways to make it better, to patch things up, dreaming of an ideal. But for every sot like me, there's ten more out there trying to tear things down. And it only takes one of them to get lucky.'

Donald flashed back to the day Thurman had given him the Order. That thick book was the start of his plummet into madness. He remembered their talk in that huge chamber, the feeling of being infected, the paranoia that something harmful and invisible was invading him. But if Erskine and Thurman were telling the truth, he'd been infected long before that.

'You weren't poisoning me that day.' He looked from the pod to Erskine, piecing something together. 'The interview with Thurman, the weeks and weeks he spent in that chamber having all of those meetings. You weren't infecting us.'

Erskine nodded ever so slightly. 'We were healing you.'

Donald felt a sudden flash of anger. 'Then why not heal *everyone*?' he demanded.

'We discussed that. I had the same thought. To me, it was an engineering problem. I wanted to build counter-measures, machines to kill machines before they got to us. Thurman had similar ideas. He saw it as an invisible war, one we desperately needed to take to the enemy. We all saw the battles we were accustomed to fighting, you see. I saw it in the bloodstream, Thurman in the war overseas. It was Victor who set the two of us straight.'

Erskine pulled a cloth from his breast pocket and removed his glasses. He rubbed them while he talked, his voice echoing in whispers from the walls. 'Victor said there would be no end to it. He pointed to computer viruses to make his case, how one might run rampant through a network and cripple hundreds of millions of machines. Sooner or later, some nano attack would get through, get out of control, and there would be an epidemic built on bits of code rather than strands of DNA.'

'So what? We've dealt with plagues before. Why would this be different?' Donald swept his arms at the pods. 'Tell me how the solution isn't worse than the problem?'

As worked up as he felt, he also sensed how much angrier he would be if he heard this from Thurman. He wondered if he'd been set up to have a kindlier man, a stranger, take him aside and tell him what Thurman thought he needed to hear. It was hard not to be paranoid about being manipulated, not to feel the strings knotted to his joints.

'Psychology,' Erskine replied. He put his glasses back on. 'This is where Victor set us straight, why our ideas would never work. I'll never forget the conversation. We were sitting in the cafeteria at Walter Reed Hospital. Thurman was there to hand out ribbons, but really to meet with the two of us.' He shook his head. 'It was crowded in there. If anyone knew the things we were discussing—'

'Psychology,' Donald reminded him. 'Tell me how this is better. More people die this way.'

Erskine snapped back to the present. 'That's where we were wrong, just like you. Imagine the first discovery that one of these epidemics was man-made – the panic, the violence that would ensue. That's where the end would come. A typhoon kills a few hundred people, does a few billion in damage, and what do we do?' Erskine interlocked his fingers. 'We come together. We put the pieces back. But a terrorist's bomb.' He frowned. 'A terrorist's bomb does the same damage, and it throws the world into turmoil.'

He spread his hands open. 'When there's only God to blame, we forgive him. When it's our fellow man, we destroy him.'

Donald shook his head. He didn't know what to believe. But then he thought about the fear and rage he'd felt when he thought he'd been infected by something in that chamber. Meanwhile, he never worried about the billions of creatures swimming in his gut and doing so since the day he was born.

'We can't tweak the genes of the food we eat without suspicion,' Erskine said. 'We can pick and choose until a blade of grass is a great ear of corn, but we can't do it with *purpose*. Vic had dozens of examples like these. Vaccines versus natural immunities, cloning versus twins, modified foods. Of course he was perfectly right. It was the man-made part that would've caused the chaos. It would be knowing that people were out to get us, that there was danger in the air we breathed.'

Erskine paused for a moment. Donald's mind was racing.

'You know, Vic once said that if these terrorists had an ounce of sense, they would've simply announced what they were working on and then sat back to watch things burn on their own. He said that's all it would take, us knowing that it was happening, that the end of any of us could come silent, invisible and at any time.'

'And so the solution was to burn it all to the ground *ourselves*?' Donald ran his hands through his hair, trying to make sense of it all. He thought of a firefighting technique that always seemed just as confusing to him, the burning of wide swathes of forest to prevent a fire from spreading. And he knew in Iran, when oil wells were set ablaze during the first war, that sometimes the only cure was to set off a bomb, to fight the inferno with something greater.

'Believe me,' Erskine said, 'I came up with my own

complaints. Endless complaints. But I knew the truth from the beginning, it just took me a while to accept it. Thurman was won over more easily. He saw at once that we needed to get off this ball of rock, to start over. But the cost of travel was too great—'

'Why travel through space,' Donald interrupted, 'when you can travel through time?' He remembered a conversation in Thurman's office. The old man had told him what he was planning that very first day, but Donald hadn't heard.

Erskine's eyes widened. 'Yes. That was his argument. He'd seen enough war, I suppose. Me, I didn't have Thurman's experiences or the professional . . . *distance* Vic enjoyed. It was the analogy of the computer virus that wore me down, seeing these nanos like a new cyber war. I knew what they could do, how fast they could restructure themselves, evolve, if you will. Once it started, it would only stop when we were no longer around. And maybe not even then. Every defence would become a blueprint for the next attack. The air would choke with our invisible armies. There would be great clouds of them, mutating and fighting without need of a host. And once the public saw this and *knew* . . .' He left the sentence unfinished.

'Hysteria,' Donald muttered.

Erskine nodded.

'You said it might not ever end, even if we were gone. Does that mean they're still out there? The nanos?'

Erskine glanced up at the ceiling. 'The world outside isn't just being scrubbed of humans right now, if that's what you're asking. It's being reset. All of our experiments are being removed. By the grace of God, it'll be a very long time indeed before we think to perform them again.'

Donald remembered from orientation that the combined shifts would last five hundred years. Half a millennium of living underground. How much scrubbing was necessary? And what was to keep them from heading down that same path a second time? How would any of them unlearn the potential dangers? You don't get the fire back in the box once you've unleashed it.

'You asked me if Victor had regrets—' Erskine coughed into his fist and nodded. 'I do think he felt something close to that once. It was something he said to me as he was coming off his eighth or ninth shift, I don't remember which. I think I was heading into my sixth. This was just after the two of you worked together, after that nasty business with silo twelve—'

'My first shift,' Donald said, since Erskine seemed to be counting. He wanted to add that it was his only shift.

'Yes, of course.' Erskine adjusted his glasses. 'I'm sure you knew him well enough to know that he didn't show his emotions often.'

'He was difficult to read,' Donald agreed. He knew almost nothing of the man he had just helped to bury.

'So you'll appreciate this, I think. We were riding the lift together, and Vic turns to me and says how hard it is to sit there at that desk of his and see what we're doing to the men across the hall. He meant you, of course. People in your position.'

Donald tried to imagine the man he knew saying such a thing. He wanted to believe it.

'But that's not what really struck me. I've never seen him sadder than when he said the following. He said . . .' Erskine rested a hand on the pod. 'He said that sitting there, watching you people work at your desks, getting to know you – he often thought that the world would be a better place with people like you in charge.'

'People like me?' Donald shook his head. 'What does that even mean?'

Erskine smiled. 'I asked him precisely that. His response was that it was a burden doing what he knew to be correct, to be sound and logical.' Erskine ran one hand across the pod as if he could touch his daughter within. 'And how much simpler things would be, how much better for us all, if we had people brave enough to do what was right, instead.'

39

• Silo 1 •

That night, Anna came to him. After a day of numbness and dwelling on death, of eating meals brought down by Thurman and not tasting a bite, of watching her set up a computer for him and spread out folders of notes, she came to him in the darkness.

Donald complained. He tried to push her away. She sat on the edge of the cot and held his wrists while he sobbed and grew feeble. He thought of Erskine's story, on what it meant to do the right thing rather than the correct thing, what the difference was. He thought this as an old lover draped herself across him, her hand on the back of his neck, her cheek on his shoulder, lying there against him while he wept.

A century of sleep had weakened him, he thought. A century of sleep and the knowledge that Mick and Helen had lived a life together. He felt suddenly angry at Helen for not holding out, for not living alone, for not getting his messages and meeting him over the hill.

Anna kissed his cheek and whispered that everything would be okay. Fresh tears flowed down Donald's face as he realised that he was everything Victor had assumed he wasn't. He was a miserable human being for wishing his wife to be lonely so that he could sleep at night a hundred years later. He was a miserable human being for denying her that solace when Anna's touch made him feel so much better.

'I can't,' he whispered for the dozenth time.

'Shhh,' Anna said. She brushed his hair back in the

darkness. And the two of them were alone in that room where wars were waged. They were trapped together with those crates of arms, with guns and ammo, and far more dangerous things.

40

• Silo 18 •

Mission wound his way towards Central Dispatch and agonised over what to do for Rodny. He felt afraid for his friend but powerless to help. The door they had him behind was unlike any he'd ever seen: thick and solid, gleaming and daunting. If the trouble his friend had caused could be measured by where they were keeping him—

He shuddered to continue that line of thought. It'd only been a few months since the last cleaning. Mission had been there, had carried up part of the suit from IT, a more haunting experience than porting a body for burial. Dead bodies at least were placed in the black bags the coroners used. The cleaning suit was a different sort of bag, tailored to a living soul that would crawl inside and be forced to die within.

Mission remembered where they had picked up the gear. It'd been a room right down the hall from where Rodny was being kept. Weren't cleanings run by the same department? He shivered. One slip of a tongue could land a body out there, rotting on the hills, and his friend Rodny was known to wag his dangerously.

First his mother, and now his best friend. Mission wondered what the Pact said about volunteering to clean in one's stead, if it said anything at all. Amazing that he could live under the rules of a document he'd never read. He just assumed others had, all the people in charge, and that they were operating by its codes in good faith.

On fifty-eight, a porter's 'chief tied to the downbound

railing caught his attention. It was the same blue pattern as the 'chief worn around his neck, but with a bright red merchant's hem. Duty beckoned, dispelling thoughts that were spiralling nowhere. Mission unknotted the 'chief and searched the fabric for the merchant's stamp. It was Drexel's, the apothecarist down the hall. Light loads and lighter pay, normally. But at least it was downbound, unless Drexel had been careless again with which rail he tied it to.

Mission was dying to get to Central where a shower and a change of clothes awaited, but if anyone spotted him with a flat pack marching past a signal 'chief, he'd hear it from Roker and the others. He hurried inside to Drexel's, praying it wasn't a round of meds going to several dozen individual apartments. His legs ached just at the thought of it.

Drexel was at the counter as Mission pushed open the apothecarist's squeaky door. A large man with a full beard and a balding head, Drexel was something of a fixture in the mids. Many came to him rather than to the doctors, though Mission wasn't sure how sound a choice that was. Often, it was the man with the most promises who got the chits, not the one who made people better.

A handful of the seemingly sick sat on Drexel's waiting-room bench, sniffling and coughing. Mission felt the urge to cover his mouth with his 'chief. Instead, he innocuously held his breath and waited while Drexel filled a small square of paper with ground powder, folding it neatly before handing it to the woman waiting. The woman slid a few chits across the counter. When she walked away, Mission tossed the signal 'chief on top of the money.

'Ah, Mish. Good to see you, boy. Looking fit as a fiddle.' Drexel smoothed his beard and smiled, yellow teeth peering out from cornrows of drooping whiskers.

'Same,' Mission said politely, braving a breath. 'Got something for me?'

'I do. One sec.'

Drexel disappeared behind a wall of shelves crammed full

of tiny vials and jars. The apothecarist reappeared with a small sack. 'Meds for down below,' he said.

'I can take them as far as Central and have Dispatch send them from there,' Mission told him. 'I'm just finishing up a shift.'

Drexel frowned and rubbed his beard. 'I suppose that'll do. And Dispatch'll bill me?'

Mission held out a palm. 'If you tip,' he said.

'Aye, a tip. But only if you solve a riddle.' Drexel leaned on the counter, which seemed to sag beneath his bulk. The last thing Mission wanted to hear was another of the old man's riddles and then not get paid. Always an excuse with Drexel to keep a chit on his side of the counter.

'Okay,' the apothecarist began, tugging on his whiskers. 'Which one weighs more, a bag full of seventy-eight pounds of feathers, or a bag full of seventy-eight pounds of rocks?'

Mission didn't hesitate with his answer. 'The bag of feathers,' he declared. He'd heard this one before. It was a riddle made for a porter, and he had thought on it long enough between the levels to come up with his own answer, one different from the obvious.

'Incorrect!' Drexel roared, waving a finger. 'It isn't the rocks—' His face dimmed. 'Wait. Did you say the feathers?' He shook his head. 'No, boy, they weigh the same.'

'The contents weigh the same,' Mission told him. 'The bag of feathers would have to be bigger. You said they were both full, which means a bigger bag with more material, and so it weighs more.' He held out his palm. Drexel stood there, chewing his beard for a moment, thrown off his game. Begrudgingly, he took two coins from the lady's pay and placed them in Mission's hand. Mission accepted them and stuffed the sack of meds into his pack before cinching it up tight.

'The bigger bag—' Drexel muttered, as Mission hurried off, past the benches, holding his breath again as he went, the pills rattling in his sack.

The apothecarist's annoyance was worth far more than

the tip, but Mission appreciated both. The enjoyment faded, however, as he spiralled down through a tense silo. He saw deputies on one landing, hands on their guns, trying to calm down fighting neighbours. The glass on the windows peeking into a shop on sixty-two was broken and covered with a sheet of plastic. Mission was pretty sure that was recent. A woman on sixty-four sat by the rails and sobbed into her palms, and Mission watched as people passed her by without stopping. On down he went as well, the stairway trembling, the graffiti on the walls warning him of what was yet to come.

He arrived at Central Dispatch to find it eerily quiet, made his way past the sorting rooms with their tall shelves of items needing delivery and went straight to the main counter. He would drop off his current package and pick out his next job before changing and showering. Katelyn was working the counter. There were no other porters queued up. Off licking their wounds, perhaps. Or maybe seeing to their families during this recent spate of violence.

'Hey, Katelyn.'

'Mish.' She smiled. 'You look intact.'

He laughed and touched his nose, which was still sore. 'Thanks.'

'Cam just passed through asking where you were.'

'Yeah?' Mission was surprised. He figured his friend would be taking a day off with the bonus from the coroner. 'Did he pick something up?'

'Yup. He requested anything heading towards Supply. Was in a better mood than usual, though he seemed miffed to have been left out of last night's adventures.'

'He heard about that, huh?' Mission sorted through the delivery list. He was looking for something upbound. Mrs Crowe would know what to do about Rodny. Maybe she could find out from the mayor what he was being punished for, perhaps put in a good word for him.

'Wait,' he said, glancing up at Katelyn. 'What do you mean he was in a good mood? And he was heading for *Supply*?' Mission thought of the job he'd been offered by

Wyck. The head of IT had said Mission wouldn't be the last to hear of the offer. Maybe he hadn't been the *first*, either. 'Where was Cam coming from?'

Katelyn touched her fingers to her tongue and flipped through the old log. 'I think his last delivery was a broken computer heading to—'

'That little rat.' Mission slapped the counter. 'You got anything else heading down? Maybe to Supply or Chemical?'

She checked her computer, fingers clacking furiously, the rest of her perfectly serene. 'We're so slow right now,' she said apologetically. 'I've got something from Mechanical back *up* to Supply. Forty-five pounds. No rush. Standard freight.' She peered across the counter at Mission, seeing if he was interested.

'I'll take it,' he said. But he didn't plan on heading straight to Mechanical. If he raced, maybe he could beat Cam to Supply and do that other job for Wyck. That was the way in he was looking for. It wasn't the money he wanted, it was having an excuse to go back to thirty-four to collect his pay, another chance to see Rodny, see what kind of help his friend needed, what sort of trouble he was truly in.

Mission made record time downbound. It helped that traffic was light, but it wasn't a good sign that he didn't pass Cam on the way. The kid must've had a good head start. Either that, or Mission had gotten lucky and had overtaken him while he was off the stairway for a bathroom break.

Pausing for a moment on the landing outside of Supply, Mission caught his breath and dabbed the sweat from his neck. He still hadn't had his shower. Maybe after he found Cam and took care of this job in Mechanical, he could get cleaned up and get some proper rest. Lower Dispatch would have a change of clothes for him, and then he could figure out what to do about Rodny. So much to think about. A blessing that it took his mind off his birthday.

Inside Supply, he found a handful of people waiting at the counter. No sign of Cam. If the boy had come and gone already, he must've flown, and the delivery must have been heading further down. Mission tapped his foot and waited his turn. Once at the counter, he asked for Joyce, just like Wyck had said. The man pointed to a heavyset woman with long braids at the other end of the counter. Mission recognized her. She handled a lot of the flow of equipment marked special for IT. He waited until she was done with her customer, then asked for any deliveries under the name of Wyck.

She narrowed her eyes at him. 'You got a glitch at Dispatch?' she asked. 'Done handed that one off.' She waved for the next person in line.

'Could you tell me where it was heading?' Mission asked. 'I was sent to relieve the other guy. His . . . his mother is sick. They're not sure if she's gonna make it.'

Mission winced at the lie. The lady behind the counter twisted her mouth in disbelief.

'Please,' he begged. 'It really is important.'

She hesitated. 'It was going six flights down to an apartment. I don't have the exact number. It was on the delivery report.'

'Six down.' Mission knew the level. One-sixteen was residential except for the handful of less-than-legal businesses being run out of a few apartments. 'Thanks,' he said. He slapped the counter and hurried towards the exit. It was on his way to Mechanical, anyway. He might be too late for Wyck's delivery, but he could ask Cam if he might pick up the pay for him, offer him a vacation chit in return. Or he could just flat out tell him an old friend was in trouble, and he needed to get through security. If not, he'd have to wait for an IT request to hit Dispatch and be the first to jump on it. And he'd have to hope that Rodny had that much time.

He was four levels down, formulating a dozen such plans, when the blast went off.

The great stairwell lurched as if thrown sideways. Mission slammed against the rail and nearly went over. He wrapped his arms around the trembling steel and held on.

There was a shriek, a chorus of groans. He watched, his head out in the space beyond the railing, as the landing two levels below twisted away from the staircase. The metal sang and cried out as it was ripped free and went tumbling into the depths.

More than one body plummeted after. The receding figures performed cartwheels in space.

Mission tore himself away from the sight. A few steps down from him, a woman remained on her hands and knees, looking up at Mission with wild and frightened eyes. There was a distant crash, impossibly far below.

I don't know, he wanted to say. There was that question

in her eyes, the same one pounding in his skull, echoing with the sound of the blast. *What the hell just happened? Is this it? Has it begun?*

He considered running up, away from the explosion, but there were screams coming from below and a porter had a duty to those on the stairwell in need. He helped the woman to her feet and bid her upward. Already the smell of something acrid and the haze of smoke were filling the air. 'Go,' he urged, and then he spiralled down against the sudden flow of upward traffic. Cam was down there. Where his friend had gone with the package and where the blast had occurred were still coincidence in Mission's rattled mind.

The landing below held a crush of people. Residents and shopkeeps crowded out of the doors and fought for a spot at the rail that they might gaze over at the wreckage one flight further down. Mission fought his way through, yelling Cam's name, keeping an eye out for his friend. A bedraggled couple staggered up to the crowded landing with hollow eyes, clutching the railing and each other. He didn't see Cam anywhere.

He raced down five turns of the central post, his normally deft feet stumbling on the slick treads, around and around. It'd been the level Cam was heading towards, right? Six down. Level one-sixteen. He would be okay. He must be okay. And then the sight of those people tumbling through the air flashed in Mission's mind. It was an image he knew he'd never forget. Surely Cam wasn't among them. The boy was late or early to everything, never right on time.

He made the last turn, and where the next landing should have been was empty space. The rails of the great spiral staircase had been ripped outward before parting. A few of the steps sagged away from the central post, and Mission could feel a pull towards the edge, the void clawing at him. There was nothing there to stop him from going over. The steel felt slick beneath his boots.

Across a gap of torn and twisted steel, the doorway to one-sixteen was missing. In its place stood a pocket of crumbling cement and dark iron bars bent outward like hands reaching for the vanished landing. White powder drifted down from the ceiling beyond the rubble. Unbelievably, there were sounds beyond the veil of dust: coughs and shouts. Screams for help.

'Porter!' someone yelled from above.

Mission carefully slid to the edge of the sloping and bent steps. He held the railing where it had been torn free. It was warm to the touch. Leaning out, he studied the crowd fifty feet above him at the next landing, searching for the person who had called out for him.

Someone pointed when they spotted him leaning out, spotted the 'chief around his neck.

'There he is!' a woman shrieked, one of the mad-eyed women who had staggered past him as he hurried down, one of those who had survived. 'The porter did it!' she yelled.

42

• Silo 18 •

Mission turned and ran as the stairway thundered and clanged with the descending mob. He stumbled downward, a hand on the inner post, watching for the return of the railing. So much had been pulled away. The stairs were unstable from the damage. He had no idea why he was being chased. It took a full turn of the staircase for the railing to reappear and for him to feel safe at such speeds. It took just as long to realize that Cam was dead. His friend had delivered a package, and now he was dead. He and many others. One glance at his blue 'chief and someone above must've thought it was Mission who'd made the delivery. It very nearly had been.

Another crowd at landing one-seventeen. Tear-streaked faces, a woman trembling, her arms wrapped around herself, a man covering his face, all looking up or down beyond the rails. They had seen the wreckage tumble past. Mission hurried on. Lower Dispatch on one-twenty was the only haven between him and Mechanical. He hurried there as a violent scream approached from above and came much too fast.

Mission started and nearly fell as the wailing person flew towards him. He waited for someone to tackle him from behind, but the sound whizzed past beyond the rail. Another person. Falling, alive and screaming, plummeting towards the depths. The loose steps and empty space above had claimed one of those chasing him.

He quickened his pace, leaving the inner post for the

outer rail where the curve of the steps was broader and smoother, where the force of his descent tugged him against the steel bar. Here, he could move faster. He tried not to think of what would happen if he came across a gap in the steel. He ran, smoke stinging his eyes, the clang and clamour of his own feet and that of the others above, not realising at first that the haze in the air wasn't from the ruin he had left behind. The smoke all around him was *rising*.

43

• Silo 1 •

D onald's breakfast of powdered eggs and shredded potatoes had long grown cold. He rarely touched the food brought down by Thurman and Erskine, preferring instead the bland stuff in the unlabelled silver cans he had discovered among the storeroom's vacuum-sealed crates. It wasn't just the matter of trust – it was the rebelliousness of it all, the empowerment that came from taking command of his own survival. He stabbed a yellowish-orange gelatinous blob that he assumed had once been part of a peach and put it in his mouth. He chewed, tasting nothing. He pretended it tasted like a peach.

Across the wide table, Anna fiddled with the dials on her radio and sipped loudly from a mug of cold coffee. A nest of wires ran from a black box to her computer, and a soft hiss of static filled the room.

'It's too bad we can't get a better station,' Donald said morosely. He speared another wedge of mystery fruit and popped it into his mouth. Mango, he told himself, just for variety.

'No station is the best station,' she said, referring to her hope that the towers of silo forty and its neighbours would remain silent. She had tried to explain what she was doing to cut off any unlikely survivors, but little of it made any sense to Donald. A year ago, supposedly, silo forty had hacked the system. It was assumed to have been a rogue head of IT. No one else could be expected to possess the expertise and access required of such a feat. By the time the camera feeds were cut, every failsafe had already been severed. Attempts had been made to terminate the silo, but there was no way to verify them. It became obvious these attempts had failed when the darkness started to spread to other silos.

Thurman, Erskine and Victor had been woken according to protocol, one after the other. Further failsafes proved ineffective, and Erskine worried the hacking had progressed to the level of the nanos, that the machines in the air were being reprogrammed, that everything was in jeopardy. After much cajoling, Thurman had convinced the other two that Anna could help. Her research at MIT had been in wireless harmonics; remote charging technology; the ability to assume control of electronics via radio.

She'd eventually been able to commandeer the collapse mechanism of the afflicted silos. Donald still had nightmares thinking about it. While she described the process, he had studied the wall schematic of a standard silo. He had pictured the blasts that freed the layers of heavy concrete between the levels, sending them like dominoes down to the bottom, crushing everything and everyone in-between. Stacks of concrete fifty feet thick had been cut loose to turn entire societies into rubble. These underground buildings had been designed from the beginning so they could be brought down like any other – and remotely. That such a failsafe was even needed seemed as sick to Donald as the solution was cruel.

All that now remained of those silos was the hiss and crackle of their dead radios, a chorus of ghosts. The silo heads in the rest of the facilities hadn't even been told of the calamity. There would be no red Xs on their schematics to haunt their days. The various heads had little contact with each other as it was. The greater worry was of the panic spreading.

But Victor had known. And Donald suspected it was this heavy burden that had led him to take his own life, rather than any of the theories Thurman had offered. Thurman was so in awe of Victor's supposed brilliance that he searched for purpose behind his suicide, some conspiratorial cause. Donald was verging on the sad realisation that humanity had been thrown to the brink of extinction by insane men in positions of power following one another, each thinking the others knew where they were going.

He took a sip of tomato juice from a punctured can and reached for two pieces of paper amid the carpet of notes and reports around his keyboard. The fate of silo eighteen supposedly rested on something in these two pages. They were copies of the same report. One was a virgin printout of the report he'd written long ago on the fall of silo twelve. Donald barely remembered writing it. And now he had stared at it so long, the meaning had been squeezed out of it, like a word that, repeated too often, devolves into mere noise.

The other copy showed the notes Victor had scrawled across the face of this report. He had used a red pen, and someone upstairs had managed to pull just this colour off in order to make both versions more legible. By copying the red, however, they had also transferred a fine mist and a few splatters of his blood. These marks were gruesome reminders that the report had been atop Victor's desk in the final moments of his life.

After three days of study, Donald was beginning to suspect that the report was nothing more than a scrap of paper. Why else write across the top of it? And yet Victor had told Thurman several times that the key to quelling the violence in silo eighteen lay right there, in Donald's report. Victor had argued for Donald to be pulled from the deep freeze, but hadn't been able to get Erskine or Thurman to side with him. So this was all Donald had: a liar's account of what a dead man had said.

Liars and dead men – two parties unskilled at dispensing the truth.

The scrap of paper with the red ink and rust-coloured bloodstains offered little help. There were a few lines that resonated, however. They reminded Donald of how horoscopes were able to land vague and glancing blows, which gave credence to all their other feints.

The One who remembers had been written in bold and

confident letters across the centre of the report. Donald couldn't help but feel that this referred to him and his resistance to the medication. Hadn't Anna said that Victor spoke of him frequently, that he wanted him awake for testing or questioning? Other musings were vague and dire in equal measure. *This is why*, Victor had written. Also: *An end to them all.*

Had he meant the why of his suicide or the why of silo eighteen's violence? And an end to all of what?

In many ways, the cycle of violence in silo eighteen was no different than what took place elsewhere. Beyond being more severe, it was the same waxing and waning of the mobs, of each generation revolting against the last, a fifteen-to-twenty-year cycle of bloody upheaval.

Victor had written much on the subject. He'd left reports behind about everything from primate behaviour to the wars of the twentieth and twenty-first centuries. There was one that Donald found especially disturbing. It detailed how primates came of age and attempted to overthrow their fathers, the alpha males. It told of chimps that committed infanticide, males snatching the young from their mothers and taking them into the trees where their arms and legs were ripped, limb from limb, from their small bodies. Victor had written that this put the females back into oestrus. It made room for the next generation.

Donald had a hard time believing any of this was true. He had a harder time making sense of a report about frontal lobes and how long they took to develop in humans. Maybe this was important to unravelling some mystery. Or perhaps it was the ravings of a man losing his mind – or a man discovering his conscience and coming to grips with what he'd done to the world.

Donald studied his old report and searched through Victor's notes, looking for the answer. He fell into a routine that Anna had long ago perfected. They slept, ate and worked. They emptied bottles of Scotch at night, one burning sip at a time, and left them standing like factory smokestacks amid the diagram of silos. In the mornings, they took turns in the shower, Anna brazen with her nakedness, Donald wishing she wouldn't be. Her presence became an intoxicant from the past, and Donald began to assemble a new reality in his mind: he and Anna were working on one more secret project together; Helen was back in Savannah; Mick wasn't making it to the meetings; Donald couldn't raise either of them because his phone wouldn't work.

It was always that his phone didn't work. Just one text getting through on the day of the convention and Helen might be down in the deep freeze, asleep in her pod. He could visit her the way Erskine visited his daughter. They would be together again once all the shifts were over.

In another version of the same dream, Donald imagined that he was able to crest that hill and make it to the Tennessee side. Bombs exploded in the air; frightened people dived into their holes; a young girl sang with a voice so pure. In this fantasy, he and Helen disappeared into the same earth. They had children and grandchildren and were buried together.

Dreams such as these haunted him when he allowed Anna to touch him, to lie in his cot for an hour before bedtime, just the sound of her breathing, her head on his chest, the smell of alcohol on both their breaths. He would lie there and tolerate it, suffer how good it felt, her hand resting on his neck, and only fall asleep after she grew uncomfortable from the cramped quarters and moved back to her own cot.

In the morning, she would sing in the shower, steam billowing into the war room, while Donald returned to his studies. He would log on to her computer where he was able to dig through the files in Victor's personal directories. He could see when these files had been created, accessed and how often. One of the oldest and most recently opened was a list with all the silos ranked in order. Number eighteen was near the top, but it wasn't clear if this was a measure of trouble or worth. And why rank them to begin with? For what purpose?

He also used Anna's computer to search for his sister Charlotte. She wasn't listed in the pods below, nor under any name or picture that he could find. But she had been there during orientation. He remembered her being led off with the other women and being put to sleep. And now she seemed to have vanished. But to where?

So many questions. He stared at the two reports, the awful, dead sound of static leaking from the radio, the weight of all the earth above pushing down upon him, and he began to wonder, if he fixated on Victor's notes too closely, if perhaps he would reach the same conclusion.

44

• Silo 1 •

W hen he could no longer look at the notes, Donald went for what had become his customary stroll among the guns and drones in the storeroom. This was his escape from the hiss of the radio static and the cramped confines of their makeshift home, and it was during these laps that he came nearest to clearing his head from his dreams, from the prior night's bottle of Scotch, and from the mix of emotions he was beginning to feel for Anna.

Most of all, he walked those laps and tried to make sense of this new world. He puzzled over what Thurman and Victor had planned for the silos. Five hundred years below ground, and then what? Donald desperately wanted to know. And here was when he felt truly alive: when he was taking action, when he was digging for answers. It was the same fleeting sense of power he had felt from refusing their pills, from staining his fingers blue and tonguing the ulcers that formed in his cheeks.

During these aimless wanderings, he looked through the many plastic crates lining the floors and walls of the huge room. He found the one with the missing firearm, the one he assumed Victor had stolen. The airtight seal was broken and the other guns inside reeked of grease. Some crates, he discovered, contained folded uniforms and suits like astronauts wore, vacuum sealed in thick plastic; others held helmets with large domes and metal collars. There were flashlights with red lenses, food and medical kits, backpacks, rounds and rounds of ammo, and myriad other devices and gadgets he could only guess at.

He had found a laminated map in one crate, a chart of the fifty silos. There were red lines that radiated from the silos, one from each, and met at a single point in the distance. Donald had traced the lines with his finger, holding the map up to catch the light spilling from the distant office. He had puzzled over it and then put it back in its place, clues to a mystery he couldn't define.

This time, he stopped during his lap to perform a set of jumping jacks in the wide aisles between the sleeping drones. The exercise had been a struggle just two days ago, but the chill seemed to be melting from his veins. And the more he pushed himself, the more awake and alert he seemed to become. He did seventy-five, ten more than yesterday. After catching his breath, he dropped down to see how many push-ups he could do on his atrophied muscles. And it was here, on the third day of his captivity, his face barely an inch above the steel floor, that he discovered the launch lift, a garage door that barely came to his waist but was wide enough to handle the wingspan of the drones lurking beneath the tarps.

Donald rose from his push-up and approached the low door. The entire storehouse was kept incredibly dim, this wall almost pitch black. He thought about going for one of the flashlights when he saw the red handle. A tug, and the corrugated door slid up into the wall. On his hands and knees, Donald explored the cavity beyond, which went back over a dozen feet. There were no buttons or levers that he could feel along the walls, no method of operating the lift.

Curious, he crawled out to grab a flashlight. As he turned, he spotted another door along the darkened wall. Donald tried the handle and found it unlocked, a dim hallway beyond. He fumbled for a light switch and the overhead bulbs flickered hesitantly. He crept inside and pulled the door shut behind him.

The hallway ran fifty paces to a door at the far end, a pair of doors on either side. More offices, he assumed, similar to the home Anna had carved out in the back of the warehouse. He tried the first door and the odour of mothballs wafted out. Inside, there were rows of bunks, the shuffle of recent footsteps in a layer of dust, and a gap where two small beds formerly lay. The absence of people could be felt. He peeked into the door across the hall and found bathroom stalls and a cluster of showers.

The next two doors were more of the same, except for a row of urinals in the bathroom. Perhaps people had lived down there to keep up with the munitions, but Donald didn't remember anyone coming to that level during his first shift. No, these were quarters kept for another time, much like the machines beneath the tarps. He left the bathroom to the ghosts and checked the door at the end of the hall.

Inside, he found sheets of plastic thrown over tables and chairs, a fine mist of dust settled on top. Donald approached one of the tables and saw the computer display beneath the sheet. The chairs were attached to the desks, and there was something familiar about the knobs and levers. He knelt and fumbled for the edge of the plastic and peeled it up noisily.

The flight controls took him back to another life. Here was the stick his sister had called a yoke, the pedals beneath the seat she had called something else, the throttle and all the other dials and indicators. Donald remembered touring her training facility after she graduated from flight school. They had flown to Colorado for her ceremony. He remembered watching a screen just like this as her drone took to the air and joined a formation of others. He remembered the view of Colorado from the nose of her graceful machine in flight.

He glanced around the room at the dozen or so stations. The obvious need for the place slammed into him. He imagined voices in the hallway, men and women showering and chatting, towels being snapped at asses, someone looking to borrow a razor, a shift of pilots sitting at these desks where coffee could lie perfectly still in steaming mugs as death was rained down from above.

Donald returned the plastic sheet. He thought of his sister, asleep and hidden some levels below where he couldn't find her, and he wondered if she hadn't been brought there as a surprise for him at all. Maybe she had been brought as a surprise for some future *others*.

And suddenly, thinking of her, thinking of a time lost to dreams and lonely tears, Donald found himself patting his pockets in search of something. Pills. An old prescription with her name on it. Helen had forced him to see a doctor, hadn't she? And Donald suddenly knew why he couldn't forget, why their drugs didn't work on him. The realisation came with a powerful longing to find his sister. Charlotte was the why. She was the answer to one of Thurman's riddles.

45

• Silo 1 •

'I want to see her first,' Donald demanded. 'Let me see her, and then I'll tell you.'

He waited for Thurman or Dr Sneed to reply. The three of them stood in Sneed's office on the cryopod wing. Donald had bargained his way down the lift with Thurman, and now he bargained further. He suspected it was his sister's medication that explained why he couldn't forget. He would exchange this discovery for another. He wanted to know where she was, wanted to see her.

Something unspoken passed between the two men. Thurman turned to Donald with a warning. 'She will not be woken,' he said. 'Not even for this.'

Donald nodded. He saw how only those who made the laws were allowed to break them.

Dr Sneed turned to the computer on his desk. 'I'll look her up.'

'No need,' Thurman said. 'I know where she is.'

He led them out of the office and down the hall, past the main shift rooms where Donald had awoken as Troy all those years ago, past the deep freeze where he had spent a century asleep, all the way to another door just like the others.

The code Thurman entered was different; Donald could tell by the discordant four-note song the buttons made. Above the keypad in small stencilled letters he made out the words *Emergency Personnel*. Locks whirred and ground like old bones, and the door gradually opened.

Steam followed them inside, the warm air from the

hallway hitting the mortuary cool. There were fewer than a dozen rows of pods, perhaps fifty or sixty units in total, little more than a full shift. Donald peered into one of the coffin-like units, the ice a spiderweb of blue and white on the glass, and saw inside a thick and chiselled visage. A frozen soldier, or so his imagination told him.

Thurman led them through the rows and columns before stopping at one of the pods. He rested his hands on its surface with something like affection. His exhalations billowed into the air. It made his white hair and stark beard appear as though they were frosted with ice.

'Charlotte,' Donald breathed, peering in at his sister. She hadn't changed, hadn't aged a bit. Even the blue cast of her skin seemed normal and expected. He was growing used to seeing people this way.

He rubbed the small window to clear the web of frost and marvelled at his thin hands and seemingly fragile joints. He had atrophied. He had grown older while his sister had remained the same.

'I locked her away like this once,' he said, gazing in at her. 'I locked her away in my memory like this when she went off to war. Our parents did the same. She was just little Charla.'

Glancing away from her, he studied the two men on the other side of the pod. Sneed started to say something, but Thurman placed a hand on the doctor's arm. Donald turned back to his sister.

'Of course, she grew up more than we knew. She was killing people over there. We talked about it years later, after I was in office and she'd figured I'd grown up enough.' He laughed and shook his head. 'My kid sister, waiting for *me* to grow up.'

A tear plummeted to the frozen pane of glass. The salt cut through the ice and left a clear track behind. Donald wiped it away with a squeak, then felt frightened he might disturb her.

'They would get her up in the middle of the night,' he

said. 'Whenever a target was deemed . . . what did she call it? *Actionable.* They would get her up. She said it was strange to go from dreaming to killing. How none of it made sense. How she would go back to sleep and see the video feeds in her mind – that last view from an incoming missile as she guided it into its target—'

He took a breath and gazed up at Thurman.

'I thought it was good that she couldn't be hurt, you know? She was safe in a trailer somewhere, not up there in the sky. But she complained about it. She told her doctor that it didn't feel right, being safe and doing what she did. The people on the front lines, they had fear as an excuse. They had self-preservation. A reason to kill. Charlotte used to kill people and then go to the mess hall and eat a piece of pie. That's what she told her doctor. She would eat something sweet and not be able to taste it.'

'What doctor was this?' Sneed asked.

'My doctor,' Donald said. He wiped his cheek, but he wasn't ashamed of the tears. Being by his sister's side had him feeling brave and bold, less alone. He could face the past and the future, both. 'Helen was worried about my re-election. Charlotte already had a prescription, had been diagnosed with PTSD after her first tour, and so we kept filling it under her name, even under her insurance.'

Sneed waved his hand, stirring the air for more information. 'What prescription?'

'Propra,' Thurman said. 'She'd been taking propra, hadn't she? And you were worried about the press finding out that you were self-medicating.'

Donald nodded. 'Helen was worried. She thought it might come out that I was taking something for my . . . wilder thoughts. The pills helped me forget them, kept me level. I could study the Order, and all I saw were the words, not the implications. There was no fear.' He looked at his sister, understanding finally why she had refused to take the meds. She wanted the fear. It was necessary somehow, had made her feel more human.

'I remember you telling me she was on them,' Thurman said. 'We were in the bookstore—'

'Do you remember your dosage?' Sneed asked. 'How long were you on it?'

'I started taking it after I was given the Order to read.' He watched Thurman for any hint of expression and got nothing. 'I guess that was two or three years before the convention. I took them nearly every day right up until then.' He turned to Sneed. 'I would've had some on me during orientation if I hadn't lost them on the hill that day. I think I fell. I remember falling—'

Sneed turned to Thurman. 'There's no telling what the complications might be. Victor was careful to screen psychotropics from administrative personnel. Everyone was tested—'

'I wasn't,' Donald said.

Sneed faced him. 'Everyone was tested.'

'Not him.' Thurman studied the surface of the pod. 'There was a last-minute change. A switch. I vouched for him. And if he was getting them in her name, there wouldn't have been anything in his medical records.'

'We need to tell Erskine,' Sneed said. 'I could work with him. We might come up with a new formulation. This could explain some of the immunities in other silos.' He turned away from the pod as if he needed to get back to his office.

Thurman looked to Donald. 'Do you need more time down here?'

Donald studied his sister for a moment. He wanted to wake her, to talk to her. Maybe he could come back another time just to visit.

'I might like to come back,' he said.

'We'll see.'

Thurman walked around the pod and placed a hand on Donald's shoulder, gave him a light, sympathetic squeeze. He led Donald towards the door and Donald didn't glance back, didn't check the screen for his sister's new name. He didn't care. He knew where she was, and she would always be Charlotte to him. She would never change.

'You did good,' Thurman said. 'This is real good.' They stepped into the hall, and he shut the thick door behind them. 'You may have stumbled on why Victor was so obsessed with that report of yours.'

'I did?' Donald didn't see the connection.

'I don't think he was interested in what you wrote at all,' Thurman said. 'I think he was interested in *you*.'

46

• Silo 1 •

They rode the lift to the cafeteria rather than drop Donald off on fifty-four. It was almost dinnertime, and he could help Thurman with the trays. While the lights behind the level numbers blinked on and off, following their progress up the shaft, Thurman's hunch about Victor haunted him. What if Victor had only been curious about his resistance to the medication? What if there wasn't anything in that report at all?

They rode past level forty, its button winking bright and then going dark, and Donald thought of the silo that had done the same. 'What does this mean for eighteen?' he asked, watching the next number flash by.

Thurman stared at the stainless steel doors, a greasy palm print there from where someone had caught their balance.

'Vic wanted to try another reset on eighteen. I never saw the point. But maybe he was right. Maybe we give them one more chance.'

'What's involved in a reset?'

'You know what's involved.' Thurman faced him. 'It's what we did to the world, just on a smaller scale. Reduce the population, wipe the computers, their memories, try it all over again. We've done that several times before with this silo. There are risks involved. You can't create trauma without making a mess. At some point, it's simpler and safer to just pull the plug.'

'End them,' Donald said, and he saw what Victor had been up against, what he had worked to avert. He wished he could speak to the old man. Anna said Victor had spoken of him often. And Erskine had said Victor had wished people like Donald were in charge.

The lift opened on the top level. Donald stepped out and immediately felt strange to be walking among those on their shifts, to be present and at the same time removed from the day-to-day life of silo one.

He noticed that no one here looked to Thurman with deference. He was not that shift's head, and no one knew him as such. Just two men, one in white and one in beige, grabbing food and glancing at the ruined wasteland on the wall screen.

Donald took one of the trays and noticed again that most people sat facing the view. Only one or two ate with their backs to it. He followed Thurman to the lift while longing to speak to these handful, to ask them what they remembered, what they were afraid of, to tell them that it was okay to be afraid.

'Why do the other silos have screens?' he asked Thurman, keeping his voice down. The parts of the facility he'd had no hand in designing made little sense to him. 'Why show them what we did?'

'To keep them in,' Thurman said. He balanced the tray with one hand and pressed the call button on the express. 'It's not that we're showing them what we did. We're showing them what's out there. Those screens and a few taboos are all that contain these people. Humans have this disease, Donny, this compulsion to move until we bump into something. And then we tunnel through that something, or we sail over the edge of the oceans, or we stagger across mountains—'

The lift arrived. A man in reactor red excused himself and stepped between the two of them. They boarded and Thurman fumbled for his badge. 'Fear,' he said. 'Even the fear of death is barely enough to counter this compulsion of ours. If we didn't show them what was out there, they would go look for themselves. That's what we've always done as a race.'

Donald considered this. He thought about his own compulsion to escape the confines of all that pressing concrete, even if it meant death out there. The slow strangulation inside was worse.

'I'd rather see a reset than extinguish the entire silo,' Donald said, watching the numbers race by. He didn't mention that he'd been reading up on the people who lived there. A reset would mean a world of loss and heartache, but there would be a chance at life afterwards. The alternative was death for them all.

'I'm less and less eager to gas the place, myself,' Thurman admitted. 'When Vic was around, all I did was argue against wasting our time with any one silo like this. Now that he's gone, I find myself pulling for these people. It's like I have to honour his last wishes. And that's a dangerous trap to fall into.'

The lift stopped on twenty and picked up two workers, who ceased a conversation of their own and fell silent for the ride. Donald thought about this process of cleansing a silo only to watch the violence repeat itself. The great wars of old were like this. He remembered two wars in Iran, a new generation unremembering so that sons marched into the battles their fathers had already fought.

The two workers got off at the rec hall, resuming their conversation as the doors closed. Donald remembered how much he enjoyed punishing himself in the weight room. Now he was wasting away with little appetite, nothing to push against, no resistance.

'It makes me wonder sometimes if that was why he did what he did,' Thurman said. The lift slid towards fifty-four. 'Vic calculated everything. Always with a purpose. Maybe his way of winning this argument of ours was to ensure that he had the last word.' Thurman glanced at Donald. 'Hell, it's what finally motivated me to wake you.'

Donald didn't say out loud how crazy that sounded. He thought Thurman just needed some way to make sense of the unthinkable. Of course, there was another way Victor's death had ended the argument. Not for the first time, Donald imagined that it hadn't been a suicide at all. But he didn't see where such doubts could get him except in trouble.

They got off on fifty-four and carried the trays through the aisles of munitions. As they passed the drones, Donald thought of his sister, similarly sleeping. It was good to know where she was, that she was safe. A small comfort.

They ate at the table in the war room. Donald pushed his dinner around his plate while Thurman and Anna talked. The two reports sat before him – just scraps of paper, he thought. No mystery contained within. He had been looking at the wrong thing, assuming there was a clue in the words, but it was just Donald's *existence* that Victor had remarked upon. He had sat across the hall from Donald and watched him react to whatever was in their water or their pills. And now when Donald looked at his notes, all he saw was a piece of paper with pain scrawled across it amid specks of blood.

Ignore the blood, he told himself. The blood wasn't a clue. It had come after. There were several splatters in a wide space left in the notes. Donald had been studying the senseless. He had been looking for something that wasn't there. He may as well have been staring off into space.

Space. Donald set his fork down and grabbed the other report. Once he ignored the large spots of blood, there was a gap in the notes where nothing had been written. This was what he should've been focused on. Not what was there, but what wasn't.

He checked the other report – the corresponding location of that blank space – to see what was written there. When he found the right spot, his excitement vanished. It was the paragraph that didn't belong, the one about the young inductee whose great-grandmother remembered the old times. It was nothing.

Unless—

Donald sat up straight. He took the two reports and placed them on top of each other. Anna was telling Thurman about her progress with jamming the radio towers, that she would be done soon. Thurman was saying that they could all get off shift in the next few days, get the schedule back in order. Donald held the overlapping reports up to the lights. Thurman looked on curiously.

'He wrote *around* something,' Donald muttered. 'Not *over* something.'

He met Thurman's gaze and smiled. 'You were wrong.' The two pieces of paper trembled in his hands. 'There is something here. He wasn't interested in me at all.'

Anna set down her utensils and leaned over to have a look.

'If I had the original, I would've seen it straight away.' He pointed to the space in the notes, then slid the top page away and tapped his finger on the one paragraph that didn't belong. The one that had nothing to do with silo twelve at all.

'Here's why your resets don't work,' he said. Anna grabbed the bottom report and read about the shadow Donald had inducted, the one whose great-grandmother remembered the old days, the one who had asked him a question about whether those stories were true.

'Someone in silo eighteen remembers,' Donald said with confidence. 'Maybe a bunch of people, passing the knowledge in secret from generation to generation. Or they're immune like me. They remember.'

Thurman took a sip of his water. He set down the glass and glanced from his daughter to Donald. 'More reason to pull the plug,' he said.

'No,' Donald told him. 'No. That's not what Victor thought.' He tapped the dead man's notes. 'He wanted to find the one who remembers, but he didn't mean me.' He turned to Anna. 'I don't think he wanted me up at all.'

Anna looked up at her father, a puzzled expression on her face. She turned to Donald. 'What are you suggesting?'

Donald stood and paced behind the chairs, stepping over the wires that snaked across the tiles. 'We need to call eighteen and ask the head there if anyone fits this profile, someone or some group sowing discord, maybe talking about the world we—' He stopped himself from saying *destroyed*.

'Okay,' Anna said, nodding her head. 'Okay. Let's say they do know. Let's say we find these people over there like you. What then?'

He stopped his pacing. This was the part he hadn't considered. He found Thurman studying him, the old man's lips pursed.

'We find these people—' Donald said.

And he knew. He knew what it would take to save these people in this distant silo, these welders and shopkeeps and farmers and their young shadows. He remembered being the one on a previous shift to kill in order to save.

And he knew he would do it again.

47

• Silo 18 •

Mission's throat itched and his eyes stung, the smoke growing heavier and the stench stronger as he approached one-twenty and Lower Dispatch. The pursuit from above seemed to have faltered, perhaps from the gap in the rails that had claimed a life.

Cam was dead, of that he felt certain. And how many others had suffered the same fate? A twinge of guilt accompanied the sick thought that the fallen would have to be carried up to the farms in plastic bags. A porter would have to do that job, and it wouldn't be a pretty one.

He shook this thought away as he got within a level of Dispatch. Tears streamed down his face and mixed with the sweat and grime of the long day's descent. He bore bad news. A shower and clean clothes would do little to alleviate the weariness he felt, but there would be protection there, help in clearing up the confusion about the blast. He hurried down the last half-flight and remembered, perhaps due to the rising ash that reminded him of a note torn to confetti, the reason he'd been chasing after Cam in the first place.

Rodny. His friend was locked away in IT, and his plea for help had been lost in the din and confusion of the explosion.

The explosion. Cam. The package. The *delivery*.

Mission wobbled and clutched the railing for balance. He thought of the ridiculous fee for the delivery, a fee that perhaps was never meant to be paid. He gathered himself and hurried on, wondering what was going on in that locked room in IT, what kind of trouble Rodny might be in and how to help him. How, even, to *get* to him.

The air grew thick and it burned to breathe as he arrived at Dispatch. A small crowd huddled on the stairway. They peered across the landing and into the open doors of one-twenty. Mission coughed into his fist as he pushed his way through the onlookers. Had the wreckage from above landed here? Everything seemed intact. Two buckets lay on their sides near the door, and a grey fire hose snaked over the railing and trailed inside. A blanket of smoke clung to the ceiling; it trailed out and up the wall of the stairwell shaft, defying gravity.

Mission pulled his 'chief up over his nose, confused. The smoke was coming from *inside* Dispatch. He breathed in through his mouth, the fabric pressing against his lips and lessening the sting in his throat. Dark shapes moved inside the hallway. He unsnapped the strap that held his knife in place and crossed the threshold, keeping low to stay away from the smoke. The floors were wet and squished with the traffic from deeper inside. It was dark, but beams of light from flashlights danced around further down the hallway.

Mission hurried towards the lights. The smoke was thicker, the water on the floor deeper. Bits of pulp floated on the surface. He passed one of the dormitories, the sorting hall, the front offices.

Lily, an elder porter, ran by in slaps and spray, recognis-able only at the last moment as the beam from her flashlight briefly lit her face. There was someone lying in the water, pressed up against the wall. As Mission approached and a passing light played over the form, he saw that they weren't lying there at all. It was Hackett, one of the few dispatchers who treated the young shadows with respect and never seemed to take delight in their burdens. Half of his face remained unscathed, the other half was a seething red blister. Deathdays. Lottery numbers flashed in Mission's vision.

'Porter! Get over here.'

It was Morgan's voice, Mission's former caster. The old

man's cough joined a chorus of others. The hallway was full of ripples and waves, splashes and hacks, smoke and commands. Mission hurried towards the familiar silhouette, his eyes burning.

'Sir? It's Mission. The explosion—' He pointed at the ceiling.

'I know my own shadows, boy.' A light was trained on Mission's eyes. 'Get in here and give these lads a hand.'

The smell of cooked beans and burned and wet paper was overpowering. There was a hint of fuel behind it all, a smell Mission knew from the down deep and its generators. And there was something else: the smell of the bazaar during a pig roast, the foul and unpleasant odour of burned flesh.

The water in the main hall was deep. It lapped up over Mission's halfboots and filled them with muck. Drawers of files were being emptied into buckets. An empty crate was shoved into his hands, beams of light swirling in the mist, his nose burning and running, tears on his cheeks unbidden.

'Here, here,' someone said, urging him forward. They warned him not to touch the filing cabinet. Piles of paper went into the crate, heavier than they should be. Mission didn't understand the rush. The fire was out. The walls were black where the flames must have licked at them, and the grow plots along the far wall where rows of beans had run up tall trestles had turned to ash. The trestles stood like black fingers, those that stood at all.

Amanda from Dispatch was there at the filing cabinets, her 'chief wrapped around her hand, managing the drawers as they were emptied. The crate filled up fast. Mission spotted someone emptying the wall safe of its old books as he turned back towards the hallway. There was a body in the corner covered by a sheet. Nobody was in much of a hurry to remove it.

He followed the others to the landing, but they did not go all the way out. The emergency lights in the dorm room were on, mattresses stacked up in the corner. Carter, Lyn and

Joel were spreading the files out on the springs. Mission unloaded his crate and went back for another load.

'What happened?' he asked Amanda as he reached the filing cabinets. 'Is this some sort of retribution?'

'The farmers came for the beans,' she said. She used her 'chief to wrestle with another drawer. 'They came for the beans and they burned it all.'

Mission took in the wide swathe of damage. He recalled how the stairwell had trembled during the blast, could still see in his mind the people falling and screaming to their deaths. The months of growing violence had sparked alive as if a switch had been flipped.

'So what do we do now?' Carter asked. He was a powerful porter, in his early thirties, when men find their strength and have yet to lose their joints, but he looked absolutely beat. His hair clung to his forehead in wet clumps. There were black smears on his face, and you could no longer tell what colour his 'chief had been.

'Now we burn their crops,' someone suggested.

'The crops we eat?'

'Just the upper farms. They're the ones who did this.'

'We don't know who did this,' Morgan said.

Mission caught his old caster's eye. 'In the main hall,' he said. 'I saw . . . Was that . . . ?'

Morgan nodded. 'Roker. Aye.'

Carter slapped the wall and barked profanities. 'I'll kill 'em!' he yelled.

'So you're . . .' Mission wanted to say *Lower chief*, but it was too soon for that to make sense.

'Aye,' Morgan said, and Mission could tell it made little sense to him either.

'People will be carrying whatever they like for a few days,' Joel said. 'We'll appear weak if we don't strike back.' Joel was two years older than Mission and a good porter. He coughed into his fist while Lyn looked on with concern.

Mission had other concerns besides appearing weak. The

people above thought a porter had attacked them. And now this assault from the farmers, so far from where they'd been hit the night before. Porters were the nearest thing to a roaming sentry and they were being taken out by someone, purposefully, he thought. Then there were all those boys being recruited into IT. They weren't being recruited to fix computers; they were being hired to break something. The spirit of the silo, perhaps.

'I need to get home,' Mission said. It was a slip. He meant to say up top. He worked to unknot his 'chief. The thing reeked of smoke, as did his hands and his overalls. He would have to find different overalls, a different colour to wear. He needed to get in touch with his old friends from the Nest.

'What do you think you're doing?' Morgan asked. His former caster seemed ready to say something else as Mission tugged the 'chief away. Instead, the old man's eyes fell to the bright red weal around Mission's neck.

'I don't think this is about us at all,' Mission said. 'I think this is bigger than that. A friend of mine is in trouble. He's at the heart of all that's going wrong. I think something bad is going to happen to him or that he might know something. They won't let him talk to anyone.'

'Rodny?' Lyn asked. She and Joel had been two years ahead at the Nest, but they knew Mission and Rodny, both.

Mission nodded. 'And Cam is dead,' he told the others. He explained what'd happened on his way down, the blast, the people chasing him, the gap in the rails. Someone whispered Cam's name in disbelief. 'I don't think anyone cares that we know,' Mission added. 'I think that's the point. Everyone's supposed to be angry. As angry as possible.'

'I need time to think,' Morgan said. 'To plan.'

'I don't think there *is* much time,' Mission said. He told them about the new hires at IT. He told Morgan about seeing Bradley there, about the young porter applying for a different job.

'What do we do?' Lyn asked, looking to Joel and the others.

'We take it easy,' Morgan said, but he didn't seem so sure. The confidence he displayed as a senior porter and caster seemed shaken now that he was a chief.

'I can't stay down here,' Mission said flatly. 'You can have every vacation chit I own, but I've got to get up top. I don't know how, but I have to.'

48

• Silo 18 •

Before he went anywhere, Mission needed to get in touch with friends he could trust, anyone who might be able to help, the old gang from the Nest. As Morgan urged everyone on the landing back to work, Mission slunk down the dark and smoky hallway towards the sorting room, which had a computer he might be able to use. Lyn and Joel followed, more eager to find out about Rodny than to clean up after the fire.

They checked the monitor at the sorting counter and saw that the computer was down, possibly from the power outage the night before. Mission remembered all those people with their broken computers earlier that morning at IT and wondered if there would be a working machine anywhere on five levels. Since he couldn't send a wire, he picked up the hard line to the other Dispatch offices to see if they could get a message out for him.

He tried Central first. Lyn stood with him at the counter, her flashlight illuminating the dials, piercing the haze of smoke in the room. Joel splashed among the shelves, moving the reusable sorting crates on the bottom higher up to keep them from getting wet. There was no response from Central.

'Maybe the fire got the radio too,' she whispered.

Mission didn't think so. The power light was on and the speaker was making that crackling sound when he squeezed the button. He heard Morgan splash past in the hallway, yelling and complaining that his workforce was disappearing.

Lyn cupped her hand over her flashlight. 'Something is going on at Central,' he told Lyn. He had a bad feeling.

The second way station he tried up top finally won a response. 'Who's this?' someone asked, their voice shaking with barely concealed panic.

'This is Mission. Who's this?'

'Mission? You're in big trouble, man.'

Mission glanced up at Lyn. 'Who is this?'

'This is Robbie. They left me alone up here, man. I haven't heard from anybody. But everyone's looking for you. What's going on down there in Lower?'

Joel stopped with the crates and trained his flashlight on the counter.

'Everyone's looking for *me*?' Mission asked.

'You and Cam, a few of the others. There was some kind of fight at Central. Were you there for that? I can't get word from anyone!'

'Robbie, I need you to get in touch with some friends of mine. Can you send out a wire? Something's wrong with our computers down here.'

'No, ours are all kind of sideways. We've been having to use the terminal up at the mayor's office. It's the only one working.'

'The mayor's office? Okay, I need you to send a couple of wires, then. You got something to write with?'

'Wait,' Robbie said. 'These are official wires, right? If not, I don't have the authority—'

'Dammit, Robbie, this is important! Grab something to write with. I'll pay you back. They can dock me for it if they want.' Mission glanced up at Lyn, who was shaking her head in disbelief. He coughed into his fist, the smoke tickling his throat.

'All right, all right,' Robbie said. 'Who'm I sending this to? And you owe me for this piece of paper because that's all I have to write on.'

Mission let go of the transmit button to curse the kid. He thought about who would be most likely to get a wire and send it along to the others. He ended up giving Robbie three names, then told him what to write. He would have his friends meet him at the Nest, or meet each other if he couldn't make it there himself. The Nest had to be safe. Nobody would attack the school or the Crow. Once the gang was together, they could figure out what to do. Maybe the Crow would know what to do. The hardest part for Mission would be working out how to join them.

'You got all that?' he asked Robbie when the boy didn't reply.

'Yeah, yeah, man. I think you're gonna be over the character limit, though. This better come out of your pay.'

Mission shook his head in disbelief.

'Now what?' Lyn asked as he hung up the receiver.

'I need overalls,' Mission said. He splashed around the counter and joined Joel by the shelves, began searching through the nearest crates. 'They're looking for me, so I'm gonna need new colours if I'm getting up there.'

'We,' Lyn told him. '*We* need new colours. If you're going to the Nest, I'm coming with you.'

'Me too,' Joel said.

'I appreciate that,' Mission said, 'but company might make it more dangerous. We'd be more conspicuous.'

'Yeah, but they're looking for you,' Lyn said.

'Hey, we have a ton of these new whites.' Joel pulled the lid off a sorting bin. 'But they'll just make us stand out, won't they?'

'Whites?' Mission headed over to see what Joel was talking about.

'Yeah. For Security. We've been moving a ton of these lately. Came down from Garment a few days ago. No idea why they made up so many.'

Mission checked the overalls. The ones on top were covered in soot, more grey than white. There were dozens of them stacked in the sorting crate. He remembered all the new hires. It was as if they wanted half the silo dressed in white and the other half fighting one another. It made no sense. Unless the idea was to get everyone killed.

'Killed,' Mission said. He splashed down the shelves to another crate. 'I've got a better idea.' He found the right bin – he and Cam had been given one of these just a few days ago. He reached in and pulled out a bag. 'How would you two like to make some money?'

Joel and Lyn hurried over to see what he'd found and Mission held up one of the heavy plastic bags with the bright silver zipper and the hauling straps.

'Three hundred and eighty-four chits to divide between you,' he promised. 'Every chit I own. I just need you for one last tandem.'

The two porters played their lights across the object in his hands. It was a black bag. A black bag made for carrying the dead.

49

• Silo 18 •

Mission sat on the counter and worked the laces on his boots free. They were soaked, his socks as well. He shucked them off to keep the water out of the bag and to save the weight. Always a porter, thinking about weight. Lyn handed him one of the Security overalls, an extra precaution. He wiggled out of his porter blues and tugged the whites on while Lyn looked the other way. His knife he strapped back to his waist.

'You guys sure you're up for this?' he asked.

Lyn helped him slide his feet into the bag and worked the inside straps around his ankles. 'Are *you* sure?' she asked, cinching the straps.

Mission laughed, his stomach fluttering with nerves. He stretched out and let them work the top straps under his shoulders. 'Have you both eaten?'

'We'll be fine,' Joel said. 'Stop worrying.'

'If it gets late—'

'Lie your head back,' Lyn told him. She worked the zipper up from his feet. 'And don't talk unless we tell you it's okay.'

'We'll take a break every twenty or so,' Joel said. 'We'll bring you into a bathroom with us. You can stretch and get some water.'

Lyn worked the zipper up over his chest to his chin, hesitated, then kissed the pads of her fingers and touched his forehead the same way he'd seen countless loved ones and priests bless the dead. 'May your steps rise to the heavens,' she whispered.

Her wan smile caught in the spill of Joel's flashlight before the bag was sealed up over Mission's face.

'Or at least until Upper Dispatch,' Joel added.

They carried him outside and down the hall, and the porters made way for the dead. Several hands reached out and touched Mission through the black plastic, showing respect, and he fought not to flinch or cough. It felt as though the smoke was trapped in the bag with him.

Joel took the lead, which meant Mission's shoulders were pressed against his. He faced upward, his body swaying in time to their steps, the straps beneath his armpits pulling the opposite way from what he was used to. It grew more comfortable as they hit the stairs and began the long spiral up. His feet were lowered until the blood no longer pooled in his head. Lyn carried her half of his weight from several steps below.

The dark and quiet overtook him as they left the chaos of Lower Dispatch. The two porters didn't talk as some tandems might. They saved their breath and kept their thoughts to themselves. Joel set an aggressive pace. Mission could sense it in the gentle swaying of his body, suspended above the steel treads.

As the steps passed, the journey grew more and more uncomfortable. It wasn't the difficulty breathing, for he had been shadowed well to manage his lungs on a long climb. He could also handle the stuffiness from the plastic pressed against his face. Nor was it the dark, for his favourite hour for porting had always been the dim-time, time alone with his thoughts while others slept. It wasn't the stench of plastic and smoke, the tickle in his throat or the pain of the straps.

It was the act of lying still. Of being carried. Of being a burden.

The straps pinched his shoulders until his arms fell numb, and he swayed in the darkness, the sounds of boots on steel, of Joel and Lyn's heavy breathing, as he was lifted up the stairwell. *Too great a burden*, he thought.

He thought of his mother carrying him for all those

months with no one to confide in and no one to support her. Not until his father had found out, and by then it was too late to terminate the pregnancy. He wondered how long his father had hated the bulge in her belly, how long he had wanted to cut Mission out like some kind of cancer. Mission had never asked to be carried like that. And he had never wanted to be ported by anyone ever again.

Two years ago to the day. That was the last time he had felt this, this sense of being a burden to all. Two years since he had proved too much for even a rope to bear.

It was a poor knot he had tied. But his hands had been trembling and he had fought to see the knot through a film of tears. When it failed, the knot didn't come free so much as slide, and it left his neck afire and bleeding. His great regret was having jumped from the lower stairwell in Mechanical, the rope looped over the pipes above. If he had gone from a landing, the slipping knot wouldn't have mattered. The fall would've claimed him.

Now he was too scared to try again. He was as scared of trying again as he was of being a burden to another. Was that why he avoided seeing Allie, because she longed to care for him? To help support him? Was that why he ran away from home?

The tears finally came. His arms were pinned, so he couldn't wipe them away. He thought of his mother, about whom he could only piece together a few details. But he knew this of her: she hadn't been afraid of life or death. She had embraced both in an act of sacrifice, giving her own blood for his, a trade he would never feel worthy of.

The silo spun slowly around him; the steps sank one at a time; and Mission endured the suffering. He laboured not to sob, seeing himself for the first time in that utter darkness, knowing his soul more fully in that deathly ritual of being ported to his grave, this sad awakening on his birthday.

50

• Silo 1 •

Finding one among ten thousand should've been more difficult. It should have taken months of crawling through reports and databases, of querying the head of eighteen and asking for personality profiles, of looking at arrest histories, cleaning schedules, who was related to whom, and all the gossip and chatter compiled from monthly reports.

But Donald found an easier way. He simply searched the database for a facsimile of *himself*.

One who remembered. One full of fear and paranoia. One who tries to blend in but is subversive. He looked for a fear of doctors, teasing out those residents who never went to see them. He looked for someone who shunned medication and found one who did not even trust the water. A part of him expected he might find several people to be causing so much havoc, a pack, and that locating one among them would lead to the rest. He expected to find them young and outraged with some way of handing down what they knew from generation to generation. What he found instead was both eerily similar and not like him at all.

The next morning, he showed his results to Thurman, who stood perfectly still for a long while.

'Of course,' he finally said. 'Of course.'

A hand on Donald's shoulder was all the congratulations he got. Thurman explained that the reset was well underway. He admitted that it had been underway since Donald had been woken, that the head of eighteen had taken on new recruits, had sown the seeds of discord. Erskine and Dr Sneed were working through the night to make changes, to come up with a new formulation, but this component might take weeks. Looking over what Donald had found, he said he was going to make a call to eighteen.

'I want to come with you,' Donald said. 'It's my theory after all.'

What he wanted to say was that he wouldn't take the coward's way. If someone was to be executed on his account – one life for the sake of many – he didn't want to hide from the decision.

Thurman agreed.

They rode the lift almost as equals. Donald asked why Thurman had started the reset, but he thought he knew the answer.

'Vic won,' was Thurman's reply.

Donald thought of all the lives in the database that were now thrown into chaos. He made the mistake of asking how the reset was going, and Thurman told him about the bombs and the violence, how the groups who wore different colours were warring with one another, how these things typically went downhill fast with the barest of nudges, that the formula was as old as time.

'The combustibles are always there,' Thurman said. 'You'd be surprised at how few sparks it takes.'

They exited the lift and walked down a familiar hallway. This was Donald's old commute. Here, he had worked under a different name. He had worked without knowing what he was doing. They passed offices full of people tapping on keyboards and chatting with one another. Half a millennium of people coming on and off shifts, doing what they were told, following orders.

He couldn't help himself as they approached his old office: he paused at the door and peered in. A thin man with a halo of hair that wrapped from ear to ear, just a few wisps on top, looked up at him. He sat there, mouth agape, hand resting on his mouse, waiting for Donald to say or do something.

Donald nodded a sympathetic hello. He turned and

looked through the door across the hall where a man in white sat behind a similar desk. The puppeteer. Thurman spoke to him, and he got up from his desk and joined them in the hall. He knew that Thurman was in charge.

Donald followed the two of them to the comm room, leaving the balding man at his old desk to his game of solitaire. He felt a mix of sympathy and envy for the man – for those who didn't remember. As they turned the corner, Donald thought back to those initial bouts of awareness on his first shift. He remembered speaking with a doctor who knew the truth, and having this sense of wonder that anyone could cope with such knowledge. And now he saw that it wasn't that the pain grew tolerable or the confusion went away. Instead, it simply became familiar. It became a part of you.

The comm room was quiet. Heads swivelled as the three of them entered. One of the operators in orange hurriedly removed his feet from his desk. Another took a bite of his protein bar and turned back to his station.

'Get me eighteen,' Thurman said.

Eyes turned to the other man in white, the one supposedly in charge, and he waved his consent. A call was patched through. Thurman held half a headset to one ear while he waited. He caught the expression on Donald's face and asked the operator for another set. Donald stepped forward and took it while the cable was slotted into the receiver. He could hear the familiar beeping of a call being placed, and his stomach fluttered as doubts began to surface. Finally, a voice answered. A shadow.

Thurman asked him to get Mr Wyck, the silo head.

'He's already coming,' the shadow said.

When Wyck joined the conversation, Thurman told the head what Donald had discovered, but it was the shadow who responded. The shadow knew the one they were after. He said he knew the person well. There was something in his voice, some shock or hesitation, and Thurman waved at the operator to get the sensors in his headset going. Suddenly, the monitors were providing feedback like a Rite of Initiation. Thurman conducted the questioning and Donald watched a master at work.

'Tell me what you know,' he said. Thurman leaned over the operator and peered at a screen that monitored skin conductivity, pulse and perspiration. Donald was no expert at reading the charts, but he knew something was up by the way the lines spiked up and down when the shadow spoke. He feared for the young man. He wondered if someone would die then and there.

But Thurman took a softer approach. He got the boy speaking of his childhood, had him admitting to the rage he harboured, a sense of not belonging. The shadow spoke of an upbringing both ideal and frustrating, and Thurman was like a gentle but firm drill sergeant working with a troubled recruit: tearing him down, building him back up.

'You've been fed the truth,' he told the young man, referring to the Legacy. 'And now you see why the truth must be divvied out carefully or not at all.'

'I do.'

The shadow sniffed as though he were crying. And yet: the jagged lines on the screen formed less precipitous peaks, less dangerous valleys.

Thurman spoke of sacrifice, of the greater good, of individual lives proving meaningless in the far stretch of time. He took that shadow's rage and redirected it until the torture of being locked up for months with the books of the Legacy was distilled down to its very essence. And through it all, it didn't sound as though the silo head breathed once.

'Tell me what needs to be fixed,' Thurman said, after their discussion. He laid the problem at the shadow's feet. Donald saw how this was better than simply handing him the solution.

The shadow spoke of a culture forming that overvalued individuality, of children that wanted to get away from their families, of generations living levels apart and independence stressed until no one relied on anyone and everyone was dispensable.

The sobs came. Donald watched as Thurman's face tightened, and he wondered again if he was about to see the young man put out of his misery. Instead, Thurman released the radio and said to those gathered around, simply, 'He's ready.'

And what started as an inquiry, a test of Donald's theory, concluded this boy's Rite of Initiation. A shadow became a man. Lines on a screen settled into steel cords of resolve as his anger was given a new focus, a new purpose. His childhood was seen differently. Dangerously.

Thurman gave this young man his first order. Mr Wyck congratulated the boy and told him he would be allowed to go, would be given his freedom. And later, as Donald and Thurman rode the lift back towards Anna, Thurman declared that in the years to come, this Rodny would make a fine silo head. Even better than the last.

51

• Silo 1 •

That afternoon, Donald and Anna worked to restore order to the war room. They made it ready in case it was called upon in a future shift. All their notes were taken off the walls and filed away into airtight plastic crates, and Donald imagined these would sit on another level somewhere, in another storeroom, to gather dust. The computers were unplugged, all the wiring coiled up, and these were hauled off by Erskine on a cart with squeaky wheels. All that was left were the cots, a change of clothes and the standard-issue toiletries. Enough to get them through the night and to their meeting with Dr Sneed the following day.

Several shifts were about to come to a close. For Anna and Thurman, it had been a long time coming. Two full shifts. Almost a year awake. Erskine and Sneed would need a few weeks to finish their work, and by that time the next head would come on, and the schedule would return to normal. For Donald, it had been less than a week awake after a century of sleep. He was a dead man who had blinked his eyes open for a brief moment.

He took his last shower and his first dose of the bitter drink so that no one would think anything was amiss. But Donald didn't plan on going under again. If he went back to the deep freeze, he knew they would never wake him again. Unless things were so bad that he wouldn't want to be woken anyway. Unless it were Anna once more, lonely, wishing for company and willing to subject him to abuse in order to get it.

That wasn't sleep. That was a body and a mind stored

away. There were other choices, more final escapes. Donald had discovered this resolve by following the trail of clues left behind by Victor, and he would soon join him in death.

He walked a final lap amid the guns and drones before finally retiring to his cot. He thought of Helen as he lay there listening to Anna sing in the shower one last time. And he realised the anger he had felt for his wife having lived and loved without him had now dissipated, wiped away by his guilt for coming to find solace in Anna's embrace. And when she came to him that night, straight from the shower with water beading on her flesh, he could not resist any longer. They had the same bitter drink on their breath, that concoction that prepped their veins for the deep sleep, and neither of them cared. Donald succumbed. And then he waited until she had returned to her cot and her breathing had softened before he cried himself to sleep.

When he woke, Anna was already gone, her cot neatly made. Donald did the same, tucking the sheets beneath the mattress and leaving the corners crisp, even though he knew the sheets would be mussed as the cots were returned to their rightful place in the barracks. He checked the time. Anna had been put under during the early morning so as not to be spotted. He had less than an hour before Thurman would come for him. More than enough time.

He went out to the storeroom and approached the drone nearest the hangar door. Yanking the tarp off sent a cloud of dust into the air. He dragged out the empty bin from under one of the wings, opened the low hangar door, and arranged the bin so that it was slightly inside the lift. He lowered the door onto the bin to keep the hangar open.

Hurrying down the hallway, past the empty barracks, he pulled the plastic sheet off the station at the very end. Flipping the plastic cover off the lift switch, he threw it into the up position. The first time he'd done this, the door to the lift would no longer open, but he could hear the platform rumbling upward on the other side of the wall. It hadn't taken long to figure out a solution.

Replacing the plastic sheet, he hurried down the hall, turned the light off and shut the door. He pulled the other bin from under the drone's left wing. Donald stripped and tossed his clothes under the drone. He pulled the thick plastic suit from the bin and sat down to work his feet into the legs. The boots went on next, Donald being careful to seal the cuffs around them. Standing up, he gripped the dangling shoelace stolen from an extra boot. The end had been tied to the zipper on the back of the suit. He pulled it over his shoulder and tugged upward, made sure the zipper went to the top before grabbing the gloves, flashlight and helmet from the bin.

Suited up, he closed the bin and slid it back under the wing, covered the drone with the tarp. There would only be a single bin out of place when Thurman arrived. Victor had left a mess to discover. Donald would hardly leave a trace.

He crawled inside the lift, pushing the flashlight ahead of him. He could hear the motor straining against the pinned bin like an angry hive of bees. Turning on the flashlight, he took a last look at the storeroom, braced himself, then kicked the plastic tub with both boots.

It budged. He kicked again and there was a thunderous racket as the door slammed shut, and then the shudder of movement. The flashlight jittered and danced. Donald corralled it between his mitts and watched his exhalations fog the inside of his helmet. He had no idea what to expect, but he was causing it. He would control his own fate.

52

• Silo 1 •

The ride up took much longer than he anticipated. There were moments when he wasn't sure whether or not he was moving. He grew worried that his plan had been discovered, that the misplaced bin had led them to his tracks in the dust, that he was being recalled. He urged the lift to hurry along.

His flashlight gave out. Donald tapped the cylinder in his mitt and worked the switch back and forth. It must've been on a weak charge from its long storage. He was left in the dark, no way of knowing which way was up or down, whether he was rising or falling. All he could do was wait. He knew that this was the right decision. There was nothing worse than being trapped in the darkness, in that pod, unable to do anything more than wait.

Arrival came with a jarring clank. The persistent hum of the motor disappeared, the ensuing quiet haunting. There was a second clank, and then the door opposite the one he'd entered rose slowly. A metal attachment the size of a fist slid forward on a track. Donald scrambled after this, seeing how the drone might be guided forward.

He found himself in a sloping launch bay. He hadn't known what to expect, thought maybe he'd simply arrive above the soil on a barren landscape. But he was in a shaft. Above him, up the slope, a slit was opening, a dim light growing stronger. Beyond this slit, Donald spotted the roiling clouds he knew from the cafeteria. They were the bright grey that came with the sunrise. The doors at the top of the slope continued to slide apart like a maw opening wide.

Donald crawled up the steep slope as quickly as he could. The metal car in the track stopped and locked into place. Donald hurried, imagining he didn't have much time. He stayed off the track in case the launch sequence was automated, but the car never moved, never raced by. He arrived at the open doors exhausted and perspiring and pulled himself out.

The world spread out before him. After a week of living in a windowless chamber, the scale and openness were inspiring. Donald felt like tearing off his helmet and sucking in deep breaths. The oppressive weight of his silo imprisonment had been lifted. Above him were only clouds.

He stood on a round concrete platform. Behind the opening for the launch ramp was a cluster of antennae. He went to these, held on to one of them and lowered himself to the wide ledge below. From here it was a scramble on his belly, trying to hold on to the slick edge with bulky gloves, and then a graceless drop to the dirt.

He scanned the horizon for the city – had to work his way around the tower to find it. From there, he aimed forty-five degrees to the left. He had studied the maps to make sure, but now that he was there, he realised he could've done it by memory. Over there was where the tents had stood, and here the stage, and beyond them the dirt tracks through the struggling beginnings of grass as ATVs buzzed up the hillside. He could almost smell the food that'd been cooking, could hear the dogs barking and children playing, the anthems in the air.

Donald shook off thoughts of the past and made his time count. He knew there was a chance – a very good chance – that someone was sitting at breakfast in the cafeteria. At this very moment, they would be dropping their spoon and pointing at the wall screen. But he had a head start. They would have to wrestle with suits and wonder if the risk was worth it. By the time they got to him, it would be too late. Hopefully, they would simply leave him be.

He worked his way up the hillside. Movement was a struggle inside the bulky suit. He slipped and fell several times in the slick soil. When a gust of wind hammered the landscape, it peppered his helmet with grit and made a noise like the hiss of Anna's radio. There was no telling how long the suit would last. He knew enough of the cleaning to suspect it wouldn't be for ever, but Anna had told him that the machines in the air were designed to attack only certain things. That's why they didn't destroy the sensors, or the concrete, or a properly built suit. And he suspected the suits in silo one would have been built properly.

All he hoped for as he laboured up the hill was a view. He was so obsessed and determined to win this that he never thought to look behind him, slipping and scrambling, crawling on his hands and knees the last fifty feet, until he was finally at the summit. He stood and staggered forward, exhausted, breathing heavily. Reaching the edge, he peered down into the adjacent bowl. There, a concrete tower stood like a gravestone, like a monument to Helen. She was buried beneath that tower. And while he could never go to her, never be buried alongside her, he could lie down underneath the clouds and be close enough.

He wanted his helmet off. First, though, his gloves. He tugged one of them free – popping the seal – and dropped it to the soil. The heavy winds sent the glove tumbling down the slope, and the swirling grit stung his hand. The peppering of fine particles burned like a day on a windy beach. Donald began tugging on his other glove, resigned to what would come next, when suddenly he felt a hand grip his shoulder – and he was pulled back from the edge of that gentle rise and the view of his wife's last resting place.

53

• Silo 1 •

D onald stumbled and fell. The shock of being touched sent his heart into his throat. He waved his arms to free himself but someone had a grip on his suit. More than one person. They dragged him back until he could no longer see beyond the ridge.

Screams of frustration filled his helmet. Couldn't they see that it was too late? Couldn't they leave him be? He flailed and tried to lunge out of their grip, but he was being pulled inexorably down the hill, back towards silo one.

When he fell the next time, he was able to roll over and face them, to get his arms up to defend himself. And there was Thurman standing over him – wearing nothing more than his white overalls, dust from the dead earth gathering in the old man's grey brow.

'It's time to go!' Thurman yelled into the heavy wind. His voice seemed as distant as the clouds.

Donald kicked his feet and tried to crawl back up the hill but there were three of them there, blocking his way. All in white, squinting against the ferocity of the driving wind and pelting soil.

Donald screamed as they seized him again. He tried to grab rocks and fistfuls of soil as they pulled him along by his boots. His helmet knocked against the lifeless pack of dirt. He watched the clouds boil overhead as his fingernails were bent back and broken in his struggle for some purchase.

By the time they got him to the flats, Donald was spent. They carried him down a ramp and through the airlock where more men were waiting. His helmet was tossed aside before the outer door fully shut. Thurman stood in a far corner and watched as they undressed him. The old man dabbed at the blood running from his nose. Donald had caught him with his boot.

Erskine was there, Dr Sneed as well, both of them breathing hard. As soon as they got his suit off, Sneed plunged a needle into Donald's flesh. Erskine held his hand and seemed sad as the liquid spread through Donald's veins.

'A bloody waste,' someone said as the fog settled over him.

'Look at this mess.'

Erskine placed a hand on Donald's cheek as Donald drifted deeper into the black. His lids grew heavy and his hearing distant.

'Be better if someone like you were in charge,' he heard Erskine say.

But it was Victor's voice he heard. It was a dream. No, a memory. A thought from an earlier conversation. Donald couldn't be sure. The waking world of boots and angry voices was too busy being swallowed by the mist of sleep and the fog of dreams. And this time – rather than with a fear of death – Donald went into that darkness gladly. He embraced it, hoping it would be eternal. He went with a final thought of his sister, of those drones beneath their tarps, all those things he hoped would never be woken.

54

• Silo 18 •

Mission felt buried alive. He fell into an uncomfortable trance, the bag growing hot and slick as it trapped his heat and exhalations. Part of him feared he would pass out in there and Joel and Lyn would discover him dead. Part of him hoped.

The two porters were stopped for questioning on one-seventeen, the landing below the blast that took Cam. Those working to repair the stairwell were on the lookout for a certain porter. Their description was part Cam, part Mission. Mission held deathly still while Joel complained of being stopped with so sensitive and heavy a load. It seemed that they might ask for the bag to be opened, but there were some things nearly as taboo as talk of the outside. And so they were sent on their way with a warning that the rail was out above and that one person had already fallen to their death.

Mission fought off a coughing fit as the voices receded below. He wiggled his shoulders and struggled to cover his mouth to muffle the sound. Lyn hissed at him to be quiet. In the distance, Mission could hear a woman wailing. They passed through the wreckage from hours earlier, and Joel and Lyn gasped at the sight of an entire landing torn free from the stairwell.

Above Supply, on one-zero-seven, they carried Mission into a bathroom, opened the bag and let him work the blood back into his arms. Mission used one of the stalls, took a few sips of water and assured Joel and Lyn that he was fine in there. All three of them were damp with sweat, and there were still thirty-odd levels to go to Central Dispatch. Joel especially seemed weary from the climb, or perhaps from seeing the damage wrought by the blast. Lyn was holding up better but was anxious to get going again. She fretted for Rodny and seemed as eager as Mission to get to the Nest.

Mission caught a glance of himself in the mirror with his white overalls and his porter's knife strapped to his waist. He was the one they were looking for. He drew his knife, held a handful of his hair and cut through a clump close to his scalp. Lyn saw what he was doing and helped with her own knife. Joel grabbed the trash can from the corner to collect the hair.

It was a rough job, but he looked less like the one they wanted. Before putting his knife away, he cut a few slits in the black bag, right by the zipper. He peeled off his undershirt and wiped the inside of the bag dry before throwing the shirt in the trash can. It reeked of smoke and sweat anyway. Crawling back inside, helping with the straps, they zipped him up and carried him back to the stairway to resume their ascent. Mission was powerless to do anything but worry.

He ran over the events of a very long day. That morning, he had watched the clouds brighten over breakfast, had visited the Crow and delivered her note to Rodny. And then Cam – he had lost a friend. The exhaustion of it all caught up with him and Mission found himself sliding into unconsciousness.

When he started awake, it felt but a moment later. His overalls were damp, the inside of the bag slick with condensation. Joel must have felt him jerk, as he quickly shushed Mission and told him they were coming up on Central.

Mission's heart pounded as he came to and remembered where he was, what they were doing. It felt difficult to breathe. The slits he had cut were lost in the folds of the plastic. He wanted the zipper cracked, just a slice of light, a whisper of fresh air. His arms were pinned and numb from the straps around his shoulders. His ankles were sore from where Lyn was hoisting him from below.

'Can't breathe,' he gasped.

Lyn told him to be quiet. But there was a pause, an end to the swaying. Someone fumbled with the bag over his head, a series of tiny clicks from the zipper being lowered a dozen notches.

Mission sucked in cool gasps. The world resumed its swaying, boots striking the stairs in the distance – a commotion somewhere above or below, he couldn't tell. More fighting. More dying. He pictured bodies spinning through the air. He saw Cam leaving the farm sublevels just the day before, a bonus in his pocket, no thought of how little time he had left for spending it.

They rested at Central Dispatch. Mission was let out in the main hallway, which was frighteningly empty. 'What the hell happened here?' Lyn asked. She dug her finger into a hole in the wall surrounded by a spiderweb of cracks. There were hundreds of holes like them. Boots rang on the landing and continued past.

'What time is it?' Mission asked, keeping his voice down.

'It's after dinner,' Joel said. It meant they were making good time.

Down the hall, Lyn studied a dark patch of what looked to be rust. 'Is this blood?' she hissed.

'Robbie said he couldn't reach anyone down here,' Mission said. 'Maybe they scattered.'

Joel took a sip from his canteen. 'Or were driven off.' He wiped his mouth with his sleeve.

'Should we stay here for the night? You two look beat.'

Joel shook his head. He offered Mission his canteen. 'I think we need to get past the thirties. Security is everywhere. Hell, you could probably dash up with what you've got on the way they're running about. Might need to clean up your hair a bit.'

Mission rubbed his scalp and thought about that. 'Maybe I should,' he said. 'I could be up there before the dim-time.' He watched as Lyn disappeared into one of the bunk rooms down the hall. She emerged almost immediately with her hand over her mouth, her eyes wide.

'What is it?' Mission asked, pushing up from a crouch and joining her.

She threw her arms around him and held him away from the door, buried her face into his shoulder. Joel risked a look.

'No,' he whispered.

Mission pulled away from Lyn and joined his fellow porter by the door.

The bunks were full. Some lay sprawled on the floor, but it was obvious by the tangle of their limbs – the way arms hung useless from bunks or were twisted beneath them – that these porters weren't sleeping.

They discovered Katelyn among them. Lyn shook with silent sobs as Joel and Mission retrieved Katelyn's body and loaded her into the bag. Mission felt a pang of guilt that she'd been chosen as much for her size as how well loved she'd been. While they were securing the straps and zipping her up, the power in the hallway went out, leaving them in the pitch black.

'What the hell?' Joel hissed.

A moment later, the lights returned but flickered as though an unsteady flame burned in each bulb. Mission wiped the sweat from his forehead and wished he still had his 'chief.

'If you can't make it all the way to the Nest tonight,' he said to the others, 'stop and stay at the way station and check on Robbie.'

'We'll be fine,' Joel assured him.

Lyn squeezed his arm before he went. 'Watch your steps,' she said.

'And you,' Mission told them.

He hurried towards the landing and the great stairway beyond. Overhead, the lights flickered like little flames. A sign that something, somewhere, was burning.

55

• Silo 18 •

Mission hurried upbound amid a fog of smoke, his throat on fire. An explosion in Mechanical was whispered to have been the reason for the blackout. Talk swirled of a bent or broken shaft and that the silo was on backup power. He heard such things from half a spiral away as he took the steps two and sometimes three at a time. It felt good to be out and moving, good to have his muscles aching rather than sitting still, to be his own burden.

And he noticed that when anyone saw him, they either fell silent or scattered beyond their landings, even those he knew. At first, he feared it was from recognition. But it was the Security white he wore. Young men just like him thundered up and down the stairwell terrorising everyone. Only yesterday, they had been farmers, welders and pumpmen – now they brought order with their dark weapons.

More than once, a group of them stopped Mission and asked where he was going, where his rifle was. He told them that he had been a part of the fighting below and was reporting back. It was something he'd heard another claim. Many of them seemed to know as little as he did and so they let him pass. As ever, the colour you wore said everything. People thought they could know you at a glance.

The activity grew thicker near IT. A group of new recruits filed past, and Mission watched over the railing as they kicked in the doors to the level below and stormed inside. He heard screams and then a sharp bang like a heavy steel rod falling to metal decking. A dozen of these bangs, and then less screaming.

His legs were sore, a stitch in his side, as he approached the farms. He caught sight of a few farmers out on the landing with shovels and rakes. Someone yelled something as he passed. Mission quickened his pace, thinking of his father and brother, seeing the wisdom for once in his old man's unwillingness to leave that patch of dirt.

After what seemed like hours of climbing, he reached the quiet of the Nest. The children were gone. Most families were probably holed up in their apartments, cowering together, hoping this madness would pass like others had. Down the hall, several lockers stood open, and a child's backpack lay on the ground. Mission staggered forward on aching legs towards the sound of a familiar, singing voice and the horrid screech of steel on tile.

At the end of the hall, her door stood as welcome and open as always. The singing came from the Crow, whose voice seemed stronger than usual. Mission saw that he wasn't the first to arrive, that his wire had gone out. Frankie and Allie were there, both in the green and white of farm security. They were arranging desks while Mrs Crowe sang. The sheets had been thrown off the stacks of desks kept in storage along one wall. Those desks now filled the classroom the way Mission remembered from his youth. It was as though the Crow were expecting them to be filled at any time.

Allie was the first to notice Mission's arrival. She turned and spotted him at the door, her bright eyes shining amid her farmer freckles, her dark hair tied back in a bun. She rushed over, and Mission saw how her overalls were bunched up around her boots, the straps knotted at her shoulders to make them shorter. They must've been Frankie's overalls. As she threw herself into his arms, he wondered what the two of them had risked to meet him there.

'Mission, my boy.' Mrs Crowe stopped her singing, smiled and waved him by her side. After a moment, Allie reluctantly loosened her grip.

Mission shook Frankie's hand and thanked him for coming. It took a moment to realise something was different, that his hair had been cut short as well. They both rubbed their scalps and laughed. Humour came easy in humourless times.

'What is this I hear about my Rodny?' the Crow asked. Her chair twitched back and forth, her hand working the controls, her faded blue nightgown tucked under her narrow bones.

Mission drew a deep breath, smoke lingering in his lungs, and told them everything he had seen on the stairwell, about the bombs and the fires and what he had heard of Mechanical, the security forces armed with rifles – until the Crow dispelled his frenzied chatter with a wave of her frail arms.

'Not the fighting,' she said. 'The fighting I've seen. I could paint a picture of the fighting and hang it from my walls. What of Rodny? What of our boy? Has he got them? Has he made them pay?' She made a small fist and held it aloft.

'No,' Mission said. 'Got who? He needs our help.'

The Crow laughed, which took him aback. He tried to explain. 'I gave him your note, and he passed me one in return. It begged for help. They have him locked up behind these great steel doors—'

'Not locked up,' the Crow said.

'—like he'd done something wrong—'

'Something *right*,' she said, correcting him.

Mission fell silent. He could see knowledge shining behind her old eyes, a sunrise on the day after a cleaning.

'Rodny is in no danger,' she said. 'He is with the old books. He's with the people who took the world from us.'

Allie squeezed Mission's arm. 'She's been trying to tell us,' she whispered. 'Everything's going to be okay. Come, help with the desks.'

'But the note . . .' Mission said, wishing he hadn't turned it to confetti.

'The note you gave him was to give him strength. To let him know it was time to begin. Our boy is in a place to hurt them good for what they've done.' There was a wildness in the Crow's eyes.

'No,' Mission said. 'Rodny was afraid. I know my friend, and he was afraid of something.'

The Crow's face hardened. She relaxed her fist and smoothed the front of her faded dress. 'If that be the case,' she said, her voice trembling, 'then I judged him most wrongly.'

56

• Silo 18 •

The dim-time approached while they arranged desks and the Crow resumed her singing. Allie told him a curfew had been announced, and so Mission lost hope that the others would show up that night. They pulled out mats from the cubbies to rest and plan, and decided to give the others until daybreak. There was much Mission wanted to ask the Crow, but she seemed distracted, her thoughts elsewhere, possessed with a joyousness that made her giddy.

Frankie felt certain he could get them through security and deeper into IT if only he could reach his father. Mission told them how well he'd been able to move about with the whites on. Maybe he could reach Frankie's dad in a pinch. Allie produced fresh fruits harvested from her plot and passed them around. The Crow drank one of her dark green concoctions. Mission grew restless.

He wandered out to the landing, torn between waiting for the others and his anxiety to get going. For all he knew, Rodny was being marched up to his death already. Cleanings tended to settle people down, to follow bouts of unrest, but this was unlike any of the spates of violence he had seen before. This was the burning his father spoke of, the embers of distrust and crumbling trade that jumped up all at once. He had seen this coming, but it had approached with the swiftness of a knife plummeting from the up top.

Out on the landing, he heard the sounds of a mob echoing from far below. Holding the landing rail, he could feel the hum of marching boots. He returned to the others and said nothing of it. There was no reason to suspect those boots were coming for them.

Allie looked as though she'd been crying when he got back. Her eyes were moist, her cheeks flushed. The Crow was telling them an Old Time story, her hands painting a scene in the air.

'Is everything all right?' Mission asked.

Allie shook her head as if she'd rather not say.

'What is it?' he said. He held her hand, heard the Crow speaking of Atlantis, another tale of the crumbling and lost city of magic beyond the hills, a bygone day when those ruins shone like a wet dime.

'Tell me,' he said. He wondered if the stories were affecting her the way they sometimes did him, making her sad and not knowing why.

'I didn't want to say anything until after,' she cried, fresh tears welling up. She wiped them away and the Crow fell silent, her hands dropping into her lap. Frankie sat quietly. Whatever it was, the two of them knew as well.

'Father,' Mission said. It had to do with his father. He was gone, he knew it instantly. Allie was close to his father in a way that Mission had never been. And suddenly, he felt a powerful regret for ever having left home. While she wiped her eyes, the words unable to form on her trembling lips, Mission imagined himself on his hands and knees, in the dirt, digging for forgiveness.

Allie bawled, and the Crow hummed a tune of above-ground days. Mission thought of his father, gone, all he longed to say, and wanted nothing more than to hurl himself at the posters on the walls, to tear them down and rip to shreds their urgings to go and be free.

'It's Riley,' Allie finally said. 'Mish, I'm so sorry.'

The Crow ceased her humming. All three of them watched him.

'No,' Mission whispered.

'You shouldn't have told him—' Frankie began.

'He ought to know!' Allie demanded. 'His father would want him to know.'

Mission gazed at a poster of green hills and blue skies. That world blurred with tears as surely as it might with dust. 'What happened?' he whispered.

She told him that there'd been an attack on the farms. Riley had begged to go and help fight, had been told no, and had then disappeared. He'd been found with a knife from the kitchen still clutched in his hands.

Mission stood and paced the room, tears splashing from his cheeks. He shouldn't have left. He should have been there. He hadn't been there for Cam, either. Death preceded him in all the places he couldn't be. He had done the same to his mother. And now the end was coming for them all.

A rumble grew from the landing and filled the hallway – the sound of approaching boots. Mission wiped his cheeks. He had given up on any of the others coming and thought it might be Security with their guns. They would ask him where his own gun was before realising he was an impostor, before shooting them all.

He pushed the door shut, saw that the Crow had no lock on the thing, and wedged a desk under the handle. Frankie hurried to Allie, told her to get behind the Crow's desk. He grabbed the back of the Crow's wheelchair – the overhead wire swinging dangerously – but she insisted she could manage herself, that there was nothing to be afraid of.

Mission knew better. This was Security coming for them – Security or some other mob. He'd travelled the stairwell, knew what was out there.

There was a knock on the door. The handle jiggled. The boots outside quietened as they gathered around. Frankie pressed his finger to his lips, his eyes wide. The wire overhead creaked as it swung back and forth.

The door budged. Mission hoped for a moment that they would go away, that they were just making their rounds. He thought about hiding under the sheets used to cover the desks, but the thought came too late. The door was shoved open, a desk screeching as it skittered across the floor. The first person through was Rodny.

His appearance was as sudden and jarring as a slapped cheek. Rodny wore white overalls with the creases still in them. His hair had been cut short, his face newly shaved, a nick on his chin.

Mission felt as though he were staring into a mirror, the two of them in costume. More men in white crowded behind Rodny in the hallway, rifles in hand. Rodny ordered them back and stepped into the room where all those empty desks lay neatly arranged.

Allie was the first to respond. She gasped with surprise and hurried forward, arms wide as if for an embrace. Rodny held up a palm and told her to stop. His other hand held a small gun, the same the deputies wore. His eyes were not on his friends but on the Old Crow.

'Rodny—' Mission began. His brain attempted to grasp his friend's presence. They had all come together to rescue him, but he looked in little need of it.

'The door,' Rodny said over his shoulder.

A man twice Rodny's age hesitated before doing as he was asked and pulling the door shut. This was not the demeanour of a prisoner. Frankie lurched forward before the door shut all the way, calling 'Father!' as if he'd seen his old man in the hall with the others.

'We were coming for you,' Mission said. He wanted to approach his friend, but there was something dangerous in Rodny's eyes. 'Your note—'

Rodny finally looked away from the Crow.

'We were coming to help—' Mission said.

'Yesterday, I needed it,' Rodny said. He circled around the desks, the gun at his side, his eyes flicking from face to face. Mission backed up and joined Allie in standing close to the Crow – whether to protect her or feel protected, he couldn't say.

'You shouldn't be here,' Mrs Crowe said with a lecturing tone. 'This is not where your fight is. You should be hurting *them.*' A thin finger pointed at the door.

The gun in Rodny's hand rose a little.

'What're you doing?' Allie asked, her wide eyes on the gun.

Rodny pointed at the Crow. 'Tell them,' he said. 'Tell them what you've done. What you do.'

'What've they done to you?' Mission asked. His friend had changed. It was more than the haircut and uniform. It was in his eyes.

'They showed me—' Rodny swept his gun at the posters on the wall. 'That these stories are true.' He laughed and turned to the Crow. 'And I was angry, just like you said I would be. Angry at what they did to the world. I wanted to tear it all down.'

'So do it,' the Crow insisted. 'Hurt them.' Her voice creaked like a door about to slam.

'But now I know. They told me. We got a call. And now I know what you've been doing here—'

'What's this about?' Frankie asked, still in the middle of the room. He moved towards the door. 'Why is my father—'

'Stay,' Rodny told him. He pushed one of the desks out of the way and moved down the aisle. 'Don't you move.' His gun swung from Frankie to the Crow, whose chair shivered in time with her palsied hand. 'These sayings on the wall, the stories and songs – you made us what we are. You made us angry.'

'You *should* be,' she screeched. 'You damn well should be!'

Mission moved closer to the Crow. He kept his eye on the gun. Allie knelt and held the old woman's hand. Rodny stood ten paces away, the gun angled at their feet.

'They kill and they kill,' the Crow said. 'And this will go the way it always has. Wipe it all clean. Bury and burn the dead. And these desks—' Her arm shot up, her quivering finger aimed at the empty desks newly arranged. 'These desks will be *full* again.'

'No,' Rodny said. He shook his head. 'No more. It ends here. You won't terrify us any more—'

'What're you saying?' Mission asked. He stepped close to the Crow, a hand on her chair. 'You're the one with the gun, Rodny. You're the one scaring us.'

Rodny turned to Mission. '*She* makes us feel this way. Don't you see? The fear and hope go hand in hand. What she sells is no different than the priests, only she gets to us *first*. This talk of a better world. It just makes us hate *this* one.'

'No—' Mission hated his friend for uttering such a thing.

'Yes,' Rodny said. 'Why do you think we hate our fathers? It's because she makes us hate them. Gives us ideas to break free from them. But this won't make it better.' He waved his hand. 'Not that it matters. What I knew yesterday had me terrified for my life. For all of us. What I know now gives me hope.' His gun came up. Mission couldn't believe it. His friend pointed the barrel at the Old Crow.

'Wait—' Mission raised a hand.

'Stand back,' Rodny said. 'I have to do this.'

'No!'

His friend's arm stiffened. The barrel was levelled at a defenceless woman in a mechanical chair, the mother to them all, the one who sang them to sleep in their cribs and on their mats, whose voice followed them through their sha-dowing days and beyond.

Frankie shoved a desk aside and lurched towards Rodny. Allie screamed. Mission threw himself sideways as the gun roared and flashed. There was a punch to his stomach, a fire in his gut. He crashed to the floor as the gun thundered a second time, the Crow's chair lurching to the side as a spasm gripped her hand.

Mission landed heavily, clutching his stomach. His hands came away sticky and wet.

Lying on his back, he saw the Crow slump over in her chair, a chair that no longer moved. Again, the gun roared. Needlessly. Her body twitched as it was struck. Frankie flew into Rodny and the two men went tumbling. Boots stormed into the room, summoned by the noise.

Allie was there, crying. She kept her hands on Mission's stomach, pressing so hard, and looked back at the Crow. She wailed for them both. Mission tasted blood in his mouth. It reminded him of the time Rodny had punched him as a kid, only playing. They'd only ever been playing. Costumes and pretending to be their fathers.

There were boots everywhere. Shiny and black boots on some, scuffed with wear on others. Those who had fought before and those just learning.

Rodny appeared above Mission, his eyes wide with worry. He told him to hang in there. Mission wanted to say he'd try, but the pain in his stomach was too great. He couldn't speak. They told him to stay awake, but all he'd ever wanted was to sleep. To not be. To not be a burden to anyone.

Hush my Darling, don't you cry
I'm going to sing you a lullaby
Though I'm far away it seems
I'll be with you in your dreams.

Hush my Darling, go to sleep
All around you angels keep
In the morn and through the day
They will keep your fears at bay.

Sleep my Darling, don't you cry
I'm going to sing you a lullaby

57

Three Years Later

• Silo 18 •

M ission changed out of his work overalls while Allie readied dinner. He washed his hands, scrubbed the dirt from beneath his fingernails and watched the mud slide down the drain. The ring on his finger was getting more and more difficult to remove, his knuckles sore and stiff from the hoeing of planting season.

He soaped his hands and finally managed to work the ring off. Remembering the last time he'd lost it down the drain, he set it aside carefully. Allie whistled in the kitchen while she tended the stove. When she cracked the oven, he smelled the pork roast inside. He'd have to say something. They couldn't go buying roasts on no occasion.

His overalls went into the wash. There were lighted candles on the table when he got back to the kitchen. They were for emergencies, for the times when the fools below switched generators and worked on the busted main. Allie knew this. But before he could say anything about the roast or the candles, or tell her that the bean crop wouldn't be what he'd hoped come harvest, he saw the way she was beaming at him. There was only one thing to be that happy about – but it was impossible.

'No,' he said. He couldn't allow himself to believe it.

Allie nodded. There were tears in her eyes. By the time he got to her, they were coursing down her cheeks.

'But our ticket is up,' he whispered, holding her against him. She smelled like sweet peppers and sage. He could feel her trembling.

Allie sobbed. Her voice broke from being overfull of joy. 'Doc says it happened last month. It was in our window, Mish. We're gonna have a baby.'

A surge of relief filled Mission to the brim. Relief, not excitement. Relief that everything was legal. He kissed his wife's cheek, salt to go with the pepper and sage. 'I love you,' he whispered.

'The roast.' She pulled away and hurried to the stove. 'I was gonna tell you after dinner.'

Mission laughed. 'You were gonna tell me now or have to explain the candles.'

He poured two glasses of water, hands trembling, and set them out while she fixed the plates. The smell of cooked meat made his mouth water. He could anticipate the way the roast would taste. A taste of the future, of what was to come.

'Don't let it get cold,' Allie said, setting the plates.

They sat and held hands. Mission cursed himself for not putting his ring back on.

'Bless this food and those who fed its roots,' Allie said.

'Amen,' said Mission. His wife squeezed his hands before letting go and grabbing her utensils.

'You know,' she said, cutting into the roast, 'if it's a girl, we'll have to name her Allison. Every woman in my family as far back as we can remember has been an Allison.'

Mission wondered how far back her family could remember. It'd be unusual if they could remember very far.

He chewed and thought on the name. 'Allison it is,' he said. And he thought that eventually they would call her Allie too. 'But if it's a boy, can we go with Cam?'

'Sure.' Allie lifted her glass. 'That wasn't your grandfather's name, was it?'

'No. I don't know any Cams. I just like the way it sounds.'

He picked up his glass of water, studied it awhile. Or did he know a Cam? Where did he know that name from? There were bits of his past shrouded and hidden from him. There were things like the mark on his neck and the scar on his stomach that he couldn't remember coming to be.

Everyone had their share of these things, parts of their bygone days they couldn't recall, but Mission more than most. Like his birthday. It drove him crazy that he couldn't remember when his birthday was. What was so hard about that?

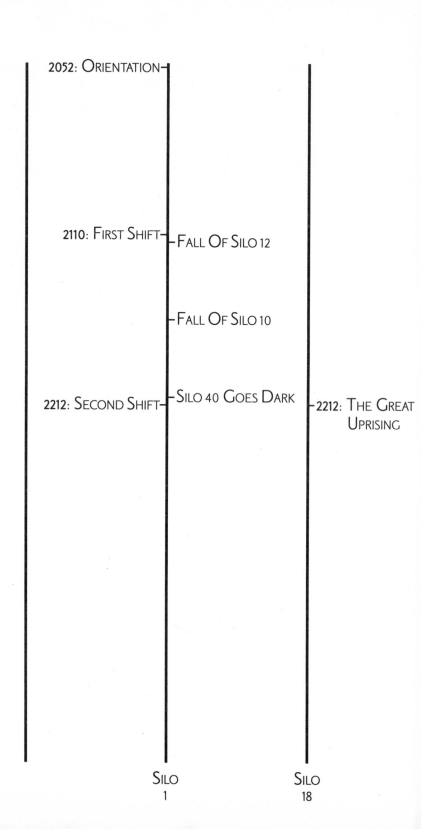

2052: ORIENTATION

2110: FIRST SHIFT— FALL OF SILO 12

FALL OF SILO 10

2212: SECOND SHIFT— SILO 40 GOES DARK

2212: THE GREAT UPRISING

SILO
1

SILO
18

THIRD SHIFT – PACT

'**S**ir?'

There was a clatter of bones beneath his feet. Donald stumbled through the dark.

'Can you hear me?'

The haze parted, an eyelid cracking just like the seal of his pod. A bean. Donald was curled inside that pod like a bean.

'Sir? Are you with me?'

Skin so cold. Donald was sitting up, steam rising from his bare legs. He didn't remember going to sleep. He remembered the doctor, remembered being in his office. They were talking. Now he was being woken up.

'Drink this, sir.'

Donald remembered this. He remembered waking over and over, but he didn't remember going to sleep. Just the waking. He took a sip, had to concentrate to make his throat work, had to fight to swallow. A pill. There was supposed to be a pill, but it wasn't offered.

'Sir, we had instructions to wake you.'

Instructions. Rules. Protocol. Donald was in trouble again. Troy. Maybe it was that Troy fellow. Who was he? Donald drank as much as he could.

'Very good, sir. We're going to lift you out.'

He was in trouble. They only woke him when there was trouble. A catheter was removed, a needle from his arm.

'What did I—'

He coughed into his fist. His voice was a sheet of tissue paper, thin and fragile. Invisible.

'What is it?' he asked, shouting to form a whisper.

Two men lifted him up and set him into a wheelchair. A third man held it still. There was a soft blanket instead of a paper gown. There was no rustling this time, no itching on his skin.

'We lost one,' someone said.

A silo. A silo was gone. It would be Donald's fault again. 'Eighteen,' he whispered, remembering his last shift.

Two of the men glanced at each other, mouths open.

'Yes,' one of them said, awe in his voice. 'From silo eighteen, sir. We lost her over the hill. We lost contact.'

Donald tried to focus on the man. He remembered losing someone over a hill. *Helen.* His wife. They were still looking for her. There was still hope.

'Tell me,' he whispered.

'We're not sure how, but one of them made it out of sight—'

'A cleaner, sir—'

A cleaner. Donald sank into the chair; his bones were as cold and heavy as stone. It wasn't Helen at all.

'—over the hill—' one said.

'—we got a call from eighteen—'

Donald raised his hand a little, his arm trembling and still half numb from the sleep. 'Wait,' he croaked. 'One at a time. Why did you wake me?' It hurt to talk.

One of the men cleared his throat. The blanket was tucked up under Donald's chin to stop him from shivering. He hadn't known he was shivering. They were being so reverent with him, so gentle. What was this? He tried to clear his head.

'You told us to wake you—'

'It's protocol—'

Donald's eyes fell to the pod, still steaming as the chill escaped. There was a screen at the base, empty readouts without him in there, just a rising temp. A rising temp and a name. Not his name.

And Donald remembered how names meant nothing

unless that was all one had to go by. If nobody remembered each other, if they didn't cross paths, then a name was everything.

'Sir?'

'Who am I?' he asked, reading the little screen, not understanding. This wasn't him. 'Why did you wake me?'

'You told us to, Mr Thurman.'

The blanket was wrapped snugly around his shoulders. The chair was turned. They were treating him with respect, as if he had authority. The wheels on this chair did not squeak at all.

'It's okay, sir. Your head will clear soon.'

He didn't know these people. They didn't know him.

'The doctor will clear you for duty.'

Nobody knew anyone.

'Right this way.'

And then anyone could be anybody.

'Through here.'

Until it didn't matter who was in charge. One who might do what was correct, another who might do what was right.

'Very good.'

One name as good as any other.

59

2312 – *Hour One*
• Silo 17 •

The Loud came before the quiet. That was a Rule of the World, for the bangs and shouts need somewhere to echo, just as bodies need space in which to fall. Jimmy Parker was in class when the last of the great Louds began. It was the day before a cleaning. Tomorrow, they would be off from school. For the death of a man, Jimmy and his friends would be gifted a few extra hours of sleep. His father would work overtime down in IT. And tomorrow afternoon, his mother would insist that they go up with his aunt and cousins to watch the bright clouds drift over the clear view of the hills until the sky turned dark as sleep.

Cleaning days were for staying in bed and for seeing family. They were for silencing unrest and quietening the Louds. That's what Mrs Pearson told them as she wrote the rules from the Pact up on the blackboard. Her chalk clacked and squeaked and left dusty trails of all the whys for which a man could be put to death. Civics lessons on a day before a banishment. Warnings on the eve of graver warnings. Jimmy and his friends fidgeted in their seats and learned rules. Rules of the World that very soon would no longer apply.

Jimmy was sixteen. Many of his friends would move off and shadow soon, but he would need another year of study to follow in his father's footsteps. Mrs Pearson marked the blackboard and moved on to the seriousness of choosing a life partner, of registering relationships according to the Pact. Sarah Jenkins turned in her seat and smiled back at Jimmy. Civics lessons and biology lessons intermingled, hormones spoken of alongside the laws that governed their excesses. Sarah Jenkins was cute. Jimmy hadn't thought so at the beginning of the year, but now he was seeing it. Sarah Jenkins was cute and would be dead in just a few hours.

Mrs Pearson asked for a volunteer to read from the Pact, and that's when Jimmy's mother came for him. She burst in unannounced. An embarrassment. The end of Jimmy's world began with hot cheeks and a burning collar and everyone watching. His mom didn't say anything to Mrs Pearson, didn't excuse herself. She just stormed through the door and hurried among the desks the way she walked when she was angry. She pulled Jimmy from his desk and led him out with his arm in her fist, causing him to wonder what he'd done this time.

Mrs Pearson didn't speak. Jimmy looked back at his best friend Paul, caught him smiling behind his palm, and wondered why Paul wasn't in trouble too. They rarely got in or out of a fix alone, he and Paul. The only person to utter a word was Sarah Jenkins. 'Your backpack!' she cried out just before the classroom door slammed shut, her voice swallowed by the quiet.

There were no other mothers pulling their children down the hallway. If they came, it would be much later. Jimmy's father worked among the computers and knew things. His father knew things before anyone else. This time, it was only moments before. There were others scrambling on the stairwell already. The noise was frightening. The landing outside the school level thrummed with the vibrations of distant and heavy traffic. A bolt in one of the railing's stanchions rattled as it worked its way loose. It felt as though the silo would simply shake itself apart. Jimmy's mom took him by the sleeve and pulled him towards the spiral staircase as if he was still twelve.

Jimmy pulled against her for a moment, confused. In the past year, he had grown bigger than his mom, as big as his father, and it was strange to be reminded that he had this power, that he was nearly a man. He had left his backpack and his friends behind. Where were they going? The banging from below seemed to be getting louder.

His mother turned as he gave resistance. Her eyes, he saw, were not full of anger. There was no glare, no furrowed brow. They were wide and wet, shiny like the times Grandma and Grandpa had passed. The noise below was frightful, but it was the look in his mother's eyes that placed fear in Jimmy's bones.

'What is it?' he whispered. He hated to see his mother upset. Something dark and empty – like that stray and tailless cat that nobody could catch in the upper apartments – clawed at his insides.

His mother didn't say. She turned and pulled him down the stairs, towards the thundering approach of something awful, and Jimmy realised at once that he wasn't in trouble at all.

They all were.

60

2312 – Hour One

• Silo 17 •

J immy had never felt the stairs tremble so. The entire
spiral staircase seemed to sway. It turned to rubber the
way a length of charcoal appears to bend between jiggled
fingers, a parlour trick he'd learned in class. Though his feet
rarely touched the steps – racing as he was to keep up with
his mother – they tingled and felt numb from vibrations
transmitted straight from steel to bone. Jimmy tasted fear in
his mouth like a dry spoon on his tongue.

There were angry screams from below. Jimmy's mother
shouted her encouragement, told him to hurry, and down the
staircase they spiralled. They raced towards whatever bad
thing was marching upward. 'Hurry,' she cried again, and
Jimmy was more scared of the tremor in her voice than the
shuddering of a hundred levels of steel. He hurried.

They passed twenty-nine. Thirty. People ran by in the
opposite direction. A lot of people in overalls the colour of
his father's. On the landing of thirty-one, Jimmy saw his first
dead body since his grandpa's funeral. It looked as if a tomato
had been smashed on the back of the man's head. Jimmy had
to skip over the man's arms, which stuck out into the stairwell.
He hurried after his mother while some of the red dripped
through the landing and splattered and slicked the steps below.

At thirty-two, the shake of the stairs was so great that
he could feel it in his teeth. His mother grew frantic as the
two of them bumped past more and more people hurrying
upward. Nobody seemed to see anyone else. Everyone was
looking out for themselves.

The stampede could be heard, a din of a thousand boots. There were loud voices among the ringing footfalls. Jimmy stopped and peered over the railing. Below, as the staircase augered into the depths, he could see the elbows and hands of a jostling crowd jutting out. He turned as someone thundered by. His mother called for him to hurry, for the crowd was already upon them, the traffic growing. Jimmy felt the fear and anger in the people racing past and it made him want to flee upward with them. But there was his mom yelling for him to come along, and her voice cut through his fear and to the centre of his being.

Jimmy shuffled down and took her hand. The embarrassment of earlier was gone. Now he wanted her clutching him. The people who ran past shouted for them to go the other way. Several held pipes and lengths of steel. There were some who were bruised and cut. Blood covered the mouth and chin of one man. A fight somewhere. Jimmy thought that only happened in the Deeps. Others seemed simply to be caught up in it all. They were without weapons and were looking over their shoulders. It was a mob scared of a mob. Jimmy wondered what had caused it. What was there to be afraid of?

Loud bangs rang out among the footfalls. A large man knocked into Jimmy's mom and sent her against the railing. Jimmy held her arm, and the two of them stuck to the inner post as they made their way down to thirty-three. 'One more to go,' she told him, which meant it was his father they were after.

The growing throngs became a crush a few turns above thirty-four. People pressed four wide where there was only room for two. Jimmy's wrist banged against the inner rail. He wedged himself between the post and those forcing their way up. Moving a few inches at a time – those beside him shoving, jostling and grunting with effort – he felt certain they would all become stuck like that. People crowded in and he lost his grip on her arm. She surged forward while he remained pinned in place. He could hear her yelling his name below.

A large man, dripping with sweat, jaw slack with fear, was trying to force his way up the downbound side. 'Move!' he yelled at Jimmy, as if there were anywhere to go. There was nowhere to go but up. He flattened himself against the centre post as the man brushed past. There was a scream by the outer rail, a jolt through the crowd, a series of gasps, someone yelling 'Hold on!' and another yelling to let them go, and then a shriek that plummeted away and grew faint.

The wedge of bodies loosened. Jimmy felt sick to his stomach at the thought of someone falling so near to him. He wiggled free and climbed up onto the inner rail, hugged the central post and balanced there, careful not to let his feet slip into the six inches of space between the rail and the post, that gap that kids liked to spit into.

Someone in the crowd immediately took his place on the steps. Shoulders and elbows knocked into his ankles. He remained crouched there, the undersides of the steps above him transmitting the scrapes of shuffling boots from those overhead. He slid his feet along the narrow bar of steel made slick by the rubbing of thousands of palms and worked his way down the railing after his mom. His foot slipped into the gap by the centre post. It seemed eager to swallow his leg. Jimmy righted himself, fearful of falling onto the lurching crowd, imagining how he could be tossed across their frenzied arms and slip out into space.

He was half a circuit around the inner post before he found his mom. She had been forced towards the outside by the crowds. 'Mom!' he yelled. Jimmy held the edge of the steps above his head and reached over the crowd for her. A woman in the middle of the steps screamed and disappeared, her head sinking below those who took her place. As they trampled her, the woman's screams disappeared. The crowd surged upward. They carried Jimmy's mom a few steps with them.

'Get to your father!' she screamed, cupping her hands around her mouth. 'Jimmy!'

'Mom!'

Someone knocked into his shins, and he lost his grip on the stairs overhead. Jimmy waved his arms once, twice, in little circles, trying to keep his balance. He fell inward on the sea of heads and rolled. Someone punched him in the ribs as they protected themselves from his fall.

Another man threw Jimmy aside. He tumbled outward across an undulating platform of sharp elbows and hard skulls, and time slowed to a crawl. There was nothing but empty space and a long fall beyond the crowd, now packed five wide. Jimmy tried to grab one of the hands pushing and shoving at him. His stomach lurched as the space grew nearer. He couldn't see the rail. He heard his mother's voice, a screech recognisable above all the others, as she watched, helpless. Someone screamed to help that boy as he slid down the spiral of heads, rolling and grasping. That boy they were screaming after was him.

Jimmy rolled into open space. He was thrown aside by those trying to protect themselves. He slid between two people – a shoulder catching him in the chin – and he saw the railing at last. He clutched for it, got one hand wrapped around the bar. As his feet tumbled over his head he was twisted around, his shoulder wrenched painfully, but he kept his grip. He hung there, clutching the railing with one hand and one of the vertical stanchions with the other, his feet dangling in the open air.

Someone's hip pinched his fingers against the rail and Jimmy cried out. Hands scrambled at his arms to help, but these people and their concerns were pushed upward by the madness below.

Jimmy tried to pull himself up. He looked down past his kicking feet at the crowds jostling beyond the rail below him. Two turns down was the landing to thirty-four. Again he tried to hoist himself, but there was a fire in his wrenched shoulder. Someone scratched his forearm as they tried to help and then they too were gone, surging upward.

Peering down his chest, between his feet, Jimmy saw that the landing to thirty-four was packed. A crowd spilled out of the jammed stairs and tried to shove their way back in again. Someone barged out of the doors to IT with a cleaning suit on, helmet and everything. They threw themselves into the crowd, silvery arms swimming amid the flesh, everyone trying to get up, more of the bangs and shouts from down below, a sudden pop like the balloons from the bazaar but much, much louder.

Jimmy lost his grip on the railing – his shoulder was too injured to bear the weight any longer. He clutched the stanchion with his other hand as he slid down, sweaty palm on steel adding one more squeal to the uproar of the mob. He was left clutching the edge of the steps at the base of the stanchion. With his feet, he tried to feel for the railing one turn below, but all he felt were angry arms knocking his boots aside. His busted shoulder was alive with pain. He swung down on one hand, dangling for an instant.

Jimmy cried out in alarm. He cried out for his mother, remembering what she'd told him.

Get to your father.

There was no way he was getting back up on the stairwell. He didn't have the strength. There was no room. Nobody was going to help him. A surging crowd, and yet he hung there all alone.

Jimmy took a deep breath. He dangled a moment longer, glanced down at the packed landing below him, and let go.

2312 – Hour One
• Silo 17 •

Two turns of the spiral staircase flew by. Two turns of wide eyes among the packed and crushing crowd. Jimmy felt the swoosh of wind on his neck grow and grow. His stomach flew up into his throat, and there was a glimpse of a face turning in alarm to watch him plummet past.

Slamming into the crowd on the landing below, he hit with a sickening thud. The man in the silver suit, faceless behind his small visor, was pinned beneath him.

People yelled at him. Others crawled out from underneath him. Jimmy rolled away, an electric shock in his ribs where he'd hit someone, a throbbing pain in one knee, his shoulder burning. Limping, he hurried towards the double doors as another person barged out, a bundle in their arms. They pulled to a halt at the sight of the crowd on the stairs. Someone yelled about the forbidden Outside, and nobody seemed to care. Tomorrow, there was to be a cleaning. Maybe it was too late. Jimmy thought of the extra hours his dad had been putting in. He wondered how many more people would be sent out for all this violence.

He turned back to the stairs and searched for his mom. The screams and shouts for people to move, to get out of the way, made it impossible to hear. But her voice still rang in his ears. He remembered her last command, the plaintive look on her face, and hurried inside to find his father.

It was chaos beyond the doors, people running back and forth in the halls, loud voices arguing. Yani stood by the security gate, the large officer's hair matted with sweat. Jimmy ran towards him. He clutched his elbow to pin his arm to his chest and keep his shoulder from swinging. The sting in his ribs made it difficult to take in a full breath. His heart was still pounding from the rush of the long fall.

'Yani—' Jimmy leaned against the security gate and gasped for air. It seemed to take a moment for the guard to register his existence. Yani's eyes were wide; they darted back and forth. Jimmy noticed something in his hand, a pistol like the sheriff wore. 'I need to get through,' Jimmy said. 'I need to find Dad.'

The officer's wild eyes settled on Jimmy. Yani was a good man, a friend of his father's. His daughter was just two years younger than Jimmy. Their family came over for dinner around the holidays sometimes. But this was not that Yani. Some sort of terror seemed to have him by the throat.

'Yes,' he said, bobbing his head. 'Your father. Won't let me in. Won't let any of us in. But you—' It seemed impossible, but Yani's eyes grew wilder.

'Can you buzz me—' Jimmy started to ask, nudging the turnstile.

Yani grabbed Jimmy by his collar. Jimmy was no small boy, was growing into his adult frame, but the massive guard practically lifted him over the turnstile as if he were a sack of dirty laundry.

Jimmy struggled in the man's fierce grip. Yani pressed the end of the pistol against Jimmy's chest and dragged him down the hall. 'I've got his boy!' he yelled. To whom, it wasn't clear. Jimmy tried to twist free. He was hauled past offices in disarray. The entire level looked cleared out. He thought of all the overalls in silver and grey on the stairway earlier and feared for a moment that his father had been among those he'd passed. The crowd had been littered with people from this level, as though they'd been leading the charge – or were the ones being chased.

'I can't breathe—' he tried to tell Yani. He got his feet beneath him, clutched the powerful man's forearm, anything to take the pinch off his collar.

'Where'd you assholes go?' Yani screamed, glancing up and down the halls. 'I need a hand with this—'

There was a clap like a thousand balloons popping at once, a deafening roar. Jimmy felt Yani lurch sideways as if kicked. The guard's grip relaxed, allowing the blood to rush back to Jimmy's head. Jimmy danced sideways as the large man tumbled over. He crashed to the floor, gurgling and wheezing, the black pistol skittering across the tile.

'Jimmy!'

His father was at the end of the hall, half around a corner, a long black object under his armpit, a crutch that didn't quite reach the floor. The end of this too-short crutch smoked as if it were on fire.

'Hurry, son!'

Jimmy cried out in relief. He stumbled away from Yani, who was writhing on the floor and making awful, inhuman sounds. He ran to his father, limping and clutching his arm.

'Where's your mother?' his dad asked, peering down the hall.

'The stairs—' Jimmy fought for a breath. His pulse had blurred into a steady thrum. 'Dad, what's going on?'

'Inside. Inside.' He pulled Jimmy down the hall towards a large door of stainless steel. There were shouts from around the corner. Jimmy could see the veins standing out in his father's forehead, trickles of sweat beading beneath his thinning hair. His father keyed a code into the panel by the massive door and there was a whirring and a series of clunks before it opened a crack. His dad leaned into the door until there was room for the two of them to squeeze through. 'C'mon, son. Move.'

Down the hall, someone yelled at them to stop. Boots clomped in their direction. Jimmy squeezed through the crack, was worried his dad might close him up in there, all alone, but his old man worked his way through as well then leaned against the inside of the door.

'Push!' he said.

Jimmy pushed. He didn't know why they were pushing,

but he'd never seen his dad frightened before. It made his insides feel like jelly. The boots outside stomped closer. Someone yelled his father's name. Someone yelled for Yani.

As the steel door slammed shut, a slap of hands hit the other side. There was a whir and a clunk once more. His dad keyed something into the pad, then hesitated. 'A number,' he said, gasping for breath. 'Four digits. Quick, son, a number you'll remember.'

'One two one eight,' Jimmy said. Level twelve and level eighteen. Where he went to school and where he lived. His father keyed in the digits. There were muffled yells from the other side, soft ringing sounds from palms slapping futilely against the thick steel.

'Come with me,' his father said. 'We've got to keep an eye on the cameras, have to find your mother.' He slung the black machine over his back, which Jimmy now saw was a bigger version of the pistol. The end was no longer smoking. His father hadn't kicked Yani from a distance; he had shot him.

Jimmy stood motionless while his father set off through the room of large black boxes. It dawned on him that he'd heard of this place, that his father had told him stories of a room full of servers. The machines seemed to watch him as he stood there by the door. They were black sentries, quietly humming, standing guard.

Jimmy left the wall of stainless steel with its muffled slaps and muted shouts and hurried after his father. He had seen his dad's office before, back down the hall and around a bend, but never this place. The room was huge. He favoured one leg as he ran the full length of it, trying to pick his way through the servers and keep track of where his dad had gone. At the far wall, he rounded the last black box and found his dad kneeling on the floor as if in prayer. Bringing his hands up around his neck, his dad dug inside his overalls and came out with a thin black cord. Something silver danced on the end of it.

'What about Mom?' Jimmy asked. He wondered how

they would let her in with the rest of those guys outside. He wondered why his father was kneeling on the floor like that.

'Listen carefully,' his dad said. 'This is the key to the silo. There are only two of these. Do not ever lose sight of it, okay?'

Jimmy watched as his father inserted the key into the back of one of the machines. 'This is the comm hub,' his dad said. Jimmy had no idea what a comm hub was, only that they were going to hide inside of one. That was the plan. Get inside one of the black boxes until the noise went away. His dad turned the key as if unlocking something, did this three more times in three more slots, then pulled the panel away. Jimmy peered inside and watched his dad pull a lever. There was a grinding noise in the floor nearby.

'Keep this safe,' his father said. He squeezed Jimmy's shoulder and handed him the lanyard with the key. Jimmy accepted it and studied the jagged piece of silver amid the coil of black cord. One side of the key formed a circle with three wedges inside – the symbol of the silo. He teased the lanyard into a hoop and pulled it down over his head, then watched his dad dig his fingers into the grating by their feet. He lifted out a small rectangle of flooring to reveal darkness underneath.

'Go on. You first,' his father said. He waved at the hole in the ground and began unslinging the long pistol from his back. Jimmy shuffled forward and peered down. There were handholds along one wall. It was like a ladder, but much taller than any he'd ever seen.

'C'mon, son. We don't have much time.'

Sitting on the edge of the grating, his feet hanging in the void, Jimmy reached for the steel rungs below and began the long descent.

The air beneath the floor was cool, the light dim. The horror and noise of the stairwell seemed to fade, and Jimmy was left with a sense of foreboding, of dread. Why was he being given this key? What was this place? He climbed down mostly using his good arm, made slow but steady progress.

At the bottom of the ladder, he found a narrow passage-way. There was a dim pulse of light at the far end. Looking up, he could see the outline of his father making his way down.

'Through there,' his father said, indicating the slender hallway. He left the long pistol propped up against the ladder.

Jimmy pointed up. 'Shouldn't we cover the—'

'I'll get it on my way out. Let's go, son.'

Jimmy turned and worked his way through the passage. There were wires and pipes running in parallel across the ceiling. A light ahead beat crimson. After twenty paces or so, the passage opened on a space that reminded him of the school stockroom. There were shelves along two walls. Two desks as well: one with a computer, the other with an open book. His dad went straight for the computer. 'You were with your mother?' he asked.

Jimmy nodded. 'She pulled me out of class. We got separated on the stairs.' He rubbed his sore shoulder while his father collapsed heavily into the chair in front of the desk. The computer screen was divided into four squares.

'Where did you lose her? How far up?'

'Two turns above thirty-four,' he said, remembering the fall.

Rather than reach for the mouse or keyboard, his father grabbed a black box studded with knobs and switches. There was a wire attached to the box that trailed off to the back of the monitor. In one corner of the screen, Jimmy saw a moving picture of three men standing over someone lying still on the floor. It was real. It was an image, a window, like the cafeteria wall screen. He was seeing a view of the hallway they'd just left.

'Fucking Yani,' his father muttered.

Jimmy's eyes fell from the screen to stare at the back of his dad's head. He'd heard his old man curse before, but never that word. His father's shoulders were rising and falling as he took deep breaths. Jimmy returned his attention to the screen.

The four windows had become twelve. No, sixteen. His father leaned forward, his nose just inches from the monitor, and peered from one square to the next. His old hands worked the black box, which clicked as the knobs and dials were adjusted. Jimmy saw in every square the turmoil he'd witnessed on the stairway. From rail to post, the treads were packed with people. They surged upward. His father traced the squares with a finger, searching.

'Dad—'

'Shhh.'

'—what's going on?'

'We've had a breach,' he said. 'They're trying to shut us down. You said it was two turns above the landing?'

'Yeah. But she was being carried up. It was hard to move. I went over the rail—'

The chair squeaked as his father turned and sized him up. His eyes fell to Jimmy's arm, pinned against his chest. 'You fell?'

'I'm okay, Dad, what's going on? Trying to shut what down?'

His father returned his focus to the screen. A few clicks from the black box and the squares flickered and changed. They now seemed to be peering through slightly different windows.

'They're trying to shut down our silo,' his father said. 'The bastards opened our airlock, said our gas supply was tainted— Wait. There she is.'

The many little windows became one. The view shifted slightly. Jimmy could see his mother pinned between a crush of people and the rail. Her mouth and chin were covered in blood. Gripping the rail and fighting for room, she lurched down one laborious step as the crowd coursed in the other direction. It seemed as though everyone in the silo were trying to get topside, as if that were the only escape.

Jimmy's father slapped the table and stood abruptly. 'Wait here,' he said. He stepped towards the narrow passage, stopped, looked back at Jimmy, seemed to consider something. There was a strange shine in his eyes.

'Quick, now. Just in case.' He hurried in the other direction, past Jimmy and through a door leading out of the room. Jimmy hurried after him, frightened, confused and limping.

'This is a lot like our stove,' his father said, patting an ancient thing in the corner of the next room. 'Older model, but it works the same.' There was a wild look in his father's eyes. He spun and indicated another door. 'Storehouse, bunkroom, showers, all through there. Food enough to last four people for ten years. Be smart, son.'

'Dad . . . I don't understand—'

'Tuck that key in,' his father said, pointing at Jimmy's chest. Jimmy had left the lanyard outside his overalls. 'Do not lose that key, okay? What's the number you said you'd never forget?'

'Twelve-eighteen,' Jimmy said.

'Okay. Come in here. Let me show you how the radio works.'

Jimmy took a last look around this second room. He didn't want to be left alone down there. That's what his father was doing, leaving him down between the levels, hidden in the concrete. The world felt heavy all around him.

'I'll come with you to get her,' he said, thinking of those men slapping their hands against the great steel door. His father couldn't go alone, even with the big pistol.

'Don't open the door for anyone but me or your mother,' his father said, ignoring his son's pleas. 'Now watch closely. We don't have much time.' He indicated a box on the wall. The box was locked behind a metal cage, but there were some switches and dials on the outside. 'Power's here.' His father tapped one of the knobs. 'Keep turning this way for volume.' His father did this and the room was filled with an awful hiss. He pulled a device off the wall and handed it to Jimmy. It was attached to the noisy box by a coil of stretchy cord. His dad grabbed another device from a rack on the wall. There were several of them there.

'Hear this? Hear this?' His father spoke into the portable device, and his voice replaced the loud hiss from the box on the wall. 'Squeeze that button and talk into the mic.' He pointed to the unit in Jimmy's hands. Jimmy did as he was told.

'I hear you,' Jimmy said hesitantly, and it was strange to hear his voice emanate from the small unit in his father's hands.

'What's the number?' his dad asked.

'Twelve-eighteen,' Jimmy said.

'Okay. Stay here, son.' His father appraised him for a moment, then stepped forward and grabbed the back of Jimmy's neck. He kissed his son on the forehead, and Jimmy remembered the last time his father had kissed him like that. It was right before he had disappeared for three months, before his father had become a shadow, back when Jimmy was a little boy.

'When I put the grate back in place, it'll lock itself. There's a handle below to reopen it. Are you okay?'

Jimmy nodded. His father glanced up at the red, pulsing lights and frowned.

'Whatever you do,' he said, 'do not open that door for anyone but me or your mother. Understand?'

'I understand.' Jimmy clutched his arm and tried to be brave. There was another of the long pistols leaning up against the wall. He didn't understand why he couldn't come as well. He reached for the black gun. 'Dad—'

'Stay here,' his father said.

Jimmy nodded.

'Good man.' He rubbed Jimmy's head and smiled, then turned and disappeared down that dark and narrow corridor. The red lights overhead winked on and off, throbbing like a pulse. There was the distant clang of boots on metal rungs, swallowed by the darkness, which soon became silent. And then Jimmy Parker was alone.

• Silo 1 •

Donald couldn't feel his toes. His feet were bare and had yet to thaw. They were bare, but all around him were boots. Boots everywhere. Boots on the men pushing him through aisles of gleaming pods. Boots standing still while they took his blood and told him to pee. Stiff boots that squeaked in the lift as grown men shifted nervously in place. And up above, a frantic hall greeted them where men stomped by in boots, a hall laden with shouts and nervous, lowered brows. They pushed him to a small apartment and left him alone to clean up and thaw out. Outside his door, more boots clomped up and down, up and down. Hurrying, hurrying. A world of worry, confusion and noise in which to wake.

Donald remained half asleep, sitting on a bed, his consciousness floating somewhere above the floor. Deep exhaustion gripped him. He was back to aboveground days, back when stirring and waking were two separate things. Mornings when he gained consciousness in the shower or behind the wheel on his way into work, long after he had begun to move. The mind lagged behind the body; it swam through the dust kicked up by numb and shuffling feet. Waking from decades of freezing cold felt like this. Dreams of which he was dimly aware slipped from his grasp, and Donald was eager to let them go.

The apartment they'd brought him to was down the hall from his old office. They had passed it along the way. That meant he was on the operations wing, a place where he used to work. An empty pair of boots sat at the foot of the bed. Donald stared at them numbly. The name 'Thurman' wrapped around the back of each ankle in faded black marker. Somehow, these boots were meant for him. They had been calling him Mr Thurman since he woke up, but that was not who he was. A mistake had been made. A mistake or a cruel trick. Some kind of game.

Fifteen minutes to get ready. That's what they'd said. Ready for what? Donald sat on the double cot, wrapped in a blanket, occasionally shivering. The wheelchair had been left with him. Thoughts and memories reluctantly assembled like exhausted soldiers roused from their bunks in the middle of the night and told to form ranks in the freezing rain.

My name is Donald, he reminded himself. He must not let that go. This was the first and most primal thing. Who he was.

Sensation and awareness gathered. Donald could feel the dent in the mattress the size and shape of another's body. This depression left behind by another tugged at him. On the wall behind the door, a crater stood where the knob had struck, where the door had been flung open. An emergency, perhaps. A fight or an accident. Someone barging inside. A scene of violence. Hundreds of years of stories he wasn't privy to. Fifteen minutes to get his thoughts together.

There was an ID badge on the bedside table with a bar code and a name. No picture, fortunately. Donald touched the badge, remembered seeing it in use. He left it where it was and rose shakily on creaky legs, held the wheelchair for support and moved towards the small bathroom.

There was a bandage on his arm where the doctor had drawn his blood. Dr Wilson. He'd already given a urine sample but he needed to pee again. Allowing his blanket to fall open, he stood over the toilet. The stream was pink. Donald thought he remembered it being the colour of charcoal on his last shift. When he finished, he stepped into the shower to wash off.

The water was hot, his bones cold. Donald shivered in a

fog of steam. He opened his mouth and allowed the spray to hit his tongue and fill his cheeks. He scrubbed at the memory of poison on his flesh, a memory that made it impossible to feel clean. For a moment, it wasn't the scalding water burning his skin – it was the air. The outside air. But then he turned off the flow of water and the burning lessened.

He towelled off and found the overalls left out for him. They were too big. Donald shrugged them on anyway, the fabric rough against skin that had lain bare for who knew how long. There was a knock at the door as he worked the zipper up to his neck. Someone called a name that was not his, a name scrawled around the backs of the boots lying perfectly still on the bed, a name that graced the badge sitting on the bedside table.

'Coming,' Donald croaked, his voice thin and weak. He slid the badge into his pocket and sat heavily on the bed. He rolled up his cuffs, all that extra material, before pulling the boots on one at a time. He fumbled with the laces, stood, and found that he could wiggle his toes in the space left behind by another.

Many years ago, Donald Keene had been elevated by a simple change in title. Power and importance had come in an instant. For all his life, he had been a man to whom few listened. A man with a degree, a string of jobs, a wife, a modest home. And then one night, a computer tallied stacks of ballots and Donald Keene became Congressman Keene. He became one of hundreds with his hand on some great tiller – a struggle of hands pushing, pulling and fitfully steering.

It had happened overnight, and it was happening again.

'How're you feeling, sir?'

The man outside his apartment studied Donald with concern. The badge around his neck read *Eren*. He was the Ops head, the one who manned the shrink's desk down the hall.

'Still groggy,' Donald said quietly. A gentleman in bright blue overalls raced by and disappeared around the bend. A gentle breeze followed, a stir of air that smelled of coffee and perspiration.

'Are you good to walk? I'm sorry about the rush, but then I'm sure you're used to it.' Eren pointed down the hall. 'They're waiting in the comm room.'

Donald nodded and followed. He remembered these halls being quieter, remembered them without the stomping and the raised voices. There were scuff marks on the walls that he thought were new. Reminders of how much time had passed.

In the comm room, all eyes turned to him. Someone was in trouble – Donald could feel it. Eren led him to a chair, and everyone watched and waited. He sat down and saw that there was a frozen image on the screen in front of him. A button was pressed and the image lurched into motion.

Thick dust tumbled and swirled across the view, making it difficult to see. Clouds flew past in unruly sheets. But there, through the gaps, a figure in a bulky suit could be seen on a forbidding landscape, picking their way up a gentle swell, heading away from the camera. It was someone outside.

He wondered if this was *him* out there, all those years ago. The suit looked familiar. Perhaps they'd caught his foolish act on camera, his attempt to die a free man. And now they'd woken him up to show him this damning bit of evidence. Donald braced for the accusation, for his punishment—

'This was earlier this morning,' Eren said.

Donald nodded and tried to calm himself. This wasn't him on the screen. They didn't know who he was. A surge of relief washed over him, a stark contrast to the nerves in the room and the shouts and hurrying boots in the hallway. Donald remembered being told that someone had disappeared over a hill when they'd pulled him from the pod. It was the first thing they'd told him. This was that person on the screen. This was why he'd been woken. He licked his lips and asked who it was.

'We're putting a file together for you now, sir. Should have it soon. What we do know is that there was a cleaning scheduled in eighteen this morning. Except . . .'

Eren hesitated. Donald turned from the screen and caught the Ops head looking to the others for help. One of the operators – a large man in orange overalls with wiry hair and headphones around his neck – was the first to oblige. 'The cleaning didn't go through,' the operator said flatly.

Several of the men in boots stiffened. Donald glanced around the room at the crowd that had packed into the small comm centre, and he saw how they were watching him. Waiting on him. The Ops head looked down at the floor in defeat. He appeared to be in his mid thirties, the same age as Donald, and yet he was waiting to be chastised. These were the men in trouble, not him.

Donald tried to think. The people in charge were looking to *him* for guidance. Something was wrong with the shifts, something very wrong. He had worked with the man they thought he was, the man whose name graced his badge and his boots. Thurman. It felt like yesterday that Donald had stood in that very same comm room and had felt that man's equal but for a moment. He had helped save a silo on his previous shift. And even though his head was groggy and his legs were weak, he knew it was important to uphold this charade. At least until he understood what was going on.

'What direction were they heading?' he asked, his voice a whisper. The others held perfectly still so that the rustle of their overalls wouldn't compete with his words.

A man from the back of the room answered. 'In the direction of seventeen, sir.'

Donald composed himself. He remembered the Order, the danger of letting anyone out of sight. These people in their silos with a limited view of the world thought that they were the only ones alive. They lived in bubbles that must not be allowed to burst. 'Any word from seventeen?' he asked.

'Seventeen is gone,' the operator beside him said, dispensing more bad news with the same flat voice.

Donald cleared his throat. 'Gone?' He searched the faces of the gathered. Foreheads creased with worry. Eren studied Donald, and the operator beside him adjusted his bulk in his seat. On the screen, the cleaner disappeared over the top of the hill and out of view. 'What did this cleaner do?' he asked.

'It wasn't her,' Eren said.

'Seventeen was shut down shifts ago,' the operator said.

'Right, right.' Donald ran his fingers through his hair. His hand was trembling.

'You feeling all right?' the operator asked. He glanced at the Ops head, then back to Donald. He knew. Donald sensed that this man in orange with the headphones around his neck knew something was wrong.

'Still a bit woozy,' Donald explained.

'He's only been up for half an hour,' Eren told the operator.

There were murmurs from the back of the room.

'Yeah, okay.' The operator settled back into his seat. 'It's just . . . he's the Shepherd, you know? I pictured him waking up chewing nails and farting tacks.'

Someone just behind Donald's chair chuckled.

'So what're we supposed to do about the cleaner?' a voice asked. 'We need permission before we can send anyone out after her.'

'She can't have gotten far,' someone said.

The comm engineer on the other side of Donald spoke up. He had one half of his headphones still on, the other half pulled off so he could follow the conversation. A sheen of sweat stood out on his forehead. 'Eighteen is reporting that her suit was modified,' he said. 'There's no telling how long it'll last. She could still be out there, sirs.'

This caused a chorus of whispers. It sounded like wind striking a visor, peppering it with sand. Donald stared at the screen, at a lifeless hill as seen from silo eighteen. The dust came in dark waves. He remembered what it had felt like out there on that landscape, the difficulty of moving in one of those suits, the hard slog up that gentle rise. Who was this cleaner, and where did she think she was going?

'Get me the file on this cleaner as soon as you can,' he said. The others fell still and stopped their whispering arguments. Donald's voice was commanding because of its quietude, because of who they thought he was. 'And I want whatever we have on seventeen.' He glanced at the operator, whose brow was furrowed by either worry or suspicion. 'To refresh my memory,' he added.

Eren rested a hand on the back of Donald's chair. 'What about the protocols?' he asked. 'Shouldn't we scramble a drone or send someone after her? Or shut down eighteen? There's going to be violence over there. We've never had a cleaning not go through before.'

Donald shook his head, which was beginning to clear. He looked down at his hand and remembered tearing off a glove once, there on the outside. He shouldn't be alive. He wondered what Thurman would do, what the old man would order. But he wasn't Thurman. Someone had told him once that people like Donald should be in charge. And now here he was.

'We don't do anything just yet,' he said, coughing and clearing his throat. 'She won't get far.'

The others stared at him with a mixture of shock and acceptance. There finally came a handful of nods. They assumed he knew best. He had been woken up to control the situation. It was all according to protocol. The system could be trusted – it was designed to just *go*. All anyone needed to do was their own job and let others handle the rest.

2345

• Silo 1 •

It was a short walk from his apartment to the central offices, which Donald assumed was the point. It reminded him of a CEO's office he'd once seen with an adjoining bedroom. What had seemed impressive at first became sad after realising why it was there.

He rapped his knuckles on the open door marked *Office for Psychological Services*. He used to think of these people as shrinks, that they were here to keep others sane. Now he knew that they were in charge of the insanity. All he saw on the door any more was 'OPS'. Operations. The head of the head of the heads. The office across the hall was where the drudge work landed. Donald was reminded how each silo had a mayor for shaking hands and keeping up appearances, just as the world of before had presidents who came and went. Meanwhile, it was the men in the shadows who wielded the true power, those whose terms had no limits. That this silo operated by the same deceit should not be surprising; it was the only way such men knew how to run anything.

He kept his back to his former office and knocked a little louder. Eren looked up from his computer and a hard mask of concentration melted into a wan smile. 'Come in,' he said as he rose from his seat. 'You need the desk?'

'Yes, but stay.' Donald crossed the room gingerly, his legs still half asleep, and noticed that while his own whites were crisp, Eren's were crumpled with the wear of a man well into his six-month shift. Even so, the Ops head appeared vigorous and alert. His beard was neatly trimmed by his neck and only peppered with grey. He helped Donald into the plush chair behind the desk.

'We're still waiting for the full report on this cleaner,' Eren said. 'The head of eighteen warned that it's a thick one.'

'Priors?' Donald imagined anyone sent to clean would have priors.

'Oh, yeah. The word is that she was a sheriff. Not sure if I'm buying it. Of course, it wouldn't be the first lawman to want out.'

'But it would be the first time anyone's gotten out of sight,' Donald said.

'From what I understand, yeah.' Eren crossed his arms and leaned against the desk. 'Nearest anyone got before now was that gentleman you stopped. I reckon that's why protocol says to wake you. I've heard some of the boys refer to you as the Shepherd.' Eren laughed.

Donald flinched at the nickname. 'Tell me about seventeen,' he said, changing the subject. 'Who was on shift when that silo went down?'

'We can look it up.' Eren waved a hand at the keyboard.

'My, uh, fingers are still a little tingly,' Donald said. He slid the keyboard towards Eren, who hesitated before getting off the desk. The Ops head bent over the keys and pulled up the shift list with a shortcut. Donald tried to follow along with what he was doing on the screen. These were files he didn't have access to, menus he was unfamiliar with.

'Looks like it was Cooper. I think I came off a shift once as he was coming on. Name sounds familiar. I sent someone down to get those files for you as well.'

'Good, good.'

Eren raised his eyebrows. 'You went over the reports on seventeen on your last shift, right?'

Donald had no clue if Thurman had been up since then. For all he knew, the old man had been awake when it happened. 'It's hard to keep everything straight,' he said, which was solid truth. 'How many years has it been?'

'That's right. You were in the deep freeze, weren't you?'

Donald supposed he was. Eren tapped the desk with his finger, and Donald's gaze drifted to the man across the hall, sitting behind his computer. He remembered what it had been like to be that man nominally in charge, wondering what the doctors in white were discussing across the way. Now he was one of those in white.

'Yes, I was in the deep freeze,' Donald said. They wouldn't have moved his body, would they? Erskine or someone could've simply changed entries in a database. Maybe it was that simple. Just a quick hack, two reference numbers transposed, and one man lives the life of another. 'I like to be near my daughter,' he explained.

'Yeah, I don't blame you.' The wrinkles in Eren's brow smoothed. 'I've got a wife down there. I still make the mistake of visiting her first thing every shift.' He took a deep breath then pointed at the screen. 'Seventeen was lost over thirty years ago. I'd have to look it up to be exact. The cause is still unclear. There wasn't any sign of unrest leading up to it, so we didn't have much time to react. There was a cleaning scheduled, but the airlock opened a day early and out of sequence. Could've been a glitch or tampering. We just don't know. Sensors reported a gas purge in the lower levels and then a riot surging up. We pulled the plug as they were scrambling out of the airlock. Barely had time.'

Donald recalled silo twelve. That facility had ended in similar fashion. He remembered people scattering on the hillside, a plume of white mist, some of them turning and fighting to get back inside. 'No survivors?' he asked.

'There were a few stragglers. We lost the radio feed and the cameras but continued to put in a routine call over there, just in case anyone was in the safe room.'

Donald nodded. By the book. He remembered the calls to twelve after it went down. He remembered nobody answering.

'Someone did pick up the day the silo fell,' Eren said. 'I think it was some young shadow or tech. I haven't read the transcripts in for ever.' He paged down on the shift report.

'It looks like we sent the collapse codes soon after that call, just as a precaution. So even if the cleaner gets over there, she's gonna find a hole in the ground.'

'Maybe she'll keep walking,' Donald said. 'What silo sits on the other side? Sixteen?'

Eren nodded.

'Why don't you go give them a call?' Donald tried to remember the layout of the silos. These were the kinds of things he'd be expected to know. 'And get in touch with the silos on either side of seventeen, just in case our cleaner takes a turn.'

'Will do.'

Eren stood, and Donald marvelled again at being treated as if he were in charge. It was already beginning to make him feel as if he really were. Just like being elected to Congress, all that awesome responsibility foisted on him overnight—

Eren leaned across the desk and hit two of the function keys on the keyboard, logging himself out of the computer. The Ops head hurried out into the hall while Donald stared at a login and password prompt.

Suddenly he felt very much less in charge.

• Silo 1 •

Across the hall, a man sat behind a desk that once had belonged to Donald. Donald peered up at this man and found him peering right back. Donald used to gaze across that hallway in the opposite direction. And while this man in his former office – who was heavier than Donald and had less hair – likely sat there playing a game of solitaire, Donald struggled with a puzzle of his own.

His old login of Troy wouldn't work. He tried old ATM codes and they were just as useless. He sat, thinking, worried about performing too many incorrect attempts. It felt like just yesterday that this account had worked. But a lot had happened since then. A lot of shifts. And someone had tampered with them.

It pointed back to Erskine, the old Brit left behind to coordinate the shifts. Erskine had taken a liking to him. But what was the point? What was he expecting Donald to do?

For a brief moment, he thought about standing up and walking out into the hallway and saying, *I am not Thurman or Shepherd or Troy. My name is Donald, and I'm not supposed to be here.*

He should tell the truth. He should rage with the truth, as senseless as it would seem to everyone else. *I am Donald!* he felt like screaming, just as old man Hal once had. They could pin his boots to a gurney and put him back to glorious sleep. They could send him out to the hills. They could bury him like they'd buried his wife. But he would scream and scream until he believed it himself, that he was who he thought he was.

Instead, he tried Erskine's name with his own passkey. Another red warning that the login was incorrect, and the desire to out himself passed as swiftly as it had come.

He studied the monitor. There didn't seem to be a trigger for the number of incorrect tries, but how long before Eren came back? How long before he had to explain that he couldn't log in? Maybe he could go across the hall, interrupt the silo head's game of solitaire and ask him to retrieve his key. He could blame it on being groggy and newly awake. That excuse had been working thus far. He wondered how long he could cling to it.

On a lark, he tried the combination of Thurman and his own passkey of 2156.

The login screen disappeared, replaced by a main menu. The sense that he was the wrong person deepened. Donald wiggled his toes. The extra space in his loose boots gave him comfort. On the screen, a familiar envelope flashed. Thurman had messages.

Donald clicked the icon and scrolled down to the oldest unread message, something that might explain how he had arrived there, something from Thurman's prior shift. The dates went back centuries; it was jarring to watch them scroll by. Population reports. Automated messages. Replies and forwards. He saw a message from Erskine, but it was just a note about the overflow of deep freeze to one of the lower cryopod levels. The useless bodies were stacking up, it seemed. Another message further down was starred as important. Victor's name was in the senders column, which caught Donald's attention. It had to be from before Donald's second shift. Victor was already dead the last time Donald had been woken. He opened the message.

Old friend,

I'm sure you will question what I'm about to do, that you will see this as a violation of our pact, but

I see it more as a restructuring of the timeline. New facts have emerged that push things up a bit. For me, at least. Your time will come.

I have in recent days discovered why one of our facilities has seen more than its share of turmoil. There is someone there who remembers, and she both disturbs and confirms what I know of humanity. Room is made that it might be filled. Fear is spread because the clean-up is addicting. Seeing this, much of what we do to one another becomes more obvious. It explains the great quandary of why the most depressed societies are those with the fewest wants. Arriving at the truth, I feel an urge from older times to synthesise a theory and present it to roomfuls of professionals. Instead, I have gone to a dusty room to procure a gun.

You and I have spent much of our adult lives scheming to save the world. Several adult lives, in fact. That deed now done, I ponder a different question, one that I fear I cannot answer and that we were never brave nor bold enough to pose. And so I ask you now, dear friend: was this world worth saving to begin with? Were *we* worth saving?

This endeavour was launched with that great assumption taken for granted. Now I ask myself for the first time. And while I view the cleansing of the world as our defining achievement, this business of saving humanity may have been our gravest mistake. The world may be better off without us. I have not the will to decide. I leave that to you. The final shift, my friend, is yours, for I have worked my last. I do not envy you the choice you will have to make. The pact we formed so long ago haunts me as never before. And I feel that what I'm about to do . . . that this is the easy way.

—Vincent Wayne DiMarco

Donald read the last paragraph again. It was a suicide note. Thurman had known. All along, while Donald wrestled with Victor's fate on his last shift, Thurman had known. He had this note in his possession and hadn't shared it. And Donald had almost grown convinced that Victor had been murdered. Unless the note was a fake— But no, Donald shook that thought away. Paranoia like that could spiral out of control and know no end. He had to cling to something.

He backed out of the message with a heavy heart and scrolled up the list, looking for some other clue. Near the top of the screen was a message with the subject line: *Urgent – The Pact*. Donald clicked the message open. The body was short. It read, simply:

Wake me when you get this.
—Anna
(Locket 20391102)

Donald blinked rapidly at the sight of her name. He glanced across the hall at the silo head and listened for footsteps coming his way. His arms were covered in goosebumps. He rubbed them, wiped underneath his eyes and read the note a second time.

It was signed *Anna*. It took him a moment to realise that it wasn't to him. It was a note between daughter and father. There was no send date listed, which was curious, but it was sorted near the very top. Perhaps it was from before their last shift together? Maybe the two of them had been awake recently. Donald studied the number at the bottom. *20391102*. It looked like a date. An old date. Inscribed on a locket, perhaps? Something meaningful between the two of them. And what of the mention in the header of this Pact? That was the name the silos used for their constitutions. What could be urgent about that?

Footsteps in the hallway broke his concentration. Eren rounded the corner and covered the office in a few steps. He circled the desk and placed two folders by the keyboard, then glanced at the screen as Donald fumbled with the mouse to minimise the message. 'H-How'd it go?' Donald asked. 'You got through to everyone?'

'Yeah.' Eren sniffed and scratched his beard. 'The head of sixteen took it badly. He's been in that position a long time. Too long, I think. He suggested closing down his cafeteria or shutting off the wall screen, just in case.'

'But he's not going to.'

'No, I told him as a last resort. No need to cause a panic. We just wanted them to have a heads-up.'

'Good, good.' Donald liked someone else thinking. It took the pressure off him. 'You need your desk back?' He made a show of logging off.

'No, actually, you're on if you don't mind.' Eren checked the clock in the corner of the computer screen. 'I can take the afternoon shift. How're you feeling, by the way? Any shakes?'

Donald shook his head. 'No. I'm good. It gets easier every time.'

Eren laughed. 'Yeah. I've seen how many shifts you've taken. And a double a while back. Don't envy you at all, friend. But you seem to be holding up well.'

Donald coughed. 'Yeah,' he said. He picked up the topmost of the two folders and read the tab. 'This is what we have on seventeen?'

'Yep. The thick one is your cleaner.' He tapped the other folder. 'You might want to check in with the head of eighteen today. He's pretty shaken up, is shouldering all the blame. Name's Bernard. There are already grumblings from his lower levels about the cleaning not going through, so he's looking at a very probable uprising. I'm sure he'd like to hear from you.'

'Yeah, sure.'

'Oh, and he doesn't have an official second right now. His last shadow didn't work out, and he's been putting off a replacement. I hope you don't mind, but I told him to hurry that through. Just in case.'

'No, no. That's fine.' Donald waved his hand. 'I'm not here to get in your way.' He didn't add that he had absolutely no clue why he was there at all.

Eren smiled and nodded. 'Great. Well, if you need anything, call me. And the guy across the hall goes by Gable. He used to hold down a post over here but couldn't cut it. Opted for a wipe instead of a deep freeze when given the choice. Good guy. Team player. He'll be on for a few more months and can get you anything you need.'

Donald studied the man across the hall. He remembered the empty sensation of manning that desk, the hollow pit that had filled him. How Donald had ended up there had seemed unusual, a last-minute switch with his friend Mick. It never occurred to him how all the others were selected. To think that any might volunteer for such a post filled him with sadness.

Eren stuck out his hand. Donald studied it a moment, then accepted it.

'I'm really sorry we had to wake you like this,' he said, pumping Donald's hand. 'But I have to admit, I'm damn sure glad you're here.'

2312 – Day One
• Silo 17 •

The box on the wall was unrelenting. His father had called it a radio. The noise it made was like a person hissing and spitting. Even the steel cage surrounding it looked like a mouth with its lips peeled back and iron bars for teeth.

Jimmy wanted to silence the radio but was scared to touch it or adjust anything. He waited to hear from his father, who had left him in a strange room, a hidden warren between the silo's levels.

How many more of these secret places were there? He glanced through an open door at the other room his dad had shown him, the one like a small apartment with its stove, table and chairs. When his parents got back, would they all stay there overnight? How long before the madness cleared from the stairs and he could see his friends again? He hoped it wouldn't be long.

He glared at the hissing black box, patted his chest and felt for the key there. His ribs were sore from the fall, and he could feel a knot forming in his thigh from where he'd landed on someone. His shoulder hurt when he lifted his arm. He turned to the monitor to search for his mother again, but she was no longer on the screen. A jostling crowd moved in jerks and fits. The stairwell shook with more traffic than it was ever meant to hold.

Jimmy reached for the box with the controls his father had used. He twisted one of the knobs and the view changed. It was an empty hall. A faint number '33' stood in the lower left corner of the screen. Jimmy turned the dial once more and got a different hallway. There was a trail of clothes on the ground as if someone had walked by with a leaking laundry bag. Nothing moved.

He tried a different dial and the number on the bottom changed to '32'. He was going *up the levels*. Jimmy spun the first dial until he found the stairwell again. Something flashed down and off the bottom of the screen. There were people leaning over the railing with their arms outstretched, mouths open in silent horror. There was no sound, but Jimmy remembered the screams from the woman who fell earlier. This was too far up to be his mother, he consoled himself. His dad would find her and bring her back. His dad had a gun.

Jimmy spun the dials and tried to locate either of his parents, but it seemed that not every angle was covered. And he couldn't figure out how to make the windows multiply. He was decent on a computer – he was going to work for IT like his father someday – but the little box was as unintuitive as the Deeps. He dialled it back down to '34' and found the main hallway. He could see a shiny steel door at the far end of a long corridor. Sprawled in the foreground was Yani. Yani hadn't moved, was surely dead. The men standing over him were gone, and there was a new body at the end of the hall, near the door. The colour of his overalls assured Jimmy that it wasn't his father. His father had probably shot that man on his way out. Jimmy wished he hadn't been left alone.

Overhead, the lights continued to blink angry and red, and the image on the screen remained motionless. Jimmy grew restless and paced in circles. He went to the small wooden desk on the opposite wall and flipped through the thick book. It was a fortune in paper, perfectly cut and eerily smooth to the touch. The desk and chair were both made of real wood, not painted to look like that. He could tell by scratching it with his fingernail.

He closed the book and checked the cover. The word *Order* was embossed in shiny letters across the front. He reopened it, and realised he'd lost someone's place. The radio nearby continued to hiss noisily. Jimmy turned and checked the computer screen, but nothing was happening in the hallway. That noise was getting on his nerves. He thought about adjusting the volume, but was scared he might accidentally turn it off. His dad wouldn't be able to get through to him if he messed something up.

He paced some more. There was a shelf of metal containers in one corner that went from floor to ceiling. Pulling one out, Jimmy felt how heavy it was. He played with the latch until he figured out how to open it. There was a soft sigh as the lid came loose, and he found a book inside. Looking at all the containers filling the shelves, Jimmy saw what a pile of chits was there. He returned the book, assuming it was full of nothing but boring words like the one on the desk.

Back at the other desk, he examined the computer underneath and saw that it wasn't turned on. All the lights were dim. He traced the wire from the black box with all the switches and found a different wire led from the monitor to the computer. The machine that made the windows – that could see far distances and around corners – was controlled by something else. The power switch on the computer did nothing. There was a place for a key. Jimmy bent down to inspect the connections on the back, to make sure everything was plugged in, when the radio crackled.

'—need you to report in. Hello—'

Jimmy knocked his head on the underside of the desk. He ran to the radio, which was back to hissing. Grabbing the device at the end of the stretchy cord – the thing his dad had named Mike – he squeezed the button.

'Dad? Dad, is that you?'

He let go and looked to the ceiling. He listened for footsteps and waited for the lights to stop flashing. The monitor showed a quiet hallway. Maybe he should go to the door and wait.

The radio crackled with a voice: 'Sheriff? Who is this?'

Jimmy squeezed the button. 'This is Jimmy. Jimmy Parker. Who—' The button slipped out of his hand, the static returning.

His palms were sweaty. He wiped them on his overalls and got the device under control. 'Who is this?' he asked.

'Russ's boy?' There was a pause. 'Son, where are you?'

He didn't want to say. The radio continued to hiss.

'Jimmy, this is Deputy Hines,' the voice said. 'Put your father on.'

Jimmy started to squeeze the button to say that his father wasn't there, but another voice chimed in. He recognised it at once.

'Mitch, this is Russ.'

Dad! There was a lot of noise in the background, people screaming. Jimmy held the device in both hands. 'Dad! Come back, please!'

The radio popped with his father's voice. 'James, be quiet. Mitch, I need you to—' Something was lost to the background noise. '—and stop the traffic. People are getting crushed up here.'

'Copy.'

That was his father talking to the deputy. The deputy was acting as though his old man were in charge.

'We've got a breach up top,' his father said, 'so I don't know how long you've got, but you're probably the sheriff until the end.'

'Copy,' Mitch said again. The radio made his voice sound shaky.

'Son—' His father was yelling now, fighting to be heard over some obnoxious din of screams and shouts. 'I'm going to get your mother, okay? Just stay there, James. Don't move.'

Jimmy turned to the monitor. 'Okay,' he said. He hung the Mike back on its hook, his hands trembling, and returned to the black box with all the controls. He felt helpless and alone. He should be out there, lending a hand. He wondered how long it would be before his parents returned, before he could see his friends again. He hoped it wouldn't be long.

66

2312 – Day One
• Silo 17 •

Hours passed, and Jimmy wanted to be anywhere but in that cramped room. He crept down the dark passage to the ladder and peered up at the grating, listening. There was a faint buzzing sound coming and going that he couldn't place. The hiss of the radio could barely be heard from the end of the corridor. He didn't want to be too far away from the radio, but he worried his dad might need him by the door as well. He wanted to be in two places at once.

He went back to the room with the desks. He looked at the long gun propped against the wall, the same as the one his father had used to kill Yani. Jimmy was afraid to touch it. He wished his father hadn't left. It was all Jimmy's fault for being separated from his mom. They should've made it down together. But then he remembered the crush of people on the stairs. If only he'd been faster, they wouldn't have gotten caught up in the crowds. And it occurred to Jimmy that the only reason his mother was there at all was because she had come for him. If it weren't for that, his parents would be down in that room, together and safe.

'James—'

Jimmy spun around. His father's voice was there in the room with him. It took a moment to realise the static from the radio was gone.

'—son, are you there?'

He lunged for the radio, grabbed the Mike at the end of the cord. It had seemed like hours since he'd heard voices.

Too long. As he squeezed the button, a flash of movement caught his eye. Someone was moving on the monitor.

'Dad?' He stretched the cord across the small room and looked closer. His father was outside the steel door, standing at the end of the hall. Yani was still in the foreground, unmoving. The other body was gone. His father had his back to the camera, the portable radio in his hand. 'I'm coming!' Jimmy yelled into the radio. He dropped the Mike and dashed for the corridor and the ladder.

'Son! No—'

His father's shouts were cut off by a grunt. Jimmy wheeled around, his boots squeaking. He clutched the desk for balance. On the screen, another man had emerged from around the corner, and his father was doubled over in pain. This man held the long pistol, stooped to retrieve something from the ground, held it to his mouth. It was the portable his father had taken from the room.

'Is this Russ's boy?'

Jimmy stared at the man on the screen. 'Yes,' he said to the screen. 'Don't hurt my dad.'

The room was full of static. The lights overhead continued to throb red.

Jimmy cursed himself. They couldn't hear him. He pushed away from the desk and grabbed the dangling Mike. 'Please don't hurt him,' he said, squeezing the button.

The man turned and looked directly at the camera. It was one of the security guards. There was a bit of movement peeking out from around the corner of the hall, more people out of sight.

'James, is it?'

Jimmy nodded. He watched his dad regain his composure and stand. His father made a gesture to someone out of sight, patted the air with his palm as if to calm someone.

'What's the new code?' the man with the radio asked.

Jimmy didn't want to tell him. But he wanted his father back inside. He wasn't sure what to do.

'The code,' the man said. He aimed the gun at Jimmy's

dad. Jimmy watched his father say something, then gesture for the portable. The security guard hesitated a moment before handing it over. His father lifted the unit to his mouth.

'They'll kill you,' his father said, calm as if he were telling his son to tie his boots. The man with the gun waved an arm, and someone rushed into view to wrestle with his father. 'They'll kill us all anyway,' his father shouted, struggling to keep hold of the radio. 'And they'll kill you the moment you open this door!'

Jimmy screamed as one of the men punched his father. His dad fought back but they punched him again. And then the man with the gun waved the other guy away. The room was full of static, so he couldn't hear the shot, but Jimmy could see the flashes of flame leap out, could see the way his father jerked as he was hit, watched him slump to the ground and become as still as Yani.

Jimmy dropped the Mike and grabbed the edges of the monitor. He yelled at this cruel window on the world while the guards in the silver overalls surveyed the man who had been his father. And then more men appeared from around the corner. They dragged Jimmy's mom behind them, kicking and silently screaming.

67

2312 – Day One
• Silo 17 •

'No, no, no, no—'
The room was static and pulse. The two men wrestled with Jimmy's mother, who lifted herself off the ground and writhed in their jerking grasps. Her feet kicked and whirled. Jimmy's father lay still as stone beneath her.

'Open this goddamn door!' the man with the portable yelled. The radio on the wall was deafening. Jimmy hated the radio. He ran to it, reached for the dangling cord, then thought better and grabbed the other portable from the rack. One of the knobs said *Power*. He twisted it until it made the hissing sound, turned to the screen and held the small radio to his mouth.

'Don't,' Jimmy said, and he realised he was crying. Tears splashed his overalls. 'I'm coming.'

It was hard to tear himself away from the view of his mother. As he rushed down the dark corridor, he continued to see her kicking and screaming, her boots in the air. He could hear her yelling in the background as the man radioed again: 'Tell me the code!'

Jimmy held the portable's wrist strap between his teeth and attacked the ladder, ignoring the pain in his shoulder and knee. He found the release for the grating and threw it aside with a clang. Tossing the portable out, he scrambled after it on his knees. The lights above were on fire. His chest was on fire. His father was as dead as Yani.

'Coming, coming,' he said into the radio.

The man yelled something back. All Jimmy could hear was his mother screaming and his heartbeat ringing in his ears. He ran beneath the pulsing lights and between the dark machines. The laces on one of his boots had come undone. They whipped about while he ran, and he thought of his mother's legs, up in the air like that, kicking and fighting.

Jimmy crashed into the door. He could hear muffled shouts on the other side. They came through the radio as well. Jimmy slapped the door with his palm and shouted into his portable: 'I'm here, I'm here!'

'The code!' the man screamed.

Jimmy went to the control pad. His hands were shaking, his vision blurred. He imagined his mother on the other side, the gun aimed at her. He could feel his father lying a few feet away, just on the other side of that steel door. Tears streamed down his cheeks. He put in the first two numbers, the level of his home, and hesitated. That wasn't right. It was twelve-eighteen, not eighteen-twelve. Or was it? He put in the other two numbers, and the keypad flashed red. The door didn't open.

'What did you do?' the man yelled through the radio. 'Just tell me the code!'

Jimmy fumbled with the portable, brought it to his lips. 'Please don't hurt her—' he said.

The radio squawked. 'If you don't do as I say, she's dead. Do you understand?'

The man sounded terrified. Maybe he was just as scared as Jimmy. Jimmy nodded and reached for the keypad. He entered the first two numbers correctly, then paused and thought about what his father had said. They would kill him. They would kill him and his mother both if he let these men inside. But it was his mom—

The keypad blinked impatiently. The man on the other side of the door yelled for him to hurry, yelled something about three wrong tries in a row and having to wait another day. Jimmy did nothing, paralysed with fear. The keypad flashed red and fell silent.

There was a bang on the other side of the door, a blast from a gun. Jimmy squeezed the radio and screamed. When he let go, he could hear his mom shrieking on the other side.

'The next one won't be a warning,' the man said. 'Now don't touch that pad. Don't touch it again. Just tell me the code. Hurry, boy.'

Jimmy blubbered and tried to form the sounds, to tell the man the numbers in the right order, but nothing came out. With his forehead pressed against the wall, he could hear his mother struggling and fighting on the other side.

'The code,' the man said, calmer now.

Jimmy heard a grunt. He heard someone yell 'Bitch', heard his mother scream for Jimmy not to do it, and then a slap on the other side of the wall, someone pressed up against it, his mother inches away. And then the muffled beeps of numbers being entered, four quick taps of the same number, and an angry buzz from the keypad as a third attempt failed.

More shouts. And then the roar of a gun, louder and angrier with his head pressed to the door. Jimmy screamed and beat his fists against the cold steel. The men were yelling at him through the radio. There were screams coming through the portable, screams leaking through the heavy steel door, but none were made by his mother.

Jimmy slid to the floor, buried the portable against his belly and curled into a ball as the angry yelling bled through the steel door. His body quivered with sobs, the floor grating rough against his cheek. And while the violence raged, the lights overhead continued to throb at him. They throbbed steady. They weren't like a pulse at all.

68

2345

• Silo 1 •

There was a plastic bag waiting on Donald's bunk when he got back to his room. He shut the door to block out the cacophony of traffic and office chatter, searched for a lock and saw that there wasn't one. Here was a lone bedroom among workspaces, a place for men who were always on call, who were up for as long as they were needed.

Donald imagined this was where Thurman stayed when he was called forth in an emergency. He remembered the name on his boots and realised he didn't have to imagine; it was happening.

The wheelchair had been removed, he saw, and a glass of water stood on the nightstand. He tossed the folders Eren had given him on the bed, sat down beside them and picked up the curious plastic bag.

Shift, it read, in large stencilled letters. The clear plastic was heavily wrinkled, a few items appearing inside as inscrutable bulges. Donald slid the plastic seal to the side and peeled open the bag. Turning it over, there was a jingle of metal as a pair of dog tags rattled out, a fine chain slithering after them like a startled snake. Donald inspected the tags and saw that they were Thurman's. Dented and thin, and without the rubber edging he remembered from his sister's tags, they seemed like antiques. Which he supposed they were.

A small pocketknife was next. The handle looked like ivory but was probably a substitute. Donald opened the blade and tested it. Both sides were equally dull. The tip had been snapped off at some point, used to prise something open, perhaps. It had the look of a memento, no longer good for cutting.

The only other item in the bag was a coin, a quarter. The shape and heft of something once so common made it difficult for him to breathe. Donald thought of an entire civilisation, gone. It seemed impossible for so much to be wiped out, but then he remembered Roman coins and Mayan coins sitting in museums. He turned this coin over and over and contemplated the only thing unusual about him holding a trinket from a world fallen to ashes – and that was him being around to marvel at the loss. It was supposed to be people who died and cultures that lasted. Now it was the other way around.

Something about the coin caught Donald's attention as he turned it over and over. It was heads on both sides. He laughed and inspected it more closely, wondering if it was a joke item, but the feel of the thing seemed genuine. On one of the sides, there was a faint arc where the stamp had missed its mark. A mistake? Perhaps a gift to Thurman from a friend in the Treasury?

He placed the items on the bedside table and remembered Anna's note to her father. He was surprised not to find a locket in the bag. The note had been marked urgent and had mentioned a locket with a date. Donald folded the bag marked *Shift* and slid it beneath his glass of water. People hurried up and down the hall outside. The silo was in a panic. He supposed if the real Thurman were there, the old man would be storming up and down as well, barking orders, shutting down facilities, ordering lives to be taken.

Donald coughed into the crook of his arm, his throat tickling. Someone had put him in this position. Erskine, or Victor beyond the grave, or maybe a hacker with more nefarious designs. He had nothing to go on.

Lifting the two folders, he thought of the panic roused by a person meandering out of sight. He thought about the violence brewing in the depths of another silo. These were not his mysteries, he thought. What he wanted to know was why he was awake, why he was even *alive*. What exactly was out there beyond those walls? What was the plan for the world once these shifts were over? Would there be a day when the people underground would be set free?

Something didn't sit right with him, imagining how that last shift would play out. There was a nagging suspicion that things wouldn't end so simply. Every layer he'd peeled back so far possessed its share of lies, and he didn't think he was done uncovering them. Perhaps someone had placed him in Thurman's boots to keep digging.

He recalled what Erskine had said about people like himself being in charge. Or was it Victor who said it to Erskine? He couldn't remember. What he did know, patting his pocket for the badge there – a badge that would open doors previously locked to him – was that he was very much in charge now. There were questions he wanted answers to. And now he was in a position to ask them.

Donald coughed into his elbow once more, an itch in his throat that he couldn't quite soothe. He opened one of the folders and reached for his glass. Taking a few gulps of water and beginning to read, he failed to notice the faint stain left behind, the spot of blood in the crook of his elbow.

69

2312 – Week One

• Silo 17 •

Jimmy didn't want to move. He couldn't move. He remained curled on the steel grating, the lights flashing overhead, on and off, on and off, the colour of crimson. People on the other side of the door yelled at him and at each other. Jimmy slept in fits and starts. There were dull pops from guns and zings that rang against the door. The keypad buzzed. Only a single digit entered, and it buzzed. The whole world was angry with him.

Jimmy dreamed of blood. It seeped under the door and filled the room. It rose up in the shape of his mother and father, and they lectured him, mouths yawning open in anger. But Jimmy couldn't hear.

The yelling on the other side of the door came and went. They were fighting, these men. Fighting to get inside where it was safe. Jimmy didn't feel safe. He felt hungry and alone. He needed to pee.

Standing was the hardest thing he'd ever done. Jimmy's cheek made a tearing sound as he lifted it from the grating. He wiped the drool from the side of his face and felt the ridges there, the deep creases and the places his skin puckered out. His joints were stiff. His eyes were crusted together from crying. He staggered to the far corner of the room and tugged at his overalls, tried to get them free before he accidentally wet himself.

Urine splashed through the grating and trickled down on bright runs of wires in neat channels. His stomach rumbled and spun inside his belly, but he didn't want to eat. He wanted to waste away completely. He glared up at the lights overhead that drilled into his skull. His stomach was angry with him. Everything was angry with him.

Back at the door, he waited for someone to call his name. He went to the keypad and pressed the number '1'. The door buzzed at him immediately. It was angry too.

Jimmy wanted to lie back down on the grating and curl back into a ball, but his stomach said to look for food. Below. There were beds and food below. Jimmy walked in a daze between the black machines. He touched their warm skin for balance, heard them clicking and whirring as if everything were normal. The red lights flashed over and over. Jimmy weaved his way between them until he found the hole in the ground.

He lowered his feet to the rungs of the ladder and noticed the buzzing noise. It came and went in time with the throbbing red lights. He pulled himself out of the shaft and crawled across the floor in pursuit of the sound. It was coming from the server with its back off. His father had called it a comm hub – whatever that was. He patted his chest and felt the key against his breastbone. The buzzing from the machine came and went with the flashing lights in perfect synchrony. He peered inside. There was a headset hanging on a hook with a wire dangling down from it. The piece on the end looked like something from computer class. He searched for a place to plug it in and saw a bank of sockets. One of them was blinking. The number '40' was lit up above it.

Jimmy adjusted the headset around his ears. He lined up the jack with the socket and pressed it in until he felt a click. The lights overhead stopped their incessant throbbing and a voice came through, like the radio, only clearer.

'Hello?' the voice said.

Jimmy didn't say anything. He waited.

'Is anyone there?'

Jimmy cleared his throat. 'Yes,' he said, and it felt strange to talk to an empty room. Stranger even than the radio with its hissing. It felt as though Jimmy were talking to himself.

'Is everyone okay?' the voice asked.

'No,' Jimmy said. He remembered the stairs and falling and Yani and something awful on the other side of the door. 'No,' he said again, wiping tears from his cheeks. 'Everyone is *not* okay!'

There was muttering on the other side of the line. Jimmy sniffled. 'Hello?' he said.

'What happened?' the voice demanded. Jimmy thought it was an angry voice. Just like the people outside the door.

'Everyone was running—' Jimmy said. He wiped his nose. 'They were all heading up. I fell. Mom and Dad—'

'There were casualties?' the man from level forty asked.

Jimmy thought of the body he'd seen on the stairway with the awful wound on his head. He thought of the woman who had gone over the rails, her scream fading to a crisp silence. 'Yes,' he said.

The voice on the line spat an angry curse, angry but faint. And then: 'We were too late.' Again, it sounded distant, as if the man were talking to someone else.

'Too late for what?' Jimmy asked.

There was a click, followed by a steady tone. The light above the socket marked '40' went out.

'Hello?'

Jimmy waited.

'Hello?'

He searched inside the box for some button to press, some way to make the voices come back. There were sockets with fifty numbers above them. Why only fifty levels? He glanced at the server behind him and wondered if there were other comm stations to handle the rest of the silo. This one must be for the up top. There would be one for the mids and another for the down deep. He unplugged the jack and the tone in the headset fell silent.

Jimmy wondered if he could call another level. Maybe one of the shops near home. He ran his finger down the row looking for '18' and noticed that '17' was missing. There was no jack for '17'. He puzzled over this as the overhead lights began to flash once more. Jimmy glanced at level forty's socket, but it remained dark. It was the top level calling. The light over the number '1' blinked on and off. Jimmy glanced at the jack in his hand, lined it up with the socket and pressed it in until he heard a click.

'Hello?' he said.

'What the hell is going on over there?' a voice demanded.

Jimmy shrank within himself. His father had yelled at him like this before, but not for a long time. He didn't answer because he didn't know what to say.

'Is this Jerry? Or Russ?'

Russ was his dad. Jerry was his dad's boss. Jimmy realised he shouldn't be playing with these things.

'This is Jimmy,' he said.

'Who?'

'Jimmy. The guy on level forty said they were too late. I told him what happened.'

'Too late?' There was some distant talking. Jimmy jiggled the cord in the socket. He was doing something wrong. 'How did you get in there?' the man asked.

'My dad let me in,' he said, the truth frightened out of him.

'We're shutting you down,' the voice said. 'Shut them down right now.'

Jimmy didn't know what to do. There was a hiss somewhere. He thought it was from the headset until he noticed the white steam coming from the vents overhead. A fog descended towards him. Jimmy waved his hand in front of his face, expecting the sting of smoke like he'd smelled from a fire once as a kid, but the steam didn't smell of anything. It just tasted like a dry spoon in his mouth. Like metal.

'—on my goddamn shift—' the person in his headset said.

Jimmy coughed. He tried to say something back but he had swallowed wrong. The steam stopped leaking from the vents.

'That did it,' the man on the other end of the line muttered. 'He's gone.'

Before Jimmy could say anything else, the winking lights inside the box went dark. There was a click in the headset and then it too fell silent. He pulled the headset off just as a louder *thunk* rang out in the ceiling and the lights in the room turned off. The whirring and clicking of the tall servers around him wound down. The room was pitch black and totally silent. Jimmy couldn't see his own nose, couldn't see his hand as he waved it in front of his face. He thought he'd gone blind, wondered if this was what being dead was like, but then he heard his pulse, a *thump-thump, thump-thump* in his temples.

Jimmy felt a sob catch in his throat. He wanted his mother and father. He wanted his backpack, which he'd left behind in his classroom like an idiot. For a long while, he sat there, waiting for someone to come to him, for an idea to form on what he should do next. He thought of the ladder nearby and the room below. As he began to crawl towards that hole, cautiously patting the grating ahead of him so he wouldn't fall down the long drop, the clunking in the ceiling came back. There was a blinding flash as the lights overhead wavered, shimmered, blinked on and off several times, then burned steady.

Jimmy froze. The red lights were back to flashing. He went back to the box and looked inside. It was the light over '40' ticking on and off. He thought about answering it, seeing what these people were so angry about, but maybe the power was a warning. Maybe he'd said something wrong.

The lights overhead were like bright heat. They reminded him of the farms, of the time years ago that his class had gone on a trip to the mids and planted seeds beneath those grow lights.

Jimmy turned to the server with the open back and fumbled for the jack inside. He hated the flashing lights, but he didn't want to get yelled at. So he jabbed the headphone jack into the socket marked '40' until he felt a click.

The lights stopped blinking immediately. There was a muffled voice from the headset, which lay in the bottom of the server. Jimmy ignored that. He took a step away from the machine, watched the overhead lights warily, waited on the bright white ones to shut off again or the angry red ones to return. But everything stayed the same. The jack sat in its socket, the wire dangling, the voice in the headset distant now, unable to be heard.

70

2312 – Week One
• Silo 17 •

J immy worked his way down the ladder, wondering how long it'd been since he last ate. He couldn't remember. Breakfast before school, but that was a day ago, maybe two. Halfway down the ladder, he thought of himself as a piece of food sliding through some great metal neck. This was what a swallowed bite felt like. At the bottom of the ladder, he stood for a moment in the bowels of the silo, a hollow thing lost in a hollow thing. There would be no end to the silo's hunger, chewing on something empty like him. They would both starve, he thought. His stomach grumbled; he needed to eat. Jimmy staggered down the dark corridor and through the silo's guts.

The radio on the wall continued to hiss. Jimmy turned the volume down until the spitting noise could barely be heard. His father wouldn't be calling him ever again. He wasn't sure how he knew this, but it was a Rule of the World.

He entered the small apartment. There was a table big enough for four with the pages of a book scattered across it, a needle and thread coiled on top like a snake guarding its nest. Jimmy thumbed the pages and saw that the place where the pages met was being repaired. His stomach hurt, it was so empty. His mind was beginning to ache as well.

Across the room, the ghost of his father stood and pointed out doors, told him what was behind each. Jimmy patted his chest for the key, took it out, and used it to unlock the pantry across from the stove. Food enough for two people for ten years, that was what his father had told him. Was that right?

The room made a sucking sound as he cracked the pantry door, and there was the tickle of a breeze against his neck. Jimmy found the light switch on the outside of the door – as well as a switch that ran a noisy fan. He turned the fan off, which only reminded him of the radio. Inside the room, he found shelves bulging with cans that receded so far he had to squint to see the back wall. These were cans like he'd never seen before. He squeezed between the tight shelves and searched up and down, his stomach begging him to choose and be quick about it. *Eat, eat*, his belly growled. Jimmy said to give him a chance.

Tomatoes and beets and squash, stuff he hated. Recipe food. He wanted *food* food. There were entire shelves of corn with labels like colourful sleeves of paper, not the black ink scrawled on a tin that he was used to. Jimmy grabbed one of the cans and studied it. A large man with green flesh smiled at him from the label. Tiny words like those printed in books wrapped all around. The cans of corn were identical. They made Jimmy feel out of place, like he was asleep and dreaming every bit of this.

He kept one of the corn and found an aisle of labelled soups in red and white, grabbed one of those as well. Back in the apartment, he rummaged for an opener. There were drawers around the stove full of spatulas and serving spoons. There was a cabinet with pots and lids. A bottom drawer held charcoal pencils, a spool of thread, batteries bulging with age and covered in grey powder, a child's whistle, a screwdriver and myriad other things.

He found the can opener. It was rusty and appeared as if it hadn't been used in years. But the dull cutter still sank through the soft tin when he gave it a squeeze, and the handle turned if given enough force. Jimmy worked it all the way around and cursed when the lid sank down into the soup. He fished a knife out of the drawer to lever the lid out with the tip. Food. Finally. He placed a pot onto the stove and turned the burner on, thinking of his apartment, of his mother and father. The soup heated. Jimmy waited, stomach growling, but some part of him was dimly aware that there was nothing he could put inside himself to touch the real ache, this mysterious urge he felt every moment to scream at the top of his lungs or to collapse to the floor and cry.

While he waited for the soup to bubble, he inspected the sheets of paper the size of small blankets hanging on one wall. It looked as if they'd been hung out to dry, and he thought at first that the thick books must be made by folding up or cutting these. But the large sheets were already printed on, the drawings continuous. Jimmy ran his hands down the smooth paper and studied the details of a schematic, an arrangement of circles with fine lines inside each and labels everywhere. There were numbers over the circles. Three of them were crossed out with red ink. Each was labelled a 'silo', but that didn't make any sense.

Behind him, a hissing like the radio, like someone calling for him, the whisperings of ghosts. Jimmy turned from the strange drawing to find his soup spitting bubbles, dripping down the edge and sizzling on the glowing-hot burner. He left the large and strange drawing alone.

71

2312 – Week One

• Silo 17 •

Days passed until they threatened to make a week, and Jimmy could glimpse how weeks might eventually become months. Beyond the steel door in the upper room, the men outside were still trying to get in. They yelled and argued over the radio. Jimmy listened sometimes, but all they talked about were the dead and dying and forbidden things, like the great outside.

Jimmy cycled through camera angles of quietude and vast emptiness. Sometimes these still views were interrupted with bursts of activity and violence. Jimmy saw a man held down on the ground and beaten by other men. He saw a woman dragged down a hall, feet kicking. He watched a man attack a child over a loaf of bread. He had to turn the monitor off. His heart raced the rest of the day and into the night, and he resolved not to look at the cameras any more. That night, alone in the bunk room with all the empty beds, he hardly slept. But when he did, he dreamed of his mother.

The days would be like this, he thought the next morning. Each day would stretch out for ever, but their counting would not take long. Their counting would run out for him. His days were numbered and ticking away; he could feel it.

He moved one of the mattresses out into the room with the computer and the radio. There was a semblance of company in that room. Angry voices and scenes of violence were better than the emptiness of the other bunks. He forgot his promise to himself and ate warm soup in front of the cameras, looking for people. He listened to their soft voices bicker on the radio. And when he dreamed that night, his dreams were filled with little square views of a distant past. A younger self stood in those windows, peering back at him.

In forays to the room above, Jimmy crept silently to the steel door and listened to men argue on the other side. They tried codes, three beeping entries at a time, followed by three angry buzzes. Jimmy rubbed the steel door and thanked it for staying shut.

Padding away quietly, he explored the grid of machines. They whirred and clicked and blinked their flashing eyes, but they didn't say anything. They didn't move. Their presence made Jimmy feel even more alone, like a classroom of large boys who all ignored him. Just a handful of days like this and Jimmy felt a new Rule of the World: man wasn't meant to live alone. This was what he discovered, day by day. He discovered it and just as soon forgot, for there was no one around to remind him. He spoke with the machines instead. They clacked back at him and hissed deep in their metal throats that man wasn't supposed to live at all.

The voices on the radio seemed to believe this. They reported deaths and promised more of them for each other. Some of them had guns from the deputy stations. There was a man on the ninety-first who wanted to make sure everyone else knew he had a gun. Jimmy felt like telling this man about the storage facility his key had unlocked beyond the bunk room. There were racks and racks of guns like the one his father had used to kill Yani. And countless boxes of bullets. He felt like telling the entire silo that he had more guns than anyone, that he had the key to the silo, so please stay away, but something told him that these men would just try harder to reach him if he did. So Jimmy kept his secrets to himself.

On the sixth night of being alone, unable to sleep, Jimmy tried to make himself drowsy by flipping through the book on the desk labelled *Order*. It was a strange read, each page referencing other pages, and filled with accounts of all the horrible things that could happen, how to prevent them, how to mitigate inevitable disasters. Jimmy looked for an entry on finding oneself completely and utterly alone. There was nothing in the index. And then Jimmy remembered what was in all the hundreds of metal cases lining the bookshelf beside the desk. Maybe there was something in one of those books that could help him.

He checked the small labels on the lower portion of each tin, went to the *Li–Lo* box for 'loneliness'. There was a soft sigh as he cracked the tin, like a can of soup sucking at the air. Jimmy slid the book out and flipped towards the back where he thought he'd find the entry.

Instead, he came across the sight of a great machine with large wheels like the wooden toy dog he'd owned as a kid. Fearsome and black with a pointy nose, the machine loomed impossibly large over the man standing in front of it. Jimmy waited for the man to move, but rubbing it, he found it just to be a picture like on his dad's work ID, but one so glossy and vivid in colour that it looked to be real.

Locomotive, Jimmy read. He knew these words. The first part meant 'crazy'. The second part was a person's reason for doing something. He studied this image, wondering what crazy reason someone would have of making this picture. Jimmy carefully turned the page, hoping to find more on this loco motive—

He screamed and dropped the book when the page flopped over. He hopped around and brushed himself with both hands, waiting for the bug to disappear down his shirt or bite him. He stood on his mattress and waited for his heart to stop pounding. Jimmy eyed the flopped-open tome on the ground, expecting a swarm to fly out like the pests in the farms, but nothing moved.

He approached the book and flipped it over with his foot. The damn bug was just another picture, the page folded over and creased where he'd dropped it. Jimmy smoothed the page, read the word *locust* out loud, and wondered just what sort of book this was supposed to be. It was nothing like the children's books he'd grown up with, nothing like the pulp paper they taught with at school.

Flipping the cover over, Jimmy saw that this was different from the book on the desk, which had been embossed with the word *Order*. This one was labelled *Legacy*. He flipped through it a pinch at a time, bright pictures on every page, paragraphs of words and descriptions, a vast fiction of impossible deeds and impossible things, all in a single book.

Not in a single book, he told himself. Jimmy glanced up at the massive shelves bulging with metal tins, each one labelled and arranged in alphabetical order. He searched again for the locomotive, a machine on wheels that dwarfed a grown man. He found the entry and shuffled back to his mattress and his twisted tangle of sheets. A week of solitude was drawing to a close, but there was no chance that Jimmy would be getting any sleep. Not for a very long while.

72

2345

• Silo 1 •

Donald waited in the comm room for his first briefing with the head of eighteen. To pass the time, he twisted the knobs and dials that allowed him to cycle through that silo's camera feeds. From a single seat, he had a view of all of the world's residents. He could nudge their fates from a distance if he liked. He could end them all with the press of a button. While he lived on and on, freezing and thawing, these mortals went through routines, lived and died, unaware that he even existed.

'It's like the afterlife,' he muttered.

The operator at the next station turned and regarded him silently, and Donald realised he'd spoken aloud. He faced the man, whose bushy black hair looked as though it'd last been combed a century ago. 'It's just that . . . it's like a view from the heavens,' he explained, indicating the monitor.

'It's a view of something,' the operator agreed and took a bite of a sandwich. On his screen, one woman seemed to be yelling at another, a finger jabbed in the other woman's face. It was a sitcom without the laugh track.

Donald worked on keeping his mouth shut. He dialled in the cafeteria on eighteen and watched its people huddle around a wall screen. It was a small crowd. They gazed out at the lifeless hills, perhaps awaiting their departed cleaner's return, perhaps silently dreaming about what lay beyond those quiet crests. Donald wanted to tell them that she wouldn't be coming back, that there was nothing beyond that rise, even though he secretly shared their dreams. He longed to send up one of the drones to look, but Eren had told him the drones weren't for sightseeing – they were for dropping bombs. They had a limited range, he said. The air out there would tear them to shreds. Donald wanted to show Eren his hand, mottled and pink, and tell him that he'd been out on that hill and back. He wanted to ask if the air outside was really so bad.

Hope. That's what this was. Dangerous hope. He watched the people in the cafeteria staring at the wall screen and felt a kinship with them. This was how the gods of old got in trouble, how they ended up smitten with mortals and tangled in their affairs. Donald laughed to himself. He thought of this cleaner with her thick folder and how he might've intervened if he'd had the chance. He might've given her a gift of life if he were able. Apollo, doting on Daphne.

The comm officer glanced over at Donald's monitor, that view of the wall screen, and Donald felt himself being studied. He switched to a different camera. It was the hallway of what looked like a school. Lockers lined either side. A child stood on her tiptoes and opened one of the upper ones, pulled out a small bag, turned and seemed to say something to someone off-camera. Life going on as usual.

'The call's coming through now,' the operator behind them said. The man with the sandwich put it down and sat forward. He brushed the crumbs off his chest and switched his view of two women arguing to one of a room full of black cabinets. Donald grabbed a pair of headphones and pulled the two folders off the desk. The one on the top was two inches thick. It was about the missing cleaner. Beneath that was a much thinner folder with a potential shadow's name on it. A man's voice came through his headphones.

'Hello?'

Donald glanced up at his monitor. A figure stood behind one of the black cabinets. He was pudgy and short, unless it was the distortion from the camera lens.

'Report,' Donald said. He flipped open the folder marked *Lukas Kyle*. He knew from his last shift that the system would make his voice sound flat, make all their voices sound the same.

'I picked out a shadow as you requested, sir. A good kid. He's done work on the servers before, so his access has already been vetted.'

How meek this man. Donald reckoned he would feel the same way, knowing his world could be ended at the press of a button. Fear like that puts a man at odds with his ego.

The operator beside Donald leaned over and peeled back the top page in the folder for him. He tapped his finger on something a few lines down. Donald scanned the report.

'You looked at Mr Kyle as a possible replacement two years ago.' Donald glanced up to watch the man behind the comm server wipe the back of his neck.

'That's right,' the head of eighteen said. 'We didn't think he was ready.'

'Your office filed a report on Mr Kyle as a possible gazer. Says here he's logged a few hundred hours in front of the wall screen. What's changed your mind?'

'That was a preliminary report, sir. It came from another . . . potential shadow. A bit overeager, a gentleman we found more suited for the security team. I assure you that Mr Kyle does not dream of the outside. He only goes up at night—' The man cleared his throat, seemed to hesitate. 'To look at the stars, sir.'

'The stars.'

'That's right.'

Donald glanced over at the operator beside him, who polished off his sandwich. The operator shrugged. The silo head broke the silence.

'He's the best man for the job, sir. I knew his father. Stern sonofabitch. You know what they say about the treads and the rails, sir.'

Donald had no idea what they said about the treads and the rails. It was nothing but stair analogies from these silos. He wondered what this Bernard would say if the man ever saw a lift. The thought nearly elicited a chuckle.

'Your choice of shadow has been approved,' Donald said. 'Get him on the Legacy as soon as possible.'

'He's studying right now, sir.'

'Good. Now, what's the latest on this uprising?' Donald felt himself hurrying along, performing rote tasks so he could get back to his more pressing studies.

The silo head glanced back towards the camera. This mortal knew damn well where the eyes of gods lay hidden. 'Mechanical is holed up pretty tight. They put up a fight on their retreat down, but we routed them good. There's a . . . bit of a barricade, but we should be through it any time now.'

The operator leaned forward and grabbed Donald's attention. He pointed two fingers at his eyes, then at one of the blank screens on the top row, indicating one of the cameras that had gone out during the uprising. Donald knew what he was getting at.

'Any idea how they knew about the cameras?' he asked. 'You know we're blind over here from one-forty down, right?'

'Yessir. We . . . I can only assume they've known about them for a while. They do their own wiring down there. I've been in person. It's a nest of pipes and cables. We don't think anyone tipped them off.'

'You don't think.'

'Nossir. But we're working on getting someone in there. I've got a priest we can send in to bless their dead. A good man. Shadowed with Security. I promise it won't be long.'

'Fine. Make sure it isn't. We'll be over here cleaning up your mess, so get the rest of your house in order.'

'Yessir. I will.'

The three men in the comm room watched this Bernard remove his headset and return it to the cabinet. He wiped his forehead with a rag. While the others were distracted, Donald did the same, wiping the sweat off his brow with a handkerchief he'd requisitioned. He picked up the two folders and studied the operator beside him, who had a fresh trail of breadcrumbs down his overalls.

'Keep a close eye on him,' Donald said.

'Oh, I will.'

Donald returned his headset to the rack and got up to leave. Pausing at the door, he looked back and saw the screen in front of the operator had divided into four squares. In one, a roomful of black towers stood like silent sentinels. Two women were having a row in another.

73

2345

• Silo 1 •

D onald took his notes and rode the lift to the cafeteria. He arrived to find it was too early for breakfast, but there was still coffee in the dispenser from the night before. He selected a chipped mug from the drying rack and filled it. A gentleman behind the serving line lifted the handle on an industrial washer, and the stainless steel box opened and let loose a cloud of steam. The man waved a dishrag at the cloud, then used it to pull out metal trays that would soon hold reconstituted eggs and slices of freeze-dried toast.

Donald tried the coffee. It was cold and weak but he didn't mind. It suited him. He nodded to the man prepping for breakfast, who dipped his head in reply.

Donald turned and took in the view splayed across the wall screen. Here was the mystery. The documents in his folders were nothing compared to this. He approached the dusky vista where swirling clouds were just beginning to glow from a sun rising invisibly beyond the hills. He wondered what was out there. People died when they were sent to clean. They died on the hills when silos were shut down. But he had survived. And as far as he knew, so had the men who had dragged him back.

He studied his hand in the dim light leaking from the wall screen. His palm seemed a little pink to him, a little raw. But then, he had scrubbed it half a dozen times for the last few nights and each morning. He couldn't shake the feeling that it had been tainted. He pulled his handkerchief out of his pocket and coughed into its folds.

'I'll have potatoes ready in a few minutes,' the man behind the counter called out. Another worker in green overalls emerged from the back, cinching an apron around his waist. Donald wanted to know who these people were, what their lives were like, what they were thinking. For six months, they served three meals a day, and then hibernated for decades. Then they did it all over again. They must believe they were heading somewhere. Or did they not care? Was it a case of following the tracks laid down yesterday? A boot in a hole, a boot in a hole, round and round. Did these men see themselves as deck hands on some great ark with a noble purpose? Or were they walking in circles simply because they knew the way?

Donald remembered running for Congress, thinking he was going to do real good for the future. And then he found himself in an office surrounded by a bewildering tempest of rules, memos and messages, and he quickly learned just to pray for the end of each day. He went from thinking he was going to save the world to passing the time until . . . until time ran out.

He sat down in one of the faded plastic chairs and studied the folder in his pink hand. Two inches thick. *Nichols, Juliette* was written on the tab, followed by an ID number for internal purposes. He could smell the toner from the newly printed pages. It seemed a waste, printing out so much nonsense. Somewhere, down in the vast storeroom, supplies were dwindling. And somewhere else, down the hall from his own office, a person was keeping track of it all, making sure there were just enough potatoes, just enough toner, just enough light bulbs, to get them through to the end.

Donald glanced over the reports. He spread them out across the empty table and thought of Anna and his last shift as he did so, the way they had smothered that war room with clues. He felt a pang of guilt and regret that Anna so often entered his thoughts before Helen could.

The reports were a welcome distraction while he awaited the sunrise and his food. Here was a story about a cleaner who had been a sheriff, though not for long. One of the top reports in her folder was from the current head of eighteen, a memo on this cleaner's lack of qualifications. Donald read a list of reasons this woman should not be given a mantle of power, and it was as though he were reading about himself. It seemed the mayor of eighteen – an old woman called Jahns, a politician like Thurman – had wrangled this woman into the job, had recruited her despite the objections. It wasn't even clear that this Nichols, a mechanic from the lower levels, even *wanted* the job. In another report from the silo head, Donald read about her defiance, culminating in a walk out of sight and a refusal to clean. Again, it felt all too familiar to Donald. Or was he looking for these similarities? Isn't that what people did? Saw in others what they feared to see or hoped to see in themselves?

The hills outside brightened by degrees. Donald glanced up from the reports and studied the mounds of dirt. He remembered the video feed he'd been shown of this cleaner disappearing over a similarly grey dune. Now the panic among his colleagues was that the residents of eighteen would be filled with a dangerous sort of hope – the kind of hope that leads to violence. The far graver threat, of course, was that this cleaner had made it to another facility, that those in another silo might discover they were not alone.

Donald did not think it likely. She couldn't have lasted long, and there was little to discover in the direction she had wandered. He pulled out the other folder, the one on silo seventeen.

There had been no warning before its collapse, no increase in violence. The population graphs appeared normal. He flipped through pages of typed documents from various division heads downstairs. Everyone had their theory, and of course each saw the collapse through the lens of their own expertise, or attributed it to the incompetence of another division. Population Control blamed a lax IT department. IT blamed a hardware failure. Engineering blamed programming. And the on-duty comm officer, who liaised with IT and each individual silo head, thought it was sabotage, an attempt to prevent a cleaning.

Donald sensed something familiar about the breakdown of silo seventeen, something he couldn't place. The camera feeds had gone out, but not before a brief view of people spilling out of the airlock. There had been an exodus, a panic, mass hysteria. And then a blackout. Comm had placed several calls. The first had been answered by the IT shadow, seventeen's second-in-charge. There was a short exchange with this Russ fellow, questions fired from both ends, and then Russ had broken the connection.

The follow-up call had gone unanswered for hours. During this time, the silo went dark. And then someone else picked up the line.

Donald coughed into his handkerchief and read this unusual exchange. The officer on duty claimed the respondent sounded young. It was a male, not a shadow or the head, and he had asked a flurry of questions. One stood out to Donald. The person in seventeen, with only minutes left to live, had asked what was going on down on level forty.

Level forty. Donald didn't need to grab a schematic to check – he had designed the facilities. He knew every level like the back of his hand. Level forty was a mixed-use level with half to housing, a quarter to light agriculture, the rest to commercial. What could be going on down there? And why would this person, who must've been at the limits of survival, care?

He read the exchange again. It almost sounded as though the young man's last contact had been with level forty, as if he'd just spoken with them. Maybe he'd come from down there? It was only six levels away. Donald imagined a frightened boy storming up the stairwell with thousands of others. News of an opened airlock, of death below, people chasing upward. This young man gets to level thirty-four, and the crush of people is too much. IT has already emptied. He finds his way into the server room—

No. Donald shook his head. That wasn't right. None of that felt right. What was it about this that nagged him?

It was the blackout. Donald felt a chill run up his spine. It was the number forty. It was the silo, not the level. The report trembled in his hands. He wanted to jump up and pace the cafeteria, but all he had was the germ of a connection, the hint of an outline. He fought to connect the dots before the ideas melted away, disturbed by a rush of adrenalin.

It was *silo* forty he had spoken with. The boy had found himself at the back of seventeen's comm station. He didn't know it was a silo calling at all. That would be why he'd called it a level and had wondered what was happening down there. This blackout, this lack of contact, it was just like the silos Anna had been working on.

Anna—

Donald thought about the note she had left, asking Thurman to wake her. She was asleep below. She would know what to do. She should've been woken and put in charge, not him. He gathered the reports and papers and put them back into the proper folders. Workers were beginning to arrive from the lifts. The smell of reconstituted eggs floated out from the kitchen, the swinging doors pumping the aroma with the traffic of the bustling food staff, but Donald had forgotten his hunger.

He glanced up at the wall screen. Would anyone on shift right now know of silo forty? Maybe not. They wouldn't have made the same connection. Thurman and the others had kept the outbreak a secret, didn't want to cause a panic. But what if silo forty was still out there? What if they'd contacted seventeen? Anna said the master system had been hacked, that silo forty had hacked them. They had cut several facilities off from silo one before Anna and Thurman had been woken to terminate them all. But what if they hadn't? What if this silo seventeen wasn't destroyed? What if it was still there, and this cleaner had stumbled into the bowl to find—

Donald had a sudden urge to go see for himself, to stroll outside and dash up to the top of the hill, suit be damned. He left the wall screen and headed towards the airlock.

Perhaps he would need to wake Anna, just as Thurman had. He could set her up in the armoury. There was a blue-print for doing this from his last shift, only he didn't have anyone he could trust to help. He didn't know the first thing about waking people up. But he was in charge, right? He could demand to know.

He left the cafeteria and approached the silo's airlock, that great yellow door to the open world beyond. The outside wasn't as bad as he had been led to believe. Unless he was simply immune. There were machines in his blood that kept him stitched up when he was frozen. Perhaps they had kept him alive out there. He approached the inner airlock door and peered through the small porthole. The memory of being in there struck him with sudden violence. He tucked the two folders under his elbow and rubbed his arm where the needle had bitten into his flesh long ago, putting him to sleep. What was out there? The light spilling through the holding cell bars flickered as a dust cloud passed, and Donald realised how strange it was that they had a wall screen in silo one. The people here knew what they'd done to the world. Why did they need to see the ruin they'd left behind?

Unless—

Unless the purpose was the same as for the other silos. Unless it was to keep them from going outside, a haunting reminder that the planet was not safe for them. But what did they really know beyond the silos? And how could a man hope to see for himself?

74

• Silo 1 •

I t took a few days of planning and building up the nerve for Donald to make the request, and a few days more for Dr Wilson to schedule an appointment. During that time he told Eren about his suspicions of silo forty's involvement. The flurry of activity launched by this simple guess quickly consumed the silo. Donald signed off on a requisition for a bombing run, even though he didn't quite understand what he was signing. Little-used levels of the silo – levels familiar to Donald from before – were reawakened. Days later, he didn't feel the rumble or the ground shake, but others claimed to have. All he found was that a new layer of dust had settled over his things, shaken loose from the ceiling.

The day of his meeting with Dr Wilson, he stole down to the main cryopod floor to test his code. He still didn't fully trust the disguise offered by his loose overalls and the badge with someone else's name on it. Just the day before, he had seen someone in the gym he thought he recognised from his first shift. It put him in the habit of slinking instead of strutting. And so he shuffled down the hall of frozen bodies and entered his code into the keypad warily. He expected red lights and warning buzzes. Instead, the light above the *Emergency Personnel* label flashed green, and the lock clanked. Donald glanced down the hall to see if anyone was watching as he pulled the door open and slipped inside.

The little-used cryochamber was a fraction of the size of the others and only one level deep. Standing inside the door,

Donald could picture how the main deep freeze wrapped around this much smaller room. This was a mere bump along great walls that stretched nearly out of sight. And yet it contained something far more precious. To him, anyway.

He picked his way through the pods and peeked in at the frozen faces. It was difficult to remember being there with Thurman on his previous shift, hard to recall the exact spot, but he eventually found her. He checked the small screen and remembered thinking it didn't matter what her name was, saw that there wasn't one assigned. Just a number.

'Hey, sis.'

His fingertips sang against the glass as he rubbed the frost away. He recalled their parents with sadness. He wondered how much Charlotte knew of this place and Thurman's plans before she came here. He hoped nothing. He liked to think her less culpable than him.

Seeing her brought back memories of her visit to DC. She had wasted a precious furlough on campaigning for Thurman and seeing her brother. Charlotte had given him a hard time when she found out he'd lived in DC for two years and hadn't been to any of the museums. It didn't matter how busy he was, she'd said. It was unforgivable. 'They're free,' she told him, as if that were reason enough.

So they had gone to the Air and Space Museum together. Donald remembered waiting to get in. He remembered a scale model of the solar system on the sidewalk outside the museum entrance. Although the inner planets were located just a few strides apart, Pluto was blocks away, down past the Hirshhorn Museum, impossibly distant. Now, as he gazed at his sister's frozen form, that day in his memory felt the same way. Impossibly distant. A tiny dot.

Later that afternoon, she had dragged him to the Holocaust Museum. Donald had been avoiding going since moving to Washington. Maybe it was the reason he avoided the National Mall altogether. Everyone told him it was something he had to see. 'You must go,' they'd say. 'It's important.' They used words like 'powerful' and 'haunting'. They said it would change his life. They said this – but their eyes warned him.

His sister had pulled him up the steps, his heart heavy with dread. The building had been constructed as a reminder, but Donald didn't want to be reminded. He was on his meds by then to help him forget what he was reading in the Order, to keep him from feeling as though the world might end at any moment. Such barbarisms as that building contained were buried in the past, he'd told himself, never to be unearthed or repeated.

There had been remnants of the museum's sixtieth anniversary still hanging, sombre signs and banners. A new wing had been installed, cords and stakes holding up fledgling trees and the air scented with mulch. He remembered seeing a group of tourists file out, dabbing at their eyes and shielding themselves from the sun. He had wanted to turn and run, but his sister had held his hand and the man at the ticket booth had already smiled at him. At least it'd been late in the day, so they couldn't stay long.

Donald rested his hands on the coffin-like pod and remembered the visit. There had been scenes of torture and starvation. A room full of shoes beyond counting. Walls displayed images of naked bodies folded together, lifeless eyes wide open, ribs and genitals exposed, as mounds of people tumbled into a pit, into a hole scooped out of the earth. Donald couldn't bear to look at it. He had tried to focus on the bulldozer instead, to look at the man driving the machine, that serene face, a cigarette between pursed lips, a look of steady concentration. A job. There was no solace to be found anywhere in that scene. The man driving the bulldozer was the most horrific part.

Donald had shrunk away from those grisly exhibits, losing his sister in the darkness. Here was a museum of horrors never to be repeated. Mass burials performed with the opposite of ceremony, with complete apathy. People calmly marched into showers.

He had sought refuge in a new exhibit called *Architects*

of Death, drawn to the blueprints, to the promise of the familiar and the ordered. He'd found instead a claustrophobic space wallpapered with schematics of slaughter. That exhibit had been no easier to stomach. There was a wall explaining the movement to deny the Holocaust, even after it had happened.

The array of blueprints had been shown as evidence. That was the purpose of the room. Blueprints that had survived the frantic burnings and purges as the Russians closed in, Himmler's signature on many of them. The layout of Auschwitz, the gas chambers, everything clearly labelled. Donald had hoped the plans would give him relief from what he saw elsewhere in the museum, but then he had learned that Jewish draughtsmen had been forced to contribute. Their pens had inked in the very walls around them. They had been coerced into sketching the home of their future abuse.

Donald remembered fumbling for a bottle of pills as the small room spun around him. He remembered wondering how those people could have gone along with it, could have seen what they were drawing and not known. How could they not know, not see what it was for?

Blinking tears away, he noticed where he was standing. The pods in their neat rows were alien to him, but the walls and floor and ceiling were familiar enough. Donald had helped to design this place. It was here because of him. And when he'd tried to get out, to escape, they had brought him back screaming and kicking, a prisoner behind his own walls.

The beeping of the keypad outside chased away these disturbing thoughts. Donald turned as the great slab of steel hinged inward on pins the size of a man's arms. Dr Wilson, the shift doctor, stepped inside. He spotted Donald and frowned. 'Sir?' he called out.

Donald could feel a trickle of sweat work its way down his temple. His heart continued to race from the memory of the exhibition. He felt warm, despite being able to see his breath puff out before him.

'Did you forget about our appointment?' Dr Wilson asked.

Donald wiped his forehead and rubbed his palm on the seat of his pants. 'No, no,' he said, fighting to keep the shakiness out of his voice. 'I just lost track of time.'

Dr Wilson nodded. 'I saw you on my monitor and figured that was it.' He glanced at the pod nearest to Donald and frowned. 'Someone you know?'

'Hm? No.' Donald removed his hand, which had grown cold against the pod. 'Someone I worked with.'

'Well, are you ready?'

'Yes,' Donald said. 'I appreciate the refresher. It's been a while since I've gone over the protocols.'

Dr Wilson smiled. 'Of course. I've got you lined up with the new reactor tech coming on to his fourth shift. We're just waiting on you.' He gestured towards the hall.

Donald patted his sister's pod and smiled. She had waited hundreds of years. Another day or two wouldn't hurt. And then they would see what exactly he had helped to build. The two of them would find out together.

75

2313 – Year Two

• Silo 17 •

Jimmy couldn't bring himself to write on the paper. He was drowning in paper, but he didn't dare use even the margins for notes. Those pages were sacrosanct. Those books were too valuable. And so he counted the days using the key around his neck and the black panels of the server labelled '17'.

This was his silo, he had learned. It was the number stamped on the inside of his copy of the Order. It was the label on the wall chart of all the silos. He knew what this meant. He might be all alone in his world, *but his was not the only world.*

Every evening before he went to bed, he scratched another bright silver mark in the black paint of the massive server. Jimmy only marked off the days at night. It seemed premature to do it in the mornings.

The Project started sloppily. He had little confidence that the marks would amount to much and so he made them in the middle of the machine and much too large. Two months into his ordeal, he began to run out of room and realised he would need to start adding marks up above, so he had scratched through the ones he'd already made and had gone around to the other side of the server to start anew. Now he made them tiny and neat. Four ticks and then a slash through them, just like his mom used to mark the days in a row that he was good. Six of these in a line to mark what he now thought of as a month. Twelve of these rows with five left over, and he had a year.

He made the final mark in the last set and stepped back. A year took up half the side of a server. It was hard to believe a whole year had gone by, a year of living in the half-level below the servers. He knew this couldn't last. Imagining the other servers covered in scratches was too much to bear. His dad had said there was enough food for ten years for two or four people. He couldn't remember which. That meant at least twenty with him all alone. Twenty years. He stepped around the edge of the server and looked down the aisle between the rows. The massive silver door sat at the very end. At some point, he knew he would have to go out. He would go crazy if he didn't. He was already going crazy. The days were much too full of the same.

He went to the door and listened for some sound on the other side. It was quiet, as it sometimes was, but he could still hear faint bangs echo from his memory. Jimmy thought about entering the four numbers and peeking outside. It was the worst sensation imaginable, not being able to see what was on the other side. When the camera screens had stopped working, Jimmy had felt a primal sense stripped away. He was left with a strong urge to open the door, to crack an eyelid held shut for too long. A year of counting days. Of counting minutes within those days. A boy could only count so long.

He left the keypad alone. Not yet. There were bad people out there, people who wanted in, who wanted to know what was in there, why the power on the level still worked, who he was.

'I'm nobody,' Jimmy told them when he had the courage to talk. 'Nobody.'

He didn't have that courage often. He felt brave enough just listening to the men with the other radios fight. Brave to allow their arguments to fill his world and his head, to hear them argue and report about who had killed whom. One group was working on the farms, another was trying to stop the floods from creeping out of the mines and drowning Mechanical. One had guns and took whatever little bit the others were able to squeeze together. A lone woman called once and screamed for help, but what help could Jimmy be? By his figuring, there were a hundred or more people out there in little pockets, fighting and killing. But they would stop soon. They had to. Another day. A year. They couldn't go on fighting for ever, could they?

Maybe they could.

Time had become strange. It was a thing *believed* rather than seen. He had to trust that time was passing at all. There was no dimming of the stairwell and lights-out to signify the coming night. No trips to the top and the glow of sunshine to tell that it was day. There were simply numbers on a computer screen counting so slowly one could scream. Numbers that looked the same day and night. It took careful counting to know a day had passed. The counting let him know that he was alive.

Jimmy thought about playing chase between the servers before he went to bed, but he had done that yesterday. He thought about arranging cans in the order he would eat them, but he already had three months' worth of meals lined up. There was target practice, books to read, a computer to fiddle with, chores to do, but none of that sounded like fun. He knew he would probably just crawl into bed and stare at the ceiling until the numbers told him it was tomorrow. He would think about what to do then.

76

2313 – Year Two

• Silo 17 •

W eeks passed, scratches accumulated, and the tip of the key around Jimmy's neck wore down. He woke to another morning with crust in his eyes as though he'd been crying in his sleep and took his breakfast – one can of peaches and one of pineapple – up to the great steel door to eat. Unshouldering his gun, Jimmy sat down with his back against server number eight, enjoying the warmth of the busy machine against his spine.

The gun had taken some figuring out. His father had disappeared with the loaded one, and when Jimmy discovered the crates of arms and ammo, the method of inserting the bright casings into the machine had posed a puzzle. He made the task a Project, like his father had used to make their chores and tinkering. Ever since he was little, Jimmy had watched his dad disassemble computers and other electronics, laying out all the pieces – each screw, every bolt, the nuts spun back onto the bolts – in a neat pattern so he knew where they went again. Jimmy had done the same with one of the rifles. And then with a second rifle after he'd accidentally knocked the pieces from the first with his boot.

With the second, he saw where the ammo ended up and how it got there. The spring in the ammo holder was stiff, which made it difficult to load. Later, he learned that this was called a 'clip', after reading the entry for 'gun' under *G* in the tins full of books. That had come weeks after he'd figured out how the thing worked on his own, with a hole in the ceiling to show for it.

He kept the gun in his lap, across his thighs, and balanced the cans of fruit on the wide part of the stock. The pineapple was his favourite. He had some every day and watched with sadness as the supply on the shelves dwindled. He'd never heard of such a fruit, had to look the thing up in another of the books. The pineapples had led him on a dizzying tour through the book tins. *Be* for 'beach' had led to *Oc* for 'ocean'. This one confused him with its sense of scale. And then the 'fish' under *F*. He had forgotten to eat that day as he explored, and the room with the radio and his little mattress had become cluttered with open books and empty tins. It had taken him a week to get things back in order. Countless times since then, he had lost himself in such excursions.

Pulling his rusty can opener and favourite fork from his breast pocket, Jimmy worked the peaches open. There was the whispering pop of air as he made the first cut. Jimmy had learned not to eat the contents if it didn't make that pop. Luckily, the toilets had still been in operation back when he'd learned that lesson. Jimmy missed the toilets something fierce.

He worked his way through the peaches, savouring each bite before drinking down the juice. He wasn't sure if you were supposed to drink that part – the label didn't say – but it was his favourite. He grabbed the pineapples and his opener, was listening for the pop of air when he heard the keypad on the great steel door beep.

'Little early,' he whispered to his visitors. He set the can aside, licked his fork and put it back in his breast pocket. Cradling the gun against his armpit, he sat and watched for the door to move. One crack and he would open fire.

Instead, he heard four beeps from the keypad as a set of numbers was entered, followed by a buzz to signal that it was the wrong code. Jimmy tightened his grip on the gun while they tried again. The screen on the keypad only had room for four digits. That meant ten thousand combinations if you included all zeros. The door allowed three incorrect attempts before it wouldn't take any more until the following day.

Jimmy had learned these things a long time ago. He felt as if his mom had taught him this rule, but that was impossible. Unless she'd done it in a dream.

He listened to the keypad beep with another guess and then buzz once again. One more number down, which meant time was running out. Twelve-eighteen was the code. Jimmy cursed himself for even thinking the number; his finger went to the trigger, waiting. But thoughts couldn't be heard. You had to speak to be heard. He tended to forget this, because he heard himself thinking all the time.

The third and final attempt for the day began, and Jimmy couldn't wait to eat his pineapples. He and these people had this routine, these three tries every morning. Though scary, it was his only daily dose of human contact and he had come to rely on its regularity. On the server behind him, he had done the maths. He assumed they had started at 0000 and were working their way up. Three a day meant they would stumble on the right code on day 406 on the second try. That was less than a month away.

But Jimmy's counting didn't figure for everything. There was the lingering fear that they might skip some numbers, that they had started somewhere else, or that they might get lucky if they were inputting the codes at random. For all Jimmy knew, more than one code could open the door. And since he didn't pay attention to how his father had changed the code, he couldn't move it higher. And what if that only got them closer? Maybe they started at 9999. He could move it lower, of course, hoping to pass one they'd already tried, but what if they hadn't tried it yet? To take action and let them in by accident would be worse than doing nothing and then dying. And Jimmy didn't want to die. He didn't want to die, and he didn't want to kill anyone.

This is how his brain whirled as the next four digits were entered. When the keypad buzzed for the third and final time that day, he relaxed his grip on the gun. Jimmy wiped his sweaty palms off on his thighs and picked up his pineapples.

'Hello, pineapples,' he whispered. He bent his head towards his lap and punctured the can, listening closely.

The pineapples whispered back. They told him they were safe to eat.

77

2313 – Year Two

• Silo 17 •

L ife at its essence, Jimmy learned, was a series of meals and bowel movements. There was some sleep mixed in as well, but little effort was required for that. He didn't learn this great Rule of the World until the water stopped flushing. Nobody thinks about their bowel movements until the water stops flushing. And then it's all one thinks about.

Jimmy started going in the corner of the server room, as far from the door as possible. He peed in the sink until the tap ran out of water and the smell got bad. Once that happened, he tapped into the cistern. The Order told him which page to look on and what to do. It was a dreadfully boring book, but handy at times. Jimmy figured that was the point. The water in the cistern wouldn't last for ever, though, so he took to drinking as much of the juice in the bottom of the cans as he could. He hated tomato soup, but he drank a can every day. His pee turned bright orange.

Jimmy was draining the last drops out of a can of apples one morning when the men came to try their codes. It happened so fast. Four numbers, and the keypad beeped. It didn't buzz. It didn't bark or scream or sound angry. It beeped. And a light long red – red for as long as Jimmy could remember – flashed brilliant and scary green.

Jimmy started. The open can of peaches on his knee leapt away and tumbled to the ground, juice splashing everywhere. It was two days early for this. It was two days early.

The great steel door made noises. Jimmy dropped his

fork and fumbled with the gun. Safety off. A *click* with his thumb, a *thunk* from the door. Voices, voices. Excitement on one side, dread on the other. He pulled the gun against his shoulder and wished he'd practised yesterday. Tomorrow. Tomorrow was when he was gonna get ready. They were two days too early.

The door made noises, and Jimmy wondered if he'd missed a day or two. There was the time he'd gotten sick and had a fever. There was the day he fell asleep reading and couldn't remember what day it was when he woke. Maybe he'd missed a day. Maybe the people in the hall had skipped a number. The door opened a crack.

Jimmy wasn't ready. His palms were slick on the gun, his heart racing. This was one of those things expected and expected. Expected so hard, with so much fervour and concentration, like blowing up a plastic bag over and over, watching it stretch out big and thin in front of your eyes, knowing it was about to burst, knowing, knowing, and when it comes, it scares you as if it'd never been expected at all.

This was one of those things. The door opened further. There was a person on the other side. A person. And for a moment, for the briefest of pauses, Jimmy reconsidered a year of planning, a calendar of fear. Here was someone to talk to and listen to. Someone to take a turn with the screwdriver and hammer now that the can opener was broke. Someone with a new can opener, perhaps. Here was a Project Partner like his dad used to—

A face. A man with an angry sneer. A year of planning, of shooting empty tomato cans, of ringing ears and reloading, of oiling barrels and reading – and now a human face in a crack in the door.

Jimmy pulled the trigger. The barrel leapt upward. And the angry sneer turned to something else: startlement mixed with sorrow. The man fell down, but another was pushing past him, bursting into the room, something black in his hand.

Again, the barrel leapt and leapt, and Jimmy's eyes blinked

with the bangs. Three shots. Three bullets. The running man kept coming, but he had the same sad look on his face, a look fading as he fell, crumbling just a few paces away.

Jimmy waited for the next man. He heard him out there, cursing loudly. And the first man he'd shot was still moving around, like an empty can that danced and danced long after it was hit. The door was open. The outside and the inside were connected. The man who had opened the door lifted his head, something worse than sorrow on his face, and suddenly it was his father out there. His father lying just beyond the door, dying in the hallway. And Jimmy didn't know why that would be.

The cursing grew faint. The man out in the hallway was moving away, and Jimmy took his first full breath since the door had beeped and the light had turned green. He didn't have a pulse; his heart was just one long beat that wouldn't stop. A thrumming like the insides of a whirring server.

He listened to the last man slink away, and Jimmy knew he had his chance to close the door. He got up and ran around the dead man who had fallen inside the server room, a black pistol near his lifeless hand. Lowering his gun, Jimmy prepared to shoulder the door shut, when the thought of tomorrow, or that night, or the next hour occurred to him.

The retreating man now knew the number. He was taking it with him.

'Twelve-eighteen,' Jimmy whispered.

He poked his head out the door for a quick look. There was a brief glimpse of a man disappearing into an office. Just a flash of green overalls, and then an empty hall, impossibly long and bright.

The dying man outside the door groaned and writhed. Jimmy ignored him. He pulled the gun against his arm and braced it like he'd practised. The little notches lined up with each other and pointed towards the edge of the office door. Jimmy imagined a can of soup out there, hovering in the hall. He breathed and waited. The groaning man on the other side of the threshold crawled closer, bloody palms slapping a spot of floor. There was that ache in the centre of his skull, an ancient scar across his memories. Jimmy aimed at the nothingness in the hallway and thought of his mother and father. Some part of him knew they were gone, that they had left somewhere and would never return. The notches dropped out of alignment as his barrel trembled.

The man by his feet drew closer. Groans had turned to a hissing. Jimmy glanced down and saw red bubbles frothing on the man's lips. His beard was fuller than Jimmy's and soaked in blood. Jimmy looked away. He watched the spot in the hallway where his rifle was trained and counted.

He was at thirty-two when he felt fingers pawing weakly at his boots.

It was on fifty-one that a head peeked out like a sneaky soup can.

Jimmy's finger squeezed. There was a kick to his shoulder and a blossom of bright red down the hall.

He waited a moment, took a deep breath, then pulled his boot away from the hand reaching up his ankle. He placed his shoulder against a door hanging dangerously open and pushed. Locks whirred and made *thunking* sounds deep within the walls. He only heard them dimly. He dropped his gun and covered his face with his palms while nearby a man lay dying in the server room. Inside the server room. Jimmy wept, and the keypad chirped happily before falling silent, patiently waiting for yet another day.

78

2345

• Silo 1 •

Arow of familiar clipboards hung on the wall in Dr Wilson's office. Donald remembered scratching his name on them with mock ceremony. He remembered signing off on himself once, authorising his own deep freeze. There was a twinge of unease at the thought of signing those forms right then. What would he write? His hand would shake as he scribbled someone else's name.

In the middle of the office, an empty gurney brought back bad memories. A fresh sheet had been tucked military crisp on top of it, ready for the next to be put to sleep. Dr Wilson checked his computer for the next to be woken while his two assistants prepped. One of them stirred two scoops of green powder into a container of warm water. Donald could smell the concoction across the room. It made his cheeks pucker, but he took careful note of which cabinet the powder came from, how much was spooned in, and asked any question that came to mind.

The other assistant folded a clean blanket and draped it over the back of a wheelchair. There was a paper gown. An emergency medical kit was unpacked and repacked: gloves, meds, gauze, bandages, tape. It was all done with a quiet efficiency. Donald was reminded of the men behind the serving counter who laid out breakfast with the same habitual care.

A number was read aloud to confirm who they were waking. This reactor tech, like Donald's sister, had been reduced to a number, a place within a grid, a cell in a spreadsheet. As if made-up names were any better. Suddenly, Donald saw how easily his switch could've taken place. He watched as paperwork was filled out – his signature not needed – and dropped into a box. This was a part of the process he could ignore. There would be no trace of what he had planned.

Dr Wilson led them out the door. The assistants followed with their wheelchair full of supplies, and Donald trailed behind.

The tech they were waking was two levels down, which meant taking the lift. One of the assistants idly remarked that he had only three days left on his shift.

'Lucky you,' the other assistant said.

'Yeah, so be easy with my catheter,' he joked, and even Dr Wilson laughed.

Donald didn't. He was busy wondering what the *final* shift would be like. Nobody seemed to think much past the next shift. They looked forward to one ending and dreaded seeing another. It reminded him of Washington, where everyone he worked alongside hoped to make it to the next term even as they loathed running for another. Donald had fallen into that same trap.

The lift doors opened on another chilled hall. Here were rooms full of shift workers, the majority of the silo's population-in-waiting spread out across two identical levels. Dr Wilson led them down the hall and coded them through the third door on the right. A hall of sleeping bodies angled off into the distance until it met the concrete skin of the silo. 'Twenty down and four over,' he said, pointing.

They made their way to the pod. It was the first time Donald had seen this part of the procedure. He had helped put others under, but had never helped wake anyone up. Storing Victor's body away was something altogether different. That had been a funeral.

The assistants busied themselves around the pod. Dr Wilson knelt by the control panel, paused, glanced up at Donald, waiting.

'Right,' Donald said. He knelt and watched over the doctor's shoulder.

'Most of the process is automated,' the doctor admitted sheepishly. 'Frankly, they could replace me with a trained monkey and nobody would know the difference.' He glanced back at Donald as he keyed in his code and pressed a red button. 'I'm like you, Shepherd. Only here in case something goes wrong.'

The doctor smiled. Donald didn't.

'It'll be a few minutes before the hatch pops.' He tapped the display. 'The temperature here will get up to thirty-one Celsius. The bloodstream is getting an injection when this light is flashing.'

The light was flashing.

'An injection of what?' Donald asked.

'Nanos. The freezing procedure would kill a normal human being, which I suppose is why it was outlawed.'

A normal human being. Donald wondered what the hell that made him. He lifted his palm and studied the red splotchiness. He remembered a glove tumbling down a hill.

'Twenty-eight,' Dr Wilson said. 'When it hits thirty, the lid will release. Now's when I like to go ahead and reset the dial, rather than wait until the end. Just so I don't forget.' He twisted the dial below the temp readout. 'It doesn't stop the process. It only runs one direction once it starts.'

'What if something goes wrong?' Donald asked.

Dr Wilson frowned. 'I told you. That's why I'm here.'

'But what if something happened to you? Or you got called away?'

The doctor tugged his earlobe, thinking. 'I would advise putting them back under until I could get to them.' He laughed. 'Of course, the nanos might just fix what's wrong before I could. As long as you dial the temp back down, all you have to do is close the lid. But I don't see how that could come up.'

Donald did. He watched the temperature tick up to twenty-nine. The two assistants prepped while they waited for the pod to open. One had a towel set aside, along with the blanket and the paper gown. The medical kit sat in the wheelchair, the top open. Both men wore blue rubber gloves. One of them peeled off a strip of tape and hung it from the handle of the wheelchair. A packet of gauze was pre-emptively torn open, the bitter drink given a vigorous shake.

'And my code will start the procedure?' Donald asked, thinking of anything he might be missing.

Dr Wilson chuckled. He placed his hands on his knees and was slow to stand. 'I imagine your code would open the airlock. Is there anything you don't have access to?'

A glove was snapped. The hatch hissed as the lock disengaged.

The truth, Donald wanted to say. But he was planning on getting it soon enough.

The lid popped open a crack, and one of the assistants lifted it the rest of the way. A handsome young man lay inside, his cheeks twitching as he came to. The assistants went to work, and Donald tried to make note of every little part of the procedure. He thought of his sister in a hall above him, lying asleep, waiting.

'Once we get him up to the office,' said Dr Wilson, 'we'll check his vitals and take our samples for analysis. If they have any items in their locker, I send one of the boys to retrieve them.'

'Locker?' Donald watched as a catheter was removed, a needle extracted from an arm. The tape and gauze were applied while the man in the pod sucked from a straw, wincing from the bitterness as he did so.

'Personal effects. Anything set aside from their previous shift. We retrieve those for them.'

The assistants helped the man into the paper gown, then grunted as they lifted him from the steaming pod. Donald moved the medical kit and steadied the wheelchair for them. The blanket was already laid out across the seat. While they settled the man into place, Donald thought of the bag marked *Shift* left on his bed, the one with Thurman's personal effects in them. There had been a small number marked on the bag similar to the one in Anna's note. That number in the note wasn't a date at all.

And then it hit him. *Locket* was a typo. He tried to picture where the R and T were on a keyboard, if this was a likely mistake. Had she meant to say *locker* instead?

The confluence of clues cut through the chill in the room, and for a moment, the idea of waking his sister was forgotten. Other sleeping ghosts were whispering to him, clouding his mind.

Donald helped escort the groggy man up to the medical offices while one of the assistants stayed behind to scrub the pod. Not caring to see Dr Wilson take his samples, Donald volunteered to go and grab the tech's personal items. The assistant gave him directions to one of the storage levels in the heart of the silo.

There were sixteen levels of stores in all, not counting the armoury. Donald entered the lift and pressed the worn-out button for the storeroom on fifty-seven. The reactor tech's ID number had been scribbled on a piece of paper. The number from Anna's note to Thurman was vivid in his mind. He had assumed it was a date: 2 November 2039. It made the number easy to recall.

The lift slowed to a stop, and Donald stepped through the doors and into darkness. He ran his hand down the bank of light switches along the wall. The bulbs overhead sparked to life with the distant and muted *thunks* of ancient transformers and relays jolting into action. A maze of tall shelves revealed itself in stages as the lights popped on first in the distance, then close, then off to the right, like some mosaic unmasked one random piece at a time. The lockers were in the very back, past the shelves. Donald began the long walk while the last of the bulbs flickered on.

Cliffs of steel shelves laden with sealed plastic tubs swallowed him. The containers seemed to lean in over his head. If he glanced up, he almost expected the shelves to touch high above, to meet like train tracks. Huge swathes of tubs were empty and unlabelled, he saw, waiting for future shifts to fill them. All the notes he and Anna had generated on his last shift would be in tubs like these. They would preserve the tale of silo forty and all those unfortunate facilities around them. They would tell of the people of silo eighteen and Donald's efforts to save them. And maybe he shouldn't have. What if this current debacle, this vagabond cleaner, was his fault in some way?

He passed crates sorted by date, by silo, by name. There were cross-cuts between the shelves, narrow aisles wide enough for the carts used to haul blank paper and notebooks out and then bring them back in weighing just a little more from the ink. With relief from his claustrophobia, Donald left the shelves and found the far wall of the facility. He glanced back over his shoulder at how far he'd come, could imagine all the lights going out at once and him not being able to pick his way back to the lift. Maybe he would stagger in circles until he died of thirst. He glanced up at the lights and realised how fragile he was, how reliant on power and light. A familiar wave of fear washed over him, the panic of being buried in the dark. Donald leaned against one of the lockers for a moment and caught his breath. He coughed into his handkerchief and reminded himself that dying wouldn't be the worst of things.

Once the panic faded and he'd fought off the urge to sprint back to the lift, he entered the rows of lockers. There must've been thousands of them. Many were small, like post office boxes, six or so inches to a side and probably as deep as his arm judging by the width of the units. He mumbled the number from Anna's note to himself. Erskine's would be down here as well, and Victor's. He wondered if those men had any secrets squirrelled away and reminded himself to come back and check.

The numbers on the lockers ascended as he walked down one of the rows. The first two digits were far from Anna's number. He turned down one of the connecting aisles to search for the correct row and saw a group that started with 43. His ID number started with 44. Perhaps his locker was near here.

Donald imagined it would be empty, even as he found himself honing in on his ID number. He had never carried anything from shift to shift. The numbers marched in a predictable series until he found himself standing before a small metal door with his ID number on it, Troy's ID number. There was no latch, only a button. He pressed it with his knuckle, worried it might have a fingerprint scanner or something equally deserving of his paranoia. What would someone think if they saw Thurman looking in this man's locker? It was easy to forget the ruse. It was similar to the delay between hearing the Senator's name and realising Donald was the one being spoken to.

There was a soft sigh as the locker cracked open, followed by the squeak of old and unused hinges. The sigh reminded Donald that everything down there – the bins and tubs and lockers – was protected from the air. The good, normal air. Even the air they breathed was caustic and full of invisible things, like corrosive oxygen and other hungry molecules. The only difference between the good air and the bad air was the speed at which they worked. People lived and died too quickly to see the difference.

At least they used to, Donald thought as he reached inside his locker.

Surprisingly, it wasn't empty. There was a plastic bag inside, crinkled and vacuum-packed like Thurman's. Only this bag read *Legacy* across the top rather than *Shift*. Inside, he could see a familiar pair of tan slacks and a red shirt. The clothes hammered him with memories. They reminded him of a man he used to be, a world he used to live in. Donald squeezed the bag, which was dense from the absence of air, and glanced up and down the empty aisle.

Why would they keep these things? Was it so he could emerge from deep underground dressed just as he had been when he arrived? Like an inmate staggering out, blinking and shielding his eyes, dressed in outdated fashion? Or was it because storage was the same thing as disposal? There were two entire levels above this one where unrecyclable trash was compacted into cubes as dense as iron and stacked to the ceiling. Where else were they supposed to put their garbage? In a hole in the ground? They lived in a hole in the ground.

Donald puzzled over this as he fumbled with the plastic zipper at the top and slid the bag open. A faint odour of mud and grass escaped, a whiff of bygone days. He opened the bag further, and his clothes blossomed to life as air seeped inside. There was an impulse to change into his old clothes, to pretend that his world wasn't gone. Instead, he decided to shove the bag back into the locker – and then a glimmer caught his eye, a flash of yellow.

Donald dug down past his clothes and reached for the wedding ring. As he was pulling it out, he felt a hard object inside the slacks. He palmed the ring and reached inside again, felt around, squeezed the folds of his clothes. What had he been carrying that day? Not his pills. He'd lost those in a fall. Not the keys to the ATV, Anna had taken those from him. His own keys and wallet had been in his jacket, had never even made it beneath the earth to orientation—

His phone. Donald found it in the pocket of his slacks. The heft of the thing, the curve of the plastic shell, felt right at home in his hand. He returned the bag to the locker, tucked the wedding ring into the pocket of his overalls, and pressed the power button on the old phone. But of course it was dead. Long dead. It hadn't even been working properly the day he'd lost Helen.

Donald placed the phone in his pocket out of habit, the sort of habit that time could not touch. He felt the ring in his pocket and pulled it out, made sure it still fitted, and thought of his wife. Thoughts of Helen led to thoughts of Mick and her having children together. Sadness and sickness intermingled. He stuffed his clothes deep into the locker and shut the door, took the ring off and slipped it into his pocket with the old phone. Donald turned and headed off in search of Anna's locker. He still had to get the tech's personal items as well.

As he tracked down their lockers, something nagged at him, some connection, but he couldn't work out what.

Off to one side, there was a patch of the storeroom still in darkness, a light bulb out, and Donald thought of silo forty and the spread of darkness on a previous shift. Eren had brought an end to whatever was going on over there. A bomb had caused dust to shiver from overhead pipes. And now his deep mind whirred and made deeper connections. Something about Anna. Some reason he'd been drawn to his locker. He wrapped his hand around the phone in his pocket and remembered why she'd been woken the last time. He remembered her expertise with wireless systems, with hacking.

In the distance, a light went out with a pop, and Donald felt the darkness closing in on him. There was nothing down here for him, nothing but awful memories and horrible realisations. His heart pounded as it began to come together, a thing he dearly wanted to disbelieve. His phone hadn't worked properly the day the bombs fell; he hadn't been able to contact Helen. And then there were all the times before when he couldn't reach Mick, the nights he and Anna had found themselves alone.

And now they'd been left alone again, in this silo. Mick had changed places with him at the last moment. Donald remembered a conversation in a small apartment. Mick had given him a tour, had taken him down into a room and said to remember him down there, that this was what he wanted.

Donald slapped one of the lockers with his palm, the loud bang drowning out his curse. This should've been Mick over here, freezing and thawing, going steadily mad. Instead, Mick had stolen the domestic life he often teased Donald for living. And he'd had help doing it.

Donald sagged against the lockers. He reached for his handkerchief, coughed into it, imagined his friend consoling Helen. He thought of the kids and grandkids they'd had together. A murderous rage boiled up. All this time, blaming himself for not getting to Helen. All this time, blaming Helen and Mick for the life he'd missed out on. And it was Anna, the engineer. Anna who had hacked his life. She had done this to him. She had brought him here.

D onald retrieved the items from the other two lockers as if in a dream. Numb, he rode the lift back down to Dr Wilson's office and dropped off the reactor tech's personal effects. He asked Dr Wilson for something to help him sleep that night and paid careful attention to where the pills came from. When Wilson left for the lab with his samples, Donald helped himself to more of the pills. Crushing them up, he added two scoops of the powder and made a bitter drink. He had no plan. His actions followed robotically one after the other. There was a cruelness in his life that he wished to end.

Down to the deep freeze. Pushing a loaded-up wheelchair ahead of him, he found her pod effortlessly. Donald traced a finger down the skin of the machine. He touched its smooth surface warily, as if it might cut him. He remembered touching her body like this, always afraid, never quite able to give in or let go. The better it felt, the more it hurt. Each caress had been an affront to Helen.

He pulled his finger back and held it in his other hand to stop some imaginary bleeding. There was danger in being near her. Anna's nakedness was on the other side of that armoured shell, and he was about to open it. He glanced around the vast halls of the deep freeze. Crowded, and yet all alone. Dr Wilson would be in his lab for some while.

Donald knelt by the end of the pod and entered his keycode. Some small part of him hoped it wouldn't work. This was too great a power, the ability to give a life or take it. But the panel beeped. Donald steadied his hand and turned the dial just as he'd been shown.

The rest was waiting. Temperatures rose, and his anger faded. Donald retrieved the drink and gave it a stir. He made sure everything else was in place.

When the lid sighed open, Donald slid his fingers into the crack and lifted it the rest of the way. He reached inside and carefully removed the tubing from the needle in Anna's arm. A thick fluid leaked out of the needle. He saw how the plastic valve on the end worked, and turned it until the dripping stopped. Unfolding a blanket from the back of the wheelchair, he tucked it around her. Her body was already warm. Frost dripped down the inner surface of the pod and collected in little channels that served as gutters. The blanket, he realised, was mostly for him.

Anna stirred. Donald brushed the hair off her forehead as her eyes fluttered. Her lips parted and she let out a soft groan filled with decades of sleep. Donald knew what that stiffness felt like, that deep cold frozen in one's joints. He hated doing this to her. He hated what had been done to him.

'Easy,' he said as she began to grope the air with shivering limbs. Her head lolled feebly from side to side, murmuring something. Donald helped her into a sitting position and rearranged the blanket to keep her covered. The wheelchair sat quietly beside him with a medical bag and a Thermos. Donald made no move to lift her out and help her into the chair.

Blinking and darting eyes finally settled on Donald. They narrowed in recognition.

'Donny—'

He read his name on her lips as much as heard her.

'You came for me,' she whispered.

Donald watched as she trembled; he fought the urge to rub her back or wrap her in his arms.

'What year?' she asked, licking her lips. 'Is it time?' Her eyes were now wide and wet with fear. Melting frost slid down her cheeks.

Donald remembered waking like this with his most recent dreams still clouding his thoughts. 'It's time for the truth,' he said. 'You're the reason I'm here, aren't you?'

Anna stared at him blankly, her mind in a fog. He could see it in the twitch of her eyes, the way her dry lips remained parted, the processing delay he knew well from the times they'd done this to him, from the times they had woken him.

'Yes.' She nodded ever so slightly. 'Father was never going to wake us. The deep freeze—' Her voice was a whisper. 'I'm glad you came. I knew you would.'

A hand escaped from the blanket and gripped the edge of the pod as if to pull herself out. Donald placed a hand on her shoulder. He turned and grabbed the Thermos from the wheelchair. Peeling her hand from the lip of the pod, he pressed the drink into her palm. She wiggled her other arm free and held the Thermos against her knees.

'I want to know why,' he said. 'Why did you bring me *here*? To this place.' He looked around at the pods, these unnatural graves that kept death at bay.

Anna gazed at him. She studied the Thermos and the straw. Donald let go of her arm and reached into his pocket. He pulled out the phone. Anna shifted her attention to that.

'What did you do that day?' he asked. 'You kept me from her, didn't you? And the night we met to finalise the plans – all the times Mick missed a meeting – that was you as well.'

A shadow slid across Anna's face. Something deep and dark registered. Donald had expected a harsh defiance, steel resolve, denials. Anna looked sad instead.

'So long ago,' she said, shaking her head. 'I'm sorry, Donny, but it was so long ago.' Her eyes flitted beyond him towards the door as if she were expecting danger. Donald glanced back over his shoulder and saw nothing. 'We have to get out of here,' she croaked, her voice feeble and distant. 'Donny, my father, they made a pact—'

'I want to know what you did,' he said. 'Tell me.'

She shook her head. 'What Mick and I did— Donny, it

seemed like the right thing at the time. I'm sorry. But I need to tell you something else. Something more important.' Her voice was small and quiet. She licked her lips and glanced at the straw, but Donald kept a hand on her arm. 'Dad woke me for another shift while you were in the deep freeze.' She lifted her head and fixed her eyes on him. Her teeth chattered together while she collected her thoughts. 'And I found something—'

'Stop,' Donald said. 'No more stories. No lies. Just the truth.'

Anna looked away. A spasm surged through her body, a great shiver. Steam rose from her hair, and condensation raced down the skin of the pod in sudden bursts of speed.

'It was meant to be this way,' she said. The admission was in the way she said it, her refusal to look at him. 'It was meant to be. You and me together. We built this.'

Donald seethed with renewed rage. His hands trembled more than hers.

Anna leaned forward. 'I couldn't stand the thought of you dying over there, alone.'

'I wouldn't have been alone,' he hissed through clenched teeth. 'And you don't get to decide such things.' He gripped the edge of the pod with both hands and squeezed until his knuckles turned white.

'You need to hear what I have to say,' Anna said.

Donald waited. What explanation or apology was there? She had taken from him what little her father had left behind. Thurman had destroyed the world, and Anna had destroyed Donald's. He waited to hear what she had to say.

'My father made a pact,' she said, her voice gaining strength. 'We were never to be woken. We need to get out of here. I need your help—'

This again. She didn't care that she had destroyed him. Donald felt his rage subside. It dissipated throughout his body, a part of him, a powerful surge that came and went like an ocean wave, not strong enough to hold itself up, crashing down with a hiss and a sigh.

'Drink,' he told her, lifting her arm gently. 'Then you can tell me. You can tell me how I can help you.'

Anna blinked. Donald reached for the straw and steered it to her lips. Lips that would tell him anything, keep him confused, use him so that she might feel less hollow, less alone. He had heard enough of her lies, her brand of poison. To give her an ear was to give her a vein.

Anna's lips closed around the straw, and her cheeks dented as she sucked. A column of foul green surged up the straw.

'So bitter,' she whispered after her first swallow.

'Shhh,' Donald told her. 'Drink. You need this.'

She did, and Donald held the Thermos for her. Anna paused between sips to tell him they needed to get out of there, that it wasn't safe. He agreed and guided the straw back to her lips. The danger was her.

There was still some of the drink left when she gazed up at him, confused. 'Why am I . . . feeling sleepy?' she asked. Anna blinked slowly, fighting to keep her eyes open.

'You shouldn't have brought me here,' Donald said. 'We weren't meant to live like this.'

Anna lifted an arm, reached out and seized Donald's shoulder. Awareness seemed to grip her. Donald sat on the edge of the pod and put an arm around her. As she slumped against him, he flashed back to the night of their first kiss. Back in college, her with too much to drink, falling asleep on his frat house sofa, her head on his shoulder. And Donald had stayed like that for the rest of the night, his arm trapped and growing numb while a party thrummed and finally faded. They had woken the next morning, Anna stirring before he did. She had smiled and thanked him, called him her guardian angel and had given him a kiss.

That seemed several ages ago. Aeons. Lives weren't supposed to drag on so long. But Donald remembered as if it were yesterday the sound of Anna breathing that night. He remembered from their last shift, sharing a cot, her head on his chest as she slept. And then he heard her, right then in that moment as she took in one last, sudden, trembling lungful.

A gasp. Her body stiffened for a pause, and then cold and trembling fingernails sank into his shoulder. And Donald held her as that grip slowly relaxed, as Anna Thurman breathed her very last.

2318 – Year Seven
• Silo 17 •

Something bad was happening with the cans. Jimmy couldn't be sure at first. He had noticed little brown spots on a can of beets months ago and hadn't thought anything of it. Now, more and more cans were covered with them. And some of the contents tasted a little different too. That part may have been his imagination, but he was for sure getting sick to his stomach more often, which was making the server room smell awful. He didn't like going anywhere near the poop corner – the flies were getting bad over there – which meant defecating further and further out. Eventually he would be going everywhere, and the flies didn't carry away his waste as fast as he made it.

He knew he needed to get out. He hadn't heard any activity in the halls of late, no one trying the door. But the room that had once felt like a prison now felt like the only safe place to be. And the idea of leaving, once desirable, now turned his insides to water. The routines were all he knew. Doing something different seemed insane.

He put it off for two days by making a Project out of preparing. He took his favourite rifle apart and oiled all the pieces before putting it back together. There was a box of lucky ammo where very few had failed or jammed during games of Kick the Can, so he emptied two clips and filled them with only these magic bullets. A spare set of overalls was turned into a backpack by knotting the arms to the legs for loops and cinching up the neck. The zipper down the front made for a nice enclosure. He filled this with two cans of sausage, two of pineapple and two of tomato juice. He didn't think he'd be gone that long, but he couldn't know.

Patting his chest, he made sure he had his key around his neck. It never came off, but he habitually patted his chest anyway to make sure it was there. A purple bruise on his sternum hinted that he did this too often. He placed a fork and a rusty screwdriver in his breast pocket, the latter for jabbing open the cans. Jimmy really needed to find a can opener. That and batteries for his flashlight were the highest of priorities. The power had only gone out twice over the years, but both times had left him terrified of the dark. And checking to make sure his flashlight worked all the time tended to wear down the batteries.

Scratching his beard, he thought of what else he would need. He didn't have much water left in the cistern, but maybe he'd find some out there, so he threw in two empty bottles from years prior. These took some digging. He had to rummage behind the hill of empty cans in one corner of the storeroom, the flies pestering him and yelling at him to leave them alone.

'I see you, I see you,' he told them. 'Buzz off.'

Jimmy laughed at his own joke.

In the kitchen, he grabbed the large knife, the one he hadn't broken the tip off, and put that in his pack as well. By the time he worked up his nerve to leave on the second day, he decided it was too late to get started. So he took his gun apart and oiled it up one more time and promised himself that he would leave in the morning.

Jimmy didn't sleep well that night. He left the radio on in case there was any chatter, and the hissing made him dream of the air from the outside leaking in through the great steel door. He woke up more than once gasping for a breath and found it difficult to get back to sleep.

In the morning, he checked the cameras, but they were still not working. He wished he had the one of the hallway. All it showed was black. He told himself there was no one there. But soon he would be. He was about to go outside. *Outside.*

'It's okay,' he told himself. He grabbed his rifle, which reeked of oil, and lifted his home-made pack, which he thought suddenly he could wear as clothes in a pinch, if he had to. He laughed some more and headed for the ladder.

'C'mon, c'mon,' he said, urging himself as he climbed up. He tried to whistle, was normally a very good whistler, but his mouth was too dry. He hummed a tune his parents had used to sing to him instead.

The pack and the gun were heavy. Dangling from the crook of his elbow, they made it difficult to unlock the hatch at the top of the ladder. But he finally managed. He stuck his head out and paused to admire the gentle hum of the machines. Some of them made little clicking sounds as if their innards were busy. He'd taken most of the backs off over the years to peer inside and see if any contained secrets, but they all looked like the guts of the computers his dad used to build.

The stench of his own waste greeted him as he moved between the tall towers. That wasn't how you were supposed to greet someone, he thought. The black boxes radiated an awful heat, which only made the smell worse.

He stood in front of the great steel door and hesitated. Jimmy's world had been shrinking every day. First he had been comfortable on these two levels, the room with the black machines and the labyrinth beneath. And then he'd only been comfortable below. And then even the dark passageway and the tall ladder had frightened him. And soon, he had limited himself to the back room with all the beds and the storerooms with their funny smells, until the only place he felt safe was on his makeshift cot by the computer desk, the sound of the radio crackling in the background.

And now he stood before that door his father had dragged him through, the place where he'd killed three men, and he thought about his world expanding.

His palms were damp as he reached for the keypad. A part of him feared the air outside would be toxic, but he was probably breathing the same air, and people had lived for years out there, talking now and then on the radio. He keyed in the first two digits, level twelve, then thought about the next two. Eighteen. Jimmy imagined going home and getting some different clothes, using a toilet in a bathroom. He pictured his mother sitting on his parents' bed, waiting for him. He saw her lying on her back, arms crossed, nothing but bones.

His hand trembled as he reached for the 1 and hit the 4 instead. He wiped his hands on his thighs and waited for the keypad to time out with a buzz. 'There's no one on the other side,' he told himself. 'No one. I'm alone. I'm alone.'

Somehow, this comforted him.

He entered the two digits again for school, and then the digits of his home.

The keypad beeped. The door began to make noises. And Jimmy Parker took a step back. He thought of school and his friends, wondered if any of them were still alive. If *anyone* was still alive. He hooked his finger under the strap of his rifle and pulled it over his head, tucked it against his shoulder. The door clanked free. All he had to do was pull.

82

2318 – Year Seven
• Silo 17 •

There were signs of life and death waiting for him in the hall. A charred ring on the tile and a scatter of ash marked the corpse of an old fire. The outside of the steel door was lined with scratches and marked with dents. The latter reminded him of his misses during Kick the Can, the ineffectual kiss of bullet against solid steel. Right by his feet, Jimmy noticed a stain on the floor – a patch of dappled brown – and remembered a man dying there. Jimmy looked away from these signs of the living and the dying and stepped into the hall.

As he began to pull the door shut, something made him hesitate. Jimmy wondered if perhaps his code wouldn't work from the outside. What if the door locked and he could never get back in? He checked the keypad and saw the gouges around its steel plate where someone had tried to prise it off the wall. He was reminded how desperately so many others had wanted in over the years. Remembering this made him feel crazy for wanting out.

Before he could worry further, he shut the steel door and his heart sank a little as the gears whirred and the locks slid into the wall. There was a hollow *thunk*, the sound of awful finality.

Jimmy rushed to the keypad, his chest pounding in his throat, the feeling of men running down all three hallways to get him, blood-curdling screams and bludgeoning weapons held high over their heads—

He entered the code and the door whirred open. Pushing

on the handle, he took a few deep breaths of home . . . and nearly gagged on the smell of his own waste warmed by the hot servers.

There was no one running down the halls. He needed a new can opener. He needed to find a toilet that worked. He needed overalls that weren't worn to tatters. He needed to breathe and find another stash of canned food and water.

Jimmy reluctantly closed the door again. And even though he had just tested the keypad, the fear that he would never get back inside returned. The gears would be worn out. The code would only work from the outside once per day, once per year. A part of him knew – the obsessive part of him knew – that he could check the code a hundred times and still worry it wouldn't work the very next. He could check for ever and never be satisfied. His pulse pounded in his ears as he tore himself from the door.

The hallway was brightly lit. Jimmy kept his rifle against his arm and slid silently past ransacked offices. Everything was quiet except for the buzzing of one light fixture on its last leg and the flutter of a piece of paper on a desk beneath a blowing vent. The security station was unmanned. Jimmy crawled over the gate, remembering Yani, imagining the stair-well outside crowded with people, a man in a cleaning suit barging out and wading into the masses, but when he opened the door and peered outside, the landing was empty.

It was also dim. Only the green emergency lights were on. Jimmy shut the door slowly so that the rusty hinges would groan rather than squeal. There was an object on the grating by his feet. Jimmy nudged it with his boot, a white cylinder the length of his forearm with knobby ends. A bone. He recognised it from the jumble of a man who had wasted away by the servers, dragged close to his piles of shit.

Jimmy felt with keen surety that his own bones would be exposed someday. Perhaps this day. He would never make it back inside his sturdy little home beneath the servers. And this frightened him less than it should have. The heady rush of being out in the open, the cool air and the green glow of the stairwell, even the remnants of another human being, were a sudden and welcome relief from the claustrophobia of being imprisoned. What had once been his pen – the floors and levels of the silo – was now the great outside. Here was a land of infinite death and of hopeful opportunity.

83

2318 – Year Seven
• Silo 17 •

H e had no great plan, no real direction, but the tug
was upward. His flashlight was running out of juice,
so he knew to explore the levels cautiously. Groping
in an apartment, he fumbled for a toilet, relieved himself the
way God intended, and was disheartened by the lack of a
flush. The sink didn't run either. Neither did the wash nozzle
beside the toilet, which left him using a bedsheet in perfect
darkness.

He started up. There was a general store on nineteen,
just below his home. He would check there for batteries,
though he feared most useful things would have been
consumed by now. The garment district would have overalls,
though. He felt sure of that. A plan was forming.

Until a vibration in the steps altered it.

Jimmy stopped and listened to the clang of footsteps.
They were coming from above. He could see the next landing
jutting off overhead, one turn around the central post. It was
nearer than the landing below. So he ran, rifle clattering
against the jugs tied to his makeshift backpack, boots
clomping awkwardly on the treads, both fearful and relieved
not to be alone.

He yanked the doors open on the next landing and pulled
them to, leaving a small crack. Pressing his cheek against the
door, he peered through the gap, listening. The clanging grew
louder and louder. Jimmy held his breath. A figure flew by,
hand squeaking along the railing, and then another figure
close behind, shouting threats. Both were little more than

blurs. He remained in the darkness at the end of a strange and silent hall until the noise faded and he could feel things creeping across the tile towards him, hands with claws reaching through the inky black to tangle up in his wild and long hair, and Jimmy found himself back on the landing in the dull green glow of emergency lights, panting and not knowing what to believe.

He was alone, one way or the other. Even if people survived around him, the only company one found was the kind that chased you or killed you.

Upward again, listening more closely for footfalls, keeping a hand on the rail for a vibration, he spiralled his way past the water plant on thirty-two, the dirt farm on thirty-one, past sanitation on twenty-six, keeping to the green light and aiming for the general store. The muscles in his legs grew warm from the use, but in a good way. He passed familiar landmarks, levels from another life with an accumulation of wear and a tangle of wires and pipes. The world had grown as rusty as his memory of it.

He arrived at the general store to find it mostly bare, except for the remains of someone trapped under a spilled stand of shelves. The boots sticking out were small, a woman's or a child's. White ankle bones spanned the gap between boot and cuff. There were goods trapped underneath the shelf alongside the person, but Jimmy felt no urge to investigate. He searched the scattering of items on the other shelves for batteries or a can opener. There were toys and trinkets and useless things. Jimmy sensed that many a shadow had fallen over those goods. He saved his flashlight by sneaking out in the darkness.

Searching his old apartment wasn't worth the juice either. It no longer felt like home. There was a sadness inside that he couldn't name, a sense that he had failed his parents, an old ache in the centre of his mind like he used to get from sucking on ice. Jimmy left the apartment and continued up. Something still called to him from above. And it wasn't until he got within half a spiral from the schoolhouse that he knew what it was. The distant past was reaching out to him. The day it all began. His classroom, where he could last remember seeing his mother, where his friends still sat in his disordered mind, where if he remained, if he could just go back and sit at his desk and unwind events once more, they would have to come out differently.

84

2318 – Year Seven

• Silo 17 •

Jimmy kept his flashlight powered up as he made his way
to the classroom. There was no going back, he quickly
saw. There, in the middle of the room, lay his old backpack. Several of the desks were askew, the neat rows snapped
like broken bones, and Jimmy could see in his mind his friends
rushing out, could see the paths they took, could watch them
spill towards the door. They had taken their bags with them.
Jimmy's remained and lay still as a corpse.

A step inside, the room aglow from his flashlight, he felt
Mrs Pearson look up from a book, smile and say nothing.
Barbara sat at her desk, right by the door. Jimmy remembered
her hand in his during a class trip to the livestock pens. It
was on the way back, after the strange smells of so many
animals, hands reaching through bars to stroke fur and feather
and fat, hairless pigs. Jimmy had been fourteen, and something
about the animals had excited or changed him. So that when
Barbara hung back at the end of the corkscrew of classmates
making their way up the staircase and had reached for his
hand, he hadn't pulled back.

That prolonged touch was a taste of what-might-have-
been with another. He brushed the surface of Barbara's desk
with his fingertips and left tracks through the dust. Paul's desk
– his best friend's – was one of those that had been disturbed.
He stepped through the gap it left, seeing everyone leaving
at once, his mother giving him a head start, until he stood in
the centre of the room, by his bag, completely alone.

'I am all alone,' he said. 'I am solitude.'

His lips were dry and stuck together. They tore apart when he spoke as if opened for the very first time.

Approaching his bag, he noticed that it had been gutted. He knelt down and tossed open the flap. There was a scrap of plastic that his mom had used and reused to wrap his lunch, but his lunch was long gone. Two cornbars and an oatmeal brownie. Amazing how he remembered some things and not others.

He dug deeper, wondering if they'd taken much else. The calculator his father had built from scratch was still in there, as were the glass figurine soldiers his uncle had given him on his thirteenth birthday. He took the time to transfer everything from his makeshift bag to his old backpack. The zipper was stiff, but it still worked. He studied the knotted overalls and decided they were in worse shape than the ones he had on, so he left them.

Jimmy stood and surveyed the room, sweeping his flashlight across the chaos. On the blackboard, he saw someone had left their mark. He played the light across the scene and saw the word *fuck* written over and over. It looked like a string of letters like that, *fuckfuckfuckfuck*.

Jimmy found the erasing rag behind Mrs Pearson's desk. It was stiff and crusty, but the words still came off. Left behind was a smear, and Jimmy remembered the happy days of writing on the board in front of the class. He remembered writing assignments. Mrs Pearson complimented him on his poetry once, probably just to be nice. Licking his lips, he fished a nub of old chalk from the tray and thought of something to write. There were no nerves from standing before the class. No one was watching. He was well and truly all alone.

I am Jimmy, he wrote on the board, the flashlight casting a strange halo, a ring of dim light, as he wrote. The nub of chalk clicked and clacked as he made each stroke. It squeaked and groaned between the clicks. The noise was like company, and yet he wrote a poem of being alone, a mechanical act from bygone days:

The ghosts are watching. The ghosts are watching.
They watch me stroll alone.
The corpses are laughing. The corpses are laughing.
They go quiet when I step over them.
My parents are missing. My parents are missing. They
are waiting for me to come home.

He wasn't sure about that last line. Jimmy ran the light across what he'd written, which he didn't think was very good. More wouldn't make it better, but he wrote more, anyway.

The silo is empty. The silo is empty. It's full of death
from pit to rim.
My name was Jimmy, my name was Jimmy. But
nobody calls me any longer.
I am alone, the ghosts are watching, and solitude
makes me stronger.

The last part was a lie, he knew, but it was poetry, so it didn't count. Jimmy stepped away from the board and studied the words with his flickering flashlight. The words trailed off to the side and dipped down, each line sagging more than the last, the letters getting smaller towards the end of each sentence. It was a problem he always had with the blackboard. He started big and seemed to shrink as he went. Scratching the beard on his chin, he wondered what this said of him, what it portended.

There was a lot wrong with what he'd written, he thought. The fifth line was untrue, the one about nobody calling him Jimmy. Above the poem, he had written *I am Jimmy*. He still thought of himself as Jimmy.

He grabbed the stiff rag he'd left in the chalk tray, stood before his poem, and went to erase the line that wasn't right. But something stopped him. It was the fear of making the poem worse by attempting to fix it, the fear of taking a line away and having nothing good to put in its place. This was his voice, and it was too rare a thing to quash.

Jimmy felt Mrs Pearson's eyes upon him. He felt the eyes

of his classmates. The ghosts were watching, the corpses laughing, while he studied the problem on the board.

When the solution came, it brought a familiar thrill of arriving at the right place, of connecting the dots. Jimmy reached up and slapped the dusty rag against the board and erased the first thing he'd written. The words *I am Jimmy* disappeared into a white smear and a tumbling haze of powder. He set the rag aside and began to write a truth in its place.

I am Solitude, he started to write. He liked the sound of that. It sounded poetic and full of meaning. But like poetry was wont to do, the words had a mind of their own; his deep thoughts intervened, and so he wrote something different. He shortened it to two little neat circles, a swerve, and a slash. Grabbing his bag, he left the room and his old friends behind. All that remained was a poem and the call to be remembered, a mark to prove he'd been there.

I am Solo.

2345

• Silo 1 •

onald steered the empty wheelchair back to Dr
Wilson's office. A damp blanket was draped over the
armrests and dragged across the tile. He felt numb.
His dream that morning had been to give life, not take it. The
permanence of what he'd done began to set in, and Donald
found it difficult to swallow, to breathe. He stopped in the
hallway and took stock of what he'd become. Unknowing
architect. Prisoner. Puppet. Hangman. He wore a different
man's clothes. His transformation horrified him. Tears welled
up in his eyes, and he wiped them away angrily. All it took
was thinking of Helen and Mick, of the life taken from him.
Everything leading up to that point in time, to him awakening
in that silo, had been someone else's doing. He could feel parted
strings dangling from his elbows and knees. He was a loose
puppet steering an empty wheelchair back to where it belonged.

Donald parked the chair and set the brakes. He took the
plastic vial out of his pocket and considered stealing another
dose or two. Sleep would be hard to come by, he feared.

The vial went back into the cabinet full of empties.
Donald turned to go when he saw the note left in the middle
of the gurney:

You forgot this.
—Wilson

The note was stuck to a slender folder. Donald remembered
handing it to Dr Wilson along with the reactor tech's

belongings. The trip to the other two lockers had been a blur. All he could remember was clutching his phone, facts coming together, realising that Anna had played Mick and Thurman to engineer a last-minute switch that made no sense, that could only happen with a daughter bending her father's ear. Thus his life had been stolen away.

The folder had been in the locker Anna had mentioned to her father in the message. It seemed inconsequential now. Donald balled up the note from Dr Wilson and tossed it in the recycling bin. He grabbed the folder with the intention of staggering back to his cot and searching for sleep. But he found himself opening it up instead.

There was a single sheet of paper inside. An old sheet of paper. It had yellowed, and the edges were rough where bits had flaked off over the years. Below the single-spaced typing there were five signatures, a mix of florid and subdued penmanship. At the top of the document, boldly typed, it read: *RE: THE PACT.*

Donald glanced up at the door. He turned and went to the small desk with the computer, placed the folder by the keyboard and sat down. Anna's note to her father had the same words in the subject line, along with *Urgent*. He had read the note a dozen times to try and divine its meaning. And the number in the note had led him to this folder.

He was familiar enough with the Pact of the silos, the governing document that kept each facility in line, that managed their populations with lotteries, that dictated their punishments from fines to cleanings. But this was too brief to be that Pact. It looked like a memo from his days on Capitol Hill.

Donald read:

All—

    It has been previously discussed that ten facilities would suffice for our purposes, and that a time frame of one century would perform an adequate cleanse. With members of this pact both familiar with budget under-runs and how battle plans prove fruitless upon first firing, it should surprise no one that facts have changed our forecast. We are now calling for thirty facilities and a two-century time frame. The tech team assures me their progress makes the latter feasible. These figures may be revisited once again.

There was also discussion in the last meeting of allowing two facilities to reach E-Day for redundancy (or the possibility of holding one facility back in reserve). That has been deemed inadvisable. Having all baskets in one egg is better than the danger of allowing two or more eggs to hatch. As it is a source of growing contention, this amendment to the original Pact shall be hereby undersigned by all founding persons and considered law. I will take it upon myself to work E-shift and pull the lever. Long-term survivability prospects are at 42 per cent in the latest models. Marvellous progress, everyone.

—V

Donald scanned the signatures a second time. There was Thurman's simple scrawl, recognisable from countless memos and bills on the Hill. Another signature that might be Erskine's. One that looked like Charles Rhodes, the swaggering Oklahoma governor. Illegible others. There was no date on the memo.

He read over it again. Understanding dawned slowly, full of doubts at first, but solidifying. There was a list he remembered from his previous shift, a ranking of silos. Number eighteen had been near the top. It was why Victor had fought so hard to save the facility. This decision he mentioned in the memo, pulling the lever. Had he said something about this in his note to Thurman? In his admission before he killed himself? Victor had grown unsure of whether or not he could make some decision.

Baskets in one egg. That wasn't how the saying went. Donald leaned back in the chair, and one of the light bulbs in Dr Wilson's desk lamp flickered. Bulbs were not meant to last so long. They went dark, but there were redundancies.

One egg. Because what would they do to each other if more than one were allowed to hatch?

The list.

The reason it all fell together for Donald so easily was because he already knew. Had always known. How could it be otherwise? They had no plan, these bastards, of allowing the men and women of the silos to go free. No. There could be only one. For what would they do to each other if they met hundreds of years hence on the hills outside? Donald had drawn this place. He should've always known. He was an architect of death.

He thought about the list, the rankings of the silos. The one at the top was the only one that mattered. But what was their metric? How arbitrary would that decision be? All those eggs slaughtered except for one. With what hope? What plan? That the differences and struggles among a silo's people can be overcome? And yet the differences between the silos themselves was too much?

Donald coughed into his trembling hand. He understood what Anna was trying to tell him. And now it was too late. Too late for answers. This was the way of life and death, and in a place that ignored both, he'd forgotten. There was no waking anyone. Just confusion and grief. His only ally, gone.

But there was another he could wake, the one he'd hoped to from the beginning. This was a grave power, this ability to bestir the dead. Donald shivered as he realised what the Pact truly meant, this pact between the madmen who had conspired to destroy the world.

'It's a suicide pact,' he whispered, and the concrete walls of the silo closed in around him; they wrapped him like the shell of an egg. An egg never meant to be hatched. For they were the most dangerous of them all, this pit of vipers, and no world would ever be safe with them in it. The women and children were in lifeboats only to urge the men of silo one to keep working their shifts. But they were all meant to drown. Every last one of them.

S olo didn't set out one day to plumb the silo's depths – it simply happened. He headed off towards fabled Supply in search of batteries or a can opener and found instead a battleground strewn with bones and bolts. Searching the tall shelves and the darkened corridors beyond, he found a second flashlight, even better than batteries. The flashlight had been left on, was warm to the touch, and it took several moments to realise what this meant. Solo had fled from Supply with a vow never to return. He ran downward, hurrying, chased by ghosts, until his boots splashed into cold water.

Solo started and lost his grip on the rail. He slid, fought for balance and fell to one knee, water soaking him up to his crotch, his rifle slipping off his shoulder, his bag getting wet.

Cursing, he struggled to his feet. Water dripped from the barrel of his rifle, a stream of liquid bullets. His overalls were freezing cold and clung to his skin where they'd gotten soaked.

'Stupid,' he said. He retreated up a step and watched the agitated surface settle. The silo was full of water. Peering through the murky surface, he saw that the stairs spiralled out of sight and into the dark depths. Solo watched where the water met the railing and waited to see if the flood was rising. If so, it was far slower than he could tell.

One of the doors on level one-thirty-seven moved back and forth with the waves his splashing had caused. The water was two feet or more above the level of the landing. It was that high inside the door as well. The entire silo was filling up with water, he thought. It had taken years for it to get this high. Would it go on for ever? How long before it filled his home up on thirty-four? How long before it reached the top?

Thinking of slowly drowning elicited a strange sound from Solo's mouth, a noise like a sad whimper. His clothes dripped water back to where it had come from, and then Solo heard the whimpering sound again. It wasn't coming from him at all.

He crouched down and peered into the flooded level, listening. There. The sound of someone crying. It was coming from inside the flooded levels. It sounded like an infant.

Solo peered down at the water. He would have to wade through it. The dim green lights overhead lent the world a ghostly pallor. The air was cold, and the water colder.

He retreated up the steps and left his heavy pack on one of the dry treads. The cuffs of his overalls were soaked. He rolled them up over his calves, then began unknotting the laces of his boots.

He listened for the cry again. It did not come. He wondered if he would be braving the wet and cold for something he'd imagined, for another ghost who would disappear as soon as he paid it any mind. He dumped the water out of his boots before setting them aside. He pulled off his socks – his big toe poked through a hole in one of them. He squeezed and twisted these, then draped them across the railing to dry.

He left his bag four steps above the waterline and thought he heard the baby cry again. He was enough years old to have a baby, he thought. He did the maths. He rarely did this maths. Was he twenty-six? Twenty-seven? Another birthday had come and gone with no one to remind him.

He stepped into the water and waded towards the door, his feet shocked half numb from the cold. The colourful film on the surface swirled and mixed and flowed around the stanchions that held up the landing rail. Solo paused and peered beyond the landing. It seemed strange to be so high off the bottom of the silo and see this fluid stretching out to the concrete walls. If he were to fall over, would the water slow his plummet to the bottom? Or would he bob on the surface like that bit of trash over there? He thought he would sink, so he shuffled his feet cautiously. Something silver flashed beneath the grating, but he thought it was just his reflection or the dance of the metallic sheen on the surface.

'You better be worth this,' he told the ghost of some baby down the hall.

He listened for the ghost to call back, but it was no longer crying. The light beyond the doors fell away to blackness, so he pulled his flashlight out of his chest pocket and turned it on. The layer of rippling water caught the beam and magnified it. Waves of light danced across the ceiling.

'Hello?' he called out.

His voice echoed back to him. He played the light down the hall, which branched off in three directions. Two of the paths curved around as if to meet on the other side of the stairwell. It was one of the hub-and-spoke levels. Solo laughed. *Bi* for 'bicycles'. He thought of that entry and realised where the words *hub and spoke* came from.

There was a cry. For certain, this time, or he truly was losing his senses. Solo spun around and waited. Silence. The whisper of ripples as they crashed into the hallway wall. He picked his way in the direction he'd heard the noise, throwing up new waves with the push of his shins. He floated like a ghost. He couldn't feel his feet.

It was an apartment level. But why would anyone live down here with the waters seeping in? He paused outside a community rec room and dispelled pockets of darkness with his flashlight. There was a tennis table in the middle of the room. Rust reached up the steel legs as if the water had chased it there. The paddles were still on the warped surface of the rotting green table. *Green for grass*, Solo thought. The Legacy books made his own world look different to him.

Something bumped into his shin and Solo started. He

aimed his light down and saw a foam cushion floating by his feet. He pushed it away and waded to the next door.

A community kitchen. He recognised the layout of wide tables and all the chairs. Most of the chairs lay on their sides, partly submerged. A few legs stuck up where chairs had been overturned. There were two stoves in the corner and a wall of cabinets. The room was dark; almost none of the light from the stairwell trickled back this far. Solo imagined that if his batteries died, he would have to grope to find his way out. He should've brought the new flashlight, not his old one.

A cry. Louder this time. Near. Somewhere in the room.

Solo waved his flashlight about but couldn't see every corner at once. Cabinets and countertops. A spot of movement, he thought. He trained his light back a little, and something moved on one of the counters. It leapt straight up, the sound of claws scratching as it caught itself on an open cabinet above the counter, then the whisking of a bushy tail before a black shadow disappeared into the darkness.

2323 – Year Twelve

• Silo 17 •

cat! A living thing. A living thing he need not fear, that could do him no harm. Solo trudged into the room, calling, 'Kitty, kitty, kitty.' He recalled neighbours trying to corral that tailless animal that lived down the hall from his old apartment.

Something rummaged around in the cabinets. One of the closed doors rattled open and banged shut again. He could only see a spot at a time, wherever he aimed the flashlight. His shins brushed against something. He aimed the beam down to see trash and debris floating in the water. There was a squeak and a splash. Searching with the flashlight, he saw a V of ripples behind what he took for a swimming rat. Solo no longer wanted to be in that room. He shivered and rubbed his arm with his free hand. The cat made a racket inside the cabinet.

'Here, kitty,' he said with less gusto. Reaching into his breast pocket, he pulled out one of his ration bars and tore the packaging off with his teeth. Taking a stale bite for himself, he chewed and held the rest out in front of him. The silo had been dead for twelve years. He wondered how long cats lived, how this one had made it so long. And eating what? Or were old cats having new cats? Was this a new cat?

His bare feet brushed through something beneath the water. The reflection of the light made it difficult to see, and then a white bone broke the surface before sinking again. There was a loose jumble of someone's remains around his ankles.

Solo pretended it was just trash. He reached the cabinet that was making all the noise, grabbed a handle and pulled it open. There was a hiss from the shadows. Cans and rotting boxes shifted about as the cat retreated further. Solo broke off a piece of stale bar and set it on the shelf. He waited. There was another squeak from the corner of the room, the sound of water lapping at furniture, a stillness inside the cabinet. He kept the flashlight down so as not to spook the animal.

Two eyes approached like bobbing lights. They fixed themselves on Solo for a small eternity. He began to seriously wonder if his feet might fall off from the cold. The eyes drew closer and diverted downward. It was a black cat, the colour of wet shadow, slick as oil. The piece of ration bar crunched as the cat chewed.

'Good kitty,' he whispered, ignoring the scattered bones beneath his feet. He broke off another small piece of the bar and held it out. The cat withdrew a pace. Solo set the food on the edge and watched as the animal came forward more quickly this time. The next piece, the cat took from his palm. He offered the last piece, and as the cat came to accept it, Solo tried to pick it up with both hands. And this thing, this company he hoped would do him no harm, latched on to one of his arms and sank its claws into his flesh.

Solo screamed and threw up his hands. The flashlight tumbled end over end in the air. There was a splash as the cat disappeared. A shriek and a hiss, a violent noise, Solo fumbling beneath the water for the dull glow of the light, which flickered once, twice, then left him in darkness.

He groped blindly, seized a solid cylinder and felt the knobby ends where the leg sockets went into the hip. He dropped the bone in disgust. Two more bones before he found the flashlight, which was toast. He retrieved it anyway as the sound of frantic splashing approached. His arms were on fire; he had seen blood on them in the last of the spinning light. And then something was against his leg, up his shin, claws stinging his thighs, the damn cat climbing him as if he were the leg of a table.

Solo reached for the poor animal to get its claws out of his flesh. The cat was soaked and hardly felt bigger around than his flashlight. It trembled in his arms and rubbed itself against a dry patch of his overalls, mewing in complaint. It began to sniff at his breast pocket.

Solo held the animal with one forearm across his chest, making a perch, and reached inside his pocket for the other ration bar. It was perfectly dark in the room, so dark it made his ears ache. He ripped the package free and held the bar steady. Tiny paws wrapped around his hand, and there was a crunching sound.

Jimmy smiled. He worked his way towards where he thought the door might be, bumping through furniture and old bones as he went, Solo no more.

Donald's apartment had transformed into a cave, a cave where notes lay strewn like bleached bones, where the carcasses of folders decorated his walls, and where boxes of more notes were ordered up from archives like fresh kill. Weeks had passed. The stomping in the halls had dwindled. Donald lived alone with ghosts and slowly pieced together the purpose of what he'd helped to build. He was beginning to see it, the entire picture, zooming out of the schematic until the whole was laid bare.

He coughed into a pink rag and resumed examination of his latest find. It was a map he'd come across once before in the armoury, a map of all the silos with a line coming out of each and converging at a single point. Here was one of many mysteries left. The document was labelled *Seed*, but he could find nothing else about it.

Donald could hear Anna whispering to him. She had been trying to tell him something. The note in Thurman's account, she was trying to say, had been left for him. So obvious now. She could never be woken, not a woman. She needed him, needed his help. Donald imagined her piecing all of this together on some recent shift, alone and terrified, scared of her own father, no one left to turn to. So she had taken her father out of power, had entrusted Donald, had switched him with another man for the second time and had left him a note to wake her. And what did Donald do instead?

There was a knock on his door.

'Who is it?' Donald asked, his voice not sounding like his own.

The door opened a crack. 'It's Eren, sir. We've got a call from eighteen. The shadow is ready.'

'Just a second.'

Donald coughed into his handkerchief. He rose slowly and moved to the bathroom, stepping over two trays of old dishes. He emptied his bladder, flushed and studied himself in the mirror. Gripping the edge of the counter, he grimaced at his reflection, this man with scraggly hair and the start of a beard. He looked half crazed, and yet people still trusted him. That made them crazier than he was. Donald smiled a yellowing smile and thought of the long history of madmen who remained in charge simply because no one would challenge them.

Hinges squealed as Eren poked his head in the door.

'I'm coming,' Donald said. He stomped across the reports, leaving a trail of footprints behind, and a bloody palm print on the edge of the counter.

'They're calling the shadow now, sir,' Eren said to him in the hall. 'You want to freshen up?'

'No,' Donald said. 'I'm good.' He stood in the doorway, struggling to remember what this meeting was about. A Rite of Initiation. He remembered those, thought it was something Gable would handle. 'Why am I needed again?' he asked. 'Shouldn't our head be conducting this?' Donald remembered being the one to conduct such a Rite on his first shift.

Eren popped something into his mouth and chewed. He shook his head. 'You know, with all that reading you're doing in there, you could bone up on the Order a bit. It sounds like it's changed since the last time you read it. The ranking officer on shift completes the Rite. That would normally be me—'

'But since I'm up, it's me.' Donald pulled his door shut. The two of them started down the hall.

'That's right. The heads here do less and less every shift. There have been . . . problems. I'll sit in with you though, help you get through the script. Oh, and you wanted to know when the pilots were heading off shift. The last one is going under right now. They're just straightening up down there.'

Donald perked up at this. Finally. What he'd been waiting for. 'So the armoury's empty?' he asked, unable to hide his delight.

'Yessir. No more flight requisitions. I know you didn't like chancing them to begin with.'

'Right, right.' Donald waved his hand as they turned the corner. 'Restrict access to the armoury once they're done. Nobody should be able to get in there but me.'

Eren slowed his pace. 'Just you, sir?'

'For as long as I'm on shift,' Donald said.

They passed Gable in the hall, who had three cups of coffee nestled in a web of fingers. Gable smiled and nodded. Donald remembered fetching coffee for people when he was head of the silo. Now, that was near enough all the head did. Donald couldn't help but think his first shift was partly to blame.

Eren lowered his voice. 'You know the story behind him, right?' He took another bite of something and chewed.

Donald glanced over his shoulder. 'Who, Gable?'

'Yeah. He was in Ops until a few shifts back. Broke down. Tried to get himself into deep freeze. The duty doc at the time talked him into a demotion. We were losing too many people, and the shifts were starting to get some overlap.' Eren paused and took another bite. There was a familiar scent. Eren caught him watching and held out something. 'Bagel?' he asked. 'They're fresh baked.'

Donald could smell it. Eren tore off a piece. It was still warm. 'I didn't know they could make these,' he said, popping the morsel into his mouth.

'New chef just came on shift. He's been experimenting with all kinds of stuff. He—'

Donald didn't hear the rest. He chewed on memories. A cool day in DC, Helen up to visit, had the dog with her, drove all the way from Savannah. They walked around the Lincoln Memorial a week too early for the cherry blossoms, but there were still spots of colour dotted here and there. They had stopped for fresh bagels, still warm, the smell of coffee—

'Put an end to this,' Donald said, indicating the rest of Eren's bagel.

'Sir?'

They were nearly at the bend in the hall that led to the comm room. 'I don't want this chef experimenting any more. Have him stick to the usual.'

Eren seemed confused. After some hesitation, he nodded. 'Yes, sir.'

'Nothing good can come of this,' Donald explained. And while Eren agreed more strenuously this time, Donald realised he had begun to think like the people he loathed. A veil of disappointment fell over Eren's face, and Donald felt a sudden urge to take it back, to grab the man by the shoulders and ask him what the hell they thought they were doing, all this misery and heartache. They should eat memory foods, of course, and talk about the days they'd left behind.

Instead, he said nothing, and they continued down the hall in quiet and discomfort.

'Quite a few of our silo heads came from Ops,' Eren said after a while, steering the conversation back to Gable. 'I was a comm officer for my first two shifts, you know. The guy I took over for, the Ops head from the last shift, was from Medical.'

'So you're not a shrink?' Donald asked.

Eren laughed, and Donald thought of Victor, blowing his brains out. This wasn't going to last, this place. There were cracked tiles in the centre of the hall. Tiles that had no replacement. The ones at the edge were in much better shape. He stopped outside the comm room and surveyed the wear on this centuries-old place. There were scuff marks low on the walls, hand-high, shoulder-high, fewer anywhere else. The traffic patterns on the floors throughout the facility showed where people walked. The wear on that place, like on its people, was not evenly distributed.

'I believe they're waiting on us, sir.'

Donald looked away from the scuff marks to Eren, this young man with bright eyes and bagel on his breath, his hair full of colour, an upturn at the corners of his mouth, a wan smile like a scar of hope.

'Right,' Donald said. He waved Eren inside the comm room before following behind, stepping dead centre like everyone else.

• Silo 1 •

D onald familiarised himself with the script while Eren
plopped into the chair beside him and pulled a
headset on. The software would mask their voices,
make them featureless and the same. The silo heads need not
know when one man went off shift and another replaced him.
It was always the same voice, the same person, as far as they
were concerned.

The shift operator lifted a mug and took a sip. Donald
could see something written on the mug with a marker. It
said: *We're #1*. Donald wondered if whoever wrote it meant
the silo. The operator set the mug down and twirled his finger
for Donald to begin.

Donald covered his mic and cleared his throat. He could
hear someone talking on the other end of the line as a distant
headset was pulled on. There was a script to follow for the
first half. Donald remembered most of it. Eren turned to the
side and polished off the bagel guiltily. When the operator
gave them the thumbs-up, Eren gestured to Donald to do
the honours, and all Donald could think about was getting
this over with and getting down to that empty armoury.

'Name,' he said into his mic.

'Lukas Kyle,' came the reply.

Donald watched the graphs jump with readings taken
from the headset. He felt sorry for this person, signing on to
head a silo rated near the bottom. It all seemed hopeless, and
here Donald was going through the motions. 'You shadowed
in IT,' he said.

There was a pause. 'Yessir.'

The boy's temperature was up. Donald could read it on the display. The operator and Eren were comparing notes and pointing to something. Donald checked the script. It listed easy questions everyone knew the answers to.

'What is your primary duty to the silo?' he asked, reading the line.

'To maintain the Order.'

Eren raised a hand as the readouts spiked. When they settled, he gave Donald the sign to continue.

'What do you protect above all?' Even with the software helping, Donald tried to keep his voice flat. There was a jump on one of the graphs. Donald's thoughts drifted to the news of the pilots gone from his space, a space that he felt belonged to him. He would get through this and set his alarm clock. Tonight. Tonight.

'Life and Legacy,' the shadow recited.

Donald lost his place. It took a moment to find the next line. 'What does it take to protect these things we hold so dear?'

'It takes sacrifice,' the shadow said after a brief pause.

The comm head gave Donald and Eren an okay signal. The formal readings were over. Now to the baseline, to get off script. Donald wasn't sure what to say. He nodded to Eren, hoping he'd take over.

Eren covered his mic for a second as if he was about to argue, but shrugged. 'How much time have you had in the Suit Labs?' he asked the shadow, studying the monitor in front of him.

'Not much, sir. Bernar— Uh, my boss, he's wanting me to schedule time in the labs after, you know . . .'

'Yes. I do know.' Eren nodded. 'How's that problem in your lower levels going?'

'Um, well, I'm only kept apprised of the overall progress, and it sounds good.' Donald heard the shadow clear his throat. 'That is, it sounds like progress is being made, that it won't be much longer.'

A long pause. A deep breath. Waveforms relaxed. Eren glanced at Donald. The operator waved his finger for them to keep going.

Donald had a question, one that touched on his own regrets. 'Would you have done anything differently, Lukas?' he asked. 'From the beginning?'

There were red spikes on the monitors, and Donald felt his own temperature rise. Maybe he was asking something too close to home.

'Nossir,' the young shadow said. 'It was all by the Order, sir. Everything's under control.'

The comm head reached to his controls and muted all of their headsets. 'We're getting borderline readings,' he told them. 'His nerves are spiking. Can you push him a little more?'

Eren nodded. The operator on the other side of him shrugged and took a sip from his #1 mug.

'Settle him down first, though,' the comm head said.

Eren turned to Donald. 'Congratulate him and then see if you can get him emotional. Level him out and then tweak him.'

Donald hesitated. It was all so artificial and manipulative. He forced himself to swallow. The mics were unmuted.

'You are next in line for the control and operation of silo eighteen,' he said stiffly, sad for what he was dooming this poor soul to.

'Thank you, sir.' The shadow sounded relieved. Waveforms collapsed as if they'd struck a pier.

Now Donald fought for some way to push the young man. The comm head waving at him didn't help. Donald glanced up at the map of the silos on the wall. He stood, the headphone cord stretching, and studied the several silos marked out, the one there with the number '12'. Donald considered the seriousness of what this young man had just taken on, what his job entailed, how many had died elsewhere because their leaders had let them down.

'Do you know the worst part of my job?' Donald asked.

He could feel those in the comm room watching him. Donald
was back on his first shift, initiating that other young man.
He was back on his first shift, shutting a silo down.

'What's that, sir?' the voice asked.

'Standing here, looking at a silo on this map, and drawing
a red cross through it. Can you imagine what that feels like?'

'I can't, sir.'

Donald nodded. He appreciated the honest answer. He
remembered what it felt like to watch those people spill out
of twelve and perish on the landscape. He blinked his vision
clear. 'It feels like a parent losing thousands of children all at
once,' he said.

The world stood still for a heartbeat or two. The operator
and the comm head were both fixated on their monitors,
looking for a crack. Eren watched Donald.

'You will have to be cruel to your children so as not to
lose them,' Donald said.

'Yessir.'

Waveforms began to pulse like gentle surf. The comm
head gave Donald the thumbs-up. He had seen enough. The
boy had passed, and now the Rite was truly over.

'Welcome to Operation Fifty of the World Order, Lukas
Kyle,' Eren said, reading from the script and taking over from
Donald. 'Now, if you have a question or two, I have the time
to answer, but briefly.'

Donald remembered this part. He had a hand in this.
He settled back into his chair, suddenly exhausted.

'Just one, sir. And I've been told it isn't important, and I
understand why that's true, but I believe it will make my job
here easier if I know.' The young man paused. 'Is there . . .?'
A new red spike on his graph. 'How did this all begin?'

Donald held his breath. He glanced around the room,
but everyone else was watching their monitors as if any question was as good as another.

Donald responded before Eren could. 'How badly do you
wish to know?' he asked.

The shadow took in a breath. 'It isn't crucial,' he said,

'but I would appreciate a sense of what we're accomplishing, what we survived. It feels like it gives me – gives us a purpose, you know?'

'The reason *is* the purpose,' Donald told him. This was what he was beginning to learn from his studies. 'Before I tell you, I'd like to hear what you think.'

He thought he could hear the shadow gulp. 'What I think?' Lukas asked.

'Everyone has ideas,' Donald said. 'Are you suggesting you don't?'

'I think it was something we saw coming.'

Donald was impressed. He had a feeling this young man knew the answer and simply wanted confirmation. 'That's one possibility,' he agreed. 'Consider this . . .' He thought how best to phrase it. 'What if I told you that there were only fifty silos in all the world, and that we are in this infinitely small corner of it?'

On the monitor, Donald could practically watch the young man think, his readings oscillating up and down like the brain's version of a heartbeat.

'I would say that we were the only ones . . .' A wild spike on the monitor. 'I'd say we were the only ones who *knew*.'

'Very good. And why might that be?'

Donald wished he had the jostling lines on the screen recorded. It was serene, watching another human being clutch after his vanishing sanity, his disappearing doubts.

'It's because . . . It's not because we knew.' There was a soft gasp on the other end of the line. 'It's because we *did it*.'

'Yes,' Donald said. 'And now you know.'

Eren turned to Donald and placed his hand over his mic. 'We've got more than enough. The kid checks out.'

Donald nodded. 'Our time is up, Lukas Kyle. Congratulations on your assignment.'

'Thank you.' There was a final flutter on the monitors.

'Oh, and Lukas?' Donald said, remembering the young man's predilection for staring at the stars, for dreaming, for filling himself with dangerous hope.

'Yessir?'

'Going forward, I suggest you concentrate on what's beneath your feet. No more of this business with the stars, okay, son? We know where most of them are.'

90

2327 – Year Sixteen
• Silo 17 •

Jimmy wasn't sure how the algebra worked, but feeding two mouths was more than just twice the work. And yet – it felt like less than half the chore. He suspected it had to do with how nice it was to provide for something besides himself. The satisfaction of seeing the cat eat and of it growing used to him made him relish meals and travel outside more often.

It had been a rough start, though. The cat had been skittish after its rescue. Jimmy had dried himself off with a towel scavenged two levels up, and the cat had acted insane as he dried it off after. It seemed to both love and hate the process, rolling around one minute and batting at Jimmy's hands the next. Once dry, the animal had blossomed to twice its wet size. And yet he was still pathetic and hungry.

Jimmy found a can of beans beneath a mattress. The can wasn't too rusty. He opened it with his screwdriver and fed the slick pods to the cat one at a time while his own feet thawed, tingling like electricity the entire time.

After the beans, the cat had taken to following him wherever he went to see what he might find next. It made the hunt for food fun, rather than a never-ending war against his own growling stomach. Fun, but also lots of work. Up the staircase they went, him back in his boots, the cat silently pawing behind and sometimes ahead.

Jimmy had learned early on to trust the cat's balance. The first few times it rubbed itself against the outer stanchions, even twisting itself beyond them and back through as it ascended the steps, Jimmy nearly had a heart attack. The cat seemed to have a death wish, or just an ignorance of what it meant to fall. But he soon learned to trust the cat even as the cat began to trust him.

And that first night, as he lay huddled under his tarp in the lower farms, listening to pumps and lights click on and off and noises he mistook for others in hiding, the cat tucked itself under his arm and curled against the crook his belly made when his legs were bent and began to rattle like a pump on loose mounts.

'You were lonely, huh?' Jimmy had whispered. He had grown uncomfortable but was unwilling to move. A cramp had formed in his neck while a different tightness disappeared from deep in his gut, a tightness he didn't know was there until it was gone.

'I was lonely too,' he had told the cat softly, fascinated by how much more he talked with the animal around. It was better than talking to his shadow and pretending it was a person.

'That's a good name,' Jimmy had whispered. He didn't know what people named cats, but Shadow would work. Like the shadows in which he'd found the thing, another spot of blackness to follow Jimmy around. And that night, years back, the two of them had fallen asleep amid the clicking pumps, the dripping water, the buzzing insects and all the stranger sounds deep within the farms that Jimmy preferred not to name.

That was years ago. Now, cat hair and beard hair gathered together in the spines of the Legacy books. Jimmy trimmed his beard while he read about snakes. The scissors made crunching noises as he pinched a load of hair, held it away from his chin and hacked it off with the dull shears. He sprinkled most of the hair in an empty can. The rest drifted down among the pages, large swoops of meddling punctuation mingling with hair from the cat, who kept walking back and forth under his arms, arching his back and stepping across the sentences.

'I'm trying to read,' Jimmy complained. But he put down the scissors and dutifully stroked the animal from neck to tail, Shadow pressing his spine up into Jimmy's palm. He meowed and made that grumbling sound as if his heart were going to burst and begged for more.

Tiny claws clenched into little fists and punctured a photo of a corn snake, and Jimmy guided the animal towards the floor. Shadow lay on his back with his feet in the air, watching Jimmy carefully. It was a trap. Jimmy could rub his belly for only a moment before the cat would suddenly decide he hated this and attack his wrist. Jimmy didn't understand cats that well, but he'd read the entry on them a dozen times. One thing he hated to learn was that they didn't live as long as humans. He tried not to think of that day. On that day he would go back to being Solo, and he much preferred being Jimmy. Jimmy talked more. Solo was the one with the wild thoughts, the one who gazed over the rails, who spat towards the Deep and watched as his spit trembled and tore itself apart from the wild speeds of its racing fall.

'Are you bored?' Jimmy asked Shadow.

Shadow looked at him as though he were bored. It was similar to the look that said he was hungry.

'Wanna go explore?'

The cat's ear twitched, which was enough of a sign.

Jimmy decided to check up top again. He had only been once since the days went dark, and just for a peek. If there was a working can opener in the silo, it would be there. An end to crusty screwdrivers and slicing his hands on roughly opened lids.

They set out after lunch with a short break at the farms. When they got to the cafeteria, they found it perfectly silent and glowing in the green cast from the stairwell. Shadow scampered up the last steps alone, intrepid as usual. Jimmy headed straight for the kitchen and found it a looted wreck.

'Who took all the openers?' he called out to Shadow.

But Shadow wasn't there. Shadow was off to the far wall, acting agitated.

Jimmy ranged behind the serving line and sorted through the forks, eager to replace his usual one, when he heard the mewing. He peered across the wide cafeteria hall and saw Shadow rubbing back and forth against a closed door.

'Keep it down,' Jimmy yelled to Shadow. Didn't the cat know he'd only bring trouble making such a racket? But Shadow wasn't listening. He mewed and mewed and scratched his claws at the door and stretched until Jimmy relented. Jimmy hurried through the maze of upturned chairs and crooked tables to see what the fuss was about.

'Is it food?' he asked. With Shadow, it was almost always food. His companion was drawn to meals like a magnet, which Jimmy had come to find quite handy. Approaching the door, he saw the remnants of a rope looped around the handle, the years reducing it to tatters. Jimmy tried the handle and found it unlocked. He eased it open.

The room beyond was dark, none of the emergency lights lit like at the top of the stairwell. Jimmy fumbled for his flashlight while Shadow disappeared through the cracked door, his tail swishing into the void.

There was a startled hiss just as the flashlight came on. Jimmy paused, a boot nearly through the door, as the cone of his flashlight fell upon a face staring up at him with open and lifeless eyes. Bodies shifted against the door, and an arm flopped out against his foot.

Jimmy screamed and fell backward. He kicked at the pale and fleshy hand and called for Shadow, who came screeching out the door, fur standing on end. There was the taste of metal on Jimmy's tongue, a rush of adrenalin as he scrambled to get the door shut. He lifted the limp arm and shoved it back inside, the clothes disintegrating at his touch, the flesh beneath whole and spongy.

Open mouths and curled fingers were the last things he saw. Piles of bodies, as fresh as the morning dead, frozen where they'd crawled over one another, hands reaching for the door.

Once it clicked shut, Jimmy began sliding tables and

chairs against the door. He created a huge tangle of them, tossing more chairs on top of the pile, shivering and cursing beneath his beard while Shadow spun in circles.

'Gross, gross, gross,' he told Shadow, whose hair had not yet settled. He studied his barricade against the piles of dead and hoped it would be adequate, that he hadn't let out too many ghosts. The remnants of old rope swayed on the door's handle, and Jimmy thanked whomever had kept these people at bay.

'Let's go,' he said, and Shadow swished against his leg for comfort. There was no view to see on the wall screen, no food or tools of any use. He'd had quite enough of up top, which suddenly felt crowded to the walls with the dead.

91

2327 – Year Sixteen

• Silo 17 •

B esides food, Shadow had a nose for trouble. A nose for causing it. Jimmy woke one morning to an awful screeching sound, a pathetic and plaintive hiss spilling down the corridor. Jimmy had climbed the ladder half asleep to find Shadow stuck near the top rung. He didn't know how the cat had got there, and the cat didn't know how to get down. Jimmy released the hatch over their heads and threw it aside. He watched as Shadow clawed up the metal mesh behind the ladder, his back pressed against the rungs, and scampered over the top.

Two mornings later, the same thing happened, and that's when Jimmy decided to leave the hatch open all the time. He was sick of opening and closing it as he came and went, and Shadow liked being able to explore the server room whenever he liked. There hadn't been any fighting in a long time and the great steel door still winked red.

Shadow loved the servers. Most times, Jimmy would find him up on server number forty, where the metal was so hot that Jimmy could barely touch it. But Shadow didn't mind. He slept up there or peered over the edge at the ground far below, watching for bugs on which to pounce.

Other times, Jimmy found him standing in the corner where that man he'd shot all that time ago had wasted away. Shadow liked to sniff the rust stains and touch his tongue to the grating. It was for these freedoms that the hatch remained off. And this was how, when the power went out big-time, the bad men got inside. This was how Jimmy woke up one morning with a stranger standing over his bed.

The outage had woken him in the middle of the night. Jimmy slept with the lights on, keeping the ghosts at bay. He even liked a little of the radio static to fill the room, so he couldn't hear any whisperings. When the silence and darkness hit at once with a loud thump, Jimmy had started awake and scrambled for his flashlight, stepping on Shadow's tail in the process. He waited for the lights to come on, but they remained off. Too tired to think what to do, he went back to sleep, both hands wrapped around his flashlight, Shadow curling up warily against his neck.

The noise of someone coming down the ladder was what stirred him later. Jimmy was dimly aware of a presence in the room. It was a sensation he often felt, but this presence seemed to change the way the silence bounced around, the way even the noise of his breathing echoed. He opened his eyes to find a flashlight shining down on him, a man standing at the foot of his bed.

Jimmy screamed, and the man pounced as if to silence him. A bearded snarl of yellowed teeth caught the beam of light, and then the arc of a steel rod.

There was a flash of pain in Jimmy's shoulder. The man hauled back to hit him again with his length of pipe. Jimmy got his arms up to protect his head. The pipe cracked him on the wrist. There was a screech and a hiss by his head, and then a darting black shape amid the shadows.

The man with the pipe screamed and dropped his flashlight, which doused itself in the bedsheets. Jimmy scrambled away, his mind unable to come to grips with a person in his home. A person in his home. The fear of years and years became real in an instant. He had loosened his precautions. All the venturing out. *Slack, slack*, he told himself, crawling on his hands and knees.

Shadow let out an awful screech, the noise he made when his tail got stepped on. A howl of pain followed. Jimmy felt anger rise up and mix with his fear. He crawled towards the corner, banged into the desk, reached for where it should be propped—

His hands settled around the gun. It'd been years since he'd fired it. Couldn't remember if it was even loaded. But he could still swing it like a club if he had to. He cradled it against his shoulder and waved the barrel through the pitch black. Shadow screeched again. There was a thump of a small body hitting something hard. Jimmy couldn't breathe or swallow. He couldn't see anything but the dim glow of light rising up from the folds of his bed.

He pointed the barrel at a patch of blackness that seemed to move and squeezed the trigger. There was a blinding flash of light from the muzzle, a roar that filled the small space to the seams. In that brief strobe flashed the searing image of a man whirling towards him. Another wild shot. Another glimpse of this stranger in Jimmy's space, a thin man with a long beard and white eyes. And now Jimmy knew where he was, and the third shot did not zing. Its impact was lost in screams. The screams filled the darkness, and then a final shot put an end to even these.

Shadow's eyes glowed beneath the desk. He peered out warily at Jimmy and his new flashlight.

'You okay?' Jimmy asked.

The cat blinked.

'Stay here,' Jimmy whispered.

He cradled the flashlight between his cheek and shoulder and checked the clip. Before he left, he nudged the man who was bleeding on his sheets. Jimmy felt a strange numbness at seeing someone down there, even dead. He listened for more intruders as he stole his way towards the ladder.

The power outage and this attack were no coincidence, he told himself. Someone had gotten the door open. They had figured the keypad or pulled a breaker. Jimmy hoped this man had done it alone. He didn't recognise the face, but a lot of years had passed. Beards got long and turned grey. The silver overalls hinted at someone who might know how to break in. The pain in his shoulder and wrist hinted at these being no friends of his.

There was no one on the ladder. Jimmy slipped the rifle over his shoulder and doused the flashlight so no one would see him coming. His palms made the softest of rings on the metal rungs. He was halfway up when he felt Shadow slithering and clacking his way up between the ladder and the wall.

Jimmy hissed at the cat to stay put but it disappeared ahead of him. At the top of the ladder, Jimmy unslung his rifle and held it in one hand. With the other, he pressed the flashlight against his stomach and turned it on. Peeling the lens away from his overalls a little at a time, he cast just enough glow to pick his way through the servers.

There was a noise ahead of him, Shadow or another person, he couldn't tell. Jimmy hesitated before continuing on. It took for ever to cross the wide room with the dark machines like this. He could hear them still clacking, still whirring, still putting off heat. But when he got close to the door, the keypad was no longer blinking its sentinel light at him. And there was a void beyond the gleaming door – a door that stood halfway open.

More noise outside. The rustle of fabric, of a person moving. Jimmy killed the flashlight and steadied his rifle. He could taste the fear in his mouth. He wanted to call out for these people to leave him alone. He wanted to say what he had done to all those who came inside. He wanted to drop his gun and cry and beg never to have to do it again.

He poked his head into the hall and strained to see in the darkness, hoped this other person couldn't see him back. The hall contained nothing but the sound of two people breathing. There was a growing awareness that a dark space was shared with another.

'Hank?' someone whispered.

Jimmy turned and squeezed the trigger. There was a flash of light. The rifle kicked him in the shoulder. He retreated into the server room and waited for screams and stomping boots. He waited what felt like for ever. Something touched his boot and Jimmy screamed. It was Shadow purring and rubbing against him.

Chancing his flashlight, he peered around the corner and allowed some light to dribble out. There was a form there, a person on their back. He checked the deep and dark hallways and saw nothing. 'Leave me alone!' he yelled out to all the ghosts and more solid things.

Not even his echo called back.

Jimmy looked over this second man only to discover it wasn't a man at all. It was a woman. Her eyes had thankfully fallen shut. A man and a woman coming for his food, coming to steal from him. It made Jimmy angry. And then he saw the woman's swollen and distended belly and got doubly angry. It wasn't as if they were hurting for food, he thought.

Donald set his alarm for three in the morning, but there was little chance of him falling asleep. He'd waited weeks for this. A chance to give a life rather than take one. A chance at redemption and a chance for the truth, a chance to satisfy his growing suspicions.

He stared at the ceiling and considered what he was about to do. It wasn't what Erskine or Victor had hoped he would do if someone like him was in charge, but those men had got a lot wrong, least of all who he was. This wasn't the end of the end of the world. This was the beginning of something else. An end to the not knowing what was out there.

He studied his hand in the dim light spilling from the bathroom and thought of the outside. At two-thirty, he decided he'd waited long enough. He got up, showered and shaved, put on a fresh pair of overalls, tugged on his boots. He grabbed his badge, clipped it to his collar, and left his apartment with his head up and his shoulders back. Long strides took him down a hall with a few lights still on and the distant clatter of a keyboard, someone working late. The door to Eren's office was closed. Donald called for the lift and waited.

Before heading all the way down, he checked to see if it would be all for naught by scanning his badge and pressing the shiny button marked fifty-four. The light flashed and the lift lurched into motion. So far, so good. The lift didn't stop until it reached the armoury. The doors opened on a familiar darkness studded with tall shadows – black cliffs of shelves and bins.

Donald held his hand on the edge of the door to keep it from shutting and stepped out into the room. The vastness of the space could somehow be felt, as though the echoes of his racing pulse were being swallowed by the distance. He waited for a light to flick on at the far end, for Anna to walk out brushing her hair or with a bottle of Scotch in her hand, but nothing in that room moved. Everything was quiet and still. The pilots and the temporary activity were gone.

He returned to the lift and pressed another button. The lift sank. It drifted past more storage levels, past the reactor. The doors cracked open on the medical wing. Donald could feel the tens of thousands of bodies arranged all around him, all facing the ceiling, eyelids closed. Some of them were well and truly dead, he thought. One was about to be woken.

He went straight to the doctor's office and knocked on the jamb. The assistant on duty lifted his head from behind the monitor. He wiped his eyes behind his glasses, adjusted them on his nose and blinked at Donald.

'How's it going?' Donald asked.

'Hmm? Good. Good.' The young man shook his wrist and checked his watch, an ancient thing. 'We got someone going into deep freeze? I didn't get a call. Is Wilson up?'

'No, no. I just couldn't sleep.' Donald pointed at the ceiling. 'I went to see if anyone was up at the cafeteria, then figured since I was restless, I might as well come down here and see if you wanted me to finish out your shift. I can sit and watch a film as well as anyone.'

The assistant glanced at his monitor and laughed guiltily. 'Yeah.' He checked his watch again, had somehow already forgotten what it just told him. 'Two hours left. I wouldn't mind slagging off. You'll wake me if anything pops up?' He stood and stretched, covered his yawn with his hand.

'Of course.'

The medical assistant staggered out from behind the desk. Donald stepped around and pulled the seat away, sat down and propped up his feet as though he wouldn't be going anywhere for hours.

'I owe you one,' the young man said, collecting his coat from the back of the door.

'Oh, we're even,' Donald said under his breath as soon as the man was gone.

He waited for the lift to chime before launching into action. There was a plastic drink container on the drying rack by the sink. He grabbed this and filled it with water, the musical pitch of the vessel filling like a rising anxiety.

The lid came off the powder. Two scoops. He stirred with one of the long plastic tongue depressors and twisted the lid on, put the powder back in the fridge. The wheelchair wouldn't budge at first. He saw that the brakes were on, the little metal arms pressing into the soft rubber. He freed these, grabbed one of the blankets from the tall cabinet and a paper gown, tossed them onto the seat. Just like before. But he'd do it right this time. He collected the medical kit, made sure there was a fresh set of gloves.

The wheelchair rattled out the door and down the hall, and Donald's palms felt sweaty against the handles. To keep the front wheels silent, he rocked the chair back on its large rubber tyres. The small wheels spun lazily in the air as he hurried.

He entered his code into the keypad and waited for a red light, for some impediment, some blockade. The light winked green. Donald pulled the door open and swerved between the pods towards the one that held his sister.

There was a mix of anticipation and guilt. This was as bold a step as his run up that hill in a suit. The stakes were higher for involving family, for waking someone into this harsh world, for subjecting her to the same brutality Anna had foisted upon him, that Thurman had foisted upon her, on and on, a never-ending misery of shifts.

He left the wheelchair in place and knelt by the control pad. Hesitant, he lurched to his feet and peered through the glass porthole, just to be sure.

She looked so serene in there, probably wasn't plagued by nightmares like he was. Donald's doubts grew. And then he imagined her waking up on her own; he imagined her conscious and beating on the glass, demanding to be let out. He saw her feisty spirit, heard her demand not to be lied to, and he knew that if she were standing there with him, she would ask him to do it. She would rather know and suffer than be left asleep in ignorance.

He crouched by the keypad and entered his code. The keypad beeped cheerfully as he pressed the red button. There was a click from within the pod, like a valve opening. He turned the dial and watched the temperature gauge, waited for it to start climbing.

Donald rose and stood by the pod, and time slowed to a crawl. He expected someone to come find him before the process was complete. But there was another clack and a hiss from the lid. He laid out the gauze and the tape. He separated the two rubber gloves and began pulling them on, a cloud of chalk misting the air as he snapped the elastic.

He opened the lid the rest of the way.

His sister lay on her back, her arms by her sides. She had not yet moved. A panic seized him as he went over the procedure again. Had he forgotten something? Dear God, had he killed her?

Charlotte coughed. Water trailed down her cheeks as the frost on her eyelids melted. And then her eyes fluttered open weakly before returning to thin slits against the light.

'Hold still,' Donald told her. He pressed a square of gauze to her arm and removed the needle. He could feel the steel slide beneath the pad and his fingers as he extracted it from her arm. Holding the gauze in place, he took a length of tape hanging from the wheelchair and applied it across. The last was the catheter. He covered her with the towel, applied pressure and slowly removed the tube. And then she was free of the machine, crossing her arms and shivering. He helped her into the paper gown, left the back open.

'I'm lifting you out,' he said.

Her teeth clattered in response.

Donald shifted her feet towards her butt to tent her knees.

Reaching down beneath her armpits – her flesh cool to the touch – and another arm under her legs, he lifted her easily. It felt like she weighed so little. He could smell the cast-stink on her flesh.

Charlotte mumbled something as he placed her in the wheelchair. The blanket was draped across so that she sat on the fabric rather than the cold seat. As soon as she was settled, he wrapped the blanket around her. She chose to remain in a ball with her arms wrapped around her shins rather than place her feet on the stirrups.

'Where am I?' she asked, her voice a sheet of crackling ice.

'Take it easy,' Donald told her. He closed the lid on the pod, tried to remember if there was anything else, looked for anything he'd left behind. 'You're with me,' he said as he pushed her towards the exit. That was where both of them were: with each other. There was no home, no place on the earth to welcome one to any more, just a hellish nightmare in which to drag another soul for sad company.

93

• Silo 1 •

The hardest part was making her wait to eat. Donald knew what it felt like to be that hungry. He put her through the same routine he'd endured a number of times: made her drink the bitter concoction, made her use the bathroom to flush her system, had her sit on the edge of the tub and take a warm shower, then put her in a fresh set of clothes and a new blanket.

He watched as she finished the last of the drink. Her lips gradually faded to pink from pale blue. Her skin was so white. Donald couldn't remember if she'd been so pale before orientation. Maybe it had happened overseas, sitting in those dark trailers with only the light of a monitor to bathe in.

'I need to go make an appearance,' he told her. 'Everyone else will be getting up. I'll bring you breakfast on my way back down.'

Charlotte sat quietly in one of the leather chairs around the old war planning table, her feet tucked up under her. She tugged at the collar of the overalls as if they itched her skin. 'Mom and Dad are gone,' she said, repeating what he'd told her earlier. Donald wasn't sure what she would and wouldn't remember. She hadn't been on her stress medications as long or as recently as him. But it didn't matter. He could tell her the truth. Tell her and hate himself for doing it.

'I'll be back in a little bit. Just stay here and try to get some rest. Don't leave this room, okay?'

The words echoed hollow as he hurried through the warehouse and towards the lift. He remembered hearing from others as soon as they woke him that he should get some rest. Charlotte had been asleep for almost three centuries. As he scanned his badge and waited for the lift, Donald thought on how much time had passed and how little had changed. The world was still the ruin they'd left it. Or if it wasn't, they were about to find out.

He rode up to the operations level and checked in with Eren. The Ops head was already at his desk, surrounded by files, one hand tangled in his hair, his elbow on piles of paperwork. There was no steam from his mug of coffee. He'd been at his desk for a while.

'Thurman,' he said, glancing up.

Donald started and glanced down the hall, looking for someone else.

'Any progress with eighteen?'

'I, uh . . .' Donald tried to remember. 'Last I heard, they'd breached the barrier in the lowest levels. The head over there thinks the fighting will be over in a day or two.'

'Good. Glad the shadow is working out. Scary time not to have one. There was this one time on my third shift I think it was when we lost a head while he was between shadows. Helluva time finding a recruit.' Eren leaned back in his chair. 'The mayor wasn't an option; the head of Security was as bright as a lump of coal; so we had to—'

'I'm sorry to interrupt,' Donald said, pointing down the hall. 'I need to get back to—'

'Oh, of course.' Eren waved his hand, seemed embarrassed. 'Right. Me too.'

'—just a lot to do this morning. Grabbing breakfast and then I'll be in my room.' He jerked his head towards the empty office across the hall. 'Tell Gable I took care of myself, okay? I don't want to be disturbed.'

'Sure, sure.' Eren shooed him with his hand.

Donald spun back to the lift. Up to the cafeteria. His stomach rumbled its agreement. He'd been up all night without eating. He'd been up and empty for far too long.

94

2345

• Silo 1 •

He was pushing the time limit by letting her eat an
hour early, but it was difficult to say no. Donald
encouraged her to take small bites, to slow down.
And while Charlotte chewed, he brought her up to date. She
knew about the silos from orientation. He told her about the
wall screens, about the cleaners, that he had been woken
because someone had disappeared. Charlotte had a hard time
grasping these things. It took saying them several times until
they became strange even to his ears.

'They let them see outside, these people in the other
silos?' she asked, chewing on a small bite of biscuit.

'Yeah. I asked Thurman once why we put them there.
You know what he told me?'

Charlotte shrugged and took a sip of water.

'They're there to keep them from wanting to leave. We
have to show them death to keep them in. Otherwise, they'll
always want to see what's over the rise. Thurman said it's
human nature.'

'But some of them go anyway.' She wiped her mouth
with her napkin, picked up her fork, her hand trembling, and
pulled Donald's half-eaten breakfast towards her.

'Yeah, some of them go anyway,' Donald said. 'And you
need to take it easy.' He watched her dig into his eggs and
thought about his own trip up the drone lift. He was one of
those people who had gone anyway. It wasn't something she
needed to know.

'We have one of those screens,' Charlotte said. 'I remember

watching the clouds boil.' She looked up at Donald. 'Why do we have one?'

Donald reached quickly for his handkerchief and coughed into its folds. 'Because we're human,' he answered, tucking the cloth away. 'If we think there's no point in going out there – that we'll die if we go – we'll stay here and do what we're told. But I know of a way to see what's out there.'

'Yeah?' Charlotte scraped the last of his eggs onto her fork and lifted them to her mouth. She waited.

'And I'm going to need your help.'

They pulled the tarp off one of the drones. Charlotte ran a trembling hand down its wing and walked unsteadily around the machine. Grabbing the flap on the back of a wing, she worked it up and down. She did the same for the tail. The drone had a black dome and nose that gave it something like a face. It sat silently, unmoving, while Charlotte inspected it.

Donald noticed that three of the other drones were missing – the floor glossy where their tarps used to drape. And the neat pyramid of bombs in the munitions rack was missing a few from the top. Signs of the armoury's use these past weeks. Donald went to the hangar door and worked it open.

'No hardware?' Charlotte asked. She peered under one of the wings where bad things could be attached.

'No,' Donald said. 'Not for this.' He ran back and helped her push. They steered the drone towards the open maw of the lift. The wings just barely fitted.

'There should be a strap or a linkage,' she said. She lowered herself gingerly and crawled behind the drone, worked her way beneath the wing.

'There's something in the floor,' Donald said, remembering the nub that moved along the track. 'I'll get a light.'

He retrieved a flashlight from one of the bins, made sure it had a charge and brought it back to her. Charlotte hooked the drone into the launch mechanism and squirmed her way out. She seemed slow to stand and he lent her his hand.

'And you're sure this lift'll work?' She brushed hair, still wet from the shower, off her face.

'Very sure,' Donald said. He led her down the hall, past the barracks and bathrooms. Charlotte stiffened when he led her into the piloting room and pulled back the plastic sheets. He flipped the switch on the lift controls. She stared blankly at one of the stations with its joysticks, readouts and screens.

'You can operate this, right?' he asked.

She broke from her trance and stared at him a moment, then nodded her head. 'If they'll power up.'

'They will.' He watched the light above the lift controls flash while Charlotte settled behind one of the stations. The room felt overly quiet and empty with all those other stations sitting under sheets of plastic. The dust was gone from them, Donald saw. The place was recently lived in. He thought of the requisitions he'd signed for flights, each one at considerable cost. He thought of the risk of them being spotted in the wall screens, the need to fly deep in the swirling clouds. Eren had stressed the one-use nature of the drones. The air outside was bad for them, he'd said. Their range was limited. Donald had thought about why this might be as he'd dug through Thurman's files.

Charlotte flicked several switches, the neat clicks breaking the silence, and the control station whirred to life.

'The lift takes a while,' he told her. He didn't say how he knew, but he thought back to that ride up all those years ago. He remembered his breath fogging the dome of his helmet as he rose to what he had hoped might be his death. Now he had a different hope. He thought of what Erskine had told him about wiping the earth clean. He thought about Victor's suicide note to Thurman. This project of theirs was about resetting life. And Donald, whether by madness or reason, had grown convinced that the effort was more precise than anyone had rights to imagine.

Charlotte adjusted her screen. She flicked a switch, and a light bloomed on the monitor. It was the glare of the steel door of the lift, lit up by the drone's headlamp and viewed by its cameras.

'It's been so long,' she said. Donald looked down and saw that her hands were trembling. She rubbed them together before returning them to the controls. Wiggling in her seat, she located the pedals with her feet, and then adjusted the brightness of the monitor so it wasn't so blinding.

'Is there anything I can do?' Donald asked.

Charlotte laughed and shook her head. 'No. Feels strange not to be filing a flight plan or anything. I usually have a target, you know?' She looked back at Donald and flashed a smile.

He squeezed her shoulder. It felt good to have her around. She was all he had left. 'Your flight plan is to fly as far and as fast as you can,' he told her. His hope was that without a bomb, the drone would go further. His hope was that the limited range wasn't preprogrammed somehow. There was a flashing light from the lift controls. Donald hurried over to check them.

'The door's coming up,' Charlotte said. 'I think we've got daylight.'

Donald hurried back over. He glanced out the door and down the hall, thinking he'd heard something.

'Engine check,' Charlotte said. 'We've got ignition.'

She wiggled in her seat. The overalls he'd stolen for her were too big, were bunched around her arms. Donald stood behind her and watched the monitor, which showed a view of swirling skies up a sloped ramp. He remembered that view. It became difficult to breathe, seeing that. The drone was pulled from the lift and arranged on the ramp. Charlotte hit another switch.

'Brakes on,' she said, her leg straightening. 'Applying thrust.'

Her hand slid forward. The camera view dipped as the drone strained against its brakes.

'Been a long time since I've done this without a launcher,' she said nervously.

Donald was about to ask if that was a problem when she shifted her feet and the view on the screen lifted. The metal shaft vibrated and began to race by. The swirling clouds filled the viewscreen until that was all that existed. Charlotte said, 'Lift-off,' and worked the yoke with her right hand. Donald found himself leaning to the side as the drone banked and the ground came briefly into view before all was swallowed by thick clouds.

'Which way?' she asked. She flicked a switch and the terrain below stood out by radar, by something that could pierce the clouds.

'I don't think it matters,' he said. 'Just straight.' He leaned closer to watch the strange but familiar landscape slide by. There were the great divots he had helped create. There was another tower down in the middle of a depression. The remnants of the convention – the tents and fairgrounds and stages – were long gone, eaten by the tiny machines in the air. 'Just a straight line,' he said, pointing. It was a theory, a crazy idea, but he needed to see for himself before he dared say anything.

The pattern of depressions ended in the distance. The clouds thinned occasionally, giving him a true glimpse of the ground. Donald strained to see beyond the bowls when Charlotte let go of the throttle and reached for a bank of dials and indicators. 'Uh . . . I think we have a problem.' She flipped a switch back and forth. 'I'm losing oil pressure.'

'No.' Donald watched the screen as the clouds swirled and the land seemed to heave upward. It was too early. Unless he'd missed some step, some precaution. 'Keep going,' he breathed, as much to the machine as to its pilot.

'She's handling screwy,' Charlotte said. 'Everything feels loose.'

Donald thought of all the drones in the hangar. They could launch another. But he suspected the result would be the same. He might be resistant to whatever was out there, but the machines weren't. He thought of the cleaning suits, the way things were meant to break down at a certain time, a certain place. Invisible destroyers so precise that they could let loose their vengeance as soon as a cleaner hit a hill, reached a particular altitude, as soon as they dared to rise up. He reached for his cloth and coughed into it, and had a vague memory of workers scrubbing the airlock after pulling him back inside.

'You're at the edge,' he said, pointing to the last of the silos on the radar as the bowl disappeared beneath the drone's camera. 'Just a little further.'

But in truth, he had no idea how much further it might take. Maybe you could fly straight around the world and right back where you started, and that still wouldn't be far enough.

'I'm losing lift,' Charlotte said. Her hands were twin blurs. They went from the controls to switches and back again.

'Engine two is out,' she said. 'I'm in a glide. Altitude oh-two-hundred.'

It looked like far less on the screen. They were beyond the last of the hills now. The clouds had thinned. There was a scar in the earth, a trench that may have been a river, black sticks like charred bones that stuck up in sharp points like pencil lead – all that remained of ancient trees, perhaps. Or the steel girders of a large security fence, eaten away by time.

'Go, go,' he whispered. Every second aloft provided a new sight, a new vista. Here was a breath of freedom. Here was an escape from hell.

'Camera's going. Altitude oh-one-fifty.'

There was a bright flash on the screen like the shock of dying electrics. A purplish cast followed from the frying sensors, then a wash of blue where once there was nothing but browns and greys.

'Altitude fifty feet. Gonna touch down hard.'

Donald blinked away tears as the drone plummeted and the earth rushed up to meet the machine. He blinked away tears at the sight on the monitor, nothing wrong with the camera at all.

'Blue—' he said.

It was an utterance of confirmation just before a vivid green landscape swallowed the dying drone. The monitor faded from colour to darkness. Charlotte released the controls and cursed. She slapped the console with her palm. But as she turned and apologised to Donald, he was already wrapping his arms around her, squeezing her, kissing her cheek.

'Did you see it?' he asked, his voice a breathless whisper. 'Did you see?'

'See what?' Charlotte pulled away, her face a hardened mask of disappointment. 'Every gauge was toast there at the end. Blasted drone. Probably been sitting too long—'

'No, no,' Donald said. He pointed to the screen, which was now dark and lifeless. 'You did it,' he said. 'I saw it. There were blue skies and green grass out there, Charla! I saw it!'

95

2331 – Year Twenty

• Silo 17 •

Without wanting to, Solo became an expert in how things broke down. Day by day, he watched steel and iron crumble to rust, watched paint peel and orange flecks curl up, saw the black dust gather as metal eroded to powder. He learned what rubber hoses felt like as they hardened, dried up and cracked. He learned how adhesives failed, things appearing on the floor that once were affixed to walls and ceilings, objects moved suddenly and violently by the twin gods of gravity and dilapidation. Most of all, he learned how bodies rot. They didn't always go in a flash – like a mother pushed upward by a jostling crowd or a father sliding into the shadows of a darkened corridor. Instead, they were often chewed up and carried off in invisible pieces. Time and maggots alike grew wings; they flew and flew and took all things with them.

Solo tore a page from one of the boring articles in the *Ri–Ro* book and folded it into a tent. The silo, he thought, belonged to the insects in many ways. Wherever the bodies were gathered, the insects swarmed in dark clouds. He had read up on them in the books. Somehow, maggots turned into flies. White and writhing became black and buzzing. Things broke down and changed.

He threaded lengths of string into the folded piece of paper to give something to hang the weight on. This was when Shadow would normally get in the way, would come and arch his back against Solo's arm, step on whatever he was doing, make him annoyed and make him laugh at the same time. But Shadow didn't interrupt.

Solo made small knots in the string to keep them from pulling through. The paper was doubled over across the holes so it wouldn't tear. He knew well how things broke down. He was an expert in things he wished he could unlearn. Solo could tell at a glance how long it'd been since someone had died.

The people he'd killed years back had been stiff when he moved them, but this only lasted a while. People soon swelled up and stank. Their bodies let off gasses and the flies swarmed. The flies swarmed and the maggots feasted.

The stench would make his eyes water and his throat burn. And the bodies would soon grow soft. Solo had to move some bodies on the stairs once, tangled where they lay and difficult to step over, and the flesh came right apart. It became like cottage cheese he'd had back when there was still milk and goats to get it from. Flesh came apart once the person was no longer inside, holding themselves together. Solo concentrated on holding himself together. He tied the other ends of the strings to one of the small metal washers from Supply. Chewing his tongue, he made the finest of knots.

String and fabric didn't last either, but clothes stayed around longer than people. Within a year, it was clothes and bones that were left. And hair. The hair seemed to go last. It clung to bones and sometimes hung over empty and gazing sockets. The hair made it worse. It lent bones an identity. Beards on most, but not on the young or on the women.

Within five years, even the clothes would break down. After ten, it was mostly bones. These days, so very long after the silo had gone dark and quiet – over twenty years since he'd been shown the secret lair beneath the servers – it was only the bones. Except for up in the cafeteria. The rot everywhere else made those bodies behind that door all the more curious.

Solo held up his parachute, a paper tent with little strings fastened to a tiny washer. He had dozens and dozens of bits of string lying in tangles across the open book. A handful of washers remained. He gave one of the strings on his parachute a tug and thought of the bodies up in the cafeteria. Behind that door, there were dead people who wouldn't break down like the others. When he and Shadow had first discovered them, he'd assumed they'd recently passed. Dozens of them, dying together and piled on one another as though they'd been tossed in there or had been crawling atop the others. The door to the forbidden outside was just beyond them, Solo knew. But he hadn't gone that far. He had closed the door and left in a hurry, spooked by the lifeless eyeballs and the strange feeling of seeing a face other than his own peering back at him like that. He had left the bodies and not come back for a long time. He had waited for them to become bones. They never had.

He went to the rail and peered over, made sure the piece of paper was tented, ready to grab the air. There was a cool updraught from the flooded deep. Solo leaned out beyond the third-level railing, the fine paper pinched in one hand, the washer resting in his other palm. He wondered why some people rotted and others kept going. What made them break down?

'Break down,' he said aloud. He liked the way his voice sounded sometimes. He was an expert in how things broke down. Shadow should've been there, rubbing against his ankles, but he wasn't.

'I'm an expert,' Solo told himself. 'Breaking down, breaking down.' He stretched out his arms and released the parachute, watched it plummet for a moment before the strings went taut. And then it bobbed and twisted in the air as it sank into the dwindling depths. 'Down down down,' he called after the parachute. All the way to the bottom. Sinking until it splashed invisible or got caught up along the way.

Solo knew well how bodies rot. He scratched his beard and squinted after the disappearing chute, then sat back down and crossed his legs, the knee torn completely out of his old overalls. He mumbled to himself, delaying what needed to be done, his Project for the day, and instead tore another page from the shrinking book, trying not to think about yet another carcass that would soon dwindle with time.

96

2331 – Year Twenty
• Silo 17 •

There had been items Solo spent days and weeks searching for. There had been some things he'd needed that had consumed his hunts for years. Often, he found useful things much later, when he needed them no longer. Like the time he had come across a stash of razors. A great big bin of them in a doctor's office. All the important stuff – the bandages, medicine, the tape – had long ago been snagged by those fighting over the scraps. But a bin of new razors, many of the blades still shiny, taunted him. He had long before resigned himself to his beard, but there had been times before that when he would've killed for a razor.

Other times, he found a thing before he even knew he needed it. The machete was like that. A great blade found beneath the body of a man not long dead. Solo had taken it simply so nobody else would have the murderous thing. He had locked himself below the server room for three days, terrified of the sight of another still-warm body. That had been many years ago. It took a while longer for the farms to thicken up where the machete became necessary. By then, he had taken to leaving his gun behind – no longer any use for it – and the machete became a constant companion, something found before he knew he needed it.

Solo set the last of the parachutes free and watched as it narrowly missed the landing on level nine. The folded paper vanished out of sight. He thought of the things Shadow had helped him find over the years, mostly food. But there was one time when Shadow had run off with a mind of his own.

It was on a trip down to Supply when Shadow had raced ahead and had disappeared across a landing. Solo had followed with his flashlight.

The cat had mewed and mewed by a door – Solo wary of another pile of bodies – but the apartment had been empty. Up on the kitchen counter, twirling, pawing at a cabinet full of little cans. Ancient and spotted with rust, but with pictures of cats on them. A madness in Shadow, and there, with a short cord plugged into the wall, a battered contraption, a mechanised can opener.

Solo smiled and gazed over the rail, thinking on the things found and lost over the years. He remembered pressing the button on the top of that gadget the first time, how Shadow had whipped into a frenzy, how neatly the tops had come off. He remembered not being impressed at all with the food in the cans, but Shadow had a mind of his own.

Solo turned and studied the book with the torn pages, feeling sad. He was out of washers, so he left the book behind and reluctantly headed down to the farms. He was off to do what needed to be done.

Hacking at the greenery with his machete, Solo marvelled that the farms hadn't long ago rotted to ruin without people around to tend them. But the lights were rigged to come on and off, and more than half of them still could. Water continued to dribble from pipes. Pumps kicked on and off with angry buzzes and loud grumbles. Electricity stolen from his realm below was brought up on wires that snaked the stairwell walls. Nothing worked perfectly, but Solo saw that man's relationship to the crops mostly consisted of eating them. Now it was only him eating. Him and the rats and the worms.

He carried his burden through the thickest plots, needing to reach the far corners of the farm where the lights no longer burned, where the soil was cool and damp, where nothing grew any more. A special place. Away from his weekly trips to gather food. A place he would come to as a destination rather than simply pass because it was along the way.

Leaving the heat of the lights, he entered a dark place. He liked it back here. It reminded him of the room beneath the servers, a private and safe place where one could hide and not be disturbed. And there, scattered among other abandoned and forgotten tools, a shovel. A thing he needed right when he needed it. This was the other way of finding things. It was when the silo was in a gifting mood. It wasn't a mood the silo got into often.

Solo knelt and placed his burden by the edge of the three-railing fence. The body in the bag had gone into that stiff phase. Soon it would soften. After that—

Solo didn't want to think after that. He was an expert in some things he'd rather not know.

He collected the shovel and scampered over the top rail – it was too dark to hunt for the gate. The shovel growled and crunched through the dirt. He lifted each scoop into the air. Soft sighs and little piles slid out. Some things you found just when you needed them, and Solo thought of the years that had passed so swiftly with his friend. He already missed the way Shadow rubbed on his shin while he worked, always in the way but clever enough not to be stepped on, coming in a flash whenever Solo broke out in a whistle, there at just the right time. A thing found, before he even knew he needed it.

Donald's boots echoed in the lower-level shift storage, where thousands of pods lay packed together like gleaming stones. He stooped to check another nameplate. He had lost count of his position down the aisle and was worried he'd have to start over again. Bringing a rag to his mouth, he coughed. He wiped his lip and carried on. Something heavy and cold weighed down one pocket and pressed against his thigh. Something heavy and cold lay within his chest.

He finally found the pod marked *Troy*. Donald rubbed the glass and peered inside. There was a man in there, older than he seemed. Older than Donald remembered. A blue cast overwhelmed pale flesh. White hair and white brows possessed an azure tint.

Donald studied the man, hesitated, reconsidered. He had come there with no wheelchair, no medical kit. Just a cold heaviness. A slice of truth and a desire to know more. Sometimes a thing needed opening before closure was found.

He bent by the control pad and repeated the procedure that had freed his sister. He thought of Charlotte up in the barracks as he entered his code. She couldn't know what he was doing down there. She couldn't know. Thurman had been like a second father to them both.

The dial was turned to the right. Numbers blinked, then ticked up a degree. Donald stood and paced. He circled that pod with a name on it, the name of a man they'd turned him into, this sarcophagus that now held his creator. The cold in

Donald's heart spread into his limbs while Thurman warmed. Donald coughed into a rag stained pink. He tucked it back into his pocket and drew out the length of cord.

A report from Victor's files came to him as he stood there, roles reversed, thawing the Thaw Man. Victor had written of old experiments where guards and prisoners switched places, and the abused soon became the abuser. Donald found the idea detestable, that people could change so swiftly. He found the results unbelievable. But he had seen good men and women arrive on the Hill with noble intentions, had seen them change. He had been given a dose of power on this shift and could feel its allure. His discovery was that evil men arose from evil systems, and that any man had the potential to be perverted. Which was why some systems needed to come to an end.

The temperature rose and the lid was triggered. It opened with a sigh. Donald reached in and lifted it the rest of the way. He half expected a hand to shoot out and snatch his wrist but there was just a man lying inside, still and steaming. Just a man, pathetic and naked, a tube running into his arm, another between his legs. Muscles sagged. Pale flesh gathered in folds of wrinkles. Hair clung in wisps. Donald took Thurman's hands and placed them together. He looped the cord around Thurman's wrists, threaded it between his hands and around the loops of cord, then cinched a knot to draw the loops tight. Donald stood back and watched his wrinkled eyelids for any sign of life.

Thurman's lips moved. They parted and seemed to take a first, experimental gasp. It was like watching the dead become reanimated, and Donald appreciated for the first time the miracle of these machines. He coughed into his fist as Thurman stirred. The old man's eyes fluttered open, melted frost tracking from their corners, lending him a degree of false humanity. Wrinkled hands came up to wipe away the crust and Donald knew what that felt like, lids that wouldn't fully part, that felt as though they'd grown together. A grunt spilled out as Thurman struggled with the cord. He came to more fully and saw that all was not right.

'Be still,' Donald told him. He placed a hand on the old man's forehead, could feel the chill still in his flesh. 'Easy.'

'Anna—' Thurman whispered. He licked his lips, and Donald realised he hadn't even brought water, hadn't brought the bitter drink. There was no doubting what he was there to do.

'Can you hear me?' he asked.

Thurman's eyelids fluttered open again; his pupils dilated. He seemed to focus on Donald's face, eyes flicking back and forth in stunted recognition.

'Son . . . ?' His voice was hoarse.

'Lie still,' Donald told him, even as Thurman turned to the side and coughed into his bound hands. He peered at the cord knotted around his wrists, his expression confused. Donald turned and checked the door in the distance. 'I need you to listen to me.'

'What's going on here?' Thurman gripped the edge of the pod and tried to pull himself upright. Donald fished into his pocket for the pistol. Thurman gaped at the black steel as the barrel was levelled on him. His awareness thawed in an instant. He remained perfectly still, only his eyes moving as he met Donald's gaze. 'What year is it?' he asked.

'Another two hundred years before you kill us all,' Donald said. The barrel trembled with hatred. He wrapped his other hand around the grip and took half a step back. Thurman was weak and bound but Donald was taking no chances. The old man was like a coiled snake on a cold morning. Donald couldn't help but think of what he would be capable of as the day warmed.

Thurman licked his lips and studied Donald. Curls of steam rose from the old man's shoulders. 'Anna told you,' he finally said.

Donald had a sadistic urge to tell him that Anna was dead. He felt a prideful twinge and wanted to insist that he'd figured it out for himself. He simply nodded instead.

'You have to know this is the only way,' Thurman whispered.

'There are a thousand ways,' Donald said. He moved the gun to his other hand and dried his sweaty palm on his overalls.

Thurman glanced at the gun, then searched the room beyond Donald for help. After a pause, he settled back against the pod. Steam rose from within the unit, but Donald could see him begin to shiver against the cold.

'I used to think you were trying to live for ever,' Donald said.

Thurman laughed. He inspected the knotted cord once more, looked at the needle and tube hanging from his arm. 'Just long enough.'

'Long enough for what? To whittle humanity down to nothing? To let one of these silos go free and then sit here and kill the rest?'

Thurman nodded. He pulled his feet closer and hugged his shins. He looked so thin and fragile without his overalls on, without his proud shoulders thrown back.

'You saved all these people just to kill most of them. And us as well.'

Thurman whispered a reply.

'Louder,' Donald said.

The old man mimed taking a drink. Donald showed him the gun. It was all he had. Thurman tapped his chest and tried to speak again, and Donald took a wary step closer. 'Tell me why,' Donald said. 'I'm the one in charge here. Me. Tell me or I swear I'll let everyone out of their silos right now.'

Thurman's eyes became slits. 'Fool,' he hissed. 'They'll kill each other.'

His voice was barely audible. Donald could hear all the cryopods around them humming. He stepped even closer, more confident with each passing moment that this was the right thing to do.

'I know what you think they'll do to one another,' Donald said. 'I know about this great cleanse, this reset.' He jabbed the gun at Thurman's chest. 'I know you see these silos as starships taking people to a better world. I've read every note and memo and file you have access to. But this is what I want to hear from you before you die—'

Donald felt his legs wobble. A coughing fit seized him. He fumbled for his cloth but pink spittle struck the silver pod before he could cover his mouth. Thurman watched. Donald steadied himself, tried to remember what he'd been saying.

'I want to know why all the heartache,' Donald said, his voice scratchy, his throat on fire. 'All the miserable lives coming and going, the people down here you plan on killing, on never waking. Your own daughter . . .' He searched Thurman's face for some reaction. 'Why not freeze us for a thousand years and wake us when it's done? I know now what I helped you build. I want to know why we couldn't sleep through it all. If you wanted a better place for us, why not take us there? Why the suffering?'

Thurman remained perfectly still.

'Tell me why,' Donald said. His voice cracked but he pretended to be okay. He lifted the barrel, which had drooped.

'Because no one can know,' Thurman finally said. 'It has to die with us.'

'What has to die?'

Thurman licked his lips. 'Knowledge. The things we left out of the Legacy. The ability to end it all with the flip of a switch.'

Donald laughed. 'You think we won't discover them again? The means to destroy ourselves?'

Thurman shrugged his naked shoulders. The steam rising from them had dissipated. 'Eventually. Which is a longer time than right now.'

Donald waved his gun at the pods all around him. 'And so all this goes as well. We're supposed to choose one tribe, one of your starships to land, and everything else is shut down. That's the pact you made?'

Thurman nodded.

'Well, someone broke your pact,' Donald said. 'Someone put me here in your place. I'm the shepherd now.'

Thurman's eyes widened. His gaze travelled from the gun to the badge clipped on Donald's collar. Clattering teeth were silenced by the clenching and unclenching of his jaw. 'No,' he said.

'I never asked for this job,' Donald said, more to himself than to Thurman. He steadied the barrel. 'For any of these jobs.'

'Me neither,' Thurman replied, and Donald was again reminded of those prisoners and those guards. This could be him in that pod. It could be anyone standing there with that gun. It was the system.

There were a hundred other things he wanted to ask or say. He wanted to tell this man how much like a father he'd been to him, but what did that mean when fathers could be as abusive as they were loving? He wanted to scream at Thurman for the damage he'd done to the world, but some part of Donald knew the damage had been done long before and that it was irreversible. And finally, there was a part of him that wanted to beg for help, to free this man from his pod; a part that wanted to take his place, to curl up inside and go back to sleep – a part that found being the prisoner was so much easier than remaining on guard. But his sister was up above, recovering. They both had more questions that needed answering. And in a silo not far away, a transformation was taking place, the end of an uprising, and Donald wanted to see how that played out.

All this and more raced through Donald's mind. It wouldn't be long before Dr Wilson returned to his desk and possibly glanced at a screen just as the right camera cycled through. And even as Thurman's mouth parted to say something, Donald realised that waking the old man to hear his excuses had been a mistake. There was little to learn here.

Thurman leaned forward. 'Donny,' he said. He reached out with bound wrists for the pistol in Donald's hand. His arms moved slowly and feebly, not with the hope – Donald didn't think – of snatching the gun away, but possibly with the desire to pull it close, to press it against his chest or his mouth the way Victor had, such was the sadness in the old man's eyes.

Thurman reached past the lip of the pod and groped for the gun, and Donald very nearly handed it to him, just to see what he would do with it.

He pulled the trigger instead. He pulled the trigger before he could regret it.

The bang was unconscionably loud. There was a bright flash, a horrid noise echoing out across a thousand sleeping souls, and then a man slumping down into a coffin.

Donald's hand trembled. He remembered his first days in office, all this man had done for him, that meeting very early on. He had been hired for a job for which he was barely qualified. He had been hired for a job he could not at first discern. That first morning, waking up a congressman, realising he and only a handful of others stood at the helm of a powerful nation, had filled him with as much fear as accomplishment. And all along, he had been an inmate asked to erect the walls of his own asylum.

This time would be different. This time, he would accept responsibility and lead without fear. Him and his sister in secret. They would find out what was wrong with the world and fix it. Restore order to all that had been lost. An experiment had begun in another silo, a changing of the guard, and Donald intended to see the results.

He reached up and closed the lid on the pod. There was pink spittle on its shiny surface. Donald coughed once and wiped his mouth. He stuffed the pistol in his pocket and walked away from the pod, his heart racing from what he'd done. And the pod with a dead man inside – it quietly hummed.

2345 – Year Thirty-four
• Silo 17 •

Solo worked the rope through the handles of the empty plastic jugs. They rattled together and made a kind of sonorous music. He collected his canvas bag and stood there a moment, scratching his beard, forgetting something. What had he forgotten? Patting his chest, he made sure he had the key. It was an old habit from years ago that he couldn't shake. The key, of course, was no longer there. He had tucked it in a drawer when things no longer needed locking, when there was no one left to be afraid of.

He took two bags of empty soup and veggie cans with him – hardly a dent in the massive pile of garbage. With his hands full and every step causing a clang and a clatter, he carried his things down the dark passage to the shaft of light at the far end.

It took two trips up the ladder to unload everything. He passed between the black machines, many of which had gone silent over the years, succumbing to the heat, perhaps. The filing cabinet had to be moved before the door would open. The silo had no locks and no people – but no dummies, either. He pulled the heavy door, could feel his father's presence as always, and stepped out into the wide world crowded with nothing but ghosts and things so bad he couldn't remember them.

The hallways were bright and empty. Solo waved to where he knew the cameras were as he passed. He often thought that he'd see himself on the monitors one day, but the cameras had quit working for ever ago. And besides, there'd have to be two of him for that to happen. One to stand there and wave, another down by the monitors. He laughed at how silly he was. He was Solo.

Stepping out on the landing brought fresh air and a troubling sense of height. Solo thought of the rising water. How long before it reached him? Too long, he thought. He would be gone by then. But it was sad to think of his little home under the servers full of water one day. All the empty cans in the great pile by the shelves would float to the top. The computer and the radio would gurgle little bubbles of air. That made him laugh, thinking of them gurgling and the cans bobbing around on the surface, and he no longer cared if it happened or not. He tossed both bags of empty cans over the railing and listened for them to crunch down on the landing at thirty-five. They dutifully did. He turned to the stairs.

Up or down? Up meant tomatoes, cucumbers and squash. Down meant berries, corn and digging for potatoes. Down required more cooking. Solo marched up.

He counted the steps as he went. 'Eight, nine, ten,' he whispered. Each of the stairs was different. There were a lot of stairs. They had all kinds of company, all kinds of fellow stairs, like friends, to either side. More things just like them. 'Hello, step,' he said, forgetting to count. The step said nothing. He didn't speak whatever they spoke, the ringing singing of lonely boots clanging up and down.

A noise. Solo heard a noise. He stopped and listened, but usually the noises knew when he was doing that and they got shy. This was another of those noises. He heard things that weren't there all the time. There were pumps and lights wired all over the place that turned on and off at their whim and choosing. One of these pumps had sprung a leak years ago, and Solo had fixed it himself. He needed a new Project. He was doing a lot of the same ones over and over, like chopping his beard when it got to his chest, and all of these Projects were boring.

Only one break to drink and pee before he reached

the farms. His legs were good. Stronger, even, than when he was younger. The hard things got easier the more you did them. It didn't make it any more fun to do the hard things, though. Solo wished they would just be easy the first time.

He rounded the last bend before the landing on thirty, was just about to start whistling a harvest tune, when he saw that he'd left the door open. He wasn't sure how. Solo never left the door open. Any doors.

There was something propped up in the corner against the rail. It looked like scrap material from one of his Projects. A broken piece of plastic pipe. He picked it up. There was water in it. Solo sniffed the tube. It smelled funny, and he started to dump the water over the rail when the pipe slipped from his fingers. He froze and waited for the distant clatter. It never came.

Clumsy. He cursed himself for being forgetful and clumsy. Left a door open. He was headed inside when he saw what was holding it open. A black handle. He reached for it, saw that it was a knife plunged down through the grating.

There was a noise inside, deep within the farms. Solo stood very still for a moment. This was not his knife. He was not this forgetful. He pulled the blade out and allowed the door to close as a thousand thoughts flitted through his waking mind. A rat couldn't do something like this. Only a person could. Or a powerful ghost.

He should do something. He should tie the handles together or wedge something under the doors, but he was too afraid. He turned and ran instead. He ran down the stairs, jugs clattering together, his empty pack flopping on his back, someone else's knife clutched in his hand. When the jugs caught on the railing the rope snagged, and he tugged twice before giving up and letting them go. His hole. He had to get to his hole. Breathing heavily, he hurried on, the clangs and vibrations of some *other* disrupting his solitude. He didn't have to stop to listen for them. This was a loud ghost. Loud and solid. Solo thought of his machete, which had snapped in half years ago. But he had this knife. This knife. Around and around the stairs he went, sorely afraid. Down to the landing. Wrong landing! Thirty-three. One more to go. Stopped counting, stopped counting. He nearly stumbled, he ran so fast. Sweating. Home.

He slammed the doors behind him and took a deep breath, hands on his knees. Scooping the broom off the ground, he slid it through the handles on the door. It kept the quiet ghosts at bay. He hoped it would work on the noisy ones.

Solo pushed through the busted security gate and hurried down the halls. One of the lights overhead was out. A Project. But no time. He reached the metal door and heaved. Ran inside. Stopped and ran back. He leaned on the door and pushed it closed. He got low and put his shoulder into the filing cabinet, slid that against the door, an awful screech. He thought he heard footsteps outside. Someone fast. Sweat dripped off his nose. He clutched the knife and ran, through the servers. There was a squeal behind him, metal on metal. Solo was not alone. They had come for him. They were coming, coming. He could taste the fear in his mouth like metal. He raced to the grate, wished he'd left it open. At least the locks were broken. Rusted. No, that wasn't good. He needed the locks. Solo lowered himself down the ladder and grabbed the grating, began to pull it over his head. He would hide. Hide. Like the early years. And then someone was tugging the grate from his hand. He was swiping at them with the knife. There was a startled scream, a woman, breathing heavy and looking down at him, telling him to take it easy.

Solo trembled. His boot slipped a little on the ladder. But he held. He held very still while this woman talked to him. Her eyes were wide and alive. Her lips moved. She was hurt, didn't want to hurt him back. She just wanted his name. She was happy to see him. The wetness in her eyes was from being happy to see him. And Solo thought – maybe – that he himself was like a shovel or a can opener or any of those rusty things lying about. He was something that could be found. He could be found. And someone had.

Donald sat in the otherwise empty comm room. He had every station to himself, had sent the others to lunch and ordered those who weren't hungry to take a break. And they listened to him. They called him Shepherd, knew nothing else about him except that he was in charge. They came on and off shift, and they did as he ordered.

A blinking light on the neighbouring comm station signalled silo six attempting to make a call. They would have to wait. Donald sat and listened to the ringing in his headset as he placed a call of his own.

It rang and rang. He checked the cord, traced it to the jack, made sure it was plugged in correctly. Between two of the comm stations lay an unfinished game of cards, hands set aside from Donald ordering everyone out. There was a discard pile with a queen of spades on top. Finally, a click in his headset.

'Hello?' he said.

He waited. He thought he could hear someone breathing on the other line.

'Lukas?'

'No,' the voice said. It was a softer voice. And yet harder, somehow.

'Who is this?' he asked. He was used to talking to Lukas.

'It doesn't matter who this is,' the woman said. And Donald knew perfectly well. He looked over his shoulders, made sure he was still alone, then leaned forward in his chair.

'We're not used to hearing from mayors,' he said.

'And I'm not used to being one.'

Donald could practically hear the woman sneer at him. 'I didn't ask for my job,' he confided.

'And yet here we are.'

'Here we are.'

There was a pause.

'You know,' Donald said, 'if I were any good at my job, I'd press a button right now and shut your silo down.'

'Why don't you?'

The mayor's voice was flat. Curious. It sounded like a real question rather than a dare.

'I doubt you'd believe me if I told you.'

'Try me,' she said. And Donald wished he still had the folder on this woman. He had carried it everywhere his first weeks on shift. And now, when he needed it—

'A long time ago,' he told her, 'I saved your silo. It would be a shame to end it now.'

'You're right. I don't believe you.'

There was a noise in the hallway. Donald removed one of the cups from his ears and glanced over his shoulder. His comm engineer stood outside the door with a Thermos in one hand, a slice of bread in the other. Donald raised his finger and asked him to wait.

'I know where you've been,' Donald told this mayor, this woman sent to clean. 'I know what you've seen. And I—'

'You don't know the first thing about what I've seen,' she spat, her words sharp as razors.

Donald felt his temperature rise. This was not the conversation he wanted to have with this woman. He wasn't prepared. He cupped his hand over the microphone, could sense that he was both running out of time and losing her.

'Be careful,' he said. 'That's all I'm saying—'

'Listen to me,' she told him. 'I'm sitting over here in a roomful of truth. I've seen the books. I'm going to dig until I get to the heart of what you people have done.'

Donald could hear her breathing.

'I know the truth you're looking for,' he said quietly. 'You may not like what you find.'

'*You* may not like what I find, you mean.'

'Just . . . be careful.' Donald lowered his voice. 'Be careful where you go digging.'

There was a pause. Donald glanced over his shoulder at the engineer, who took a sip from his Thermos.

'Oh, we'll be careful where we dig,' this Juliette finally answered. 'I'd hate for you to hear us coming.'

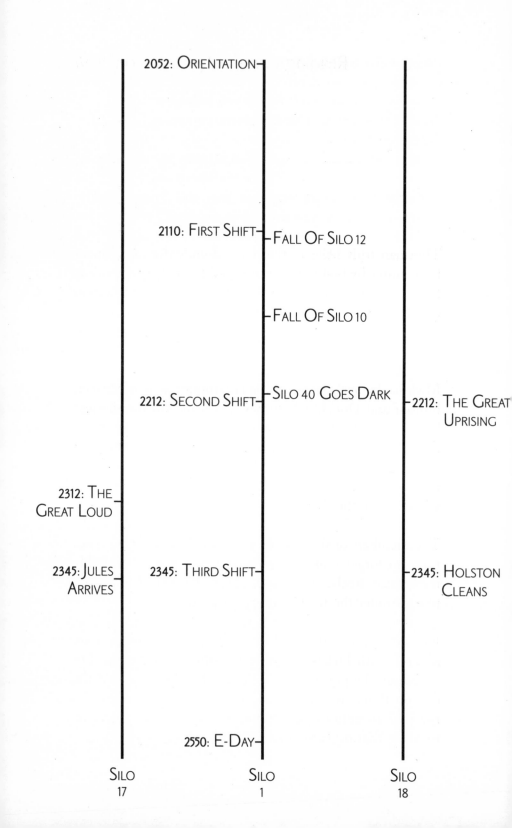

2052: ORIENTATION

2110: FIRST SHIFT — FALL OF SILO 12

FALL OF SILO 10

2212: SECOND SHIFT — SILO 40 GOES DARK — 2212: THE GREAT UPRISING

2312: THE GREAT LOUD

2345: JULES ARRIVES   2345: THIRD SHIFT   2345: HOLSTON CLEANS

2550: E-DAY

SILO 17   SILO 1   SILO 18

Reading Group Questions on *Shift*

- Thurman truly believes that he is doing what is right for his country by building the silos and forcing people inside them. Do you agree with him based on the information of the possible threat to his country? Or is acting on anything but a certainty of a threat too much of a risk to take?

- Mick is obviously aware of the last-minute switch between himself and Donald when they go down into the silo just before the rally. Of their two roles, Donald's is the more powerful, with much more responsibility, leading to him living for hundreds of years, but he is envious of Mick's relatively normal life in a silo with Helen. Whose position would you rather be in?

- The members of silo one are given medication that causes them to forget traumatic events. If you were offered this medication freely, would you take it? Or would you want to remember the truth about your past?

- Donald discovers that Anna is the reason he is in silo one, and not with Helen in a different silo, and is furious. Do you think she put him there for purely selfish reasons? Or do you think she thought he would be the best man for the job? In either case, do you believe she had the right to make that decision for him?

- The Crow is seen as a threat to the stability of the silo for generating a feeling of dissatisfaction among her pupils. Do you agree she is a threat? Would this feeling of there being something more out there be realised without her help? Consider the other silos. Does there always have to be a 'Crow' figure for an uprising?

- Mission is willing to go to any lengths to help Rodny as soon as he believes he is in danger. Would you agree that ultimately it is his own bravery at trying to save his friend that causes his reset? Are you happy that Mission can now start a new life, forgetting the troubles of his past? Or do you feel angry that such a decision was made for him without his knowledge?

- How did you feel when Thurman 'shepherds' Donald back in from the outside? Were you happy that he saved his life? Or were you behind Donald, wanting him to die a free man?

- Donald realises that it was Anna who swapped him and Thurman for the start of his third shift. Did you always suspect it was her? Was there anyone else who thought that Donald would be better than Thurman in that role? Do you agree that Donald is the best man for the job?

- Jimmy's father leaves safety behind to go in search of his wife, resulting in both of their deaths, and Jimmy being alone. Do you think he should have stayed to be with Jimmy? Could he have ever lived with the knowledge that he didn't try to save his wife?

- Donald wakes up his sister, Charlotte, because he needs her help, and as soon as she is with him, he feels happier. Would you wake your loved ones if you were in Donald's position? Or would you want to protect them from the horrors of their new existence?

- Jimmy ceases to be Solo and reclaims his identity when he meets another living thing in his silo – a cat. What gives you your identity? Is it something deep within yourself or is it about the people surrounding you? Consider yourself at Jimmy's age. Does this change how you would feel?

- When Juliette comes into contact with Donald at the end of *Shift*, she threatens him, as she sees him as a keeper of lies and secrets, and the reason for the state of her world. Was this how you felt towards those in authority as you read *Wool*? Has your opinion changed since hearing Donald's side of the story? Why?

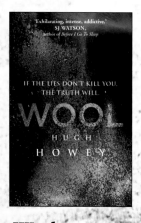 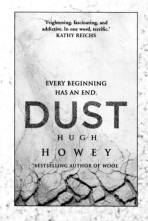